Prayers *the* Devil Answers

ALSO BY SHARYN McCRUMB

Nora Bonesteel's Christmas Past

King's Mountain

The Ballad of Tom Dooley

The Devil Amongst the Lawyers

Ghost Riders

The Songcatcher

The Ballad of Frankie Silver

The Rosewood Casket

She Walks These Hills

The Hangman's Beautiful Daughter

If Ever I Return, Pretty Peggy-O

Prayers *the* Devil Answers

A NOVEL

Sharyn McCrumb

ATRIA PAPERBACK
New York London Toronto Sydney New Delhi

ATRIA PAPERBACK
An Imprint of Simon & Schuster, Inc.
1230 Avenue of the Americas
New York, NY 10020

This book is a work of fiction. Any references to historical events, real people, or real places are used fictitiously. Other names, characters, places, and events are products of the author's imagination, and any resemblance to actual events or places or persons, living or dead, is entirely coincidental.

First Atria Paperback edition April 2017

ATRIA PAPERBACK and colophon are trademarks of Simon & Schuster, Inc.

For information about special discounts for bulk purchases, please contact Simon & Schuster Special Sales at 1-866-506-1949 or business@simonandschuster.com.

The Simon & Schuster Speakers Bureau can bring authors to your live event. For more information or to book an event, contact the Simon & Schuster Speakers Bureau at 1-866-248-3049 or visit our website at www.simonspeakers.com.

Interior design by Kyoko Watanabe

Manufactured in the United States of America

10 9 8 7 6 5 4 3 2 1

Library of Congress Cataloging-in-Publication Data is available.

ISBN 978-1-4767-7281-3
ISBN 978-1-4767-7284-4 (pbk)
ISBN 978-1-4767-7285-1 (ebook)

For Laura Eleanor

Prayers
the
Devil Answers

prologue

Years later, after the tragedy, someone remembered the Dumb Supper and what had happened there. That was the cause of it, they said, because the ritual wasn't a game after all. It really was magic, but magic has rules, and she broke them. Even when they call it a "senseless tragedy," people always try to find a reason for it.

The Dumb Supper.

The young girls who lived up the mountain in Thorn Hollow only half believed in that ancient tradition—after all, the world had come through a terrible war and into a new century unlike any other that had ever been. Surely the old ways were gone. It was a new age: an era of motorcars and flying machines, telephones and talking pictures. In light of all this mechanized magic, the old superstitions were fading into half-forgotten memories. But these traditions had been around for a long time. People said that keeping some of the old ways was a sign that you honored your forebears. New century or not, country people still nailed horseshoes above the doorways of the house and barn—a hunk of cold iron to keep out the fairy folk and the restless spirits.

The unsinkable *Titanic* went down in 1912, and Martha, the last passenger pigeon, died in 1914, but despite the changing world a few of the old ways lived on. The women in the remote mountain settlements still constructed homemade quilts out of old clothes and scraps of cloth, even though you could buy a factory-made bedspread from the mail-order catalogue for only a dollar or two. Some quilts bore intricate patterns that were centuries old. Long ago the ancestors of the mountain quilt makers had put those same designs on their coverlets, and if you looked far enough back into the origin of the tradition, those colorful geometric patterns once meant something. The designs were symbols of protection derived from ancient magic, put there to guard a loved one, perhaps a sleeping child, from whatever spirits walked abroad at night. But people had forgotten that. They kept putting the old patterns on the quilts just because that was the way their grandmothers and great-grandmothers had always made them.

The Dumb Supper was another mountain tradition, so ancient that nobody remembered how or why it had started. Some said the custom began back over the water, where the quilt patterns came from, in the birthplaces of their pioneer ancestors: Scotland or Ireland or the north of England. When people left those places and sailed away to the New World, they took with them the old customs, the tales, the ballads and fiddle tunes, and the quilt patterns, because memories and traditions were all they had left to remind them of home. After a few generations in the Southern mountains the songs and the customs began to change, as the descendants of the first settlers adapted the old tunes and the old ways to a new place.

Once a solemn ceremony intended to allow the living to contact the dead, the Dumb Supper took place on Samhain eve, when the barrier between here and the hereafter was at its weakest point. With time, as the pioneers died out and their descendants remembered the what but not the why, the tradition became watered down by other ideas, both foreign and modern.

Although the tradition of the Dumb Supper had been passed down through many generations in the mountain communities, the women would tell you now that it was only a bit of fun. Similar rituals can be found in some form among young unmarried girls everywhere—that longing to settle what is for girls of sixteen life's all-important question: *Who will I marry?* The practice was just a quaint variation of playing *He loves me, he loves me not* with daisy petals.

It was only a fanciful party, people said, not really a sacred ceremony. *Just an old wives' tale, perhaps, but . . . Why not? What if it really worked? Don't you want to know?* Everybody had heard a story about a friend of a friend of a friend who had seen the image of her future husband at a Dumb Supper held in Virginia . . . Kentucky . . . southern Ohio. The details were vague, but the story was always the same. Maybe once in a while, for some people, it worked.

⟷

Only the community's unmarried maidens observed the tradition of the Dumb Supper. Nobody else needed it. The single men never hosted one; either they did not believe in the art of prophecy, or, more likely, they weren't much interested yet in the one question the rite was designed to answer. Sometimes, though, the county's more spirited young bucks would turn up as guests at the Dumb Supper, out of curiosity or as a prank to frighten their sisters and cousins. More importantly, any unmarried fellow who had set his sights on a particular girl was expected to attend to assure his lady love that she was indeed spoken for. His attendance also staked the suitor's claim publicly so that word of his intentions would get around, and then an engagement was expected to follow. The young men jokingly called the Dumb Supper "the prisoner's last meal," because if a fellow went to one, it marked the end of his carefree days as a bachelor.

Days before the event, the girl who was being courted would give her sweetheart hints as to when and where the supper would take place, hoping that he would come. Expecting it, really. This was more guile than superstition: the girl knew that once the community learned that the young man had claimed her at the Dumb Supper, he was as good as caught.

Frivolous party or solemn ritual, there were rules to be followed. Mountain lore decreed that a Dumb Supper could not be held at someone's home; the participants had to find a remote, empty old house for the ceremony, or better still, a long-abandoned log cabin on some forgotten farmstead, being reclaimed by the forest. The farther it was from any neighbors, the better, because magic doesn't happen in the noise and bustle of everyday life.

The ritual didn't have to take place on All Hallow's Eve, as it had in olden times, but the moon had to be full, and the night warm enough for the girls to spend the dark hours in an abandoned, unheated dwelling. The ceremony must begin at midnight, even though that hour was only the threshold between days, not worlds.

Once a suitable gathering place had been chosen, the young hostesses would spend the better part of the daylight hours making preparations for the meal. Somebody's father or brother would bring six chairs and an old wooden table to the empty house; another one's mother or older sister might contribute the cutlery or a starched white tablecloth. While the sun shone, the girls laughed and chattered as they went to and fro, bringing boxes containing the plates, the glasses, and the flatware, all borrowed from home. Late in the afternoon each girl would bring the food she had cooked herself—a pot of beans, salt pork and turnips, a pound cake, or whatever her family's specialty was—that is, the same dishes they would have taken to a church supper. All these things were left in the kitchen or in a corner of the cabin, for the table would not be set, nor the food served until the stroke of midnight. Each girl tended to one setting at the table, although they would not be at the table themselves, nor using the plates and silver, nor eating any of the food. Generally, they skipped dinner altogether, perhaps from some dim memory that fasting preceded a ritual. The meal laid out at midnight was intended only for the guests, spectral or otherwise, and when the hostesses served the meal, they piled an equal amount of food on the plate of an invisible guest as they did for a mortal one.

During the daylight hours, as they laughed and talked nineteen to the dozen, making the preparations for the night's adventure, they kept an eye on the setting sun. After dark, all talking must cease. In order for the charm to work, they must keep an unbroken silence throughout the long hours of the evening until the ritual was complete.

There were six girls that night at the abandoned cabin in Thorn Hollow: the Greer sisters, who had proposed the Dumb Supper to begin with, even though they were both as stout and plain as piglets, unlikely to attract the attention of any man, living or dead; Sarah, the minister's daughter, who was only able to go because she'd told her parents she was staying the night at her best friend's house, though, of course, the best friend Ann was also a participant; Aurelia, the girl who was considered by everyone, including herself, to be the beauty of the settlement, attended in order to see how many eager young men would turn up on her behalf, perhaps even adding to the evening's excitement and the luster of her reputation by fighting one another over the single place at the table tended by her. Since it would be too dim in the candlelight to see anyone clearly, the beauty left the berry stain off her lips and the lampblack off her eyelids, but throughout the evening she made frequent use of the comb tucked in the pocket of her apron.

The last girl among them was not particularly beautiful but not quite plain either. Small and dark-haired, she was a quiet girl who never had much to say for herself, always a follower of the more strong-minded ones in any gathering, and, although she laughed and talked easily among her close friends, she was painfully shy around strangers. No one expected any young man to turn up for her.

The only thing unusual about the quiet girl was that her name was Celia, an uncommon name for then and there, chosen by her mother out of an old book of plays. As her contribution to the feast, Celia brought a pot of stew beans and fresh-baked cornbread. She was assigned the last place at the table after the others had already chosen where their suitors would sit.

The dark came, and with it the necessary silence. Outside, the wind picked up and clouds scudded back and forth across the full moon. When the cabin became cold, the girls huddled together, wrapped in their wool shawls, staring into the flickering lamplight and wishing they could have a fire to keep warm by, but the Dumb Supper rules forbade it. Even so, they might have been tempted to light it, but that afternoon, after inspecting the premises, the father of the Greer sisters insisted that the fireplace not be lit. The stone chimney of the old cabin was crumbling and would no longer draw. The danger of an outbreak of fire was too great for them to risk using the fireplace. The night air was chilly, but the cold lantern light would have to do.

Time stretched on as they waited for midnight, silent and still in the deserted cabin. Sarah, who had brought her father's pocket watch along, went out into the moonlight every now and then to see how much time was left before the Dumb Supper would begin. (Lamplight would have done just as well to illuminate the watch face, but she welcomed the excuse to stretch her legs and go outside, away from the temptation of forgetting the rules and talking. Anyway, moonlight was more in keeping with the spirit of the ancient tradition.) Because the participants were forbidden to speak, or else all would be spoiled, Sarah would come back inside after checking the time and hold up her fingers to indicate what hour it was. At last she held up both hands, fingers spread. Then closing one fist, she raised only the forefinger of her right hand. Ten plus one. The girls looked at one another and smiled. Not long now.

The last time Sarah came back, signaling that midnight had

come, each of the girls picked up the dish of food she had brought from home and carried it to the table—walking backward. This was the other rule of the ritual; besides keeping silent, the girls had to do everything backward, never turning to face the table. Some of them had practiced at home, because it was awkward and difficult to walk backward with a bowl of food held behind your back without spilling it or tripping. They found that it was best to walk backward slowly until you came up against the edge of the table, then you bent backward and eased the bowl onto the table, careful not to turn around or drop it.

They moved like shadows in the lantern light, as, one by one, they slid their platters and bowls to the center of the table. The practicing and the care they took to walk slowly served them well. No one spilled anything. That, too, might break the spell. Next they carried the earthenware water jug to the table, then the drinking gourds. Last, each girl carried a plate to the table, setting it at her appointed place, taking care not to turn and look as she did so. The last things put on the table were the knives, forks, and spoons. Each girl held the cutlery in one hand and felt behind her to locate the edge of the table and then the plate. Slowly and deliberately, each one eased the flatware into its proper place: fork on the left, knife and spoon on the right.

Finally all was ready.

Suddenly, a noise broke the silence, startling them all, and—careful not to look toward the table or to cry out in alarm—they peered over their shoulders to see what had made the sound. Nothing moved. They kept still and waited for something else to happen, but all stayed quiet. They looked at one another and shrugged. Perhaps it had been a mouse somewhere in the shadows. After a few more moments of listening, the girls went back to watching the doorway, hoping to hear the sound of arriving guests.

At her place at the corner of the table farthest from the lantern, Celia had been holding her breath, hoping that no one would realize that she was responsible for the disturbance. When it happened she nearly cried out to let the others know, but, remembering the rule of silence, she bit her lip and waited. They would be so angry if they knew.

She had tried to calm her nerves by adjusting the table setting, making sure that the plate was not too close to the edge, and that the flatware was neatly spaced on either side. When she reached behind her to straighten the knife beside the dinner plate, her hands were shaking. At the last instant, the knife slipped through her fingers, missing the chair, and striking the floor with a thump that echoed in the silence. When the others turned to see what made the sound, she slid the knife under the table with her foot, and then kept still, waiting for them to turn away again. After a few moments the others lost interest in the disruption, so she thought it might still be all right.

When she was sure no one was looking, Celia bent her knees so that she could touch the floor, and reached down, feeling under the table for the knife. There it was, a few inches from the chair. She knew she ought to tell the others what had happened, so that they could end the ritual before it could jinx them, but she kept silent. If the others knew, they would scold her, and blame her for spoiling the evening. She blinked back tears. Why tell them anything? After all it was just a silly game. Why risk their wrath and spoil their fun over a simple mistake?

Before she could make up her mind to speak, the first of the human guests arrived—Aurelia's best beau, of course, and the grinning girls took hold of his arms and gently guided him backward to his appointed place at the table. Sarah's young man came in a few minutes later and was seated next to the other suitor. The Dumb Supper had begun, and Celia's chance to admit her mistake passed.

While the others were paying attention to the young man, Celia made up her mind. She picked up the knife and wiped the blade on her skirt. Aurelia was smiling and hugging the others, overjoyed but careful to make no sound. No one noticed that Celia did not join in. No one noticed Celia much at all.

She pushed the knife back into its proper place on the table, but, worried that she might drop it again and be found out, she turned and looked at the table—only for an instant—just to make sure that the knife was not too close to the table's edge.

The Dumb Supper went on without further incident. Sarah and Aurelia's would-be suitors wolfed down the cold, unsalted food as if it were a feast, and grinned their approval, though, of course, the girls could not turn to see their expressions. The guests must eat and leave without a word or a sign to anyone. The girls whose sweethearts came were triumphant at this token of esteem; the other four chairs remained empty throughout the meal. Perhaps the ritual silence was a blessing after all; no one could make comments about the vacant chairs or boast of her own good fortune.

At the end of the supper, still four hours from daybreak, the girls gathered up their plates and the leftover food, which had gone unclaimed, and set out for home, still keeping the silence for good measure.

In the days afterward, when they did laugh and talk about the adventure, the two betrothed girls were careful not to say that no one had come for the others. Maybe someone had come for them. The ritual was a channel to old magic. It might have summoned phantom guests, invisible and silent, a sign that these girls had yet to meet their future husbands. That, too, could be good news—they might meet someone from outside the community, a rich and successful gentleman. Who knew? Perhaps these girls would be the fortunate ones after all. They might travel far from home to strange cities and distant places, instead of ending up right where they started as brides of eighteen: a worn-out woman, old at thirty-five and forever bound to a hardscrabble mountain farm.

A year later, though, at Aurelia's wedding to her dinner guest,

Celia told one of the Greer girls about dropping the knife at the Dumb Supper.

"Why didn't you say something then?" asked Eunice Greer, wide-eyed with alarm.

"Maybe no one will ever marry me," she said a little sadly.

The Greer girl nodded and managed to smile. "You're young yet, Celia. You'll meet someone one of these days." But she was thinking that if the Dumb Supper really was a magic ritual, then worse than mere spinsterhood might come from that mistake.

chapter one

If you looked close enough, you could tell he wasn't sleeping. This was something else. The sheet was rumpled and sweat-soaked from his thrashing in delirium. Sometimes he'd be burning up, and struggling to tear the covers away from himself. At other times he would shiver and moan, no matter how many quilts I put on the bed. All without waking up. No matter how often I wiped his forehead with a damp rag, beads of sweat still glistened on his brow, and when I spoke to him, he never seemed to hear. He would not come back from oblivion.

He's not even forty yet. *That thought rose unbidden to my mind, and that's when deep inside me I knew the truth that I would not admit or even think about. No matter how well I tended him or how much I cared, he was going to die. Soon.*

Soon.

I reckon things might have been different if we hadn't moved to town. Times were hard for everybody these days. Mr. Hoover's Depression had stretched on into President Roosevelt's term with no end in sight, but the fate of the stock market did not matter to the likes of us, just as long as there were jobs nearby for Albert. But all the jobs were in town, which meant a whole new set of problems. At least if you lived out in the country, you might not have any ready money or store-bought goods, but nobody ever went cold or hungry. You could always be sure there would be logs for the woodstove and food to put on the table at suppertime. Country people could hunt the fields and forest for squirrels and rabbits, same as the red hawk did. A family could eat good on rabbit stew thickened with flour, cooked with carrots, taters, and onions from the garden. It cost little enough to keep a flock of chickens if you had land enough for them to forage on, which saved the cost of feed. Chickens would give you eggs and a good Sunday dinner every now and then. Looking back on it, I can see that the country was the best place to ride out hard times.

Back then, though, moving to town seemed like the right thing to do. Albert's cousin Willis worked in the machine shop of the railroad. When he came up the mountain for that summer's dinner on the ground at the church cemetery, Albert asked him about jobs in town. The graveyard picnic was held to honor our dead kinfolk, but Albert said people ought to think about helping out the living, too. Willis saw the sense in that; he told Albert that if we were willing to move to town, he could get him hired on at the rail yard. After they talked it over, Albert asked me what I thought about it.

To me a regular paycheck sounded like an answer to prayer.

Ready money meant that we could buy food that didn't grow on the farm—oranges, coffee beans, and sugar. Money meant shoes for the boys when they outgrew their old ones, and maybe a store-bought dress for myself every once in a while, or at least a home-stitched one made with cloth that hadn't once been a flour sack. In town we might even manage to eat something for dinner besides stewed chicken or rabbit. I thought that if we could afford to eat pot roast once a week, maybe Albert could put on some weight, instead of having his ribs poking out, looking like a half-starved hound. With a little more meat on his bones, I hoped he wouldn't catch so many of those head colds that made him cough and wheeze all the way through every winter.

The town school would be better for the boys, too; no more one-room schoolhouse, where the teacher's attention had to be split up eight different ways and there weren't enough books to go around. People said that town schools had blackboards and books aplenty, and, best of all, they split the pupils up into different grades, so that they shared a class with schoolmates their own age, and there was one teacher for every single one of those classrooms. Eddie was bright, and, just like me, he loved to read, even if it was just those old dime novels about the Wild West. Georgie was still too little to read on his own, but he'd sit and listen as long as anybody cared to read to him from a storybook. I hoped that better schooling would help the boys go further in life than their daddy ever had. Albert could read and cipher well enough, but he wasn't what you would call educated. Never had the chance, coming from where we did.

Not that Albert was a bad man—he wasn't. He worked long and hard, even when he was sick as a dog, with never a word of complaint, never drinking his paycheck away, or making wagers with it. Everybody saw him as rock-steady, but he was nearing middle age now, and it was plain that no matter how hard he worked he wouldn't ever earn much more than it took to pay the bills and put food on the table. If it was the Lord's will, I wanted a better life than that for Eddie and George, and maybe a town school would make the difference.

I told Albert: "They could be anything; if they get good schooling and work as hard as you do, there's no telling what they could do in life."

We went back and forth about it for most of the week, talking in hoarse whispers in the bed so as not to be overheard through the wall. Finally Albert sighed and said, "All right, Ellendor. If you're dead set on it, why, we'll go."

Every time he moaned, I'd open my eyes and jerk back awake.

Although I tried not to, every now and then I'd catch myself dozing off in the chair. Ever since he took sick, Albert had been in our bed alone, and for all that time I had sat in that chair and watched him every minute I wasn't tending to the boys. I didn't want him to wake up and find me gone, or be in need of something and have to do without. I kept on telling myself that he would wake up—any hour now, *I thought, and then it became* any day.

But he didn't.

If there had been someone I could ask to come in and sit a spell with Albert while I got something to eat or to sleep a little in the boys' room, it would have been a blessing. But I was on my own. Even Eddie was too young to watch over his daddy. I couldn't bear to think of our boy keeping watch there alone, in case Albert should die while his son looked on. There might have been ladies I knew from church who would have sat with Albert so that I could rest, but I didn't feel like I knew any of them well enough to go asking favors. They weren't family. Cousin Willis was the only family we had in town, but he had no wife to be counted on, and besides, he had his job at the railroad yard taking up most of his time. Men are no use in a sickroom anyhow.

I must have slept sometime, but I can't remember doing it. I had worn the same clothes for days, not that it mattered compared to everything else. I kept thinking that surely Albert's fever would break soon, and once the crisis had passed, I could go and tend to myself. For days I waited for him to begin to recover on his own, but instead he seemed to sink deeper into himself, shutting out food and water, light and sound. Shutting out the world, like he was getting ready to let go.

I tried to pray every now and then, but it didn't give me any comfort. I kept asking the Lord to let my husband wake up and come back to me, but gradually I began to realize that if God had answered my prayer, then His answer had been no.

The time came when I was more afraid than hopeful. The practical side of me—the one that took me through hog killing and childbearing and doing without—told me that I ought to be thinking about a future without Albert, but I felt some kind of superstitious dread that if I started making plans for a life without him—if I so much as thought such a thing—then my acceptance of his fate would cause him to die. I know it was whistling in the dark to believe that if I didn't plan ahead he would have to recover, but it gave me a feeling of control when in fact there wasn't any. Things just happened, and nothing I could do would change what was meant to be.

Finally, it felt like our little rented house had shrunk to just this one small room.

We knew that living in town meant we would have to pay rent, of course, but we were resigned to that. At least Albert and I had the sense to make the trip down the mountain to town to look things over before we went forward with our plans to move—no use wishing for something if you can't make it so. Albert said it wasn't as if we'd be cast alone among strangers. Cousin Willis had promised to look after us, at least at first.

True to his word, Willis took Albert to work with him down at the railroad yard and managed to convince the shop foreman to hire him on. Albert was good with machinery. All the men in the Robbins family were—always tinkering with a broken clock or a misfiring gun. It just came naturally to them. I think they'd rather take a machine apart than to use it.

When we knew he would have a job with the railroad, Willis took us down to see one of the deacons from church and explained about his country kinfolk who were fixing to move to town and needed a helping hand. We just stood there like geese and let him do all the talking. Well, we were new in town then.

That church deacon said he thought there was more to religion than just praying, because the Lord told us to love one another, so he took it upon himself to help us find a place we could afford, which wasn't much. He claimed he knew everybody in town, and that if there was a house to be had, he would find it for us. When we made our minds up to rent one of the houses the deacon showed us, Albert said that the fellow's kindness made us beholden to him, so he reckoned that settled the question of where we would go to church. Country people pay what they owe—be it money or favors or meanness. Sugar for sugar; salt for salt.

It seemed like I sat there at the bedside for months instead of days. Sometimes I read the Bible, not so much for comfort as to forget all the other things I'd rather not worry about. I didn't know how Albert had caught this illness, and that made me afraid that the rest of us would get it too. Georgie was too little to survive such a sickness; maybe Eddie was too. Back when I was still in school, during the Great War that was, an epidemic of influenza hit the big cities and the army camps across the country, and it wasn't the old folks or the babies who mostly died. It was the soldiers, and strong, healthy people in their prime—like Albert was now. I worried, too, that I might be taken, but only because if I fell ill, there would be no one to look after the boys. It was for their sakes that I made myself eat when I fixed food for them, for I had no appetite and scarcely tasted anything that passed my lips.

We were lucky, I suppose, for Albert was the only one of us who took sick. I didn't feel fortunate, though, for I knew that whether the rest of us got sick or not, there were hard times ahead. Dying would be easier than what was to come. Quicker, anyhow.

When word got around that Albert and I were going away to live in town, the folks at our little mountain church prayed for us as if we were headed off to Abyssinia instead of just down the mountain and a few miles across the valley to a no-account whistle-stop railroad town.

The town had sprung up at the turn of the century in that narrow river valley around the railroad shops. We had no money to buy land or lumber to build a place of our own, so, with the kind help of that church deacon, we resolved to take what we could get. I was hoping that we would find a house with indoor plumbing—I had heard about places in town having the privy and a bathtub right inside, in a little room of their own, with piped-in water that didn't have to be boiled. But houses with marvels such as that belonged to the bankers and doctors and the foremen of the railroad shops—not to ordinary folk like us.

After looking at half a dozen places, some hardly more than shacks, the deacon took us to an across-the-tracks place that wasn't grand enough for any fancy plumbing, but that was why we could afford it in the first place. Instead of running water, the little house had a hand pump in the yard, which at least was better than an open well. There was a tin bath in a corner of the kitchen, but we had to fill it up with water that we heated on the stove. It took so much water to fill it that by the time we managed to heat enough water—a gallon at a time on the woodstove—the bath wasn't more than lukewarm.

A ways from the house on the woods side of the backyard sat an unpainted wooden outhouse. *"Four rooms and a path,"* Albert called it, trying to tease me out of my disappointment. I hadn't uttered a word of complaint, but I guess he could see it on my face.

We had seen the houses that were available, and most of them were beyond our means, so we settled on that four-room frame house a few yards from the railroad tracks. The place was small and in need of a coat of paint, but the kitchen had a cook stove, an old icebox, a pie safe, and an unvarnished pine table, which meant fewer things for us to buy. Above the dry sink, a little square of window overlooked the woods beyond the yard. What I liked best of all was that the kitchen was separate from the parlor. Next to it was a short hallway leading to two bedrooms opposite each other. We gave Eddie and George one of the rooms to share, and we took the bigger one across the hall. After all those years of being cooped up on the farm with the in-laws, I could scarcely imagine any more privacy than that.

We were happy to finally have some privacy, even after all the years that we'd been man and wife. It was better than having a kitchen all to myself.

Another disappointment for me, besides the lack of plumbing, was the fact that the house wasn't wired up for power, either, but the deacon said, "That means there won't be no electric bills to pay," and Albert happily agreed with him, as if that was good news. But he wasn't the one who had to worry about keeping food cold so that it didn't spoil and poison us, and he wouldn't be lying awake nights worrying that a kerosene lantern would get knocked over and cause a fire.

Well, there hadn't been electricity or indoor plumbing at the farm up the mountain, either, so I hadn't lost anything, but I figured if Albert and Willis were handy enough to work in a machine shop, then between the two of them they could rig up some wiring for that little house. I didn't nag him about it—not too much—but he must have known how bad I wanted it, because two months after we moved in, Albert and Willis had the house fitted with electricity so that we could dispense with the kerosene lamps. I wanted a refrigerator, too, instead of an icebox, but I knew it would take a long time to save up for that.

The best thing about leaving the family farm was that we wouldn't have to live with Henry and his wife anymore, bumping elbows with Elva when the two of us were fixing dinner, and then Albert and me trying to keep the bed from creaking in the night. That alone was worth the move to town, and Lord knows the move hadn't been too much trouble. We had lived with Albert's family for the whole of our wedded lives, so there had never been any call for us to buy furniture or dishes. What little we had to take with us fit in the bed of cousin Willis's old Ford truck, with room to spare.

Albert had started off the New Year with a hacking cough that kept both of us awake nights. By mid-February the cough had turned to wheezing, and his skin was hot to the touch. He was ailing for most of a week before he finally took to his bed and surrendered himself to the fever. He had not left it since.

Albert was never what you'd call hardy. Being thin as an arrow, like all the Robbins men, made him look taller than he was, and he had a narrow, bony face that made you think that if he wasn't sick, then he wasn't getting enough to eat. But that wasn't so. Albert could put away food like he had a furnace in his stomach—seconds on everything; four biscuits at one sitting; and all the chicken that was left after the boys and I had eaten our fill. Albert could go through twice as much food as I could eat, but he never seemed to keep it on his bones. No matter how much he ate he never put on any weight. I used to tell him that I could gain weight just watching him eat. Not that I was all that heavy either, being little and wiry, but I reckon that if I had tried to keep up with Albert, I would have swelled up like a toad inside of a month.

I always thought he would get heavier as he got older. People generally do. Running to fat is a bad thing to happen to most men and to all women, but in Albert's case, I figured the extra weight might come as a godsend as he got older. His sandy hair had flecks of gray, but they didn't show much. Being so thin made him look younger.

Sometimes he would moan in a fever dream, and I would try to talk to him. When I ran out of things to say, I'd sing, "Abide with me; fast falls the eventide . . ." *It was Albert's favorite tune. I know that the words of that old hymn were meant to be spoken to the Lord, but when I sang it then, I was really pleading with Albert himself.* Abide with me.

He seemed to turn toward me, just ever so slightly when I sang, but his eyes stayed shut, and I never did know if he heard me or not. Every now and then he'd gabble a few sounds that might have been words, but I couldn't make sense of them. Maybe they weren't words at all, but just the sound of his fever. Finally, when he had gone two days without eating anything, I tried to wake him. When I could not make him wake up to drink, I held a moistened rag to his lips so that he would get the water, but he just lay there moaning softly, his eyes shut tight as a new kitten's. Every time I held that cloth to his mouth, I thought about the Crucifixion, when someone held a sponge up to Jesus so that he could get a bit of moisture. Sometimes it's all you can do.

That was the only time I ever wondered if we had been right to leave the farm.

Hour after hour I just sat by the bedside, waiting, while Albert slept on. At first I was waiting for him to wake up, and then I was waiting for his condition to change one way or the other, and finally I was just waiting, because when I stopped waiting, time would start again, and I'd have to go on with the rest of my life.

Every now and again Eddie would remind me, mostly for Georgie's sake, that they needed meals cooked for them. I'd leave the sickroom long enough to boil some potatoes, fry slices of bacon, and round off the meal with whatever we had left in the larder. No one had been to the store in a week. We mostly ate in silence. I was exhausted and I think Eddie was afraid to ask me any questions about his dad. I was afraid that if I tried to explain it to him, I'd commence to crying and never stop.

At mealtimes, if I remembered, I would eat a bite or two myself, before I went back to the chair by the bedside. The only times I'd know that I had slept were when I would jerk awake in the chair and see that outside the window the light had changed or the moon was down. It was better to look out the window than to catch sight of my reflection in the mirror—catching even a glimpse of myself made me cringe: broom-straw hair; hollow, staring eyes; a pinched face; and lips pale as a fish belly. Sometimes I caught myself hoping that Albert wouldn't wake suddenly and find me looking haggard and old. I knew he'd be too sick to care how I looked, but I still minded.

⟷

The front yard of our rented house faced a dirt road, but it was big enough to have a patch of grass and flower beds, and on one side of the house a high blackthorn hedge kept us from having to look at the ramshackle house next to ours. The other side of the house faced the woods, and that view was more to our liking.

Our backyard faced the railroad tracks, but at least it was big enough to have fifty yards of bedraggled grass and a place to put up a clothesline. That spring I laid out a flower bed next to the blackthorn hedge.

When we first moved in, we discovered that the house was so close to the railroad tracks that whenever a train went past, the windowpanes rattled and the whole house shook like a leaf in the wind. The shrill scream of the locomotive whistle cut right through your bones. The only thing I ever heard as chilling as that was the sound of the cougars—we called them painters—up on the ridge. Maybe people could get used to such things, even learn to sleep through the shuddering roar of the night train, but none of us adjusted to it quickly. Georgie would wake up screaming. A whole year passed before the rumble of a train became an ordinary night sound, disturbing no one anymore.

I figured I could plant a vegetable garden in the backyard so that we could save money on groceries. I wasn't sure about keeping chickens—not with the railroad tracks so near. If I turned them out to forage, they'd either get run over by the train, or stolen by the tramps who wandered from place to place with nothing to their names except their independence. We could have put up a chicken wire fence, but the kind of flimsy fence we could afford wouldn't do much to keep the hoboes out or the chickens in.

Albert loved the woods, even that scraggly patch of weed trees near us that didn't amount to more than a couple of acres. I thought that maybe he wouldn't mind living in town so much if he lived near some woods and didn't have to feel crowded in by other houses. We moved because he needed a job to support us, but I didn't really know if he liked being a town dweller or not. He never said. We never did talk much about feelings or wherefores; mostly it was just *"What's for supper?"* or *"Do you have anything that needs sewn while I'm doing the mending?"*

I guess it really didn't matter whether Albert liked it here or not, though, because we were doing what we had to, but even if that had not been the case, I had no intention of going back up the mountain and living on sufferance from Henry and Elva. We would manage in town on our own.

⟷

After I had spent three days tending him, scarcely leaving the room except to see to Eddie and George, Albert stopped thrashing and his breathing changed. That's when I truly became afraid and gave up trying to care for him on my own. Digging two quarters out of my change purse in the dresser drawer, I called for Eddie and told him to fetch the doctor.

"Eddie, your daddy's took bad," *I said, as if he didn't know that already.* "You go and fetch the doctor, and if he's busy, you stay with him until he can come with you, so you can show him the way."

"And so he won't go tending to somebody else first," *said Eddie.*

"That too. Give him the quarters. Tell him it's all we got."

We had some jars of blackberry jam left over from summer, and I thought I'd give the doctor one of those along with the quarters. People pay what they can these days, and I reckon by now the doctor is used to taking his fee in vegetables or fresh-killed chickens. He was raised in these parts, so maybe he took these things so that his patients wouldn't feel beholden to him or feel shamed by charity. Most people's pride walled them away from anybody except family, and when illness struck, they tended their own. Fetching a doctor was the last resort. If a family felt ashamed to be in the doctor's debt, they'd not be sending for him again.

After Eddie set off, I stayed there by the bedside, wondering how long we could make do with just the food we had in the house. Albert hadn't got his paycheck on account of his being sick, and we had no money now to buy more. I'd had to choose, and I chose the doctor. That's what people do in town: when someone took sick, they sent for doctors. Well, poultices and herbal home remedies first, same as up home, but finally, doctors.

A passing freight train thundered past, shaking the house, its shrill whistle cutting through the silence. It shook me awake, for during my weary vigil I had nodded off in the chair. Albert did not stir. He still laid there, eyes shut tight, dead to the world, sleeping but yet not sleeping. He sank all the way into the mire of illness before I ever realized how serious it was, and before I knew that things were coming to an end. Back when Albert was still awake, when I had no inkling of what was to come, I did not try to talk to him about anything other than how he felt and whether he wanted to eat or sleep. Later on I wished I had thought to ask him bigger questions, but that would have meant admitting to myself and to him that he was not coming back. As bad as I needed to know things, I could not have done that. Taken away his hope of surviving—I could not have done that.

Anyway, I hadn't believed it myself. I kept thinking, But he can't be dying. He's not old.

But by the end, I knew that if, by the grace of God, Albert did return to life long enough to speak even a few words, I would ask him about everything. By then I'd had many waking hours to sit by the bedside in silence and dwell on the big questions, knowing that the answers to questions would have to last me the rest of my life. I needed to ask him about money, about the boys, about a future without him, whether he wanted me to stay here or go back up the mountain. So many questions, but they all boiled down to a single one: What must I do?

There had always been things we had to worry about—mostly money—but now all those day-to-day cares seemed meaningless compared to this last great sorrow that swallowed up all the rest. All I could think was: What must I do?

chapter two

Those first few months in town, even more than I feared the house shaking to pieces from the passing trains, I worried about the hoboes. They were mostly raggedy, unshaven men with gaunt faces and haunted eyes. There were so many men out of work these days: out of money, out of a place to live, and out of any hope for better times. With no homes to go back to, the hoboes roamed the country, riding in unlocked boxcars, camping out in hobo jungles near the railroad tracks. Some of them had given up on ever finding another job or a second chance at an ordinary life. They would forage, working a day or two when they could, and live off the land. Some of the vagrants were just sad husks, turned into failures by an economic disaster they did not understand, and I felt sorry for them. They were like chickens, headed for the chopping block but not knowing why. But I was uneasy about them, too, because some of them were drunks or dangerously angry men, maybe even deranged. Some of those men stole when they got the chance, so you didn't leave a door unlocked or a window open.

Somehow, the fact that some of these men were well spoken and obviously educated made it all the more terrible, because those once-respectable hoboes reminded me that our family might be only one stumble away from sharing the fate of these men: homelessness and hunger. Nothing was safe these days.

Every so often a grimy man in tattered clothes would knock politely, asking for a cup of water or any food that could be spared, offering to do chores in exchange for a meal. If I didn't think the tramp looked menacing, I would usually give him water in a tin cup and a hunk of cornbread if there was any left from supper. One day I told one of the ragged men, "We don't have much to spare. Why don't you go ask for a handout at the back door of one of those big houses on Elm Street? That's where the rich folks live—the bankers, the lawyers, and the railroad bosses. Why, I reckon those folks could give you a whole chicken and never miss it."

The fellow shook his head. "Don't you believe it, ma'am. Why, shoot, most of the time those rich folks up the hill won't give you nothing at all. Poor people will, because they know what it's like to be hungry and cold, and they realize how easy it is to get there. It's *because* they understand that they'll give a man whatever they can spare, but rich people don't think being down and out has anything to do with them or ever will. They think that being what we are is our own fault, and that maybe we're drunkards, or lazy, or feeble-minded. They won't give you a thing."

Some of the tramps tried to earn a few coins by selling intricately carved boxes fashioned with pocket knives, or they might make wooden toys or whatnots out of scrap from old orange crates and cast-off lumber. Some of their handiwork was as good as anything you'd see in a dime store, but I never did buy one. Pretty as they were, they were a reminder of someone losing everything, and I didn't want that reminder.

Albert and I had been together for what seemed like forever. We met in church when we were children, the way most folk up the mountain meet the one they will someday marry. Sixteen years back, when I was two months away from being twenty and Albert was nigh on twenty-two, we tied the knot at that same country church where we met. That wasn't why we got married there, though. That little white church had been both our families' place of worship for close to a hundred years. For us, all the ceremonies of life took place there: baptisms, weddings, funerals.

There was no room for a married couple on my family's land, not that I'd have wanted to live with them anyhow. What's the point of taking a husband unless you get to leave home? We could have built a place of our own, but there was no land to spare, because my daddy had my younger brothers to think of. The boys would be needing land for themselves one day, and keeping them living close by meant that they could still help Daddy with the family farm.

So as newlyweds Albert and I had little choice but to go back to the farm where he grew up and move in with his parents and Henry, his only surviving brother. I agreed to go because we were just starting out and there really wasn't any other choice, but our stay was never supposed to be permanent—just until we could manage to afford a place of our own—but we lived there longer than we or they ever thought we would.

Albert's older brother Virgil, the one who had been expected to take over the farm, went off with Pershing to fight the Kaiser, but mostly he went off to see the world, and the pity of it is just how little of it he got to see. Poor Virgil caught the influenza in an army camp in France just a week or so after he got there, before he even made it to the front. Virgil never came back, not even in a box to rest forever on the family land. If he had a grave somewhere in France, none of his family would ever see it. His mother put a little mound of stones at the far end of the yard, next to the wooded ridge. She wedged a wooden cross among the stones, planted flowers around it, and kept it weeded, summer and winter. Virgil wasn't there, but no one wanted to remind her of that. Later on we buried our first two babies up there beside him. Our first, a little blue-eyed girl, came too early, and she didn't thrive from the very beginning. We lost her before a month had passed. The next one, Albert Jr., died in his first winter. After that no more babies came for a few years, and I thought that was the end of it, but maybe my body just had to lie fallow for a while, same as the fields do from time to time, before things will grow there again. Sure enough, I was all of twenty-six by the time Eddie came along, and then after six more years of barrenness, we had little George.

After the passing of Virgil and our first two babies, Albert's parents seemed to get older real quick. They just began to fade out, which meant that Albert was obliged to stay and help his father with the farm work, because his other brother Henry, the change-of-life baby, had been only ten years old when we got married, so it would be another six or seven years before he could handle a man's share of the farm work.

Albert didn't want the farm, and he would just as soon have left, and I was praying that we could go anywhere else, but it wouldn't have been right. Daddy Robbins was getting too old to manage on his own, and we didn't want it on our heads if he killed himself with overwork or perished in a farming accident. So we stayed on because we had to.

After a dozen years of living with Albert's family, the farmhouse got crowded. Little Henry had finally grown up and found himself a wife. That was about the time that Albert and I had our last baby, George Albert Robbins. I had secretly been hoping for a little girl, to replace the firstborn that we lost, but everybody else was overjoyed that we had a son. Georgie was a fat and lusty summer baby, so we knew we had a good chance of keeping him.

Soon after Georgie was born Albert's father had a heart attack. He lived through it, but it left him frail, which meant that he was able to do even less work than before. I still wanted us to set out on our own, but it seemed heartless to want to abandon the family just when Daddy Robbins needed us more than ever. Besides, Albert's parents doted on the new grandbaby and it would have been cruel to take him away. So we stayed on. Somehow, for another year, we all managed to jostle along together: three families in one house, but I had started to feel like a bear on a chain, and I prayed we'd be able to leave.

When we lived up the mountain Albert would sometimes hire on to one of the logging crews so that we would have some extra money for shoes or for cans of food to stretch out our winter food supply. A paycheck meant ready cash to replace something around the farm that needed fixing or replacing. The logging jobs never lasted long, though, and neither did the money. The timber company always closed down the operation before the cold rains of November. Albert seemed happy harvesting timber or gathering ginseng in the woods to sell to the drugstore in town. He liked the countryside and working outdoors, as long as it wasn't farming. He always said that farming was like pouring sand down a rat hole: no matter how long you did it, you wouldn't get anywhere. I thought it was strange that he felt like that because his folk had been farmers nigh on all the way back to Noah.

I told him I couldn't see where logging or laying track for the railroad got you anywhere either, but Albert's answer to that was that at least the trees stayed cut down and a stretch of track didn't have to be laid but once. Farming, though, meant doing the same thing in the same place over and over, year in and year out. *"Same as housework,"* I said, and he laughed like he thought I was joking.

So we kept living on the family farm. The soil wasn't good, though, and it never produced much in the way of a living. Splitting the land between Albert and Henry would have ruined both of them. Maybe Albert knew that and just said he didn't like farming to spare his father from having to choose between them.

As bad as I wanted out of there, I tried not to complain about the close quarters and the lack of privacy, because as Albert's parents began to fade into the frailty of old age staying on seemed more like a kindness than good sense. When old Miz Robbins's sight began to fail, Henry's wife, Elva, and I took over most of the cooking and the heavy work around the house. I tended the little flower path around the memorial to Virgil because my babies were there too. Between the two of them Albert and Henry shouldered more of the farm chores as their daddy's strength ebbed away. Finally, though, the old man's heart gave out, and we buried him at the end of October—not in the family burying ground, but out beside Virgil's plot near the graves of our first two children, which is what he said he wanted. Then in late winter a bout of flu carried off Albert's mother. She slipped away so gently that it was as if she was glad to go. *"She followed him to the grave,"* people said at the funeral.

Since there were two less people living on the farm, it seemed strange that the homeplace began to feel too small to house all of us. When she first married Henry, Elva had been a quiet, biddable girl, but she grew up quick and headstrong, and now she let her temper show when she was displeased, which was often. When running the kitchen became a war of wills between Elva and me, I made up my mind to go. I told Albert that since he didn't care for farming anyhow, it was time we left the place to Henry, and started looking for somewhere else to go. Sooner or later Henry would have to manage to run the farm on his own, and he might as well start now.

By the time we were ready to leave, my parents had been dead for half a dozen years. One by one, all my brothers and sisters got married and went elsewhere—the boys to the car factories in Detroit, and the girls to their husband's house or off to try their luck at city life. We all agreed to sell the farm, and split the money among the five of us. It hadn't come to much, but I put my share in the bank to save up for the day when we would be on our own. Money was so scarce in Mr. Hoover's Depression that I reckon we were lucky to find anybody to buy the farm at all.

The friction between me and Elva was the last straw that made

Albert ask Willis about railroad jobs in town. Soon after, we headed down the mountain to make a new start. Our new place might be shabby, small, and owned by somebody else, but at least we had it all to ourselves.

I didn't see any harm in parceling out what food we could spare to the hungry men who came begging at the door, but before long Albert put a stop to my charity. All those tramps seemed so dirty and desperate, he said, you couldn't tell by looking at them which ones were dangerous and which were not. He reckoned the only safe thing to do was to trust none of them. He never said why he decided that, but maybe he had heard something down at the railroad shop. There must have been an incident; some tramp somewhere must have robbed some woman and killed her. Anyhow, one day he made me promise not to open the door to any of them anymore.

When he said that, I put down the dishrag I had been using and swung around to face him. I expect he could tell from the look on my face that I was as close to disagreeing with him as I ever got. I took a deep breath to fuel my arguing. "I seem to remember, Albert, that the Bible says we are bidden to help those in need."

He sniffed, not best pleased at having Scripture cited at him. "Well, Ellendor, as I recall, the Bible also said, 'The poor you will always have with you.' Now that is the pure truth, hon, and you can't change it with leftover cornbread. I'll allow that maybe this isn't how the Bible would have us treat the folks who are poor in spirit, but from what I hear some of those tramps are dangerous. You've only got to think of all those Christian martyrs in the Roman Coliseum getting eaten by lions to know that the Lord doesn't seem to mind if following His teachings gets you killed or not. I guess he reckons heaven is all the reward you need, but I'd rather you didn't go there just yet, darlin'."

He smiled and gave me a one-armed hug to show he wasn't spoiling for an argument about this, but when I still looked doubtful, he added, "Well, what if one of them tried to break in while you were here by yourself? And what about the boys?"

After that at least once a week Albert came home full of tales from the machine shop about some woman somewhere who was beaten and raped or found in her kitchen with her throat cut. To hear him talk, you'd think that living here in Tennessee was just as perilous as in the pioneer days, when it was the Indians you had to look out for. Finally, his stories began to get under my skin, and I took to keeping the butcher knife under a dish towel by the sink, in case one of the tramps tried to break in and attack me.

Albert had a two-dollar pistol with a rubber stock that he'd bought from a fellow at the railroad yard, but he kept it locked in a tin box in the bedroom and wouldn't let anybody else touch it. "You'd be more dangerous with that shootin' iron than ten hoboes, Ellie," he told me, laughing. "I'm afraid you'd panic and shoot one of the boys coming back from the outhouse some night."

That laugh flicked me raw. "Are you worried about me or not? You make it sound like somebody could break in here any minute, but what do we have that a hobo or anybody else would think worth taking?"

"Besides you, Ellie? Anything is worth something to them that have nothing. Hoboes get hungry, same as anybody else. They steal anything that isn't nailed down to sell so they can buy liquor."

It was no use trying to convince Albert of anything when he set his jaw like that and got a mulish look in his eyes, so I let it drop. He had to come to it on his own. Anyhow, he was probably right about the gun being more dangerous than helpful, unless I knew how to use it, so I held my peace and saved the arguments for later. I was thankful that Albert worked days, so that he would be home to protect the boys and me if anybody tried to break in at night while we were sleeping.

I said no more about it then, but after a couple of days of mulling it over on his own, Albert said maybe he ought to allow me to keep the gun where I could get to it quickly if I had to. "A pistol can stop a man faster and farther away than a butcher knife," he said, and I wondered what terrible tale he had heard at work to make him change his mind.

I didn't much care for guns; all his talk about wayfaring robbers had made me afraid, but I didn't want to rush into anything. "I think it's a good idea for me to be able to defend myself and the boys, but I never have fired a gun, you know. I wouldn't want to shoot anybody by accident because I didn't know what I was doing."

Albert smiled and kissed my cheek. "I'm fixing to teach you, hon."

One bright Saturday morning he set down his coffee mug and pushed back from the breakfast table. "Take off that apron, Ellie. We're going out in the backyard for your first shooting lesson. Last evening Eddie and I collected all the old tin cans and bottles we could find. He's already set them up on that fallen log on the edge of the woods, haven't you son?"

Eddie looked up from his breakfast and nodded happily. "Can I shoot, too, Daddy?"

"You cannot. That there gun's no toy, Eddie. It's dangerous. You stay right where you are and make sure you keep your brother in the house."

Then he turned to me and said: "Now we'll see how you do with a pistol. But you have to do as I say, Ellendor, and for the Lord's sake, don't point it at anything but those cans."

From the way he talked, you'd think I wasn't any older than Eddie. "I know to be careful, Albert."

Albert looked at Eddie and Georgie, still shoveling pancakes into their mouths. "You boys stay here in the kitchen. Both of you. Don't even go near the window." He grinned at them. "Your mama is fixing to learn how to be a crack shot, in case John Dillinger needs any help robbing banks."

They had all laughed at that, and I managed a tepid smile. Dillinger was dead: shot by lawmen in Chicago that summer, but I didn't bother to point that out, because Albert had only been teasing anyway.

So we went out in the backyard to begin the shooting lesson. The weight of the weapon did not trouble me overmuch. It wasn't as heavy as the flatiron I used to press our good clothes for church. The first time I fired, the crack of the pistol startled me, not because it was particularly loud—not compared to the whistle of a freight train, anyhow—but because the nearness of it to my ear startled me, causing me to jerk back and almost drop it.

When he saw that, Albert sighed and shook his head. He looked like he was about to tell me to quit, but before he could say anything I brought the gun up again as fast as I could and fired off a shot at a jam jar in the middle of the log. When the bullet hit it, the jar flew apart, scattering pieces all over the ground around the log.

Albert chuckled and patted my shoulder. "Well, what do you know?"

It had been luck, really. I had not even taken the time to aim the pistol the way Albert had told me to, but after a few more practice rounds, I was hitting the targets not by accident, but because I was aiming at them.

After a few more shooting lessons from Albert we both figured I could protect myself if I had to. The gun was in a drawer where I could get at it quickly, and I kept on practicing until even at twenty feet my aim was dead-on. I was ready, but no hobo ever tried to break into the house, and after months passed and nothing happened, my fear of the homeless men dwindled to a faint uneasiness. The family had finally learned to sleep through the roar of the passing trains in the night. Eddie got used to the ways of the town school, and Albert seemed happy enough working at the machine shop with Willis. As for me, I found out that the household chores—cooking, scrubbing floors, washing clothes—were the same whether you lived in town or on the mountain. I did get to buy some store-bought cloth to sew a new dress so that I wouldn't feel like such a ragamuffin when we went to church. Mostly, though, any spare money from Albert's wages went for shoes for the boys and to replace their clothes when they outgrew them.

By the time a year had passed, we had settled into the community, and we even had a few friends. Well, acquaintances, more like. Where we came from, *friend* is a word folks take pretty seriously. Albert got to know the other men from work; Eddie and George found playmates from the nearby houses, and I got acquainted with the women of the church, though I never said much. Mostly I just let them talk, figuring I'd learn something, and they seemed happy to have someone to listen to them. When I really wanted company I read a book, and I was thankful for the little public library. For all of us the town was beginning to feel like home.

Of the neighbors we had, I had got to know Annie Slocombe the best, but it wasn't because the two of us had much in common. We had both married young, and we both had little children, but that's as far as the similarities went. I was older than she was and, in every way that I could see, more fortunate. I'd see Annie out in her yard now and again, usually hanging up a clothesline full of diapers, and even when she smiled she looked like a whipped hound. I kept to myself right enough, but that was because I was satisfied with my own company. The Slocombes came from Pennsylvania, she told me once, swept along by the railroad as if it was a flooded creek carrying rootless things along its path. She never said why they left home, but neither of them had family around here, and they kept to themselves, as if they were afraid of anybody getting too close. Annie looked like she had been set down to live among crocodiles and dare not turn her back for an instant. Maybe she had reason to be leery of the world. A time or two, when our windows were open, I'd hear shouting coming from the Slocombe place—only one voice, and it wasn't hers.

Judging by the way he yelled and ordered her around, you'd have expected Annie's husband to outweigh her by fifty pounds and to be older than she was by a decade, but he wasn't a big bruiser at all. He was a wiry banty rooster of a man with slicked-back hair and a hand-rolled cigarette hanging off his lip every time I saw him. You'd think that a strong wind would blow him away, but he was like a little yappy dog, far likelier to bite than a big old hound: a big attitude in a small package. Maybe it was because he was little that he bullied his wife: it was the only chance he had to outrank anybody. He might have been a year or two older than Annie, but it was hard to tell their ages. Being slight gave him the look of a teenage boy, while Annie's youth was running out awful fast. Her hair was scraggly and dull, and she had gone from slender to scrawny sooner than she ought to have. At this rate, she'd be an old woman at thirty, and if meanness didn't get her husband killed, he'd probably still look twenty-five when he turned fifty.

She might have been one of those fair-haired women who bloom early and fade fast, but I thought her decline had more to do with how hard she worked, how close together her babies came, and how little money the family had for buying decent food and warm clothes. I never saw the children do without, but I'll bet that Annie did. Slocombe managed to earn money doing odd jobs and yard work for the railroad gentry up on the hill, but he drank up most of his wages.

She lived in fear of him—anybody could see that. Even when she was out in the sunshine and everything was quiet, she'd glance back at her house like she was waiting for it to explode. A time or two I tried to tell Albert about how Slocombe treated his wife, but Albert said it wasn't any of our business, and, besides, he said the few times he'd spoken with Slocombe he'd found him to be a quiet fellow, ready to smile at a joke, though he never had much to say for himself. I couldn't offer any arguments to the contrary, because Annie wasn't talking to anybody about it, so I had to let it go.

Things came to a head one summer evening when Albert had taken the boys with him to go fishing in the river, and I was alone. I had set a kitchen chair out in the yard so that I could shell butter beans in the cool evening breeze, but before long the peace was broken by a crash and a thump, followed by a chorus of wailing. The Slocombe babies were crying from being startled and then frightened, but their mother's screams sounded like the wailing of someone in pain.

It didn't even occur to me to try to hunt up Albert. There wasn't time. I just went inside and got the pistol and a hunk of cornbread left over from supper. I walked across the yard to the Slocombes' back door, just letting all the yelling and crying whip past me as if they were no more than a train whistle. I had to pound on the door three times to make myself heard above the din.

The shouting stopped, and after a minute or two Annie peeped out the door. Her face was streaked with tears and there was a red splotch under one eye that would be swollen and purple in an hour or so. She saw it was me and tried to hide behind the door. "This ain't a good time, Miz Robbins."

I pushed back on the door. "I see that. Let me in, Annie. You take those young'uns out into the yard and give them this cornbread to take their minds off this trouble."

The children had been clinging to her skirts anyhow, and when they spied the cornbread they were glad enough to go, and she had no choice but to go with them. When they were out of the way, I pushed the door open wider. "Mr. Slocombe! I know you're in there." I didn't think twice about calling him mister instead of using his first name. Sometimes people mistake that form of address for a sign of respect, but more often it means "I don't want to give you any cause to think we're friends."

He ambled up to within a few feet of the door, close enough for me to smell the wave of liquor and sweat he gave off. "This ain't no concern of yours," he said, like he was turning a hobo away from the door.

"If I have to listen to it, that makes it my concern."

He started toward me, and I let him see the pistol in case he had any ideas about beating up a woman other than his wife. He pulled up short, but the gun didn't seem to impress him overmuch, because he sneered. "What are you fixin' to do with that?"

"Why, I'm fixin' to use it, Mr. Slocombe. The next time I see anybody besides you from this house sporting bruises or red marks. The next time I hear any shouts, or screams, or cries of pain coming from this house, I'll come pounding on the door again. I'll be keeping an eye on this place, and if anything going on here disturbs my peace or rubs me the wrong way, I'll be over here like white on rice to straighten things out. And if I have to shoot you, Mr. Slocombe, there's not a jury in the state of Tennessee that will convict me."

He gave me a mulish glare. "A man's got a right to keep order in his own home."

"And everybody's got a right to shoot mad dogs, so look out I don't take you for one. And don't go thinking you can take this out on her." I nodded toward Annie, sitting on the grass with the children crawling all over her like puppies. "If you lay a hand on her I'll know. I'll make her tell me. And then we'll finish this."

"I'll tell *your* husband—"

I smiled. "If my husband had any idea what you're getting up to over here, you'd already be dead. Now you restrain yourself, or me and this gun'll be back." I hope I sounded like the good guy in a cowboy movie. I intended to. If I hadn't been dragged along to the movies once a week with Albert and the boys I wouldn't have had any idea how to talk to a worthless bully like Slocombe, but apparently I sounded like I knew what I was about, because he left off knocking Annie around, and I never heard any more loud arguments from over there. Of course, I wasn't exactly dear to his heart after that, but

I didn't care. Annie was grateful, but I don't know that I cared about that either. It wasn't right what he was doing, that's all, and I wouldn't stand for it. Facing him down with a pistol was a dern sight easier than making chitchat with the old biddies from church.

⟷

After we'd lived in town for a year Albert bought us a big Atwater Kent radio for the parlor, and, with the coins he put in a tin box every week, he saved up enough to get me a secondhand sewing machine for Christmas. The machine had belonged to the wife of one of the railroad shop foremen. It was a good one, but it had stopped working, so instead of trying to fix it, the foreman's wife bought a new one out of the Sears Wish Book. The foreman let Albert have the broken machine for a couple of dollars, and Albert took it to the machine shop, where he and the other men got it running again, so it worked just fine. Eddie pined for a bicycle, and I wanted an electric refrigerator to replace the old icebox in the kitchen, but Albert was set on putting as much money as we could spare away in savings, so we knew that those things would have to wait.

⟷

After we got accustomed to life in town, our lives ticked steadily along for a while. I thought we were doing well, but then Albert got restless and bored at the railroad shop. He didn't like being cooped up indoors all day, and maybe he had caught a touch of ambition from living in the town. I didn't like the change in him as much as I thought I would.

Albert waited until the boys went to bed before he told me, but he had already made up his mind.

We were sitting together in the parlor, me mending socks and Albert fidgeting. Finally he turned down the music on the radio and motioned me into the kitchen. I poured him some coffee, and he sat down at the kitchen table, rubbing the sides of his coffee mug while he worked out what to say to me. "Ellie, I'm fixing to quit the machine shop."

I kept my eyes on the sock I was darning so that he wouldn't see the look on my face. "Are they laying men off then, Albert?" I kept my voice as steady as I could so he wouldn't leave off telling me. "I know times are getting worse for everybody."

That Atwater Kent radio brought us music and even plays to help us pass the time in the evening when it could pick up the signals from distant stations, but besides all the entertainment, it also reported the news from all over the country, which was a mixed blessing. It let us know that we were not the only ones struggling through hard times, but it also proved that things were no better anywhere else, and, on account of the economic depression, there seemed to be nowhere to go to escape it, and no end in sight.

"Laying people off?" Albert shook his head. "No. Ain't nobody at the railroad yard said anything about cutting back on jobs, Ellie. Touch wood. But that doesn't mean that they won't decide to do it on a moment's notice, with not a thought in the world about what would happen to us next. But even if they don't cut jobs—well, the truth is, sometimes I wish they would. Working in that little shop is a waste of daylight. I reckon the job could pay more, too."

"It's better than no pay at all."

He sighed. "Well, I reckon that's true, hon, but I've decided that I wasn't cut out for working in a shop day in and day out. In the winter, I set off afore sunup and come home past dark. Every now and then I'd like to see sunshine somewhere besides on the other side of the window."

I kept my eyes on the darning needle. "I'd like to keep seeing food on the table, Albert."

He nodded. I knew he wouldn't be so selfish as to quit a job without giving a thought to the family he had to support. "I'm mindful of that, Ellie. I've been chewing over this for a while now, and I wouldn't think about leaving unless I had somewhere else to go. You know that. I wouldn't do anything to make you and the boys go without, and I wouldn't live on other people's charity any more than you would. I do have my sights set on another job, though, and I promise you I won't leave the railroad shop unless I get it."

Another job? That puzzled me. "But who else is hiring in this town? The railroad all but owns the place. And who but the railroad could afford to take on new help in times like these? You aren't thinking to *leave* town, are you?" I had never been anywhere else, so I don't know why I expected things to be worse in some other place, but the idea of going into flatlands among strangers frightened me more than staying here and going hungry. The only thing worse would be if Albert decided to go elsewhere to work, leaving me and the boys behind. I knew that some of the men who went to work in the car factories up in Michigan did that. Some might save up their pay and send for their families to join them. But some of them wouldn't. *Grass widows* was what people called women whose husbands took off and abandoned them. I didn't intend to be one.

I took a deep breath to keep from crying. "Are you fixing to go then?"

"No, Ellie. I am not. We're all staying put. And as for 'who but the railroad could afford to take on new help,' the answer is the same as always: the government."

"What government? Washington?"

" 'Course not. I mean the county."

I stared at him while I took it in. What jobs does the county have to give? "Tax collector?"

Albert chuckled. "Well, no, hon, I ain't stooped *that* low. And I wouldn't know how to get blood out of a turnip anyhow, which is what tax collecting must be like nowadays. No thank you. I have applied to be hired on as a deputy sheriff. The job would give me a lot of work outdoors, which I'd like, and it would be a step up in the eyes of the community, which would be good for both of us."

I stabbed at the sock with the darning needle. "Well, I suppose it would be, if you call having folks scared of you a step up. I don't believe I do."

CELIA

By the time Celia Pasten had completed her two years of college and then a year of teaching in a little county school, the memory of her mishap at the Dumb Supper had faded from her mind. The other girls might still be preoccupied with thoughts of love and marriage, but she was satisfied with the path she had chosen, and that choice had nothing to do with any possible curse arising out of the Dumb Supper. When people asked why she didn't get married, she told them that working for a living wasn't any harder than cooking and scrubbing floors for free. It might even be safer: even aside from the risk of dying in childbirth, there was the fact that more than one woman had settled for marriage and then found herself widowed or abandoned with no means of support. Celia thought she might marry someday—if she felt like it—but if so, she had no intention of being completely dependent on a husband for support. She never mentioned the fact that she had received no offers of marriage anyhow. And, sometimes at church, without quite knowing why, she prayed that someone would choose her.

Most of the other girls had been spoken for.

Shortly after high school graduation, golden Aurelia, and cunning Sarah, the minister's daughter, married their sweethearts—those same young men who had attended the Dumb Supper to make their intentions known. Their weddings took place in the little community church on consecutive Saturdays in June. Once married, both brides settled into complacent domesticity, one in a wood and cinderblock cottage on a parcel of her in-laws' farm, and the other into a small town in Georgia, close to the army base where her new husband was stationed.

The childhood circle of friends didn't see much of one another after that. With little in common anymore, the girls drifted apart, going their separate ways. Celia, who was more diligent than gifted, received a scholarship to nearby Milligan College, where she studied education so that she could get a teaching certificate.

The Greer sisters, still spinsters and likely to remain so, stayed at home, tending to their ailing mother and taking on most of the farm chores. They turned up at the others' weddings, though, throwing handfuls of rice; one of them elbowing the guests aside, trying to catch the bride's bouquet, while her sister scowled at such foolishness.

Another of the Dumb Supper girls, Ann Durner, married in August. Some of her girlhood friends served as bridesmaids, but Celia was not among them. Nevertheless, she went to the wedding, partly to wish Ann well and mostly to show that she was not bitter or envious of the bride.

At the reception afterward the dour Greer sister, who was in charge of the punch bowl, beckoned to Celia. She smiled as she handed Celia a cup of apple juice and fizzy water, but there was more sneer than happiness in that smile. "Well, Celia Pasten, remember that Dumb Supper we put on when we were foolish girls? It seems to have worked for some of us anyway." She nodded toward the bride, who had just finished cutting the wedding cake.

Celia smiled to show she didn't mind being slighted by fate. "Perhaps it did. Unless it's just coincidence."

"Do you think so?" The Greer sister raised her bushy eyebrows. "Have you noticed that we three are the only old maids left of the supper party? Me—and I don't care a bit for all the nonsense of romance; my sister, who is homely and desperate, a fatal combination for a spinster; and you. Now I find that interesting. I have given up expecting the two of us Greers to ever marry; by the time Mother passes away, we will be too old to try. We don't care much for the selection around here, anyhow, but we did think that you would have settled for somebody after all this time. You're not unattractive for your type, and some men aren't overly particular about looks."

Celia blushed. None of the community's young men had ever shown more than a passing interest in her, but she couldn't bring herself to admit that to the mocking keeper of the punch bowl. "It doesn't worry me one bit," she said. "Haven't you realized why I've stayed single? I can't be thinking about courting because I'm studying to be a teacher. The state won't allow lady schoolteachers to be married, so I guess it's no use for me to try to find somebody, unless I'm willing to give up my job and waste all that education."

"Safer, too, don't you think?" The Greer sister's sour smile stayed in place, but now her eyes narrowed, completing the spiteful image. She picked up a knife from the refreshment table and, still smiling, let it fall from her hand. It clattered on the floor and spun once, ending with the blade pointing toward Celia.

Celia glanced at it and looked away as if she had not understood the gesture. "What do you mean, safer? Safer on account of not having to go through childbirth, you mean?"

"Oh, no." The Greer sister shook her head. "There's some that go through that without ever getting married, and, wedded or not, most women manage to live through it, though I wouldn't care to risk it myself." Leaning in close she whispered in Celia's ear, "You know what I really mean, don't you? It's on account of the Dumb Supper. Remember that night?"

"What about it? It was ages ago."

"Well, I haven't forgotten any of it. You told me afterward that you had dropped your table knife on the floor, and then, when you were putting it back, you looked straight at the table. So I reckon you're cursed on account of that."

Celia shrugged. "It was only a silly game."

"That's as may be, but you can't deny that it came true for Aurelia and Sarah. Both of them married the boys who showed up for them that night at the Dumb Supper. Of course, Sarah was in the family way when she was wed, so I suppose the Fates had a little help in getting her to the altar."

"And Aurelia is beautiful. She would never lack for suitors anyhow."

"Well, those chocolate-box blondes fade early, so I think it was best for her to marry while her looks lasted. But you are another matter altogether. There's many a girl plainer than you who went to the altar at seventeen, and here you are past twenty."

"I wanted an education."

"Even so, I still think you were wise to keep clear of love and marriage. You broke the ritual. If you were to get married, there's no telling what might happen." The Greer sister looked especially pleased about that, perhaps because she was red-faced and stout, with little hope of being a bride herself, while Celia, although timid and bashful, was slender and striking.

"Nothing would happen. It was all nonsense."

"Well, I wouldn't chance it if I were you, Celia. You go on and be a spinster schoolmarm and keep out of harm's way."

Because she could not manage a smile, Celia gave her a blank stare and backed away. As more wedding guests began to hover around the table asking for punch, she murmured something and slipped through the crowd as quickly as she decently could. For the remainder of the reception Celia went on embracing the old friends who insisted on it. She listened to news about their lives, without saying much about herself. But she remembered very little of the occasion after that.

If someday she had a husband she would tell him about that silly courting tradition.

Someday.

chapter three

"*The King's life is drawing peacefully to a close.*" When we heard the news on the radio, I saw Albert's eyes fill with tears.

In the evenings after supper we usually listened to the news together, and though it made me no never mind what happened to some far-off king, Albert had to wipe his eyes when he heard it. He always felt connected to the British royal family, mostly because he had been named for the Prince Consort, Queen Victoria's late husband, even though the prince had died in England more than thirty years before Albert was born in Tennessee. Maybe that's why he was so set on giving our sons the names of princes: Edward and George. Mama Robbins, Albert's mother, had spent her life miles from town on a mountain farm, but she had been a great one for reading, so in a way the world came to her. She always said she named one of her sons for a Roman poet, and the other two for English princes. Maybe she thought giving her boys such grand names would nudge them a little higher up in the world, but about the only result of it was that Albert took an interest in the royals, as if they were his long-lost kin. Otherwise, I couldn't see where his life and theirs crossed at any point . . . except possibly now.

A month ago in England old King George had died. The radio

newsreader talked about how the king had taken ill with some lung ailment, and finally in January, his majesty took to his bed where he finally slipped into a coma and passed away. Sitting at Albert's bedside made me think of the king's death. But the king was an old man, and his dying had taken place in a castle full of servants, with the best doctor in the land sitting by his bedside, doing all he could for the royal invalid, whereas my Albert, still in his prime, lay dying in the damp chill of a matchbox house with only his wife at his side. Only a few weeks apart, though, Albert and the king. That was something, anyhow.

Finally the doctor came to call. There was just the one physician in the whole valley, and, between tending to farm accidents and difficult childbirths, he never had much time to spare for ordinary aches and pains, or for fevers and winter ailments. He did his best, though. Anyone who worked all hours of the day and night, and as often as not got paid in vegetables and homemade jam, had to be dedicated to his calling. I'd heard that when he was still a young man he had attended some medical school down south, but you could tell why he chose to practice here just by looking at him. He had the wiry frame, the dark hair, and the cold blue eyes of those who were born and bred in the Tennessee mountains. He looked like a descendant of the pioneers who settled here back in the 1700s. Surely his coming to practice in a little railroad town with too many patients and too little money could only mean that he had grown up somewhere like here. Some people didn't want to leave the mountains, even if they had the education and the skills to go elsewhere. Anyhow, the community was lucky to have him.

He turned up late on a misty afternoon, carrying his black bag, and bundled to the gills in a scarf and greatcoat. I offered to hang it up for him, but he took a deep breath of the cold, still air inside the house and said he'd just keep the overcoat on for a while, thanks all the same. I took him the few paces down the short hallway to the darkened room where his patient lay, cocooned in his fever dreams.

Albert did not stir when we came in, and when I called his name he did not respond.

The doctor stood there just watching him for a minute or two. "How long has he been like that?"

"A couple of days. At first I thought that a long sleep would be good for him, but now . . . Can't you wake him up?"

The only answer I got to my question was a slight shrug. For a while we just stood there, watching Albert sleep, and neither of us spoke.

He was buried under blankets, but there were still beads of sweat on his forehead. The doctor felt his pulse, took a stethoscope out of the leather Gladstone, and put it to Albert's chest. He leaned down, listening for a few moments to the ragged and labored breathing that had frightened me so much. Then he sighed and shook his head. "Rales," he muttered to himself, and I could tell he was hoping that I hadn't overheard him, but it didn't matter, because I didn't understand the word anyhow.

When he finally looked up, he was careful not to show emotion. Maybe he had learned from long experience that a patient's loved ones will seize upon the slightest sign to figure out whether or not there was any hope. If the doctor's face didn't match his soothing words, the relatives would believe what they saw, not what they heard—and they'd be right. I could see from his expression that the news was not good. I reckon it seldom was.

The doctor sighed and ran his hand through his hair. "Well, Mrs. Robbins, I suppose I ought to say that you should have called me sooner, but the plain truth is I doubt if it would have made any difference one way or the other. Your husband has pneumonia. Perhaps you know that."

"I hoped it wasn't. I feared as much, but I was praying that it was just a chest cold."

"It may have started out that way, but it turned into pneumonia. At this point there's not much anybody can do to help him."

Seeing that I was dismayed by this grim pronouncement, the doctor seemed to cast about for something to say to give me hope. There was always a chance he could be wrong. I'm sure he hoped so. "Well, your husband's not old yet. He may yet have the reserves of strength needed to pull him through. Sometimes I think the patient has more to do with healing than the doctor does. Have you tried putting a mustard plaster on his chest?"

"I think my mama may have known how to do that, but I never had to tend to this kind of sickness before, sir."

He looked at Albert and then back at me and sighed. "Well, you might as well try it. Unlike some of those absurd folk remedies, it does work, if the patient isn't too far gone."

"How do you make one?"

"A mustard plaster? It's a poultice, but don't you go putting it on his bare chest, or else you'll draw blisters the size of quarters. Spread the mixture on a clean piece of flannel. And if you can't find a neighbor who has fresh mustard from a plant in the garden, then go and buy some—they'll have ground mustard at the drugstore. It costs a couple of pennies, I believe. I'd give you some if I had any with me. You mix two tablespoons of the mustard powder with a handful of flour and the white of an egg. Do you keep chickens?"

"No, sir. We couldn't let them out to run on account of the railroad tracks. But I reckon one of the ladies from church will trade me an egg for some of my canned pickles or a quart of apple butter. Just the one egg, then?"

"That's right. One egg will do." He smiled a little. "Being church going folks, surely one of the ladies would give you one egg for nothing."

"Well, I expect they would, but we don't like to be beholden to anybody. We'd rather pay what we owe."

I'm sure he had heard that said often enough. "Well, Mrs. Robbins, think it over. Sometimes it's a kindness to let folks do you a favor. Makes them feel good about themselves. But one way or another get you that egg, and mix it up with flour and the mustard. It should make a sticky yellow paste. If it's too thick to spread, then add a little warm water. Are you with me so far?"

"Yes sir, I am following you. Go ahead."

"Well, once you've made the paste, you want to spoon the mixture onto the clean flannel cloth, fold it over, and put it down directly on your husband's chest, right over the lungs. But remember—not on his bare skin. Put a sheet or an old shirt over his chest and set the mustard plaster on that. That's all there is to it. Just don't leave it on for more than half an hour—any longer and it might give him blisters anyhow. Can you remember all that?"

"Flannel, flour, egg white, powdered mustard. I won't forget. But why does it work?"

He shrugged. "The herb doctors around here say it pulls the toxins out of the lungs so the invalid can breathe easier. Well, they don't phrase it that way, but that's the gist of it. When I was in medical school, one of my professors, whose hobby was folk medicine, told me that mustard paste enlarges the blood vessels, which helps the patient to breathe better. I also recommend it to patients with rheumatism, because it gets some heat to their aching joints. Who knows for sure how it works? All I need to know is that mustard plasters are not an old wives' tale. They do work. I've seen it time and again."

I looked up at him, eyes shining with tears and hope. "So, Doctor, you're saying that if I put that poultice on Albert's chest, he'll start to get better?"

"I hope so." He sighed again. "To tell you the truth, there's not much else you can do. Keep him warm, and try to get some broth in him if he should wake up. Keep putting water on his lips. But aside from that, about all you can do is wait and hope he can fight this off on his own. Keep an eye on him. Send your boy for me if anything changes."

"Thank you. I will."

As he stood up to leave, he seemed to make up his mind about something. With his hand on the doorknob he looked back at me. "One more thing, Mrs. Robbins: When I came in, I saw two boys playing outside in the yard. The older one is the boy who came to fetch me here. The little one is yours too?"

"Yes sir. That would be Edward and George. We had two more before them, but they died as babies."

"How old is the younger boy?"

"Georgie is going on four. Why? Is there a chance that they might catch this too?"

"No. It isn't that. It's just that I think you should call the children in to say good-bye to their daddy. You know—just in case worse comes to worst." He hesitated before he said quietly, "But, ma'am, don't wait too long." He hurried away then so that he wouldn't hear me weeping.

LONNIE VARDEN

Lonnie Varden would not have chosen to come back to the Tennessee mountains, but he didn't have any say in the matter, not unless he wanted to give up art and look for an ordinary job. He didn't want to do that, so perhaps it was fortunate that there were no jobs to be had on account of the stock market crash, making the federal government decide to invent some. He knew he was lucky to be hired as an artist, no matter where they sent him.

He had left the mountains before he was eighteen for a stint in the army, half a dozen years too late for the European war. He had hoped to get sent overseas—all artists yearned to see Paris, didn't they?—but he never got any farther than a stateside army camp. At least he traveled through more of the world than any of his ancestors had seen in the past two hundred years, although he had seen most of it from the window of a train. Somewhere along the way he figured out that he liked drawing almost as much as he hated farming.

Where he came from in the Southern mountains families were supposed to be close, but his kin must have been the exception. They seemed no more attached to one another than a flock of chickens. When he first went away his mother wrote him every now and again, but the letters came fewer and farther apart until finally they stopped altogether. He scarcely noticed. The one thing he had learned from his family—or perhaps inherited through the bloodline—was his father's locked-in reserve, so absolute that no one ever knew what he thought or felt about anything. He thought that might explain why he took up drawing—because he couldn't express his feelings any other way.

Close-knit family or not, after the army it had seemed natural for him to head home to the farm, but when he was within a hundred miles of it the train stopped in Knoxville, and suddenly he knew he couldn't face going back. He decided to stay in Knoxville, and take a chance on learning to be an artist. Perhaps there would have been greater opportunities in Philadelphia or New York, but to an uneducated kid from the back of beyond, Knoxville seemed a more manageable sort of place. If he did well there, maybe he could aim for bigger things. And if he failed miserably, he wasn't too far from home: he could always go back, if he had to.

He worked at laborer's jobs, saving up for art lessons, and managed to take a few classes at the university. When he told people in the art community that he wanted to paint, they all said the same thing: what a pity you didn't get here a couple of years earlier. Lloyd Branson, a master of historical paintings, lived in Knoxville, and had taken pupils at his studio on Gay Street. He was widely hailed for his two frontier paintings: *Gathering of the Overmountain Men at Sycamore Shoals* and *The Battle of King's Mountain*. The latter had been lost ten years earlier when the Hotel Imperial, which owned it, had burned to the ground, taking the painting with it. But Mr. Branson had passed away in 1925, and no one else measured up to him.

Lonnie made do with the teachers he could find and afford, and he earned his keep by preparing gesso and doing other odd jobs for working artists. That in itself had been an education, but it didn't pay as much as laborer's jobs. Still, he scraped along for four years, thinking that sooner or later he'd make enough contacts to get some well-paying commissions, or at least enough jobs to allow him to buy meat for supper every now and then.

Even if the Depression hadn't happened, he doubted he would ever have been able to support himself with his art. Very few painters ever did. One of his friends joked that the best preparation for being an artist was to be born into a wealthy family. Or perhaps he hadn't been joking. Failing that, he said, the best alternative was to ingratiate yourself to the rich and tedious, until you found someone willing to keep an artist as a pet. It had worked for Michelangelo. There weren't any Medicis around these days, and the pope wasn't hiring, but America was sufficiently endowed with steel barons and railroad tycoons to make the idea seem possible.

With an indifferent education and no skills aside from his art, Lonnie Varden faced the fact that he hadn't much chance of finding better employment to support his vocation. The Depression hadn't made any difference to him at first. He wasn't particularly fazed by the poverty that the economic disaster had spawned; as far as he could tell, for an artist, being poor was a way of life. There wasn't much call for artists even at the best of times, and as the country's hard times dragged on, people no longer had money to spend on portraits of their children, or for acquiring pretty lake and cottage scenes to hang above the parlor mantelpiece. There was another world of art out there, too—people whose work hung in museums and sold for great sums to discerning collectors—but he had none of the qualifications to join that group, least of all the ability to ingratiate himself to rich and influential people.

Despite his ardor, Lonnie wasn't a natural talent as an artist, if the opinions of his teachers and fellow painters were anything to go by. At first, he could make a portrait resemble the person who posed for it, albeit without imbuing any life or personality into the image, and his attempts at landscapes, which he intended to appear as real as a photograph, showed no particular talent for composition or theme. He worked hard at it, though, and finally he learned how to put what he felt into the work so that other people could see it too.

Before times became really hard, people had liked his early efforts well enough to shell out a couple of dollars to own one, usually to be given as a gift, but, as he learned more about the social side of art, he finally resigned himself to the fact that his work would never hang in museums or sell for fabulous sums in galleries. What he lacked was not technical precision but style. His carefully wrought paintings showed no originality; no distinctive touches set his work apart from that of anyone else. He was not bad as a draftsman—as a human camera, perhaps—but in terms of creativity he was at best mediocre, and finally he learned enough about art to realize that. Charm and social connections might have made up for that deficit, but he had found them even more difficult than learning to paint.

For a while he paid thirty cents a lesson to be taught painting by an Austrian drawing master from the university. He learned about composition, perspective, and *drawing the light*, but he was also given an assessment of his worth. Despite his doubts about his talent, he had grieved for a bit when the tutor had confirmed his fears: "In the world of art, Varden, you are not an architect, but simply a carpenter. But, as you draw passably well, you can probably offload your paintings to middlebrow persons with aspirations to culture."

Even at the loss of the thirty-cent fees, he knew the instructor had meant to discourage him with that assessment of his work, but Lonnie was not particularly ambitious, and he thought that if he could manage to eke out a living from family portraits and scenes of meadows and cottages, he would not have to take any more jobs that required a great deal of effort, like ditch-digging or selling neckties. He had left his family long ago, and he had no desire to go back. They'd had no money to give him anyhow. Even if he could have afforded a university education, he doubted he could have qualified as an engineer or a doctor. Talented or not, he enjoyed making paintings, and if he could manage to keep body and soul together by selling his work for a couple of bucks, he would settle for that. He was just past twenty; if he tired of the struggle of being an artist, there was plenty of time to choose another path.

Once after a couple of whiskies at the bar where they usually ended up after the art lessons, the drawing master had confided that there was one other benefit from being an artist that Lonnie might not have considered: it was an excellent way to meet likely-looking women, single and sometimes otherwise. It was a rare young lady who could resist the charm of an earnest and attentive gentleman who pronounced her beautiful and asked permission to paint her portrait. The drawing master advised him to take as long as possible to finish that sort of painting, gaining by that a few good dinners and sometimes, if the woman was the adventurous type, a temporary bedmate. "You will seldom make any money from those portraits, but the other benefits make up for it, eh?" said the drawing master. But that lesson, too, was lost upon Lonnie Varden. He was too shy to try it, even once.

Over time he became rather good at dog portraits, and sometimes their fond owners would give him a few dinners as well as his fee, but romantic encounters with beautiful female models never materialized. He did not live well, and, to his surprise, he began to grow tired of the city, and to find himself thinking about those mountains he came from. He was making a living after a fashion, though, and he stayed where he was. In the early thirties, when the "middlebrow persons with aspirations to culture" fell on hard times and stopped buying paintings, Lonnie heard from some of the other local artists about a new government program aimed at preserving the arts by providing jobs for writers and artists. He didn't think much of his chances, but he applied anyhow.

ELLENDOR

Sometimes in the dead of night during Albert's illness, my mind began to wander, and I tried to think of things I ought to do, though mostly I forgot about them by morning. One thing I should have done was tell the sheriff's office and maybe one of the local bureaucrats that Albert was ailing. When I did remember one of the things that needed doing, I still didn't do it. I told myself I was too busy tending to my husband to bother about civilities, and partly that was true, but mostly I was shy about talking to strangers.

I knew I ought to tell them, though, because Albert was sheriff. And he was dying.

Albert was better at talking to strangers than I'll ever be. Maybe he got used to dealing with people when he was younger, working summers at those logging camps. Then we moved to town and he took the railroad job, which gave him even more chances to become accustomed to new people. After a while, he became good at it. Whether Albert took to somebody or not, he could smile at them, find something pleasant to talk about, and look at ease, which generally made the other fellow cotton to him. He did it so well that most people didn't realize that they never got any closer to Albert than they were on the day they met him. He'd pass the time of day with anybody, acting just as friendly as a hungry pup, but he never let people see what he thought or felt. Albert seemed so sociable, though, that hardly anyone ever noticed how little of himself he gave away in conversation.

I asked him once if he thought he was acting false, being sociable to people he was indifferent to, but Albert said that was just the way you had to act if you lived in a town among strangers.

"People don't trust you if you're standoffish, Ellie. They think you have something to hide."

"What you call friendly I call brown-nosing."

He laughed. "Stubborn, ain't you? You'd better get used to town ways, hon, or else you'll get downright lonely here. Well, considering which branch of the McCourry clan you come from I don't reckon *you* ever would get lonely, but since you decided to live here in town, you're obliged to get used to talking to people. Someday you may need a favor. From a friend you might get one, but there are mighty few strangers who will put themselves out for you. They have no reason to."

"Charity?" He knew I hated the very idea. "I'd never ask anybody for a favor, Albert."

"I know you wouldn't want to, Ellendor, but someday you may have to."

Well, Albert was right. It looked like that day had come, and I wasn't prepared for it. There hadn't been time for me to get used to social ways—although maybe a lifetime wouldn't have been long enough for me. I did try, but it came easier to Albert than it did to me.

I could see that he was right about friends being useful, though, because when he needed a favor, he got one. As much as his fine record as a deputy, Albert's genial gift of *seeming* with strangers had got him elected sheriff when the job came open.

Maybe townspeople found it strange that I kept to myself, but the people where we came from know that I came by it naturally.

In the little settlement I grew up in, our branch of the McCourry family was called the Solitary McCourrys, as opposed to the Preaching McCourrys or the Fiddling McCourrys. Last names weren't much use where Albert and I came from. Every family up there was descended from the few pioneer families who had settled the mountains around the time of the revolution. For the first couple of generations every pioneer family had raised about a dozen children apiece, so, as Albert used to joke about it, *"Sooner or later one of* us *married one of* them, *so we may be just fourth or fifth cousins, but we're all family."* He reckoned that if you went back six or seven generations, you could find a common ancestor with just about everybody you knew, and many surnames were shared by people who considered one another no kin at all. With few last names for so many present-day families, the settlers' descendants had to think up other ways to tell who was from which branch of the family.

My kinfolk, the Solitary McCourrys, are known for keeping to themselves. Most of us were born that way. We weren't shy; at least most of us would claim we aren't. We can be just as helpful and friendly as anybody else when you meet us in church or at a community gathering. It is just that we don't need a lot of people around us all the time, and we tend to think that socializing is just as much hard work as chopping firewood. When it comes to strangers, my family is as elusive as deer.

We don't have any use for charity either. We never want anybody to think we are asking for anything. We fend for ourselves, and I expect that because of this most of us are particular about who we help in times of trouble. If we know you well, and if you are an honest, hardworking fellow who has fallen on hard times through some misfortune, I reckon most of us would give you whatever help you need. We have no use for shiftless people who want a handout instead of a job, though; and we downright hate those slick fellers who try to float through life on their good looks or their oily friendliness, forever trying to charm people into making life easy for them. As far as the Solitary McCourrys are concerned, being obnoxious is a grave offense. We don't ingratiate ourselves with other people, for fear of being thought pushy or scheming. We called ourselves honorable, but Albert always said we were mostly proud, and maybe he was right about that.

When I first started keeping company with Albert as a young girl, some of the nosy old biddies in the community tried to warn him that he had taken up with one of the Solitary McCourrys, as if he hadn't known that all along. He didn't mind. Up the mountain my kinfolks' proud and chilly ways didn't matter much, because from one generation to the next people came to expect it. They knew the Solitary McCourrys didn't intend to offend anybody with their remoteness; it was just that the family was made that way.

When we were newlyweds all those years ago, Albert and I could not have foreseen that one day we would be pent up in a valley town among strangers. Here people judge you by what they see, without knowing anything about the ways of your family. But, for good or ill, here we were.

It hadn't been so bad when Albert worked at the railroad yard, or even when he got hired on as a deputy sheriff. None of Albert's friends seemed to mind that I kept to myself. In fact, most of them thought I behaved just as a woman ought to: quiet, polite, and never troubling anybody with opinions. Maybe the women found me as hard to talk to as I did them, but I tried to be pleasant, and since we had two boys to raise, nobody could fault me for sticking close to home. There are others around here who could do with a lesson from me, judging by the number of catty old gossips, wayward young wives, and contentious shrews there are in town.

With George and Eddie and a husband to look after, I always kept busy—cooking, sewing, scrubbing, canning the summer pole beans and tomatoes—all of which gave me the perfect excuse to stay home.

Life changed for me when the high sheriff got shot trying to catch a nest of moonshiners in the woods, but his term had almost expired anyhow, and Albert made up his mind to put his name on the ballot for sheriff in the upcoming election. I don't think anybody else much wanted it, anyhow, seeing as how poor Buck Tyler had been the second sheriff in a row to get killed in the line of duty by lawbreakers. Everyone agreed that his death was a tragedy, but some said it was an unnecessary one. People said that with the whole country going bankrupt, you could hardly call it a crime if some poor fellows made whisky, just trying to get enough money to feed their families. It was better than begging, wasn't it? And whether it was a crime was a matter of opinion too. All it meant was that the moonshine still operators had not paid the government a tax on their whisky. There were a lot of folks who thought that if the government was allowing people to go hungry then they had a lot of damn gall asking for a cut of some poor fellow's hard-earned profits. Neither the whisky tax nor the Depression was the sheriff's fault, of course. Sheriffs didn't make the laws; they only carried out the orders of those that did, but maybe a sheriff ought to keep himself busy chasing the railroad tramps who stole chickens from honest folks, or looking into deaths that were a little too convenient for somebody. Bravery was only a virtue if you were doing something that needed doing, which, in their view, persecuting local bootleggers was not. They all said it was a shame that Sheriff Tyler got shot in the line of duty, but some of them also said that maybe the moonshiners had acted in self-defense, trying to protect what was theirs. I could see both sides of the argument, but nobody asked me what I thought, and I didn't tell them.

When Buck Tyler was killed, the county elections were less than two months away, and he had been up for reelection. With so little time left before the vote, the county officials granted Albert's request to serve as the acting sheriff until Mr. Tyler's term expired. The county's other deputies voiced no objection to that, not when they had just seen the last sheriff shot dead and buried. Between the danger and the paperwork, none of them much wanted the job, even for a few extra dollars a month in their paychecks.

Albert wanted the job, though. The first reason he gave was that he thought it might be better to take on the job rather than having to be under the direction of somebody new. With our boys eating like wolves and outgrowing their clothes at every whipstitch, he said we could use the extra money, and, danger or no danger, I couldn't argue with that. Most of all, though, I suspected that Albert wanted the job to acquire the respect and importance that came along with it. The paperwork might be difficult for him at first, but he said he reckoned that anybody could learn to do it if they put their mind to it. I think he was counting on help from me with that too.

Albert wasn't afraid of hard work. In fact, the thought of being out of work, being unable to feed his family, terrified him. So with the blessing of everyone in the department and in the county government, he took over the job of sheriff, and hired an eager young fellow named Falcon Wallace to take his old job.

By election time, Albert had worked as hard as he could, and he had proved to everyone's satisfaction that he could do the job. Maybe it was mostly good fortune that nothing terrible happened in those few weeks before election, but Albert got the credit for it. Besides that, he hadn't ruffled anyone's feathers or made a nuisance of himself. He was always soft-spoken, but he was also resolute and fair. When he let it be known that he wanted to keep the job by being duly elected, nobody objected. Being a newcomer to town, Albert was not burdened with any old family loyalties that might be troublesome in delicate situations.

With the support of the county officials, the local business leaders, and his fellow deputies, and with votes from his old workmates at the railroad yard, newcomer Albert Robbins ran for sheriff and won the election. I think he found that campaigning was harder than the job. Even in a small town like this he had to do a bit of glad-handing to campaign for office, conversing with strangers and asking for the favor of their vote, but he wanted the job bad enough to work to get it. I stood by his side—as the dutiful little woman, living testimony that the candidate was a solid family man—and I made myself smile and look as if I enjoyed talking to people.

Albert went to local civic meetings and visited a different church every week. The role of politician's wife put me in the path of strangers and I dreaded every occasion, but for Albert's sake, because he wanted it so much, I went along. I smiled until my cheeks ached and shook hands until my fingers were numb, all the while longing to be back in our little house by the railroad tracks.

The sacrifice was worth it, though. Albert wanted the job so much that I couldn't help but be glad for him when he won. Besides, the job of sheriff was perhaps the only chance he would ever have to get ahead, and for all our sakes I hoped he would do well at it.

Now no one would ever know whether or not he could have made a go of this opportunity, for he had been the high sheriff just shy of three months when he was stricken with the fever that carried him away forever. It was ironic: I had prayed so hard that Albert would be safe in the job—not be shot down by criminals nor killed in a car wreck while pursuing them—that it had not occurred to me that, young as he was, he should take ill and die of pneumonia, just the same as an ordinary person with a safer occupation. *Prayers the devil answers*, they used to call it up home: when you asked for something and your wish was granted in such a way that it did you no good at all. Albert had not been killed in the line of duty, but he died all the same.

Now he was gone, and in the space of a week—from when he first took sick until the morning he died—I could feel myself growing old. Ever after, I thought, my life would stretch on and on, with no one ever sharing my bed again, no one holding me as Albert had. No one I had known all my life and could trust completely. I was only thirty-six.

Besides all the other sorrows, the loss of Albert meant that I would have no one to shoulder the burden of coping with strangers. Eddie adjusted to town living quicker than I did, on account of his being young, but he was still just a schoolboy, mostly ignorant in the ways of grown-ups. Now he would have to grow up fast, and it made me sad to think that if Albert died one of the things that would be lost was Eddie's childhood. Georgie was so young that he might not understand about death. In a few months' time, he might even forget his father altogether. And I had lost my barrier against the world.

Albert used to try to ease me out of my shyness, but he never managed to make much headway at it. *"What are you a-scared of, Ellendor?"* he would say, winking at me to calm me down when we had to be around people outside the family. *"They're just ordinary folks, hon, same as us."*

I reckon Albert's swearing-in after the election was my trial by fire at dealing with a host of strangers. All the county dignitaries and their wives were there. Albert told me that the local bureaucrats were quietly glad he had won the election. He thought that behind the scenes they might have had a lot to do with his winning. It wasn't so much that the county officials wanted Albert to win the job of sheriff as that they wanted his opponent to lose it. We reckoned the county officials favored him in the election because they knew he was an honest man—poor folk mostly are—and he had no scores to settle. All he wanted was a steady job he couldn't get laid off from, and a decent paycheck.

His opponent in the race came from an influential family in town, bred to be aware of his own importance. His family's prosperity and connections stretched all the way back to the War Between the States, but so did the grudges and loyalties that generations of his family passed down like heirlooms. If that man had won the job of sheriff—and probably the very reason he wanted the job at all—he would use his power to benefit his friends and get even with his enemies. Since a few of the county officials were probably numbered among those enemies, they had good reason to want somebody else to get the job of sheriff. When an unassuming young deputy with no local ties put himself forth as a candidate for sheriff, they quietly pulled strings behind the scenes to see that the unconnected fellow won the election. Albert had figured all that out little by little, but since the county politicians had not asked any favors of him nor tried to influence how he enforced the laws—or on whom—he went ahead and did the job as fairly as he knew how.

Perhaps he was fortunate that some of the government bureaucrats in charge of such decisions were middlebrow themselves. They looked at samples of Lonnie's work and decided he was a talented artist; you could tell at a glance what his pictures were about, not like those painters who imitated the style of degenerate Frenchmen, and whose canvases looked like they had been scrawled by a child of six. The bureaucrats were not interested in hiring anyone who painted like those foreign daubers to produce art for a US government project. They preferred the likes of Lonnie Varden, who would give them pretty pictures that ordinary people could understand. They hired him, along with hundreds of other artists of varying degrees of talent, paid him a pittance, and sent him off to the hinterlands to paint murals on the walls of small-town post offices.

Two months later, there he was, back where he started, more or less, in a little mountain town in the backwoods of east Tennessee, assigned to depict some popular scene from local history as a mural inside the little brick post office. The portion of the blank white wall earmarked for the mural was a space above the post office boxes, perhaps eight feet high and twice as long. Too large for a simple portrait of, say, Andrew Jackson, whom he seemed to remember hailed from somewhere-or-other near that end of Tennessee; the space called for a sweeping vista, depicting a landscape as well as human figures.

His school days, punctuated all too often with farm work, left him little recollection of American history, and he had never been interested in reading about it, either, except as it was mentioned in passing in paperback westerns. Thus he had only a hazy idea of what an appropriate scene might be for that area of the state, but he asked around, first talking to the elderly widow whose spare room he rented, then chatting with the locals in the diner, then consulting the mayor and the local ministers, more for diplomatic reasons than for enlightenment. He got a couple of good dinners at the homes of these local worthies, which he valued somewhat more than the information they provided.

He had expected to hear suggestions about Civil War battle scenes, but apparently, despite all the talk he'd heard from old soldiers in the Knoxville taverns, the war had not amounted to much in the Southern mountains. He could not find a suitably dramatic, large-scale battle that would fit the bill. Shiloh, it turned out, was way on the other side of Nashville, hundreds of miles away. Sooner or later, he might make his way to that end of the state, one post office at a time, but at present he had to come up with some other subject for his first painting. He wasn't entirely displeased: trees and meadows were less challenging to paint than hand-to-hand combat.

Most people Lonnie talked to thought he ought to paint a scene from the eighteenth century, rather than the nineteenth. (They all agreed that the twentieth century was too new to merit much in the way of documentation.) In the late 1700s the region was frontier territory, dotted with log cabins and wooden forts set in an unbroken wilderness. The people who currently lived there, descendants of those early pioneers and proud of it, wanted their mural to honor those original settlers.

"You oughta paint you a fort, being attacked by Indians," said an old man, who stopped to talk to Lonnie while he was preparing the wall in the post office. He had weeks of work to do before he would make a single mark toward what would become the painting. He kept having to explain to the interested locals that he couldn't just slap up a painting on the bare wall.

"Don't see why it would take you more'n a week or two," said the postmaster. "I painted the whole living room in my house over one weekend."

Lonnie smiled. Maybe the city artists had made him feel like a dunce, but around here he could pass for Rembrandt. Perhaps style and talent were God-given traits that could not be taught, but any fool who was willing to learn could mix paint and chemicals. That was one part of the craft he had mastered as well as any of them.

That afternoon a couple of farmers, who had stopped in to pick up their mail, wanted to know when the picture was going to start appearing on the blank wall. "First I have to sand off the white paint that's already on the wall," he told them. "That will take me a couple of days. Then when I get down to the raw plaster, I'll apply the dry ground gesso." He didn't even wait for their next question. "That's the base of the painting—a foundation so the paint will stick."

"How long will it last?"

Lonnie shrugged. "The *Mona Lisa* is still going strong."

"That must be some foundation then, son. What's in it?"

"Well, sir, the formula is to mix ten parts *whiting*—chalk-white limestone, that is—with one part rabbit-skin glue crystals . . ."

"Rabbit skin?" That usually brought a grin. "Reckon you are a local feller if you're making do with that old country stuff."

"No, that's not a backwoods form of making do. Everybody uses it. Well, I suppose technically glue from any animal hide would work, but artists say that rabbit is the best choice. So I mix them up, and then I add one part titanium-white pigment powder."

"Sounds like you ought to be working in a drugstore."

"Well, I guess it's like farming, sir. Before you can grow your crops and harvest them, there's a lot of plowing and hoeing that has to be done, isn't that so?"

About that time, the spectators generally lost interest in the technical explanation of mural making and wandered away. Lonnie spent a few days in the post office lobby, scraping the paint off the plaster and chatting with passersby. He didn't mind, though. Much of his preliminary work had to be done in solitude, and, as he had explained to the farmers, in the beginning it was more like chemistry than art. He felt more like an artist talking to passersby than he did mixing the potions.

The chemical preparations required the mixing and heating of various ingredients, actions he couldn't perform in the lobby of the post office. His landlady wouldn't hear of his making any kind of a mess in her guest room, so he had to find an empty space where he could work without disturbing anybody. After his weeklong search for a decent workspace came to nothing, the postmaster finally offered him an old toolshed at the back of his house a few blocks away, and he moved his supplies there and began to prepare the mix that would be the bedrock of his work.

"I'll need to cook the mixture after I've prepared it," he told the postmaster. "Will your wife mind if I use your stove?"

"As long as you don't make a mess or blow us all up, I suppose it will be all right. After all, the government sent you here to do a job of work, so it must be my duty to help you."

For a week or so, it wouldn't matter what the subject of the mural was to be, as the preparations never varied. Limestone, rabbit glue, and titanium-white powder. He mixed the dry ingredients in one of the two metal bowls he'd bought from the feed store, and then added six parts distilled water (half the amount in proportion to the dry ingredients). When the mixture began to look like cake batter, he took the bowl to the kitchen, balanced it in a larger bowl filled with water, and placed them on the stove.

The postmaster's wife came in to inspect his efforts. "I bake my cornbread in a flat pan."

Lonnie laughed. "So would I, but nobody's going to eat what I'm cooking here. I'm melting rabbit-skin glue into limestone. It's the first layer of my mural for the post office."

"Why do you have to heat it up?"

"I'm thinning the mixture. Once it gets thin enough to spread, I'll have to hustle over to the post office and slap it up on the wall with a paintbrush—the kind people use to paint ordinary walls, I mean. Do you mind if I come and go here as I please? I'll need to do this a couple more times."

"Tonight?"

"If you don't mind."

"But the post office is closed."

"I know, but your husband very kindly lent me a key so I can work after hours. I'll be in and out of there all night. After I put up this first coat, it will take about five hours to dry, and then I can put up the next one."

She shook her head. "Doesn't sound like any kind of fancy artwork I ever heard tell of. How many times will you have to do it?"

"Three more times after this ought to be enough. It'll take me until tomorrow afternoon to finish, I suppose, but I can catch a nap while each layer is drying." He laughed. "One of the best things about being an artist is that you can set your own hours."

"In that case, why don't you just do one layer a day?"

"Well, I know I said I could set my own hours, but unfortunately art doesn't pay by the hour, so I need to finish this job before I run out of money. Besides, the truth is, I can't wait to get started on what you'd call the fancy artwork, that is, the mural itself. It's the first big thing I've ever done. I guess more people will see this painting than will ever see all the dog and lake cottage paintings I've done put together. I'm raring to go."

The postmaster's wife nodded. "I'm that way myself about making dresses. I hurry through cutting the material and fitting the pattern, so's I can watch the dress take shape. I can see how you'd be anxious to see your picture appear on the wall. What's that mural of yours gonna be about?"

"I haven't decided yet. It ought to be a historical event, but I guess I can do the color wash—"

"Color wash?" She raised her eyebrows. "First cooking and then laundry?"

"What? Oh, I see. *The wash.* That's what painters call the layer of background color that underlies the whole painting. It can be pale blue or a light ochre—"

"What's wrong with white?"

"Just about anything *except* white." He stirred the gesso, and tried to think of a way to explain it to her. "It does sound strange, doesn't it? I suppose it's because white is so important to a painting. You need some other color to paint over so that you can really see the white when you put it where you need it. Does that make sense?"

She shook her head. "Not really, but I guess I'd have a hard time explaining sewing to you, though. Anyhow, I do have an idea about what story you might base your mural on."

"What's that?"

And then, like almost everybody else he had talked to in town, the postmaster's wife launched into the tale of the Cherokee attack on the frontier fort at Sycamore Shoals.

chapter four

On the day of Albert's swearing-in, I was introduced to a raft of strangers. I exchanged pleasantries with most of the representatives of the county government, as puffed up and solemn as toads, during all the glad-handing after the oaths had been administered, but I remembered little of it, partly because I had to keep an eye on the boys, but mostly on account of my own skittishness.

After the ceremony Albert and I walked home from the courthouse, talking about the afternoon's events. A wife of one of the commissioners had brought lemonade and plates of carrot cake to the reception. I offered to help serve the cake, mainly to be doing something, because handing out cake and forks was easier than thinking up things to say to strangers. Afterward, the commissioner's wife had insisted we take some of the leftover cake home for Eddie and George. We had allowed the boys to attend the ceremony, because Albert wanted his sons to share his pride in the day, but by the time the reception began, Georgie was getting fractious, on account of missing his afternoon nap, so Eddie volunteered to go home with him so that his daddy and I could enjoy the rest of the afternoon. I might have been happier going home with the boys, but Albert wanted me there, so I stayed.

When it was finally over, we set off for home, following the little creek that ran behind the courthouse. The stream flowed south, eventually passing within sight of our little house by the railroad tracks. At first the creek bed bordered the alley in back of a line of storefronts, but when it reached the edge of town it flowed into a stand of woods. In private now, surrounded by great soaring chestnut trees, Albert took my hand, something he seldom did, because both of us were shy about showing our feelings in public.

"You did fine at the reception, hon," he told me. "The prettiest woman there, if you ask me."

I laughed. "Nobody did ask you, though. Just as well. I'm satisfied that I looked better than that lady with the little dead weasels around her neck."

"I wish the boys could have stayed."

"They saw the swearing-in, though, Albert, and I know they're as proud of you as I am. I'm glad they got to be there, but as soon as I saw that fancy assortment of people I wished that we had left them with Miz Collier for the afternoon. They were the only children there."

"Eddie would have been all right staying. He's old enough to know how to behave, but Georgie was starting to raise Cain so somebody had to take him home. I wouldn't have wanted him to embarrass us in front of all those county nabobs. Not with me just starting out on the job."

"Well, I reckon they're important gentlemen—they dress like it anyhow—but maybe they wouldn't have minded a fractious baby. They all seemed friendly, Albert."

Albert smiled. "Seeming friendly is part and parcel of the job of being a local politician. I'll allow that they're pleasant company, all right, as long as you don't put too much stock in what they say to you."

I considered this. "Don't you think they like you?"

"Like me personally, you mean? I have no idea, Ellie. I don't think that kind of thing matters to them. I know they're grateful that I ran for sheriff, on account of their deep dislike of the other candidate, and they seemed quietly glad when I won. I told you: I have a suspicion that they caused it to happen. I think those powerful fellows were behind the scenes, pulling strings on my behalf."

"You don't mean they rigged the voting?"

"No, nothing that obvious. Nothing illegal. But still, I'm pretty sure they had a lot to do with me winning."

I thought about it, but I could not imagine how powerful men might have managed to sway an election without stuffing the ballot box. They each had one vote, same as anybody else, but maybe they each had a lot of friends who would take their advice on which candidate to vote for. Or if they were bosses with a lot of men working for them, maybe they could order their employees to vote a certain way. If there were other, more dishonest ways to influence the outcome of an election, I didn't want to know what they were, because knowing would taint my pride in Albert's success. But I did want to understand why they had backed him.

"Why were those men so partial to you, Albert? Were they acquainted with you?" I knew that some of the commissioners had connections to the railroad company, much higher up than Albert had been, of course, but it was just possible that somehow they knew him from there.

"Acquainted with me?" Albert shook his head. "Until I took Mr. Tyler's place, those men didn't know me from Adam's off ox. Where power is concerned, I don't believe personal feelings come into it. It ain't so much that the county officials wanted me to win the election for sheriff as it was that they wanted the other fellow to lose it, because they were acquainted with him."

"Well, if they didn't know you at all, why would they rather have you than him?"

He laughed. "You mean aside from my handsome face and my devilish charm?"

I swatted him playfully on the arm. "Yeah. Aside from that. Come on, hon. No fooling."

Albert kicked a stone out of his way on the path. "Well, if I had to say, I reckon that my distinguished opponent was the commissioners' second choice for the job of sheriff. Their first choice was anybody else."

I laughed at that. "So you just happened to be the anybody else that ran for the office."

"That's it. Aside from that, I suppose that the county officials are partial to me because they know that I'm an honest man."

"Poor folk mostly are."

"I reckon that's why they're poor. The commissioners must think so, anyhow. But aside from their presumption of my honesty—which they were right about—I think the political fellows were most happy about the fact that I'm not from town."

"But we live here, same as everybody. You couldn't have run if you didn't live in the county."

"Yeah, but we're not from here, Ellie. In town we're strangers. Our families aren't from here."

"What would that matter? Seems to me like they'd want somebody who already knew his way around."

"They'd rather have somebody who isn't beholden to anybody. With me being a newcomer, they figured that I'd have no old scores to settle with anybody in particular. When they interviewed me, I told them right off that all I wanted was a steady job I couldn't get laid off from, and a decent paycheck so I could feed my family. They liked that."

"Well, that's the truth. I know that. What about the other fellow who was running for sheriff? That Mr. Snyder?"

"Oh, he's from here, all right. His family is dug in this town tighter than a badger in a rabbit hole. Snyder's father and uncles and cousins are lawyers and businessmen—one of them is even a state legislator. People say every man in the family is a big wheel around here, and apparently none of them lets people forget it. The Snyders around here have been rich and powerful for generations. Sometimes it seems like this town is a big spider web, and there's usually a Snyder somewhere pulling on old threads and weaving new ones. If he was to get elected, he'd be a law unto himself."

"And some of the other big wheels don't like him? I thought they were all kinda like that themselves."

"I expect they are. That's why they know that if Samuel Snyder had won the job of sheriff—and probably the very reason he wanted the job in the first place—he would use his term in office to settle old scores with some of the other local families, while he looked the other way for anything done by his own kinsmen and friends. That favoritism might have been all right with the county officials, except—"

"Except some of their kinfolks were exactly the people he wanted to settle old scores with, I bet."

Albert nodded. "Nobody came right out and said that, but that's how I see it. It took me awhile to work it out, but now I think that when a humble deputy with no local ties—in other words, me—put himself forward as a candidate for sheriff, these local politicians quietly pulled strings behind the scenes to make sure the unconnected fellow won the election."

"Albert! You knew that? Was it fair for you to take a job that you knew you were given just to spite somebody else?"

"They said they wanted an honest man, and by God they got one."

"Now that you are sheriff, I expect I'll have to learn to talk to people I don't know."

Albert smiled. "I believe you will, Ellie, but you have more courage than you know. You may have forgotten but I haven't. You carry a reminder." He let go of my hand and touched the long puckered scar on my wrist.

That was a long time ago, and nothing I cared to think back on.

I was nearly thirteen that winter, still a scrawny kid with patches on the knees of my blue jeans and my brown hair worn in a Dutch boy bob: cut straight as a stick to reach just beneath my ears and a curtain of bangs that covered my eyebrows. Albert was a string bean back then, all skin and bones, and already trying to act grown up. We went to the settlement's one-room schoolhouse with all the other kids from our side of the ridge, all of us often walking together to get there. I was two years younger than Albert, but in the same grade, because in a one-room schoolhouse, promotion depended on capability, not on the age of the pupil.

That autumn and winter Albert walked alone, because he had to leave an hour before the rest of us. When the weather turned cold, the teacher had offered him a quarter a week if he would arrive early and get the fire going in the woodstove. Getting up before daylight was a small price to pay to earn enough money to buy a skinning knife with enough left over to get his mother something store-bought for Christmas.

Albert was glad of the work, and pleased that the teacher had trusted him with the chore. Considering all the farm chores he had to do at home for nothing, even in the winter rain or darkness, building a fire in the schoolhouse woodstove was no trouble at all, and getting paid for it was manna from heaven.

Every school morning that winter before first light, Albert went along to the schoolhouse and lit the fire so that at eight the rest of us would arrive to a room already warm.

He used to say he'd never forget the mornings that fall and winter, when he walked to school alone under a field of stars, with dead leaves swirling around him in the wind. By the time the sky began to lighten, he would have started the fire and sat on a bench pulled up close to the stove, thawing his hands. He said he was tempted more than once to use one of his weekly quarters to buy some gloves, because his hands got so numb on the way to school.

On that November day that neither one of us ever forgot, he was alone, tending the fire and rearranging the logs with the iron poker, when I came in.

He looked surprised because he seldom saw anybody else until a quarter of an hour before class began. He looked past me to see if the rest of the pupils from the hollow had come with me, but I was alone.

"What brings you out so early on a cold morning?" he asked me, smiling at me, the mousy little neighbor girl, younger than him.

I hardly noticed him. I stumbled to the stove without even a word. When I flung my coat and book sack down by the teacher's desk, he saw the gash on my wrist. Blood was still oozing from it, and I reckon I was ashen-faced, but I was not crying. I was afraid I might faint.

He stared at me. "You all right, Ellendor McCourry?"

I mumbled, "Don't know," and reached for the poker.

Before he realized what I was doing, I had yanked the poker out of his hand and pulled it out of the flames. The metal tip was glowing red in the lamplight. As I held it up, I could feel the waves of heat, and Albert stepped aside to avoid it, but I was already backing away from the woodstove and from him, holding on to that poker for dear life.

I did what I had to, before I had any time to think about it, and before Albert could figure out what was going on and try to stop me. Before he could reach me or even tell me to stop, I stretched out the injured arm well away from my body. The gashes on my wrist were jagged, with blood pooled around the edges, but I didn't pause to study it. I had to be quick, before the fear caught up with me.

My hand wobbled some when I aimed the poker at the wound, but I pressed the glowing tip of the poker against the gash before I could think about it. There was a hiss and a sizzle when it touched my wrist, and a moan from Albert when he saw what I was doing, but I made no sound at all.

I kept my teeth clenched when the poker seared my wrist, but I had to keep my eyes open, to make sure the glowing tip touched the wound. When it was done, I felt dizzy and sick. I sank to the floor, and the poker clattered down beside me and rolled toward the door. I still didn't scream, but I remember trembling, keeping my eyes scrunched shut. I began to rock back and forth, gripping my wrist just above the burn mark. I made myself look at the reddening burn to be sure that it covered the cut on the underside of my wrist. My stomach heaved, and I became afraid that I would faint after all, but Albert swears I never made a sound.

Albert put the poker back beside the woodstove. Then he came over and knelt beside me, holding my burned wrist in his hands, trying to think what could be done for me. He figured he might be able to help because dealing with injuries and giving first aid were regular occurrences on a family farm.

We watched the skin pucker and redden, and it already hid the mark of the wound. I could tell Albert was bewildered, because the burn looked more serious—and certainly more painful—than the cut it had covered.

"Why did you do it?" he whispered, still staring at the blistering red streak across my wrist.

I jerked away from him, shaking my head because I still couldn't trust myself to speak. I felt tears coursing down my cheeks, and I was afraid that if I tried to speak, the sound would come out as a scream instead.

The whys of it didn't matter just then. What was done was done.

He was looking around the room, and I could see he meant to do something to help me. There was no time to wait for the teacher to arrive. *Cool the burn.* A bucket of cold water stood near the teacher's desk, a precaution in case a spark or a fragment of burning wood escaped from the stove. Another part of Albert's duties was filling that bucket from the spring every morning. He went over and hoisted that heavy bucket with both hands and carried it back to where I sat. He squatted down beside me and pushed up the sleeve of my sweater. Then he grabbed my arm and pulled it down into the bucket until the water covered it up to the elbow.

For another minute or so neither of us spoke. Albert held my hand down in the cold water until I stopped trembling. After a couple of minutes the cold water dulled the pain, and my breath stopped coming in ragged gulps.

Albert nodded toward my burned arm. "It won't kill you, Ellendor," he said. I reckon he couldn't think of any reason for me to have done it except an attempt at suicide. "It'll hurt like blazes for a good long time, but I don't reckon you'll die, if that's what you were aiming to do."

I looked up at him and sighed, wishing I didn't have to waste my strength making explanations. "I wasn't fixing to die, Albert. I was trying to live."

He waited, but I didn't say anything else. "Ellendor, everybody is going to be coming through that door in a few minutes."

"Oh all right." I figured I owed him for trying to help me. I swirled my hand around in the water, drew it out to look at the burn, and put it back. "I'll tell you what happened. I was walking to school this morning by myself because I wanted to get here early to finish my homework. Chores got in the way last night."

He nodded. "So you were walking alone."

"Yes, and as I was crossing the track that leads to the Ritters' farm, I saw a little black and tan dog standing there in the weeds looking out at me. The sky was just light enough for me to make out his shape through the morning mist. At first I thought he might be a painter or else a wolf . . ."

Albert shook his head. "Ellendor, there haven't been any wolves around here in . . ."

"I know that, Albert. *Wolf* was just a stray thought when I first spied the dark shape there next to the trace. Once I saw that it was just a little old dog, I went over to pet it. I'm partial to dogs, always wanted one. Anyhow, I leaned down and patted its head. That is, I tried to. But before I could draw my hand away, the dog tossed his head and grabbed on to my wrist. I jerked it away so it didn't get a good hold on my skin, but its teeth cut that gash just above my hand, and when I saw that it was slobbering, I started running."

Albert still looked puzzled. "Did the dog chase you?"

"No. It didn't even try. When I got a little distance away I turned to look back to see if he was coming after me, but he paid me no mind. I saw him staggering off into the weeds."

"A wild dog, then?"

"No. It turned out that he was from the Ritters' farm all right. 'Cause when I got to the part of the path next to their hayfield, I met Ned Ritter coming toward me, toting a shotgun. He waved me over and asked me if I had seen a little brown and black dog anywhere along the path. I pointed back the way I came, and he hurried on, but after a couple of steps he turned back to me and said, *'He was a good dog, but I got to put him down. He's got the rabies.'* "

"And it bit you," Albert whispered. A look passed between us, but nothing needed to be said. We knew about rabies. Sometimes a rabid fox or skunk, made fearless by pain, would stagger out of the woods, coming much closer to the house than any normal wild animal would. Sometimes you could see foam around its mouth. As soon as people spotted it in the yard, someone would have to go out and—at a safe distance—shoot the suffering animal before it could infect any livestock, and before a child tried to approach it, like I had just done. Rabies was a death sentence.

"Yes, Albert, the dog bit me. But I thought maybe I could burn out the poison before it took hold." I looked at the blistered skin on my wrist, wondering if I had been fast enough. "The burn hurts beyond words, but it's better than dying."

Before the rest of the students got to school I pulled down the sleeve of my sweater to hide the wound. Albert and I never spoke of it again. For weeks we waited to see what would happen. The scar didn't go away, but the purge by fire must have worked, because I never got the sickness.

I tried to put the whole thing out of my mind, but Albert never forgot it.

Years later, Albert traced his finger along that old scar on my wrist, white now, but still visible if you looked close enough. *"I made up my mind to marry you on account of that day, Ellie. I guess everybody else sees a quiet, ordinary girl, but I'll always know that my wife has a wellspring of courage, and the strength of chestnut wood."*

LONNIE VARDEN

After he heard more or less the same sentiment from several other local residents, Lonnie Varden decided that the Sycamore Shoals suggestion was a good one. Despite its technical difficulty, the idea of painting a frontier battle appealed to him. He envisaged a scene of buckskin-clad frontiersmen fighting off marauding redskins wielding stone axes: bodies in the nearby creek, arrows in flight, little tongues of flame at one end of the fort. Yes, it had dramatic possibilities.

In his notebook he made a quick sketch of a log-walled fort, surrounded by a canopy of trees, laid against a familiar backdrop of rounded green mountains. Perhaps he would put an eagle in the sky to symbolize the future United States. A horse somewhere in the background would add a picturesque touch; people always liked to see a horse in a painting. He could scatter a few pretty pioneer ladies somewhere about. With all these colorful elements he could create a powerful historical scene, familiar to the local community and appealing to the casual viewer. It might be hard work to depict such a complex scene, but he wouldn't mind the effort it took. Compared to everything else he had ever done, it wouldn't really be work at all.

One of the supervisors had mentioned several important historical events connected to the fort that he insisted merited commemoration, and the more Lonnie thought about those suggestions, the better he liked them. Apparently, those few acres by the river at

Sycamore Shoals had cropped up time and again in frontier history. It was there that Daniel Boone and his fellow investors had brought six wagonloads of trade goods to barter with the Cherokee for the land that became the state of Kentucky. Then, in 1776, the Cherokee attacked the fort in their anger over the influx of settlers moving into their territory in what is now east Tennessee. Four years later, during the Revolutionary War, the militias from the surrounding areas met on that same patch of ground to form a volunteer army, in response to a message from a British army officer threatening to burn their farms and kill their families. They finished the dispute—and the officer himself—in a battle a hundred miles or so southeast, but the campaign began right there at Sycamore Shoals.

He couldn't think of any place within a hundred miles of there that could rival it in historical importance. At first, he had thought of painting the gathering of the Overmountain militias during the revolution, but then he remembered that Lloyd Branson, the famous Knoxville painter, had already depicted that scene. Maybe the Cherokees' attack on the fort would be a better choice anyway for drama and visual interest. By the time the last layer of gesso had dried, he had decided to paint the 1776 battle between the frontiersmen of Fort Watauga and the Cherokee attackers. That decision seemed to please everyone. The supervisor said he had an ancestor who had helped to found that fort, and the postmaster said having that scene to look forward to at work each morning would be just like spending every day watching a cowboy movie.

Everybody was happy, most of all Lonnie Varden, who felt that he finally had his chance to become a real artist.

chapter five

Through all the days of Albert's lingering death I was too dazed to think any further ahead than getting through the next hour or two. Early on, when I still thought his fever would break, I busied myself shining his shoes for when he would go back to work, as if by preparing for it I would make it happen. For an hour or more I sat there by the bedside, rubbing the rag over a black shoe and staring out the window at the rain, just waiting for life to start up again, and go on like it always had. I stayed too tired and too busy to think about the future going any other way.

Every hour or so, day and night, I would dip a clean cloth into a bowl of water and squeeze a few drops of it into his mouth, because he couldn't take water any other way. Early on, I had tried to give him broth that way, but he moaned and made choking noises, so I was afraid to try again. After the doctor came I made the mustard plaster the way he told me to and put it on Albert's chest, but his breathing was as ragged as ever. I told myself that I hadn't waited long enough to see a difference, but the hours passed, and by nightfall nothing had changed.

Once, in his delirium, Albert's eyelids fluttered, and he began to mumble a few words. I thought it was a sign that he had come through the worst of it. Surely soon he would wake up, but after a few minutes he went quiet again and lay as still as ever. I think I knew then that it was all over but the waiting.

Just past dawn on the fifth day after he took sick, Albert died. The night before, when the boys came to the door, wanting me to put them to bed, I brought them into the bedroom and told them to say good-bye to their father.

Eddie stared at the unmoving body in the bed, at the hollowed cheeks and the sweat-soaked hair, and he went pale, but he didn't cry. "Will he hear us?"

"I don't know, son. He might." I didn't think Albert would hear them, but this leave-taking was for their sake, not his.

The boys stood there a few feet from the bed, Georgie holding on to Eddie's hand, but they didn't go any closer. Eddie saw my tears, and he seemed to understand what was happening, but Georgie reached out to the foot of the bed and tugged on the edge of the sheet. "Wake up soon, Daddy."

Eddie and I looked at each other. By now both of us knew that Albert would never awaken. After a moment Eddie put his arm around his little brother and led him off to bed. I heard him promising to tell Georgie a bedtime story about Jack, an imaginary rascal who was the hero of the tall tales Albert used to tell them.

By the time they woke up the next morning, Albert had departed this life. Just before dawn, when the ragged breathing stopped, I drew the quilt up over his head to cover his face, though he had still looked as if he were only sleeping. It felt right to cover him, but I wondered why. Are we protecting the privacy of the dead when we do that, or are we beginning our own process of letting them go?

At first light the boys found me still sitting in the chair by the bedside where I had been all night, neither sleeping nor crying—just staring at the wall on the other side of the bed. I knew that as soon as I stood up and walked away I would be heading into a life without

Albert, and I wasn't ready to face it yet. I didn't know where I was going.

Eddie stood in the doorway, holding Georgie's hand so that he shouldn't wander too close to the bed. He didn't know what had happened. Young as he was, he might not understand it for a long time.

For a while none of us made a sound. Finally Eddie said, "I'll see to breakfast, Mama."

I looked up, trying to smile. "I'll be along directly, son."

He led Georgie toward the kitchen, and I heard the scraping of the chair, as Eddie settled him at the table. We had some rice left over from a batch I had cooked the day before. They could help themselves to that easily enough. Mixed with yesterday's pint of milk and a few spoonfuls of sugar, it would do for breakfast.

Awhile later, after he had mixed the rice and got Georgie to eat, Eddie came back to the sickroom to tend to me. I could see that, for him, the end of childhood had already begun.

I was still numb with realizing that Albert's death was no longer just a possibility; it had become a fact. I'd had a few days to get used to the idea, but part of my mind had been thinking all along that it wouldn't happen.

Gone forever. That thought dazed me so that I didn't even hear Eddie come in. He stood in the doorway for a while, and, when I did not look up, he said softly, "Mama, do you want me to go fetch the doctor again?"

"Too late for that, Eddie."

"I know. I was thinking of bringing him in to look after *you*."

"No use wasting the doctor's time when there's other folks who will be in need of him. He can't cure what ails me."

"You've hardly eaten or slept for most of a week, so I reckon you need him as much as anybody."

"No. I'll try to sleep a little, and then I'll get on with all the things that need to be done."

"I can do some of it."

Perhaps I should have told him to go to school, because he had been out all week, but I wasn't ready yet to manage things alone. "I reckon you ought to go tell the reverend, son. He'll know what must be done next. Ask him to please send the undertaker. I don't want you going over there." Death is a more complicated business here in town than it is up home. If we had still been on the mountain, I would have known what to do.

"Tell the preacher." Eddie nodded. "Ask him to send the undertaker. Shall I get word to Uncle Henry?"

Henry. Like as not, Albert's brother would come as soon as he heard, but that would be more of a trial than a consolation. I should have told him sooner, but that would have meant that I had accepted Albert's death as a fact. He might still wake up, I had convinced myself, in hopes that I wouldn't have to summon Henry.

I rubbed my hand across my forehead trying to think. My head hurt and I wished all this could be left for later, but things needed to be done as quickly as possible. Seeing Eddie being so brave made me determined to bear up as well. I felt like as much of a child as the boys were—alone and frightened. If Albert could see me now, he wouldn't recognize that brave girl who had taken a red-hot poker to her wrist so long ago. This hurt worse.

I tried to keep my voice steady when I answered him. "Yes, Eddie, the family will have to be told first thing. I'm glad you remembered about your uncle Henry. After you tell the reverend, go down to the railroad yard and find Cousin Willis. Tell him I asked for him to drive up the mountain and let the folks up there know that Albert has passed away. Tell him to bring them back to town if anybody wants to come."

"Do you think they will?"

"No." Leastways I hoped not. If they intended to stay here with us, they would be intruders more than consolation.

Eddie nodded, and thought for a moment. "Anybody else?"

There weren't many people in town that I would count as friends. Up home we mostly made do with family for company, and somehow I felt that telling the sad news to those I considered acquaintances might make them feel that we were asking for something from them. I would not shame Albert by taking charity or even appearing to ask for it.

"That will do for now, Eddie. If I think of anybody else who needs telling, it can wait until later. Let me be quiet a while longer."

"You ought to sleep, Mama."

"When I can, son."

Eddie still stood on the threshold, watching me. He seemed to be waiting for me to say something else, but grief was winning over practicality, and I couldn't think of anything. I should have spent these last few days making plans in case the worst happened, but I had not. I shook my head. "Nothing else now."

Eddie shifted from one foot to the other. Finally he said, "What about the jail, Mommy?"

I turned to look at him then. *The jail.* The shock and weariness had made me forget all about Albert's job. He'd only been in charge a little more than two months, after all.

My husband was dead, but so was the sheriff of the county. I would have to work out what to do about that. Who to tell. They would wonder why I hadn't let them know before, I reckon, but the truth is I had forgotten all about them.

Eddie came back from his errands midmorning, while I was making pancakes for Georgie. I had fixed a plate for myself, too. There wasn't time to sleep now, so I figured I might as well eat. I put out another plate for Eddie.

"Did you find Cousin Willis?"

Eddie nodded. "He says he will go up the mountain this evening and tell them the news." His voice quavered a little, but he was determined not to cry.

I knew I mustn't cry either. "Thank you, Eddie. You have been a world of help. Your daddy would be proud of you."

"I told Preacher," he said, pushing bits of pancake around on his plate. "He said he was mortal sorry, and he's gonna get word to the undertaker. He said for you not to worry. They'll be along this afternoon. He said to expect more company too. Not just him."

There it was. I closed my eyes. If the Lord meant that as a blessing, I wish He had asked me first. When we moved to town, I tried my best to get used to strangers in bunches, but it didn't come naturally to me. In gatherings where there were clumps of people, I tended to talk to one person—whoever had approached me first. I can be sociable well enough that way, although I couldn't think of much to say, but that was all right. People like it when you just listen. Most of the time the strangers were so busy talking about themselves that they didn't even notice I wasn't saying anything. But sometimes I'd find myself surrounded by people, bent on trying to rope me into the conversation. I could not manage to divide my attention among them to save my life. When they began to talk about the latest books, which I had not read, and of movies playing at the theater, which mostly we had not seen, I couldn't find anything to contribute to the conversation, so mostly I would just smile and nod while I waited for them to go away. I did read books, but not the right ones, I suppose. We had a Bible, a volume of Shakespeare, and some old books Albert had bought at an auction as a birthday gift for me. I didn't much bother with the leather-bound volumes of sermons, but I liked what I read of Mark Twain, Charles Dickens, Washington Irving, and the poems of Mr. Henry Longfellow. Nobody ever seemed to talk about them, though.

As for movies, we took the boys to a show now and again, but only to westerns, and the ladies I met never did talk about those either. I guess I'm too old to get the hang of talking to strangers. I think being social is a matter of practice rather than a gift, and I never got many chances to try it out. I also had a feeling—I don't know what to call it, there's probably a fancy word for it—but to me it felt like *otherness*, that no matter what I said or did, I would never be a part of any group except family. I hadn't known that about myself before we came to live in town. Anxious as I was to leave the mountain, I never gave a thought to what it would be like to be moored forever among strangers.

Company coming. Clumps of them, all expecting me to talk. Like as not, asking me questions that would be too painful to answer.

Albert could talk to anybody. But he was gone. Now the ladies from church—I knew them by name, but they were still strangers—would come to visit, with every intention in the world of being helpful. Most of them wouldn't come empty-handed, either. They would be bringing a pound cake, a chunk of ham, perhaps a bowl of potato salad, and I knew they were the soul of kindness, but it still meant I would have to think of something to say to them beyond thank you. Maybe, though, they would take my bereavement as an excuse for the awkwardness. Some of it was.

I knew the custom, of course. It was probably as old as Moses: the bringing of food and sympathy to folk after the recent death of a loved one. We did that up home as well. I reckon everybody does, all over the world. My mother and grandmother were always the first to bake a pie or a loaf of bread to take to the grieving family, and no one ever thought of it as charity. In our settlement on the mountain that tradition was always a kindness between relatives or lifelong friends and neighbors. That kept it from feeling like a handout. Sooner or later the folks who gave and those who received would end up being the same people. But the people who would be calling on us now with bread and casseroles were not the neighbors and kin we had known forever. The news would not have reached them yet, and even so, it was too far to town for most of them to travel.

If the burying took place back up the mountain, we would see them then.

Oh, Lord, what should I do about the burial?

I was so mired in grief that I had not spared a thought for the funeral. But Preacher told Eddie he would come to call this afternoon, and I decided to ask for his advice about the funeral service and the burial. I would have to make a decision soon, but I didn't yet know my own mind. He would know best about what should be done. Albert and I had never talked about deaths and funerals. We thought we were too young yet to concern ourselves with such matters.

There were so many decisions to make. Should we hold the services here in town or in our little church up the mountain? Would Albert want to be laid to rest amid family graves on the farm now that it belonged to Henry, or would he rather stay forever in the public cemetery in this little railroad town where he had been someone important—the county sheriff—for all of about three months, anyway? Either way, I suppose he would be forgotten soon enough—except by me and the boys. It's the way of the world to let go of the past, good or ill. Dust to dust.

The boys. That was another decision I had to make quickly. Where would we go now? Back home to live on Henry's charity and under Elva's rule? Anything but that. Surely there was another choice, but we had no savings and now there would be no money coming in. We couldn't even stay in the house unless I could find some way to pay the rent. I didn't think I would ever marry again. The idea of marrying a stranger for security and support made me shudder.

Eddie could probably find some sort of job, delivering groceries or doing odd jobs around town, but I couldn't bear to let him do it. Albert wouldn't want his education disrupted for the sake of the few dollars he might earn. I knew he would offer to get work, because he felt he had to be the man of the family now, but I was bound to tell him it wasn't necessary. At least I hoped it wouldn't be.

The best solution would be for me to find work myself. The boys were getting old enough now not to need me at home all the time. But what sort of occupation was I fit for? With the Depression dragging on and on, it was hard enough for a man to find a job these days, much less a woman. I was not young anymore; I wasn't good at being around strangers; I supposed I could be a store clerk, but I'd be no good at it. I'd have to write *Smile* on the back of my hand. I never learned how to type and I didn't get enough education to be a teacher. What other job could a woman get? Being a waitress or a cleaning woman didn't pay a living wage, not if you had a family to support. What chance did I have?

Sure enough, in the afternoon, people came to call, just as Preacher said they would. I sat there in the parlor—trapped—looking past the knot of visitors, feeling as if I was waiting for something. Or someone. Sometimes I would forget that Albert had died, and I would catch myself looking at the door, waiting for him to come into the parlor and deal with all these people who were trying to talk to me. I still hadn't slept much in a long time, and, groggy as I was, I could almost convince myself that the past few days had been a nightmare, but then the cold memories would come flooding back, and every time I remembered what happened, snow melt churned in the pit of my stomach, just as it had when I realized that my husband was dying.

I was still thinking about the funeral when more visitors arrived. I forced myself to stop woolgathering and make an effort. These people meant to be kind, doing for me what they would want done for themselves in this situation.

I turned to the nearest visitor, a silver-haired woman in a lavender-flowered frock who had sat down next to me on the sofa and patted my hand. I forced a smile. I had seen her often enough in church at a distance, but the visitor's name escaped me. After a few more silent moments, I asked her a question, chosen at random out of the jumble of my thoughts. "How did you come to know about our trouble, ma'am?"

The gray lady smiled and patted my hand again. "Well, Miz Robbins, the pastor announced the sad news at services this morning after your boy went over to let him know. He knew you would need caring friends to help you through this time of grief. Oh, and Reverend McKee asked me to remind you that he will be coming over himself just as soon as he can. It's Sunday, you know, and I imagine church business will keep him occupied until midafternoon."

I had clean forgot that it was Sunday. After I had sat hour after hour in the lamplight by Albert's bedside, I suppose time, for me, had melted into one long twilight that just seemed to go on and on. It put me in mind of the world described in Genesis: no day or night until the Lord created the sun, moon, and the stars. It had been like that for me: a long twilight.

Sunday.

That explained the stream of dressed-up ladies gathered in the parlor. Of course Rev. McKee would have announced the news of Albert's passing to the congregation. He would have included it in the little talk about church business he delivered at the pulpit just before the sermon. Of course he told them, and I suppose it was their business, after all. Albert had been the sheriff.

Besides that, any pastor would consider it a kindness to let people know of the death of a church member, because most people in the congregation would welcome such an announcement. Town folk make a family out of their neighbors and church friends as well as blood kin. They would think that I felt the same as they did about the need for help and company in troubled times. I wish I did.

I couldn't tell anybody how much I dreaded the arrival of those well-meaning strangers; being sociable to them would take more effort than I could muster at the moment. I never knew what to say.

Here in town people seem to call one another "friends" on the barest acquaintance, as if anybody you said two words to was your friend right then and there. Up the mountain we measured things differently, and *friend* was a word we used sparingly. A friend was somebody you could ask a favor from without shame; somebody whose door you could approach without needing to hello the house; and somebody who wouldn't sell out your secrets for a few minutes of the limelight at some social gathering. When I could be sure that I could trust you for all that, I might call you a friend, but I was by no means sure of these people. I considered myself barely acquainted with our fellow church members. On Sundays I would smile and murmur a hasty greeting in the church, but that falls far short of confiding in any of them, after knowing them for so little time.

Albert knew lots of townspeople, though.

He had worked with dozens of men at the railroad yard and I reckon he encountered a hundred others while he served as a lawman. Barring the folks he arrested, I thought the people who knew him would mourn him sincerely. People liked Albert. I suppose the women in the congregation mostly knew him only by sight, unless one of their chickens had been stolen or some other trifling crime had sent them down to the sheriff's office for help. The men may have been better acquainted with him, but you can bet that when word of Albert's passing spread through the congregation, it was the church women who hurried home to search their own pantries for something to bring to us besides condolences. It didn't matter that they hardly knew us. I didn't think it was personal, really; it was just customary. It had more to do with how they felt about themselves than how they felt about us.

I would try to be grateful for their kindness, for it was well meant, but all the same, I hoped they wouldn't stay long. I would have liked more time alone for my own mourning. As it was, I felt trapped among strangers in my own parlor. I wondered if they would expect me to remember their names. More strangers to contend with at a time when I was least able to manage composure. I smiled and murmured thanks, and wished I could go back to the bedroom and shut the door.

Albert found it easier to be around strangers than I did, so mostly I had let him do the talking for both of us. I shouldn't have done that. I should have tried harder to get acquainted with these people who were now our neighbors. Now I was thrown into their society with no one to help me out. It had been easy, though, to let Albert be all smiles, so that I could stay quiet around most folk. No one seemed to mind a small woman who smiled but seldom spoke. But now I would have to learn another way to deal with acquaintances.

Just as my thoughts turned again to what must be done about the funeral, I realized that the silver-haired woman beside me, still toying with the white gloves in her lap, had kept on talking. I honestly couldn't remember if I had replied to anything she had said or not.

Then I began to fret about whether to offer the guests a cup of coffee and something baked—a cake or sugar cookies—but grief was taking all of my attention, leaving no time to worry about the conventional courtesies of town folk. Besides, I had neither the time nor the provisions to prepare anything. But apparently they had anticipated that, because before I knew it one of them was in the kitchen seeing to the refreshments. I could hear her talking, trying to keep her voice low, while she dispensed coffee and slices of cake to the visitors. They had brought the food with them, of course. I should have expected that.

The woman on the sofa was still talking. I dragged my attention away from the kitchen chatter and willed myself to listen.

"If there's anything that the county government can do for you, dear, you've only got to ask. As I told you, my Vernon is a county commissioner, and, if you want me to, I will certainly ask him to see what can be done for you."

I smiled and mumbled a thank you, but I did wonder if the commissioner's wife realized what a futile remark she had made. *You've only got to ask.* Me? Born and bred in a mountain settlement far from town? Not a one of the folks from up there would ask for anything—not food if they were hungry, not a rope if they were drowning. I was raised that way, and I didn't think I could ever change.

That must have occurred to her—maybe my expression told her—because then she smiled. "Well, you wouldn't ask for anything, would you dear? Pride is a fine thing, but it doesn't fill your stomach, you know. I suppose that if there is a way to help you, dear, then I will have to think of it myself. I worry about those boys of yours, poor lambs. I will see what can be done."

"It's kind of you to offer," I mumbled. And it was.

"Well, I hate to see a woman with children left on her own, with no means of support and no family to help. As Mr. Kipling says, we are sisters under the skin."

She was kind, but she was also a commissioner's wife, so maybe she felt that her social position obliged her to look after people in need. And maybe the fact that I had two little boys to raise alone now obliged me to swallow my pride and accept the help she offered. She was right: pride doesn't fill your stomach.

"Albert Robbins was a good sheriff, even though he didn't hold the job for long. The commissioners were impressed by him. When we heard of his passing, I told my husband, *'A fine, upstanding man who faithfully served our community deserves to have his family taken care of. Two little boys, now without a father. It's a pitiful shame.'*" She sighed and shook her head. "I declare, sometimes I wonder if the Lord knows what He is doing."

chapter six

By the time Sheriff's Deputy Falcon Wallace heard the sad news and went calling to pay his respects to the widow, the little parlor was crowded with ladies, some of them still in their church outfits, murmuring softly among themselves, as if loud talking would wake the dead. The widow sat with leaden stillness, silent, staring at nothing.

Falcon stood for a moment in the hall doorway, taking in the scene, and suddenly hoping that no one would make him go in. His old Sunday school teacher was in there, and probably a spinster schoolmarm as well. He wasn't afraid of steel-eyed old ladies; it's just that they always made him feel ten years old again, with lessons forgotten and a frog in his pocket.

He felt guilty that he had not come by sometime during the past week. In hindsight, it seemed thoughtless and unkind to have stayed away, but although he and Roy knew that their boss was ailing, it never crossed their minds that he was deathly ill. He would have to apologize for that. If Mrs. Robbins had needed anything while her husband was sick, she should have sent for them, but he knew she wouldn't. The sheriff might have summoned him or Roy, if he'd been able to, because he knew them well, but they were barely acquainted with his missus. She might be shy about asking for favors, or, more likely, she had not been expecting her husband to die, any more than they had. Falcon hoped that the widow would not be angry with them or feel slighted by their absence. The sheriff was dead. He still couldn't take it in. If he felt bewildered and stricken, what must poor Mrs. Robbins be feeling? He wouldn't ask her if she needed help, because she would say no. He would have to figure out on his own what the sheriff's family needed, and then he would do whatever it was without being asked.

He peeked into the parlor. It looked like a henhouse in there. It was nearly three o'clock. Most of the married ladies present must have gone home from church to serve dinner to their families before setting out again on the condolence call. (Duty must be done, but charity begins at home.)

A stout silver-haired woman whom Falcon recognized as the wife of County Commissioner Johnson, still decked out in her flowered church frock and Sunday hat, was sitting beside the sheriff's widow, dwarfing her as she huddled on the horsehair sofa, pale and silent. Occasionally when someone came near and addressed the widow directly she would nod and try to smile, but Falcon didn't think she was listening.

Four younger women, more scrawny than slender, were sitting in straight-backed wooden chairs that Eddie must have dragged in from the kitchen. Two of these matrons had fretful babies on their laps. The babies' scrunched-up red faces suggested that they were likely to erupt into howls at any moment. Falcon shuddered. Crying babies.

A few others, whose store-bought Sunday finery proclaimed them to be the wives of important men (Falcon recognized the missus of a railroad foreman and the widow of a banker), had congregated in one corner of the room, talking among themselves in low voices, as if their very presence conferred condolence, without there being any need for them to give any attention to the bereaved herself. After all, they hardly knew the poor woman. Their presence was a tribute owed to her husband's standing as a county official. Perhaps once he had been buried his wife would be nobody again.

Falcon knew most of the women present, at least by sight, but none of them well enough to make him feel less uneasy. He hadn't arrested any of their kinfolk that he knew of.

A few of them had glanced up when he came through the front door, and then, dismissing him as irrelevant, they went back to talking among themselves. Beyond a grave nod of recognition none of them took any further notice of him, as if grief were women's work, too delicate for the likes of men. Falcon agreed. He wished he could hurry away and leave them to it, because, while he was left unmoved by the tears and anger of someone he was arresting, that same outburst from a distraught and blameless woman always made him sweat and wish he were elsewhere. He generally tried not to look at weeping wives and mothers when he handcuffed the family's lawbreaker and took him off to jail. It was their man's fault that they were made to suffer, not Falcon's, but their accusing stares made him feel guilty anyhow.

It was worse to have to knock on someone's door and tell the unsuspecting householder that a loved one had been killed—usually a wreck, but sometimes a knife fight or gunplay down at the roadside tavern just outside town. He knew why the kings in ancient times wanted to kill the messenger, and if that would make his tidings somehow untrue, many people probably would. As it was, he delivered the bad news with as much haste as he decently could, and offered to fetch their minister or a neighbor to help them through the crisis.

In both cases, though, arrests and condolence calls, his presence was a duty, and despite personal discomfort he meant to see it through. Right and wrong mattered to him; that's why he took to the law, he supposed. He wondered, though, where his fellow deputy was—not in church, Falcon was sure of that. Probably still asleep from a Saturday-night bender. Roy Phillips was a good-enough deputy, but nobody would ever mistake him for a saint.

Maybe Roy didn't even know yet that the sheriff was dead. Falcon had been alone at the office when Eddie appeared that morning with the news, solemn but dry-eyed. He had hurried away again before Falcon could find out anything else. Maybe there wasn't anything else yet. It was probably too soon for funeral plans and such to have been made.

Falcon cursed himself for not hunting up Roy and the other deputies before coming to pay his respects to the sheriff's widow. He should have thought of that, mostly because the deputies had a duty to be here, but also because he could have used an ally. Being the only man in this overheated henhouse made him feel not only as if he had two left feet, but two heads as well. At twenty-four he was still unmarried, and, given his shyness around females in general, that wasn't likely to change anytime soon. Whatever this group chose to talk about would be Greek to him, and he dreaded having to think up things to say. But the ladies ignored him, having no more to say to him than he to them.

He knew he ought to make his way through the chirruping crowd and offer his sympathies to Ellendor Robbins, but he thought he would wait awhile, in hopes that some of the guests might leave. Right now the new widow had enough to contend with, and he told himself that joining the crowd around her would not be doing the poor woman a kindness. He wondered what would be.

Falcon was acquainted with the sheriff's wife, of course, from when she stopped by the office on some errand or other, and even though her husband had been in charge for only a few months, he was tolerably sure that she knew which deputy he was (*Deputy Wallace, not Deputy Phillips, Aldridge, or Madden*), but since she had as little to say as he did, there had been no conversation between them past a murmured hello. She seemed shy around people, as if she wasn't one herself, but some trapped animal put on display and hat-ing it. Falcon was sorry for her, but he had even less to say to her now: her grief shut out the voices, and he could think of no words beyond, "I'm sorry," which didn't seem like enough. Maybe if he waited awhile longer, something else would come to him.

Where the devil were Roy, Tyree, and Galen?

Finally one of the babies began to howl, and as its mother hurried out so as not to disrupt the gathering, she noticed Falcon hovering in the hall. With an exasperated sigh, she shooed him into the kitchen, pointing him toward the well-scrubbed pine table holding the food they had brought as tangible sympathy. Falcon gathered that the ladies thought men were to be fed rather than conversed with. He hadn't brought anything, but, being male, no one expected him to. He stared at the array of pies, cakes, potato salad, and deviled eggs, wondering how they managed to have food prepared on such short notice. Heretofore, all of Falcon's experience with wakes had been occasioned by the death of a relative, and the formalities of bereavement had not concerned him. But this was a social occasion, however solemn. Should he ask permission to eat something?

He was greeted by Mrs. Thompson, the grocer's wife, the woman who had taken charge of the kitchen for the afternoon. She took a long look at him, and then, without asking Falcon what he wanted, she handed him a slice of pound cake on a paper napkin, much as she would have given a dog a treat to make it behave.

When his mouth was full so that he could not reply, she whispered, "It's a terrible thing about the sheriff, isn't it? We were all sorry to hear about it, especially with . . ." she nodded toward the sheriff's youngest son, and trailed off into silence.

Falcon swallowed the last bit of cake. "Yes, ma'am, it is a pitiful shame. He wasn't with us for long, but he was a good man, fair and honest. He worked as hard as any of us. Not all sheriffs are like that."

"I expect you'll miss him all the more then. What happens now? Will they appoint one of you deputies to take his place?"

She probably had no idea who "they" might be, and he wasn't sure he knew either. "It isn't up to me, ma'am. I reckon somebody who outranks the likes of me will tell us that pretty soon now." Falcon had wondered about it, too, though, more than he was willing to let on. It seemed impolite to be concerned about official business and moving on when the poor man wasn't even dead a day yet, but he couldn't help but worry. Sometimes new sheriffs, like new brooms, swept away everything that had been there before. Mr. Robbins, when he took office, had kept the deputies on, saying that he'd appreciate their opinions on things, but his successor was almost sure to be a political choice, and he might have different ideas about how to run the department, and friends to parcel out jobs to. Falcon couldn't be sure of his post past another week or two.

Mrs. Thompson nodded. "No, I don't suppose you deputies will have any say in the matter. The people on the bottom never do. I expect that will be the county board's decision. You all must be doing a fine job, though. Our grocery store has never been robbed—knock wood—so we have never had need of your services, but all the same I hope they find a suitable replacement soon." She nodded toward the parlor. "I do wonder what *she's* going to do, though, poor thing."

Having no reply to this, Falcon nodded glumly, and looked around for someplace to eat a second slice of cake in peace.

He saw the sheriff's youngest boy on a low wooden stool in the corner near the stove, with cherry pie stains around his mouth and red streaks dribbling down his shirt. The child's ruddy, round face was tear-stained, and he was unusually quiet, but being as young as he was, he might not understand the finality of what had happened. He only knew that something was amiss, the house was full of strangers, and he had to be neither seen nor heard. The pie seemed to have taken his mind off the family's troubles, though. To be given an unending supply of desserts for the asking, with no one scolding you for eating them, was a wonderful thing, unheard of before now.

From time to time he would glance up at the table, trying to decide what he would have next.

The elder son, Eddie, came in through the back door. He nodded to Falcon, his face relaxing in relief at seeing someone he knew, someone other than another old biddy in the house. Eddie sat down on the floor and propped himself up against the pie safe—all the family's chairs had been taken into the parlor, and there still weren't enough seats to go around. Without a word, Mrs. Thompson took the boy a slice of winter apple pie on a tin plate. When she turned away, Eddie set it on the floor beside him, untouched.

Falcon sighed. This boy understood what was going on all right—his pinched face and numbed expression was proof of that. If anything, he looked worse than he had when he delivered the news that morning. He was still not wearing his Sunday clothes; his britches were worn and patched, and his faded shirt had seen better days. No one had cared this morning how he was dressed, least of all himself. He kept glancing at the back door, as if he wished he could be somewhere else, and was only waiting for the chance to bolt outside again and make a run for the woods. The boy was dry-eyed, though, a sturdy little fellow with his daddy's chiseled face and cold blue eyes.

For his part Falcon was relieved to find another male in the house. He knew Eddie better than he knew anyone else in the sheriff's family. A few weeks after Albert Robbins became sheriff, Eddie took to stopping by the office after school a few times a week. The newsreels and magazines were full of tales about daring outlaws robbing banks and staging gun battles with law officers. Obviously the boy thought there was a chance of such excitement happening here in town, although he didn't seem aware of the danger that would pose. He saw it like a movie, exciting, but just harmless make-believe. Still, Eddie was proud of his father's important new job, and somehow or other he wanted to be part of it.

The boy soon learned that being the sheriff in a sleepy rural county bore little resemblance to the responsibilities of the federal G-men, who chased bank robbers like John Dillinger and had shoot-outs with outlaws. Still, Eddie was proud of his father, and he was happy to mop the jail cells or empty the prisoners' slop buckets, determined to be useful enough for his father to let him stay. After all, something might happen one day. You never knew.

He was a helpful, well-mannered boy, skinny and short for his age, but usually talkative and chipper around people he knew. Now, of course, his burden of grief made him somber and quiet. He stared at the blank wall opposite—or perhaps at his little brother, who was sitting on the wooden stool by the sink wall, still gobbling pie. Apart from the nod to Falcon when he first came in, the boy took no notice of anyone.

Falcon watched him for a few moments while Mrs. Thompson sliced another cake in anticipation of more visitors. He carried his second slice of pound cake over to where Eddie was sitting, and eased himself down next to him on the bare wood floor. He had intended to put his hand on the boy's shoulder, as a condolence, but at the last moment he thought better of it. Eddie was encased in a shell of grief, not to be broken.

After a companionable silence, Falcon said, "I'm real sorry about your daddy. He was a good sheriff, and a good man."

The boy nodded, staring down at his plate. "We knew he was ailing and this past week he got worse, but we never thought it would come to this."

"Yeah. Nobody could have foreseen it."

Mrs. Thompson stood over them. "If you boys are all right here, I'll just go into the parlor and see if Mrs. Robbins or any of the others would like a bite to eat."

"You go on, ma'am. We'll be just fine here." Falcon waited until she bustled away before he spoke again. "How are you faring, Eddie?"

The boy shrugged. "I'm bearing up all right, I reckon. Maybe it hasn't sunk in yet. I keep thinking there must be some way to change what happened."

"Most people would wish that in times of trouble." Falcon wanted to ask about the funeral arrangements, but Eddie did not need to be reminded of such things. Anyway he judged that it was too soon yet. There hadn't been time to make those decisions, certainly not time for the children to know about it. He decided to tell Roy that they all ought to offer to be pallbearers; he thought the sheriff would have liked that. "Are you managing here all right?"

Eddie shrugged. "I have to, don't I? Somebody's got to stay clear-headed enough to take care of Mama and Georgie, and there ain't nobody else here but me. Reckon in a week or so I'll have to hunt up a job somewhere."

Falcon was sorry to hear a quaver in the boy's voice, but he thought it was even sadder to see Eddie's stoic determination to take on his father's responsibilities. Eddie was a brave kid, but he was in over his head, trying to swallow his own grief because he had decided that he had to be the man of the family now. Sometimes it was hard to tell courage from pigheadedness.

Falcon picked up Eddie's plate of untouched pie and handed it to him. Who knew when the kid had last eaten? "Better eat this. Never turn down a meal, especially in times like this. You're going to need your strength to cope with what's to come. Has your mother eaten anything?"

"Miz Thompson tried to make her take a plate. So did I. She keeps saying she'll eat later, but I don't think she wants to." Eddie picked up the slice of pie and chewed it mechanically, his thoughts elsewhere. A tear slid down his cheek. "How can I take care of Mama and Georgie if I can't even remember to eat?"

"You're still a kid, son. It's not your job to take care of everybody else. As for going to work, you'd best stay in school. Your daddy would have wanted you to. I do know that. He set a store by education. He said he wished he'd had more of it himself."

Falcon wished someone had given him the advice he had just given Eddie. He was older when his own father passed away, but he had felt just the way Eddie did—that everything now was up to him. If he hadn't tried to take on a man's responsibilities before he was old enough to shave, maybe he could have worked his way through some local college. Then he might have become a lawyer instead of a county lawman. He patted the boy's shoulder. "Yessir, Eddie, you do the best you can in your schoolwork, look out for your little brother there, and leave the rest of it to the grown-ups. Most of the folks in this town are good people. I'm sure they will see that you boys and your mama are all right." He wasn't entirely sure about that, but he hoped it would be the case.

Falcon tried to think of some way to help. He didn't have any money to give the family, but he thought he might offer to get firewood for them and chop it if they needed him to do it.

"I'll think it over," said Eddie.

"And you can still come by the jail and help us out after school. I reckon we can afford to pay you." Even if it came out of his own pocket, Falcon would see that the sheriff's son got paid for his work. He wondered if anybody else was looking out for the family.

"Do you have any kinfolk around, Eddie? Someone we can send word to?"

"My uncle Henry. Daddy's brother. He farms the old homeplace. We sent word."

"Well, that's good. Maybe you boys and your mother can go stay with him on the farm."

After a long pause Eddie said, "Maybe," but he didn't sound like he believed it, or maybe he didn't want to go.

Falcon wondered what the story was there.

Georgie, who had eaten all the pie that hadn't stuck to his face and clothes, headed toward the bedroom, calling out for his father to help him.

Eddie sighed. "Georgie's gotta pee. We don't let him go outside by himself on account of the train tracks." He stood up and hurried after him, to head him off before the little fellow could reach the door of their parents' room.

Falcon watched as Eddie led his younger brother out the back door and across the yard to the outhouse. After a few moments he got to his feet. He had postponed his duty long enough. It was time to pay his respects to the sheriff's widow.

The rays of the winter sun slanted through the parlor window, too feeble to make the dust motes dance or to disturb the occupants of the room with an unwelcome blaze of light. It did, however, remind them that it was late afternoon. Through meaningful glances at one another, the ladies passed the signal that the visit could come to a close. Soon they began to drift away, one or two at a time. There was supper to fix at home.

A plump blond woman, one of the younger ones without a baby in tow, took her leave of Mrs. Robbins, crying and dabbing at her eyes with a paper handkerchief. "I can't believe he's gone," she said. "I can't believe it."

Ellendor Robbins looked up sharply. It was the first time all day that Falcon had seen her actually paying attention. She didn't say anything to the blonde, though. She just nodded and the woman turned and walked away, still weeping.

When Falcon finally edged into the parlor, the last of the visitors took it as an excuse to take her leave. Nodding briskly at Falcon, she headed for the door. In the kitchen doorway Mrs. Thompson was putting on her coat, getting ready to leave as well.

Where the devil were Roy and the others?

Duty was duty, but the prospect of being alone with a woman who might become hysterical made Falcon sweat. The widow was now alone, sitting on the horsehair sofa, staring at nothing. Each departing woman had shaken her hand or hugged her, murmuring one last bit of sympathy, and urging Ellendor to send for them if she needed anything. Falcon wondered if she had even noticed.

"I came as soon as I could, ma'am." He sat down on the straight chair beside the sofa. He would have kept standing out of politeness, but, because he was tall, Mrs. Robbins would have had to crane her neck back to look up at him, and the distance would have required them to speak louder than he thought fitting under such solemn circumstances. He doubted that this poor haggard woman would care to stand on ceremony.

"We didn't know."

"No. Nobody did. I didn't send for you because Albert was young and strong. I kept thinking he was going to get better. I couldn't imagine him gone. We never thought on it, him and me."

"Hardly anybody ever does, ma'am. Many's the time we've been called out to the scene of an accident. Some poor fellow killed in a road accident, or a farmhand caught in the machinery; a hunter shot by his buddies, after a drop too much to drink. Then it would fall to one of us to go and inform the families that the man was gone." He shook his head. "The way most of those folks carry on, you'd think that practically everybody lived forever. Never a thought in the world for worse coming to worst."

"No. You can't think like that—not for long. It would drive you mad to dwell on the possibility." She kept twisting her hands together in her lap, and her voice quavered, but she did not cry.

"It ought to be done, though, ma'am. I don't have a family myself, but I've resolved that if I ever do, I'll see to it they make some kind of plan for themselves, if I'm no longer around. But maybe everybody tells himself that, and then he never gets around to it."

He ran out of things to say, and her attention drifted away again. She stared out the window for a few moments before she turned back to him and said quietly, "Mr. Wallace, who was that woman who just left?"

He hesitated just a second too long. "Which one, ma'am? Seems to me like a whole crowd of them just left."

"The . . . blond woman who was crying." He wondered what words of description she had considered before she settled on "blond." *Dumpy? Cheap-looking? Brazen?* All of them fit.

"Oh, you mean that hefty gal in the green dress?"

She nodded.

"Well, that was just Shelley. She's a waitress. I almost didn't recognize her without an apron and a coffeepot in her hand."

"She seemed awful upset."

"Well, all of us are, ma'am. We set a store by Sheriff Robbins. I reckon some folks just show their feelings more than others. Wearing their hearts on their sleeves, my mama used to call it. And that Shelley—why, she'd be in tears if you swatted a fly."

"I see." She seemed to be thinking about that, and then she said, "What happens now?"

"Now?" The question, and her way of asking it, took Falcon by surprise. Surely the minister had been to see her by now to settle all that. "Well . . . the funeral, I reckon," he stammered. "You need to let people know when and where that will be so they can pay their last respects. We'd be proud to act as pallbearers—the other deputies and I—if you need any."

"Thank you. I believe Albert would have liked that. But . . . I meant afterward. The job."

"Oh, do you mean who will be sheriff now? That's not up to us, but if it matters to you, you should ask one of the commissioners, but I don't think you ought to worry about that. You need to set this family to rights."

"Yes."

"If there's any way I can help you . . . Chopping wood, maybe.

I'm right good at fixing things. And come spring I could dig you a garden plot out back—" Falcon shifted from one foot to the other, wondering why it embarrassed him to make the offer.

At the offer of help Ellendor blushed and turned away. "No. It's kind of you, but we couldn't ask you for any favors like that."

"Well, it's early days, ma'am. I know you'll try to make do on your own, but it would be no shame if you can't manage it. If you change your mind, all you have to do is ask."

She nodded, just to say that she understood—not meaning that she ever would would take him up on the offer. She tried again. "When will they decide what happens now about Albert's job?"

Falcon shook his head. "I don't know. Soon, I guess. All I know is that I don't want it."

"Why? Because it's dangerous?"

"No. It's no more dangerous than being a deputy, maybe less so, since we do most of the legwork. But as for taking on the job of sheriff, it's the paperwork that would do me in. All sorts of reports to fill out and warrants to read . . . I never was much good at spelling in school. I can read all right, but I'd rather be outdoors, using my eyes and ears instead of my writing hand, not cooped up behind a desk."

Ellendor nodded. Since she had heard Albert say something of the sort about Deputy Wallace, she was not surprised. "What about Mr. Phillips and the others?"

"Roy? I don't believe he'd care for the extra duties or the paperwork, either, but what would really put Roy off is the politicking. Being the official, elected or appointed, means having to smile and go to receptions and be sociable with the rich folks and the bureaucrats."

"Yes. I'd consider that the hard part myself. But Albert took it in stride."

"Roy says that, if the truth be told, some of those people are just as much lawbreakers as the burglars and bootleggers we do arrest. But rich people mostly don't get prosecuted. That's what Roy says, anyhow. I never heard Sheriff Robbins opine on that particular subject, though."

"No. You wouldn't. Most of the time my husband didn't let people know what he thought. Not even me sometimes. If there were anything about the job he didn't care for, he wouldn't let on. I know the paperwork was a trial to him. I helped him some with that."

After a short, strained silence, Falcon said, "Why do you want to know who'll take Sheriff Robbins's place?"

"Well, I'd like to inquire as to who gets to decide that."

"Oh, I see." Falcon didn't see at all, but he'd rather talk county politics with the grieving widow than have to hand her handkerchiefs while she wept. "Who does the deciding? Let's see . . . when Mr. Tyler died, they appointed your husband to take his place until the election, didn't they? And then he got elected himself. So like as not, the county will appoint somebody to take on the job now—if they can find somebody who will take it."

"Yes. I see that. I can't remember who exactly did the appointing when Albert took over. It didn't matter to me then; all I really cared about was the extra money in his pay envelope. Who did the appointing? Do you remember?"

"Well, like I told you before, I think it was the county board of commissioners. That's who managed the swearing-in, anyhow. You must have met them then."

"I don't recall."

"Well, you can always ask Mr. Johnson. He's the head of the board."

"Mr. Johnson?"

"Yes. Vernon Johnson. His wife was here awhile ago. The gray-haired lady in the purple-flowered dress. Mr. Johnson is one of the railroad bosses, I think, if he's not retired. But he spends a lot of time in the commissioner's office in the courthouse. Why do you want to know, ma'am?"

Ellendor Robbins shrugged. "Just asking."

LONNIE VARDEN

Once he had decided that he would paint the 1776 battle between the settlers and the Cherokee at Sycamore Shoals, Lonnie Varden plunged headlong into the project, begrudging every moment he had to waste eating or sleeping. The day after Lonnie settled on the fort scene, he sketched out a rough plan in charcoal on a long sheet of butcher paper in his room. This drawing was for his own benefit, useful mainly to illustrate the relative positions of the various figures, so that he could decide whether or not the composition was properly balanced. On the far right he placed a shallow, rocky riverbed, and a few feet to the left of it he put an X to symbolize the fort itself. In the left foreground, he made smaller Xs representing the dense forest from which the Indian attack would come. The center of the mural would be taken up by the details of the battle: men fighting in the grassy field, bodies strewn here and there, and in the background, a ripple of dark-green mountains bounding the scene like a natural frame, with perhaps a few inches at the top of the wall allotted to an eggshell-blue sky and some fleecy clouds. He hadn't decided yet where to put the eagle. He would have to find a picture of one in a book somewhere before he could even begin to sketch it.

When he had plotted out the logistics of the work to his satisfaction, he went off in search of books with illustrations that would give him the general idea of what a frontier scene should look like. He knew that as he went along he would also need studies, from books or from life, to show him the configurations of horses, rifles, chestnut trees—just about anything that called for detail. The postmaster's wife expressed surprise when he asked if she had any books with pictures of horses and such that he could look at. He had grown up on a farm surrounded by all of these things, hadn't he? Surely he knew what a horse looked like. Yes, of course he did, he told her, but seeing a horse in order to make it seem real in a painting required a different kind of knowledge from merely being able to recognize a horse when he saw one. Objects are shapes and angles, light and shadow, but you don't notice those details unless you are trying to reproduce those effects on paper.

It was always easier to draw something you could look at rather than having to make it all up in your head. As for depicting the Indians, he figured he could always go to the local theater and watch a cowboy movie.

Each day at five o'clock as soon as the post office closed he would hurry there, drag the stepladder out of the broom closet in the back, and continue the preliminary work on the mural. First he applied the light-green wash to the blank expanse of wall, and then he alternated between sketchbook drawings and limning the shapes into their allotted positions with sticks of burnt charcoal.

His main difficulty was the fact that he had no idea what an eighteenth-century Tennessee fort looked like, or what clothing the Indians wore. If his schoolbooks had contained illustrations of such scenes, he had long forgotten them. He didn't have to be too accurate, of course; artistic license allowed for considerable alteration in a scene for visual effect, but he did have to make an effort to produce a recognizable scene. He couldn't paint, say, a medieval stone fortress set among palm trees, but he thought that taking a few liberties here and there would be permissible. Most of the people who saw his post office mural would have images of historical scenes in their heads that were as hazy as his own. Just as in religious art, it would be better to meet their emotional expectations than to be perfectly accurate and contradict their imaginings.

He found no books to suit his needs in the little community library, which set him back a bit at first—apparently the convenience of city life had affected him more than he'd realized—but after some thought, he decided that rather than make a long, time-consuming trip to the closest large town, his best bet would be to visit a local schoolhouse and ask the schoolmarm if he could borrow any history books with illustrations.

That was how he met Celia.

When Lonnie Varden walked into the schoolhouse that afternoon the pupils had already gone home, and the moderately pretty young teacher was alone, grading papers at her desk. She couldn't have been much older than some of her students, slender and small-boned with mousy brown hair tied up in a chignon at the back of her head. It was an old-fashioned style; most young women now wore their hair bobbed or in a pageboy cut, but he decided that long hair would suit her if she wore it down, which perhaps she did after work hours. Round faces needed a bit of embellishment to soften them.

She looked up with a smile that turned at once into bewilderment when she saw that the visitor was not one of her students or even a concerned parent. She had the tentative smile of a shy and unassuming person, someone who was more at home with young children than with a roomful of brash, opinionated adults. Lonnie doubted that the lessons in this schoolhouse were taught to the tune of a hickory stick.

For some reason her diffidence reassured him. He would experience no harsh questions from her about why he needed the loan of a book. He said hello, but went no nearer the desk; she looked like she might take flight if he made any sudden moves. He smiled back. "I was hoping you could help me, ma'am. I'm not here to enroll or anything."

She blushed. "No, of course you aren't. At least I hope not! But I don't quite see—"

"I finished my schooling a few years back, such as it was. The schoolroom looked a lot like this, in fact. Right now I just need some learned advice on local history."

"Well, I don't know how learned I am. One of the local ministers is an amateur historian. If it's the Civil War you're interested in . . . Are you a writer?"

"No. An artist." Whenever he said that he wondered if he glowed with pride. He never meant the statement to be boastful; it simply felt good to be content with his role in life and to be able to say so. It wasn't just a matter of opinion anymore, either, because the US government was paying him a salary to paint, and if that didn't make it official, he didn't know what would.

"My name is Lonnie Varden. Don't bother looking me up in an art book if you have such a thing on your bookshelves. You won't find me listed, not even as a footnote. I'm not one of the famous artists—yet. Maybe someday."

"I wish some of my students could meet you. They love to draw."

How many times had he heard a variation of that? He smiled again, "You been teaching long, Miss—er?"

She paused for a moment, and he wondered if she was trying to make up her mind whether or not to trust him. Hardly anyone except her pupils would ever stop by the remote schoolhouse, and perhaps she wondered if he was selling something or—surely not—there to steal something . . . or worse. But, after all, it was the middle of the afternoon. She would notice that he didn't look like one of those traveling bums people were always warning her about, and that he wasn't drunk or agitated. In fact, rather than menacing, he hoped she might think him pleasant and good-looking, in an ordinary way.

"Are you from around here?" she asked. "Your accent . . ."

"Well, I'm not altogether a stranger, but I grew up about half a dozen counties away from here. I was living in Knoxville for a couple of years though, lately."

"I've never met a real artist before."

He laughed. "Well, I hope you have now. The name is Lonnie Varden—I'm repeating that in case I do turn out to be important someday."

"I'm Miss Pasten." She came out with it automatically, and then she blushed. "Celia Pasten, that is, and I haven't been teaching long, but I'll help you with your question if I can. Is it about art?"

"More about history, really."

"Oh. History. I didn't study history very much at college. They expect future grammar school teachers to concentrate their course work on pedagogy; that is, on learning to teach little children to read and spell and do their sums."

"I don't really have any questions for you, ma'am. I just need to look in some history books, so you don't have to tell me anything. Books with pictures, I mean. Do you have any?"

She pointed toward a small bookshelf on the wall near the window, behind a circle of small chairs. "We call that our study library. Sometimes people give us old books, mostly the ones left behind when a relative dies, and a few of the others over there are mine. You're welcome to look through them."

He walked over to the bookshelf and began to study the titles. She hovered a few feet behind him, perhaps hoping he would ask for help. When the silence became awkward, he glanced back at her and said, "How do you like school teaching?"

"It's all right, I guess. I never really tried anything else." Even when she smiled she managed to look serious. "Most of the children aren't keen on learning, but I do my best. I was lucky to get the job. The last teacher left to get married. What about you? Have you been painting long?"

"Well, I've been drawing all my life, if that counts," he said, paging through a battered old leather-bound volume. No illustrations at all. He put it back. "For as long as I could hold a pencil, anyhow. It just came naturally to me." Not as naturally as all that, he admitted to himself, but he always did have a yen to do it as more than a pastime.

"That's quite a blessing—knowing from the beginning of your life what it is that you want to be."

He flipped through the pages of an old cookery book. (You never knew your luck.) "Well, being an artist isn't a blessing if you're set on making any money. Pity I wasn't born with a knack for being a railroad tycoon." He pulled another leather-bound volume off the shelf and began to leaf through it. "Anyhow, I started out as a kid with pencil drawing. I even took art lessons for a while in Knoxville, and tried to make it on my own as an independent artist, until I ran out of money—along with the rest of the country."

"But you've kept at it? You're still painting?"

"I got lucky, I guess. In fact, maybe the economic troubles were the best thing that could have happened to me. The federal government started a program to pay artists to do paintings and sculptures and such, and I got one of those jobs. So, yes, I'm still an artist, after a fashion. More so than ever, maybe. I'm painting murals in local post offices."

"At a post office? Really? The one here in town?"

"That's it. It won't make me rich, but I won't go hungry either. Besides, I get to keep practicing my art instead of digging ditches until the country gets back on its feet. When the hard times go away, the government may cancel the program, so in a way I hope things don't improve for a long time. That's a selfish point of view, I guess."

"It's human nature, surely, to be glad when things turn out well for you and sorry when they don't. You said you needed some help concerning history. Are you looking for ideas for the picture you're planning to put up there in our post office?"

"That's it. I figure I'm all right on depicting the look of the land itself. Things haven't changed much around here in the past couple of centuries. Same humpbacked mountains and big shade trees." He was still turning pages as he talked. Sometimes he would stop and stare for a moment at a line drawing, and then he would sigh and begin to leaf through the book again. "This mural is what they call a historical tableau, and it has to pertain to the area where the post office is. I talked to some of the people in town, and they all suggested that I paint a scene from local history. Pioneer days."

She nodded. "Yes, around here they set a store by frontier history. So many local families have been here since then, and so they feel very connected to those old stories. My students love to hear tales from the olden days, especially when one of the names is the same as one of theirs."

"I hope people will like it. I'm trying to do my best to get it right." He found a promising-looking drawing in the Tennessee history book he had been paging through and set it open on the floor. "This drawing of a woman in pioneer dress. That might be useful." He pulled a postcard-sized notebook and a stub of pencil from the pocket of his jacket and began to sketch rapidly. "Any idea what color that dress might have been?"

She thought about it for a moment. "Some shade of brown, like as not. Blue dyes were hard to come by, and you wouldn't wear yellow or white on a frontier farm. It wouldn't be practical. What scene did you have in mind?"

"The attack on the fort at Sycamore Shoals," he said, making broad strokes with the pencil. "Practically everybody I talked to about the mural came up with that suggestion sooner or later, and I decided it has all the elements of a colorful and dramatic tableau, so I'm going to take a crack at it. That means I have to draw a fort, with some Indians attacking it, and a few frontiersmen shooting back. Mountain landscape, of course, and a forest and a river, each on either side of the fort. Horses and maybe a deer at the edge of the woods. I suppose the women would all be inside the fort for safety, but I'll try to figure out a way to put a couple of them in the scene."

"That's easy enough. There were some women outside the fort at the start of that battle. I do know that story pretty well. I teach it to the fifth grade in Tennessee history. The first governor of the state fought there."

"That sounds like just what I need. What were the women doing outside the fort?"

"Trying to milk the cows. You see, they had been warned to expect an attack, and the whole settlement left their farms and took refuge in the fort. But there wasn't room in that little wooden fort for the cattle, so they left them outside to graze in the nearby fields. But after a couple of days the cows needed to be milked, but the Indians had showed up and were lurking in the woods, keeping an eye on the fort."

"So a woman went out to milk the cows?"

"Several of the young girls did. They needed the milk inside the fort for the babies. Off they went with wooden buckets to see to the bawling cows, and of course—"

"The Cherokee pounced on them."

"Yes. The girls dropped their pails and ran back to the fort, but the only survivor that I know of was a girl called Bonnie Kate. She later became the first lady of Tennessee. How's that for historical significance?"

He smiled. "What a great story. I think I hit the jackpot here."

"Maybe you could draw a couple of girls running back to the fort with the Indians chasing them, with the field of cows somewhere in the background."

"It would make a good scene, all right. I sure would like to see that fort. It's easier to paint things if you can look at them and make some sketches from life. The fort is long gone, I suppose?"

"Oh, yes. Ages ago. Everybody knows where it is, but there's nothing left. It was all made of wood, you see."

"I figured as much. That's why I'm here. Since I can't see it for real, then I need to find pictures that show how the scene should look: the architecture of the fort, how the Indians dressed, and what sort of firearms the frontiersmen carried. I thought you might have a book with illustrations of how they think it looked."

"There should be something in *Tennessee History*. Let me look." She took a small green volume out of the desk drawer. "Chapter two or three, I think. Yes—here it is."

He walked back to her desk and took the book she was holding out. A rough black-and-white engraving depicted a log fort surrounded by running figures, some in frontier costume and some in loincloths over breeches.

"There'll be a river close by, too," she said. "No use having a fort if you don't have access to water."

He nodded and made a note on a page in his sketchbook. "This is just what I need. Another half hour or so and I think I can get enough down to get me started. Or I could come back tomorrow, if you have to get home."

"I can stay. There are always papers to grade."

He didn't speak again for another ten minutes. They sat in companionable silence, each absorbed in their respective paperwork, and he filled up five pages in his sketchbook before he stopped. "Well, this has been a good day's work," he said, scrambling to his feet. "It's a starting point, anyway."

She looked up and smiled. "Can I see?"

He flipped the pages of the sketchbook back to the first drawing—the one of the woman in pioneer costume—and laid it on the desk in front of her. He had carefully sketched the long dress, the white apron, and the large-brimmed poke bonnet worn by countrywomen of that era, but the most detailed aspect of the drawing was the face he had given to the pioneer woman: Celia Pasten's own.

She was startled to recognize herself, but she blushed with pleasure. "It's wonderful," she whispered. "It looks like me."

The wonder was that it didn't—quite. Lonnie had captured the shape of her face, the arch of her eyebrows, the full mouth, and the small tip-tilted nose—but somehow he had managed to alter the features just enough to make an idealized version of the ordinary woman. This was Celia as she might have hoped to look, or at least as she might have hoped to be seen by others. But the smile of pleasure that the drawing brought did make her look pretty, and he found himself attracted to her.

Later he was to reflect that the myth of Pygmalion might have been a cautionary tale: that it is a great danger for an artist to idealize his creation, because seeing can indeed be believing, but pictures *do* lie. They both made images that day: she in her mind and he on sketch paper, and, while neither of these portraits were entirely true, they formed the basis of an understanding that would lead from attraction to marriage, and ultimately, to tragedy.

chapter seven

Henry and Elva arrived just after dark. The last of the town ladies had gone home and, at the pastor's behest, the undertaker's men had come and taken Albert away, still wrapped in the blanket from our bed. They told me that I could come to the mortuary later, when I was prepared to discuss the funeral arrangements. Not too late, though. Seeing as how it was Sunday, tomorrow would be best. They didn't mention how much it would cost, and I didn't think to ask. We would manage somehow.

I had already said my good-byes by then, and Eddie had taken Georgie out into the backyard to play with his ball so that he wouldn't have to see his father taken away. I stayed calm when the undertaker's men carried his body down the hall on the stretcher. Even so, one of the men had suggested I might want the doctor to come back and give me something to calm me down. Maybe that was something he always suggested to the grieving relatives. Most new widows welcomed something to help them sleep, he said. But I told him no. Medicine was for when you were sick in body, not to encourage spiritual weakness. If the Lord had sent this trial to me, I would bear it alone.

Deputy Falcon Wallace was the last to leave, and although I had been glad to see him, I was every bit as glad when he left. Now it was just me and Eddie and George. I thought that finally we could spend the evening in peace. I thought I would read them a happy story to help them sleep. There had been enough sorrow for them that day.

I was in the kitchen, spooning up a plate of cold food for Georgie, but he had been eating pie for most of the afternoon, and wasn't hungry. A hot supper of pancakes with syrup and two scrambled eggs would have been comforting for us. It was a favorite meal of Eddie's, and I would have welcomed the chance to prepare a hot supper from scratch to distract us from our grief. Instead, though, we would eat the cold food that the day's visitors had brought. I had been raised not to let good food go to waste, even though serving food brought by near strangers came too close to charity for my liking. But now practicality had to take place over sentiment. Without an icebox to store it in, the food would spoil quickly. Albert had been saving up to buy us a refrigerator, but time ran out before we could afford one. I guess we'll never have one now.

I loaded each plate with cold ham, potato salad, a deviled egg, and a biscuit. The boys knew the rule: if they ate all of the first helping, they could have more. For their sake, I had to be frugal. Every meal I could make with the food brought by the well-wishers stretched our provisions even further. I knew I had to make what little money we had left from savings last for as long as I could. A sinkhole had opened up underneath our secure and peaceful future. Now I felt I couldn't see any further than the next sunset. It was all I could do to put one foot in front of the other and try not to think.

Just as I was about to spoon helpings of food onto the fourth plate, I remembered about Albert. Habit. I couldn't trust it anymore. Now every move would have to be thought out until I got used to our new life. After I wiped my eyes, I rinsed the plate and put it back in the cupboard. The fourth place setting of flatware went back in the drawer beside the sink. My hands were shaking.

Three plates, I told myself. *From now on.*

It was full dark outside when we sat down in silence to eat the supper that none of us wanted.

"Eddie, you may say grace."

He looked up, surprised. His father had always said the blessing before meals. Now the responsibility was his.

Neither one of us had any more of an appetite than Georgie did, but we dutifully picked at our food. We had to make the effort to get our lives back to normal. I didn't yet know what normal would turn out to be, but the one sure thing about it was that I had to get past the debility of grief—soon, for the sake of the boys, who needed me to be calm and steady to keep them from being afraid. Sorrow aside, the practical obligations of a death in the family would occupy me in the days to come. Suddenly I had to decide where Albert's final resting place should be, see about arranging the funeral, and at the same time sort through the bills and the bank book to see what there was left to live on.

When I got past all that, I would have to decide what came next. People said that when Queen Victoria's Albert died, she shut herself right away for a couple of years and then stayed in mourning for the rest of her life. I never heard of any woman—even a queen with a houseful of servants—who could find the leisure to keep mourning year after year. The queen had a country to run and nine or ten children: What had she done about them? I couldn't decide whether I envied Victoria for being able to indulge that steadfast grief or if I thought her selfish for wallowing in her own sorrow and neglecting everything else. That was a choice I did not have. Besides, it wouldn't have done any good for me to fast and weep over my own Albert; he wouldn't have wanted me to carry on that way. He would have considered it an embarrassment, not a tribute.

He suffered the loss of both his parents without once giving way to mourning. According to him, an excess of grief was undignified—

less a measure of the mourner's sorrow than a self-indulgent display of emotion. He would have wondered what such transports of sorrow really meant—a guilty conscience perhaps. If I had seen fit to carry on that way, it would have made him cringe.

The three of us ate our meal in silence: me because I was too exhausted to think of anything to say to the boys, and I reckon Eddie was quiet because he was afraid he might say the wrong thing and make me cry. Georgie set his moods by watching what his elders were doing. He stared down at his plate, knowing that our silence meant trouble.

When the front door opened and closed, Eddie and I stiffened and looked at each other, but before we could make a move Henry and Elva appeared in the hall, peering into the kitchen, as if to make sure that no company was present. They were in no mood to be sociable with strangers either, I suppose.

Henry looked more ill at ease than grief-stricken, but when he saw that there was no one present except his brother's widow and their boys, his scowl relaxed into a tight-lipped stare.

I was startled to see him. Even though we had been here more than a year, this was the first time they had come to our house. Albert and I would go to see them when we paid a visit home. We usually made the trip as a daylong excursion in good weather, planned to coincide with a special event at their old church: revival, homecoming, Easter. The rest of the time we stayed in town and attended services there, but it wasn't the same.

I wondered if Henry had any trouble finding the house. He knew about Albert's new job, though; perhaps they had stopped at the sheriff's office to ask for directions. Anyhow, it was a small town; you couldn't get lost for long. Or maybe Albert had told his brother where we lived. He often invited them to visit us, and though Henry always promised he'd come soon, he never did.

Looking at Henry now, it was hard to remember the winsome

little boy he had been back when Albert and I were first married. There were frown lines at the corners of his mouth and he was already running to fat, with a fringe of thinning hair high on his forehead. It was as if he had turned forty fifteen years too early, and would just keep on looking that way for decades to come. I suppose he can't help what he looks like, but he's soured on life, too. Maybe it's because times are so hard for farmers right now, or maybe being married to Elva was as bad as I figured it would be, but he always seemed to be in a bad mood. I don't know what he had to be angry about. He never wanted to do anything except marry Elva and tend that farm, and he got his wish. I wonder if he regretted not wishing for something else instead.

Elva stood beside him, holding the strap of her purse with both hands, as if she was afraid the town was such a dangerous place that there might be robbers lurking in our kitchen. You could look at her for a week and never see one sign of the sweet, quiet girl she had seemed at seventeen. Her hair was crinkled into brassy waves, and she always seemed to have a faint sneer on her face. She was still quiet, but it was because she was always watching things, like a cat at a mouse hole, waiting to pounce.

She was looking around the room, not at us, probably comparing it to what she had back on the farm. Her faint sneer meant she thought she had won. I suppose that was because after they put in electricity Henry had bought her a refrigerator to replace the old icebox. I don't think she gave him much choice in that. Any other time I might have minded that sneer, but what did it matter now?

They must have heard the news, or else they wouldn't have come, but neither of them was dressed for a formal call, even by family standards. Henry wore his old suit jacket over the khaki pants and one of the shirts I remember him putting on when he did farm chores. His shoes were clean and free of mud, though. Under her blue winter coat Elva had on a faded print housedress that lacked only an apron to make her look as if she was ready to start a day's baking or canning. Henry must have heard the news and insisted on leaving at once, otherwise Elva would have put on her Sunday suit, silk stockings, and high heels. She'd have dabbed on red lipstick and rouged her cheeks. Now, though, Elva, with her unadorned face like a boiled potato, looked dowdy. Well, what of it, though? I don't suppose I looked any better myself. For most of the week I'd hardly slept. There hadn't ever been time for a full bath, so I did what I could with lye soap and a washcloth. I changed my dress if I happened to think of it, which was seldom. I have no doubt that my hair was unkempt and my clothing rumpled, but I couldn't worry about that. Everything else seemed to matter more right now.

With scarcely a glance toward me, Henry stepped forward and held out his hand to Eddie. "You're sprouting up like a locust tree, Eddie. Pretty soon you'll be as tall as your daddy was."

Eddie was still solemn, but I could see the comparison pleased him. "I hope so, Uncle Henry."

"You're well on your way, son. And those blue eyes of yours. They're the spitting image of your daddy's."

Eddie turned away, blinking back tears.

After Henry had patted Georgie's head and presented him with a stick of penny candy from his coat pocket, he turned his attention to me. "Well, Ellendor, we came as soon as we heard," he said, giving his excuse for their informal attire. "The minute we got the news from Willis Blevins, we put out the lights and walked straight out the front door. Left our dinner right there on the kitchen table."

I nodded toward the plates of food on the kitchen counter. "Do you want me to fix you a plate?"

He went right on talking as if I hadn't spoken. "As soon as Willis heard the news, he drove right up the mountain and over to the farm to let us know. I admit I thought people were fools for going to the trouble of putting in a telephone, but I'll allow that the contraption would have been a blessing today, or in case of an emergency. Now I'm thinking about getting one myself. On a farm you never know when there'll be an accident, and being able to summon the doctor in a hurry might save a life one day."

I nodded. "I expect it would be worth it for you to get one, when they get around to stringing the wires up the mountain, that is. But of course I knew you weren't on the telephone. That's why we asked Willis to drive up and get word to you."

Henry looked pale and shaken, but his voice was grim. "But why didn't you send for us *before* he passed, Ellendor, instead of after?"

I tried not to show it, but I sighed. As if the day had not been long enough already—now this. Of all the day's visitors, only our own relatives had not offered us any sympathy. It made me wonder if Henry was one of those people who always wanted to find someone else to blame for any misfortune, even if it was an act of God.

The fact was that I didn't think it would help to have the two of them underfoot, but I gave him another answer that was equally true. "I didn't tell you any sooner, Henry, because I didn't think Albert was dying. Did you expect me to send for you every time one of us took sick?"

I scraped the rest of my dinner into the garbage and set the plate on the drain board beside the sink. Perhaps I ought to have insisted that Henry and Elva have something to eat. Family or not, they were still guests, and after all, they had traveled a long way and abandoned their own dinner in their haste to get to town. We still had plenty of food on hand, thanks to the kindness of the local ladies, but nothing in Henry's forbidding expression made me think that their visit was intended to be a comfort to us.

Eddie went over and shook hands solemnly with his aunt, but neither of them said anything. Then Georgie, still sticky from pie and penny candy, ran to hug Elva. He wrapped himself around her legs and looked up at her with his sly grin. Georgie had taken to hugging every woman who came into the house. Earlier in the day, when all the strangers crowded into the parlor, one of the first ladies to arrive had given him a stick of peppermint from her purse; Georgie had been trying his luck with visitors ever since. Henry had shaken hands with him, but Elva only patted his head absentmindedly, without so much as a glance down at him. Small children made Elva nervous, perhaps because she didn't care for them and they seemed to know it. It was either by design or else heaven's blessing that Elva and Henry never had any of their own.

Without a word Elva pulled the fourth chair from its place at the table and dragged it farther away from us before she sat down. The strained silence went on. Eddie kept looking from one grown-up to another. I must have looked as pale and exhausted as I felt, and his uncle looked like thunder. Elva was just sitting there, jiggling her foot and staring at nothing, like somebody waiting for a train. Eddie backed away from them, and sat back down at the table. He picked up his fork and began to push the ham and potato salad around on his plate, still not eating much, but trying to look busy. He was pretending that he wasn't listening. I wished he didn't have to. It was dark now, and the night had come in cold, so I couldn't send them out in the yard while we talked.

Henry reddened. "No, Ellendor, I certainly don't expect to be notified every time one of you is taken ill, but surely you knew how serious this was. You had the doctor in to look at Albert, didn't you? What did he tell you?"

"The doctor reckoned it was pneumonia, Henry, but Albert wasn't old, and his constitution has always been strong. He hardly ever got more than a cold. You know that. I kept thinking he'd get better." Maybe the doctor had said otherwise, but I couldn't let myself believe it. Somehow I felt that making preparations for Albert's death would seal his fate. Sending for family would have meant that I had given up and accepted that his death was inevitable. Henry and Elva wouldn't have been any comfort anyway. Their high and mighty attitude since they showed up proved I had been right to dread their arrival.

Henry was puffed up like a Pouter pigeon with indignation. "I would have liked to have seen my brother one last time before he passed away." He didn't sound like he was grieving, though. He looked angry, as if he had been done out of his rights. Not for the first time I marveled at the difference between Henry and Albert.

"It would have done no good to call you, Henry. You couldn't have told him good-bye. Albert was unconscious almost from the beginning after he took to his bed."

"And when was that?"

"Nearly a week ago, I think."

"Nearly a week." His eyes narrowed into a piggy squint. "I should have been notified, Ellendor."

I shrugged. "Maybe so, but I didn't have time to think about anything except taking care of Albert and seeing that the boys had hot meals and clean clothes. I could have used some help, but I didn't think I'd get it from you."

"I'm not a nurse, Ellendor. Neither is Elva. We do have a farm to run." Apparently, hardship did not interest Henry unless he experienced it himself. Right now he was focused on his grievance and would not be distracted from it. "Since you did not have the courtesy to let me say my good-byes while Albert lived, then I want to see my brother's body."

I glanced at the boys. Eddie was cutting a deviled egg into dozens of tiny pieces, careful not to look up, but his hand was shaking and his cheeks were red. Much more of this and he'd lose the composure that had got him through the day. Even Georgie looked alarmed. He couldn't grasp what was going on, but he did understand tones of voice, and our raised voices and angry expressions had put him close to tears. Any moment now he would start to howl, and that would only make things worse for everybody.

"Eddie, please take Georgie to your room and put him to bed. Tell him a story if you're up to it. He needs to be settled down."

We waited in silence while Eddie put their plates beside the sink. With a mumbled goodnight, he led Georgie away down the hall. Elva had not said a word. She kept looking around with a bored, blank expression as if this was a movie she hadn't particularly wanted to see.

When we heard the door close, Henry resumed the attack. "I want to see my brother, Ellendor. Is he back there in the other bedroom?"

"No. Not anymore, Henry. The undertaker's men came and took him away late this afternoon. They said they will keep the body at the mortuary until the funeral, but I reckon it would be closed by this time of a Sunday evening."

"I might have known, Ellendor." He sounded like he thought I had arranged for Albert's body to be moved not out of necessity, but simply to vex him.

"You could go first thing tomorrow, though, Henry." In fairness I had to say it, but I hoped he wouldn't take that to be an invitation for them to stay here at the house.

He glanced at Elva, and she shook her head slightly. I wasn't surprised. The farmhouse was twice as big as our house here, and she had thought it too small to contain the both of us.

He turned back to me, still looking like thunder. "Well, Ellendor, I'll grant that you are pale and haggard enough, but I see no sign of tears. How much are you really grieving?"

I could have blazed back at him and asked what business it was of his, and who was he to judge how I felt, but this was probably as close to grief as Henry could feel for his brother. I would give him more consideration than he gave me. I stared back at him until he looked away. "Let's pretend you didn't say that, Henry."

He reddened. "I just think you look like you've come through the ordeal well enough."

"Well, maybe it hasn't altogether hit me yet that Albert is gone.

I haven't had much time to think—nor to eat and sleep, for that matter. I am also bone-tired from sitting by his sickbed for most of the past week."

He sniffed, not satisfied with my answer, but finding no way to fault it. "All right. What about my brother's funeral then? Have you given any thought to that?"

"Not yet, Henry. I guess I'll talk it over with the man at the funeral home tomorrow."

"Undertakers!" He spat out the word. "We never bothered with such foolishness up home. The Bible says dust to dust, and that's the way it ought to be."

I wasn't going to argue the Bible with him. "Well, it's done now. It's how folks do things in town. I think there's a law that says you have to have it done if you want to bury the deceased in the town cemetery."

"Surely Albert would want to be buried on the farm with our family. Where our mommy and daddy are laid to rest. We could lay him to rest out next to our brother Virgil."

I was tired. My patience was wearing thin. "Strictly speaking, Henry, in order to bury Albert next to Virgil, they'd have to dig him a grave somewhere in France."

I should have kept my temper, though. There was no point in quarreling with Henry when his anger was just another way of grieving, because men weren't supposed to cry. But between exhaustion and despair, I had no stomach for putting up with anybody right now, whether his anger was grief or not. As we talked, a part of my mind kept waiting for Henry to get past his own bitterness and sorrow and express anything resembling sympathy for me and the boys, who had just lost their father, but he never did.

"The funeral . . ." he said again.

He was right. I hadn't really considered it. Everything else kept getting in the way and planning seemed to be the only thing that could wait. I rubbed my eyes and stifled a yawn. "I don't know where Albert would want to be laid to rest, Henry. I haven't had any time to think about it. We never talked about it, because . . ." I could feel the tears sting my eyes, but I would not cry in front of Henry. "He wasn't old. It was all so sudden . . . I wasn't sure what to do, what he'd want."

"Well, now that we are here, we can talk about it."

I ignored him. "The preacher at our church here in town came to call this afternoon. He said I could count on him to help us in any way he could—with the undertaker, the cemetery—whatever we needed. I reckon he'd do the funeral service if I was to ask him to. That way the people in town could come. Folks here set a store by Albert. They'll want to be there."

Albert and I had never even thought about dying or what either of us would want done afterward, much less the details of a funeral. What hymn would he have liked to have sung at the funeral? What inscription on his grave marker? We should have had decades to come up with those answers. I might have asked him toward the end of his illness, when I began to fear the worst, but by then it was too late. Albert never woke up.

When the preacher came by to express his condolences and offer to help, he didn't pressure me to work out the practical details of a death in the family. He could see I was not up to the task of decision-making. I expect he had seen enough bereaved families to know not to rush them into deciding things straight away.

"Don't trouble yourself about those things now," he'd told me. *"There will be time enough for planning in another day, or the one after that. Whenever you find that the first shock of grief has begun to wear off."* I had resolved to do that. *"There is some urgency at the funeral and burial plans, of course. You mustn't leave it too long, but don't worry about the inscription on the grave marker yet. They won't put a permanent headstone on the grave until the ground settles, which will be about six months from now."*

"Town preacher!" Henry's scowl looked likely to become permanent. He wasn't even thirty yet, and already his face was etched with grooves marking the shape of his bitterness and anger. "Surely you must realize that Albert's real church is the one up the mountain that he attended for most of his life, Ellendor? It's your church, too, come to that. Brother Cavendish, who has known Albert and the rest of us since we were little, ought to be the one to lay him to rest. That's what Albert would want."

"I'll think about it, Henry." I didn't know where Albert would have wanted to be buried, or who he would want to conduct the funeral service. Maybe he would want a grave on the family farm far from the new life we'd made, but he never seemed homesick or anxious to go back there. Town was his home now. He might have preferred to be buried in the public cemetery on the hill above the town. And even if he had a preference, what did it matter now? Surely Albert was now past caring where he ended up. If you ask me, graves are for the living. The decision ought to be mine.

Maybe all Henry really cared about was winning this family argument, but aside from that piddling little victory, I didn't think the location of Albert's grave would matter to him one bit. He spent precious little time at Virgil's. After he took over running the farm, he didn't even see to it that his wife took care of the graves. The flowers their mother planted there were long since dead, and the family plot was overgrown with weeds. What was the point of burying Albert there, to be forgotten along with the rest of them?

I stopped mulling over the possibilities and turned back to Henry. "If we buried Albert here in town, the boys and I could visit him more often."

Henry's anger nearly made him unable to speak. I wished it had. "In town? Away from family? More importantly, could you afford a cemetery plot here? Why, they must cost twenty-five dollars or more. I hope you wouldn't expect us to contribute to such foolishness.

Buying a plot in town when you can have a perfectly good one for free would certainly be throwing away good money, no matter how well off you think you are. Did the county insure Albert's life when he became sheriff? Will they pay for his burial?"

I shook my head. "I haven't asked, but I don't expect they will. There is no insurance, either. We could have bought a policy ourselves, but Albert said he didn't see the need to waste any money insuring people who were young and healthy like us. There were things we needed more, he reckoned. Mostly things for George and Eddie—shoes, winter coats. But we do have a little money put by from his pay, and I reckon I could use some of it to buy him a place in the burying ground."

Henry shut his eyes and heaved a weary sigh. "Well, I can't think of a greater waste of money. Leave it to a woman to make a hash of practical matters once she is on her own. It's a good thing we came to tell you what to do before it was too late."

Elva spoke up, perhaps to prove that she could be practical despite being female. "Bury him *in town*, Ellendor? But where is the sense in that?"

Not that it's any of your business, I thought. "The sense is this, Elva: when he died, Albert was the county sheriff. He made friends here—men from the railroad shop, the church, the neighbors—enough well-wishers to get him elected to office, in fact. People here respected him. He was the sheriff, and he was proud of that. Here he was somebody."

"Somebody, indeed! He wasn't sheriff for long, was he? Not even three months. I think you'll find that people have short memories, Ellendor, especially when it comes to dead men who were no kin to them. Three months from now in a town cemetery Albert would be lying forgotten in an untended grave."

"He will not. I will be here to tend it. And the boys and I would visit him. That's all that matters, really."

"You'll visit him?" Henry was still glowering. "That brings up another matter, doesn't it? I took it for granted that you'd agree with me about Albert being buried at the homeplace, not only because that is where he belongs—with family—but also because the three of you will be moving back there yourselves."

I looked away. "That hasn't been decided." But where would we go now? That was another thing I had not had the time or the will to think about. Moving in with Henry and Elva again. I supposed that it did seem inevitable to everyone. What else could I do? Now Henry was forcing me to think about it. I looked over at Elva's smug face and pictured myself going back to sharing a kitchen with her . . . only this time I wouldn't be there as an equal. Now that Albert wasn't around to stand up for me, I wouldn't put it past Elva to treat me like a servant. What was there to stop her from doing it? Albert was dead, and everyone would expect us to go back to live with family.

Family . . . But I couldn't stand it there, and the boys weren't close to Henry either. He seldom took any notice of them. Since they were too young to help with the farm chores, Henry had no use for them, and consequently no interest in them. I knew that regardless of what I felt, all that mattered was what was best for Eddie and George. Should I take them back to their father's homeplace on the mountain, where they could count on having a roof over their heads and enough to eat, however grudgingly it was given? At least they would be safe that way. But if I took them back to the farm Eddie would have to attend the settlement's one-room schoolhouse that hadn't changed since Albert and I went there: just one teacher for all eight grades and not enough books to go around. As for Georgie, with the farm's nearest neighbors a mile away, he would have no one to play with, and without Albert to teach him skills, Georgie would never learn the pleasures of living in the country: hunting, fishing. Henry had no interest in any of that. He had never learned those things himself.

And I would be no better off than the boys. Henry's attitude made it plain that we would be living back at the farm on sufferance, an object of charity. The thought of being somebody's "poor relation" made me shudder. I suppose with times being hard and money being tight, Henry had good reason to resent three more mouths to feed. After all, I wasn't blood kin to Albert's brother, and there was no one in my family who could take us in. My folks were dead, and my brothers and sisters were scattered between here and Detroit, none of them prosperous enough to take on extra mouths to feed.

Then there was my dread of sharing the house again with Elva, only this time Elva would be in charge absolutely, and she'd never let me forget it either.

I glanced at my sister-in-law, who was more of a stranger to me than an Eskimo. I never knew what she was thinking, but you could tell from her expression that it wasn't good. Elva was staring up at the ceiling with her arms crossed, her body rigid, and her mouth set in a tight frown. She said nothing, but her disapproval radiated from every pore. Apparently, it had not occurred to her that we might be coming back to the farm. Obviously Henry had not discussed the future plans with her, and knowing Elva, she would spend most of the drive back to the farm expressing her displeasure.

"Since you are my brother's widow, Ellendor, I—that is, we—" he amended with a wary glance at his wife. "*We* think it is our Christian duty to give you a home with us." Henry's tone of voice made it clear that rather than a family member to share his home with, he considered me and the children his cross to bear. No matter how hard I might try to be useful, no matter how meekly I accepted my position as a "poor relation," I would never be welcome. It would never be home.

"It is unfortunate that Albert lacked the foresight to provide insurance to support you after his death . . ." Henry was saying. "I would have thought he had more sense than that."

And suddenly I knew. It wasn't for the sake of Eddie's education or Georgie's future. It wasn't a reasoned decision, or a careful weighing of pros and cons. It wasn't even a sign of self-confidence on my part, much less ambition. It was just that anything on earth would be better than going back to that farm without Albert, where I would be unwanted and considered a burden. My life there would be an unchanging round of drudgery that would go on and on until I finally ran out of time and joined Albert again.

"We're staying here, Henry. Albert will be buried up the hill in the town cemetery, and we'll keep on living here. I don't know what we'll live on, but one way or another, the boys and I will manage without your charity. So y'all can go home and stop worrying about us. We're not your problem. We'll be fine."

Henry's smile was grim. "When you are homeless and starving, you can come and apologize to me and Elva for your uncivil attitude, and then, for the sake of Albert's sons, we'll take you in."

I stood up, finally feeling more angry than tired. Instead of shouting at him, I took a deep breath and motioned them toward the front door. "Don't hold your breath, Henry."

chapter eight

"Well, ma'am, first let me say how sorry I am, Mrs. Robbins. Your Albert was a good man, and his loss will be felt by all of us."

I nodded, wondering if I ought to sit down in the visitor's chair in front of the desk, but I decided against it. This was Mr. Johnson's office; it was only proper to wait until the commissioner invited me to be seated. I stood there, and he must have realized that I was still standing.

"Ma'am, you put me in mind of a child called on the carpet for some bit of mischief and expecting a whipping." With a faint smile he motioned me toward the chair. "Very formal, you mountain people. Though on the whole that's not a bad thing at all."

"Thank you for the loan of your umbrella yesterday." I handed it to him across the desk.

He took it and waved away my awkward attempt to thank him. "I'd have been happy for you to keep it, ma'am."

The silence stretched on after that, making both of us uneasy, I think. I was still standing, gripping the back of the wooden chair, and trying to think of some casual remark that would continue the conversation with this prosperous-looking gentleman, but I had gone so long on ragged bits of sleep that my mind could not summon up any suitable words. Finally, for want of anything else to do, I sat down.

I saw him looking at my clothes. I had put on an old black cloth coat over a homemade brown church dress; that was as close to mourning as my wardrobe allowed. I hoped he understood that. I had worn the same outfit to Albert's funeral, not for a lack of grief, but because I thought that buying a black dress for that one occasion would have been a sinful waste of money. Albert might have wanted me to buy some proper mourning clothes, and perhaps a dark suit for Eddie as well so that what we wore would reflect well on his position as a county official. Albert considered the rules of etiquette to be laws that must be obeyed as surely as those on the law books. Even when we were having nothing for supper but soup beans and cornbread, he still expected ironed cloth napkins and serving bowls on the table, because dishing the food straight out of the pot was not *fitten*—a word he used more and more often as he adapted himself to town ways and learned its rules.

Albert had been quick to figure out that the most important laws in life are the unwritten ones.

To please him, I did my best to follow the rules as he saw them, but mostly I didn't really care what people thought. If they judged you by your clothes, I figured they weren't worth knowing. Besides, meeting people's expectations usually meant that you wanted something from them, even if it was only a bit of respect, but I don't think I ever wanted favors from anyone. I already had a husband, a home, and two healthy children, which was all I wanted. Why bother to ingratiate yourself to society people if you didn't want anything from them?

I might have to change my ways now, though, and try to be more sociable like Albert. Pride does not come cheap, and I could no longer afford it.

As for the proper attire befitting a town funeral, now that Albert was gone I would please myself. Funerals were for the living, because, one way or another, the dead were past caring. Either they were in the hereafter with other things to occupy their minds or they were nowhere, so what they would have wanted no longer mattered. I wouldn't indulge in the foolishness of expensive mourning finery when the rent needed paying and the larder was almost empty.

I would try to do as Albert wished, as long as it was practical, but really I had my own ideas about the rules to be followed after a death in the family. My rules weren't printed in etiquette books; they were born of long tradition, and they had nothing to do with the opinions of town-bred strangers.

First I had to record Albert's death in the family Bible, alongside his name and the date of his birth. Some town people must still do that as well, since many of them set such a store by their bloodlines. Did they also open a window and put a dish of salt on the windowsill? Did they drape a cloth over the mirror? I never heard anyone mention it here, but I didn't think so.

A few hours after Albert took his last breath, I opened the boys' bedroom window, which was on the backside of the house facing the railroad tracks. That way people coming to the house would not see it and want to know why in the chill of early March I had left a window open. The old people up home said that when there was a death in the family someone had to open a window in order for the soul of the departed to leave the house and pass on. The salt on the windowsill was to prevent other spirits from getting in.

If we had kept bees in the yard I would have gone out to the hives to tie a bit of crape on each one and tell them about Albert's death. You must do this if there is a death in the family or else the bees will swarm—leave the hives and go elsewhere. That was true. Every beekeeper I ever knew swore by it, but none of them ever explained how the bees knew or why they cared.

I wasn't sure about needing to put the salt on the windowsill.

I did that mainly because it was an old custom in my family. People do a lot of things not because they believe in them, but because these things had always been done that way—like saying "Bless you" when someone sneezes. I was glad for an excuse to cover the mirror, though, so that I wouldn't catch sight of my own pale, gaunt reflection in it. I looked half-dead myself.

I didn't know if those old-fashioned death rituals would have mattered to Albert or not. He never said anything about it one way or the other. It was just what people did, and that was good enough for him, I suppose. We'd had no reason to talk about the finer points of death customs. We thought we had decades left to settle those things. But if Albert was still lingering on this earth, seeing and hearing what was happening, I wanted him to know that I honored his memory by following the old customs, just in case it mattered. Rituals with salt and mirrors didn't cost anything. Mourning clothes did.

We had buried Albert the day before my meeting with Vernon Johnson, in a biting March wind, beneath a clabbered sky that kept spitting rain. The wet wind battened down the flowers and chilled those of us gathered at the graveside. I had used some of our savings to put a down payment on a burial plot as close to the top of the hill as they had available. Albert would like the thought of having a view of the sky and mountains, like we had up home. The ground would have to settle for six months before they could put in a headstone, and I hoped by then I'd be able to afford one. It was a double burial plot, so that when the time came the boys could lay me to rest there beside their father.

I judged there to be a good half a hundred people there, some of them friends or fellow church members. The doctor had come, and two of the deputies from the jail. But some of those present had been people I knew only by sight, if at all: the bank president, some office people representing the railroad, and an assortment of local officials, all there to pay respects to the sheriff, which I realized was not quite the same as honoring Albert Robbins for himself. He would have been pleased, though. Some of them had even brought flowers to lay on the mound of bare earth after the service. They were mostly daffodils and crocuses, because it was too early in the spring to get anything else from the gardens.

Vernon Johnson had been there. He had come alone, but I remembered his wife, that nice lady in lavender who had come by the house the day Albert died and offered to help. You could tell just by looking at Mr. Johnson at the graveside that he was someone important. He was standing near the minister, wearing a dark belted raincoat, and scrunched up under a black umbrella to protect his fedora from the rain. When he saw that the boys and I had no protection from the elements, he stepped forward and handed the umbrella to me, silently motioning for me to take it. His black shoes shone like a pond in the moonlight, despite the mud in the burying ground, and the suit just visible under his store-bought black trench coat looked like fine-spun wool. I thought it fit him too well to have been bought sight unseen from the Wish Book, like Albert's was: the one he wore on Sundays, the one that would now go into the ground with him forever.

I stopped thinking back on the funeral. I knew I mustn't dwell on it now, because if I began to cry, Mr. Johnson would be embarrassed. He would probably be so anxious for me to leave that he wouldn't listen to what I had to say. I had to make him listen, because I had decided he was the one person I needed to talk to. The well-meaning condolences of the others might comfort me for the moment, but it was the future that mattered.

Mr. Johnson told me after the service that he had attended the funeral as the representative of the county government. Before he left he shook my hand with his gloved one and murmured his condolences. He shook Eddie's hand, too, and patted Georgie's head, but there were other people waiting to speak to me, and before I had a chance to say anything to him beyond a word of thanks or give him back his umbrella, he had moved away, edged aside by some of our neighbors from the mountain who had come down for the burying. Then a few people from town patted my shoulder or shook my hand as they left. The minister's wife rushed forward to embrace me, tearfully exclaiming that the ways of the Lord were mysterious indeed, but that she trusted we would understand it all once we arrived in heaven. I nodded, trying to hide my impatience. A few yards away I saw Falcon Wallace talking to the stocky blond woman who had been at the house when all the other ladies had paid their condolence calls. I had wanted to have a word with Falcon, to thank him for his kindness, but I was looking toward the departing commissioner, wishing I could run after him—but as Albert would have said, *"It wouldn't have been fitten."*

Georgie recognized Falcon, and slipped his hand out of mine to go and hug his friend. With a nod at me, Eddie hurried after him, probably as much to see Falcon himself as to tend to his little brother. The two of them surrounded Falcon, Georgie wrapping his little arms around the deputy's legs so that he couldn't escape them if he wanted to, although to give him credit, he gave no sign of being impatient with them. The blond woman, blocked now by the boys, smiled uncertainly and wandered away in my direction. When she noticed me, she stopped and said, "Oh!" as if she hadn't expected to see me, or maybe she didn't know who I was. *A woman in black with two tearful young'uns in tow; who else could I be?*

"It's you, Miz Robbins. In all this rain, well . . . anyhow, I'm real sorry about Albert, ma'am." She had thin blond hair crinkled into tight permanent waves, damp now and frizzing in the mist, and a lot of black eye makeup and red lipstick, like those Kewpie dolls you can win at the sideshow at the fair. She wasn't dressed in a flashy way, though, as far as I could tell; just a plain brown coat with a rabbit-fur collar and clunky high-heel shoes, muddied halfway up the sides.

"Yes."

"We just thought the world of Albert down at the diner. He used to come in late of an evening for his coffee and pie, and we felt safe just having him sitting there."

"Why?"

"Well, in case somebody tried to come in and rob the till while we were closing up, I guess. Anyway, he was always a welcome sight for sore eyes. He was a one, that Albert Robbins. Always ready with a smile and a joke."

When Albert worked in the machine shop at the railroad he used to say that sometimes you could tell when there was something wrong with a machine just by listening to it. Something in the way it ran might be just the least bit off, but if you didn't figure out right then what was wrong with it, it would break down altogether sooner or later. I had that same feeling as the blond woman went on talking to me, but I didn't have the time or the presence of mind to give it any thought then. I just nodded, until more people surged past her to shake my hand and tell me how sorry they were.

"Albert would have been proud to know that you came," I said—over and over. The stocky blond woman walked away, and I forgot about her.

When I looked back across the field, Vernon Johnson was nowhere to be seen. I had hoped he would come by the house, where Mrs. Thompson presided again over a cold collation for the mourners, cobbled together from the food brought by Sunday's visitors. Henry and Elva had attended the funeral and the graveside service, but when it was over they nodded to me and walked away. They did not come by the house afterward. Mr. Johnson did not appear, either, and I decided I would have to hunt him up in his office, sooner rather than later.

"Is there some way I can help you, Mrs. Robbins?" Vernon Johnson's expression was politely blank, but his eyes were wary, as if he was expecting a bout of hysterics from me, the new widow, and that he wished me anywhere but in his little courthouse office. He was still standing, perhaps out of courtesy, but also so that he could escort me quickly to the door if I became distraught.

I smiled and tried to look calm and unafraid.

I had given it a lot of thought since the funeral, and finally I remembered meeting Vernon Johnson at the swearing-in ceremony back in January, when Albert, as the newly elected sheriff, had taken the oath with the other incoming officials. As Albert's wife, I was allowed to hold the Bible that he put his left hand on while he took the oath of office. "Just like the president's wife," he had said later, and I think that little gesture pleased him as much as anything else that day.

Mr. Johnson had worn the same black suit then, watching the ceremony alongside a crowd of other well-dressed, and therefore important, local men. I remembered taking note of what the county officials wore, wondering if Albert would need a suit like that. If so, I knew we'd better start saving up for it then, because it would have cost him a month's pay, at least.

I wasn't worried about my outfit. The ladies present were dressed mostly alike, in below-the-knee wool skirts and matching jackets with shoulder pads in them. They were fashionable these days, but they put me in mind of scarecrows. As a woman, I was interested in seeing their finery, but not envious. And the outfit worn by one of the officials' wives looked too outlandish even for a scarecrow. She was a stringy red-haired lady wearing a dark-green wool suit, pretty much like those the other women wore, but wrapped around her shoulders like a furry shawl was a circle of reddish-brown pelts, about the same color as her hair. I couldn't help it: I kept staring at those little weaselly-looking animals with their glass-eyed heads still attached and their tiny feet dangling. They looked like little pine martens to me, but I think they were minks, though I'd never seen one alive. The ladies' magazines talk about mink coats sometimes, but I'd never heard of this style before. Four or five dead minks were fastened together to form the wrap: the head of one clamped on the tail of the animal in front of it, and its own tail gripped by the one behind it. At first I thought, despite her red hair, which in any case looked dyed, that the fur-wearing lady was an Indian, but since then I have seen several women wearing pelts that way—a fur stole, they call it—and, remembering the women's magazines, I decided the wrap must be some fashionable city notion, seeing as the news of it had not made it up the mountain to the settlement. Just as well, though. I expect they'd have laughed fit to kill to see such a sight. I had no desire to be encircled by dead weasels, but I would have liked to have the green wool suit with a little gold flower pin on the lapel instead. Such extravagances for myself were past praying for, though. There were better ways to spend Albert's salary: first, on the boys; then on Albert; then things for the kitchen, and, finally, clothes for me, if there was any money left over. There never was.

I wish Albert could have had a suit as fine as Mr. Johnson's. I guess he wouldn't have had it long, but having it would have made him so happy. I tried to remember if I'd spoken to Mr. Johnson at the swearing-in. I exchanged pleasantries with most of the solemn representatives of the county government during all the glad-handing after the oaths had been administered, but, between my nervousness and having to keep an eye on the boys, I remembered very little of it. After all that had happened since that day, that event seemed like years ago instead of a couple of months. By now Mr. Johnson was as strange to me as an apparition, sitting there expressionless, patiently waiting to be told why I had come. I hoped I could summon up the courage to tell him.

When the silence became uncomfortable, he tried to reassure me of the county's concern, in case that was what I had come about. "If there's anything that the county government can do for you, ma'am, you've only got to ask. I assume that's why you're here."

"In a way." I was blushing and still trying not to look afraid.

After more silence, he tried again. "This must be a mighty hard time for you, losing your husband so suddenly. I can certainly understand that. Now, seeing as how he was one of our local elected officials, your loss concerns all of us in the county government. We all thought a lot of Sheriff Robbins, ma'am. He didn't hold the job for long, but we were impressed with what we saw. Now tell me what is it I can help you with?"

He thought I was after money. "I haven't come to ask for charity," I told him. "Won't take it."

In spite of the awkwardness and my plain speaking, Vernon Johnson smiled. "Well, I believe I already knew that, Mrs. Robbins. You hail from one of those communities up the mountain, same as your husband, don't you? I remember him saying once that none of the families from up there would ask for anything—not food if they were hungry, not a rope if they were drowning. I've seen enough of them in my years with the railroad to believe that."

"It's true enough. We don't like to be beholden."

"Beholden." He smiled at the word, which probably sounded quaint to him, but I couldn't think of a better one. "Well, I wouldn't think of it that way, if I were you. For a start you have your sons to think of. Their well-being should take precedent over pride, shouldn't it?"

"It's a painful choice, sir."

"I hope it won't be. You know, since your late husband was a good sheriff—a public servant—you could say that he deserved to have his family taken care of, even if he didn't perish in the line of duty. So why don't you tell yourself that maybe we owe you?"

I nodded. Maybe they did.

chapter nine

Seeing Vernon Johnson at the graveside made me wonder if Albert's passing meant that the other fellow, that Samuel Snyder that nobody liked much, would call for a special election and get the job after all. If Albert was right about the politics surrounding the job, I didn't think the county officials would want that to happen. At least I hoped they wouldn't, because here was Commissioner Johnson sitting at his big oak desk, still watching me warily, and twiddling his fingers while he waited to hear what I had to say.

I could see that this visit from me—the sheriff's widow—was giving Mr. Vernon Johnson the fidgets. I looked calm enough, but I expect he thought any minute now I would give way to noisy grief, and there he would be, helpless and mortified, while a poor bereaved woman screamed or sobbed or—worst of all—fainted right there in front of his desk. I was sure that the commissioner was equal to most of the situations he might encounter. He'd know which fork to use at a dinner party and how to talk to a lawyer and understand what they said back, and I'll bet he could fire an employee without missing a beat, but it was plain that he had no earthly idea how to handle a crying woman. I'll bet he hoped he wouldn't have to figure it out. Granted that I had every right to be distraught, of course, but no doubt he'd be praying that I wouldn't give way right there in his office.

He was smiling pleasantly enough, but if he was like most men, he was wishing he could be anywhere but here; however, he was a county official and that made him obligated to hear me out. His wife, the kindly silver-haired woman who had come to the house with the other ladies, told me then that she'd ask her husband to give us whatever help he could. I hoped she had remembered to do that. It would be easier to talk to him if he had some idea that I was coming. He probably supposed that I'd come to ask for money, but it wouldn't be as easy as that.

I tried to push a stray lock of hair out of my face, wishing I had thought to put on rice powder and lip rouge so I wouldn't look so much like a scarecrow, but I didn't care to look in the mirror these days if I could help it. I was never much of a beauty, and I neither wanted nor could afford much in the way of makeup or fancy clothes, but I knew I looked a fright now. In a matter of days grief had made me old. Exhaustion and missing nearly a week of meals hadn't helped my appearance either. I supposed it would pass, though, when I got used to things being the way they were now. Later, when the dark circles under my eyes faded and the pallor and the haggard look left my face, I might be a passably attractive woman again. Now, though, I looked like a whipped hound. I waited until the silence felt like noise, but I still couldn't find a way to begin telling him exactly why I had come.

He smiled. "You needn't be nervous, ma'am. I know that except on social occasions you ladies are not used to having to talk to—well, men of business like me. And it's no wonder. The sheriff gave us to understand that the both of you came from a remote little settlement up the mountain, and that they were more or less shy around strangers. Is that right?"

"Pretty much. Where we come from, people are known for being as economical with their emotions as if they thought they would be charged for them. Albert always said they acted like real life were a type of telegram costing two cents a word."

Mr. Johnson sighed. "I wish some of the people in our committee meetings felt that way."

"It's hard to get used to being any different. At least you needn't worry about me giving way here while I'm talking to you. We don't make a show of our feelings, however strong those feelings might be. Now, I'll grant you that I am still trying to cope with the sorrow of my husband's passing, but now I'm able to put that to one side in order to tend to practical matters."

He was fidgeting again. "As soon as this, Mrs. Robbins? Perhaps you should wait a few days?"

"I've thought about it, but I have my sons to think of. I'd rather start moving forward. It's no use trying to hang on to the past."

He nodded. "Perhaps that's best. I've seen many people postponing practical matters until their distress thaws enough to let them think about the future, and then they face a second grief, because that is when they realize that they have financial worries to contend with in addition to their personal loss."

"Most of the people I know can't afford to wait, Mr. Johnson. Even if they wanted to."

"So you've decided to face the future now, have you? Then I admire your courage."

He might have admired it, but he still didn't quite believe it. I knew he would ease as gradually as time allowed into the painful subject of the Robbins family's future without their breadwinner, because local politics had made Vernon Johnson a diplomat.

I was right. He spent a few more minutes asking about Eddie and George and making remarks about the weather, but finally he decided it was time to come to the point. "Well, I hope you'll excuse my plain speaking, ma'am. I don't mean to be overly inquisitive, but before we discuss some ways that we could address your situation, there are things I need to know on behalf of the county."

"Yes, sir." I was going to save him the trouble of a long discussion by telling him my idea, but before I could figure out a way to frame it, he plunged right on ahead.

"The main concerns are did Sheriff Robbins carry any insurance and do you have any family that can take you in?"

"Family? No sir. There's just my brothers and sisters left now, and they are pretty well scattered from here to Michigan. With times being as hard as they are, none of them could afford to take in three more people. And I wouldn't ask them to." I didn't want to move away and live in some far-off city, anyhow, but I wouldn't say that unless I had to.

Vernon Johnson steepled his fingers and scrunched his forehead so I'd know he was thinking. "But what about your husband's people?"

I knew that question would be coming, and I had worked out what to say so that I wouldn't sound too harsh, but still made it clear that we weren't going back there. I didn't want to sound troublesome, just firm. "There's just his brother Albert. He offered to let us go back to the farm, but . . ."

"But other people there feel differently?"

"Yes. It's plain as a pikestaff that his wife wouldn't like it. Neither would he, really. I don't intend to go where we'd be a burden."

"Is there another alternative, Mrs. Robbins?"

"I could stay put."

That startled him. "You would prefer to stay here?"

"Here in town? Yes sir, I would."

"Alone? That might be difficult. May I ask why?"

I wondered if I should tell him any more about the biggest reason I wanted to stay. Unless Elva could persuade Henry not to let us move in, she would make my life a misery in hopes of forcing us to go elsewhere. It had been hard to put up with Elva even at the best of times, but now I knew I would have no energy to contend with her, and no one to take my side in the inevitable arguments anymore. Not with Albert gone. The boys didn't need to grow up in a house full of quarreling and bitter silences.

"I'd like to stay in town on account of the boys," I told him, and it was true enough. "The schools are better here. Besides, there's no one we can count on to take us in. Nobody we'd care to ask."

"Can you afford to stay on?"

"Not as we are now. You asked about insurance. We didn't have any, because Albert said we couldn't afford it yet."

"We're too young to need it, Ellie," he had told me. *"Let's spend our money on things we need in the here and now. Like new shoes and winter coats for Eddie and George."*

Well, Albert had been wrong about us not needing insurance, but we weren't to know then that he would be dead before he ever saw forty. He had been right about the expense, anyhow. We had so little money to spare that to spend it betting on something that was not likely to happen for decades did seem like an unnecessary waste. Unfortunately, we lost that bet.

Vernon Johnson sighed again. "Yes, I thought it might be like that. It's human nature to take care of the present and hope that the future will see to itself."

"Seems like the very people who need insurance the most are the ones who can't afford to have it."

"Indeed. It's a pitiful shame, but there it is. I wish the county had some sort of pension plan for employees, like the railroad does, but alas we can't afford it either."

"We always thought we were too young to need insurance, but Albert had been thinking about it again, since he got elected sheriff, on account of the dangers of the job. It's just that he never did get around to taking out a policy. It has only been a couple of months since he won the election, you know. Maybe if he had been in the job longer . . ."

"I understand." He was looking alarmed. I think my voice must have quavered. "None of us likes to think about dying, so making plans for it feels like asking for trouble, don't you think? It's a natural reaction. People don't like making wills for the same reason. But now the future has arrived and plans have to be made. Have you thought about what you want to do now?"

I was still too numb to feel much of anything, even hope, and I didn't trust anybody, really, but the man seemed sincere in his willingness to help, and, after all, where else did I have to turn? I know I must have looked red-eyed and weary, but I tried to sound confident anyway. "I have given it a lot of thought, sir."

"And what would you like to do, if you don't mind my asking?"

"I'm glad you asked, sir. You're the very person I had to tell. I want my husband's job."

Vernon Johnson leaned back in his leather chair, and I think that for once he had been rendered speechless. He kept opening and closing his mouth like a fish. I almost smiled. Finally he stammered, "Your husband's *job*? Well . . . that is a facer, ma'am. Frankly, what I was expecting was a request for a sum of money—I expect the county could manage fifty dollars—to enable you and your children to move somewhere else. I had hoped you would be going back to family, but from what you tell me, that is not in the cards." He shook his head. "We had not anticipated this. The other commissioners and I, I mean."

"No, sir. I don't suppose many widows would ask for such a thing."

He picked up a pencil and started tapping his desk with it. He looked like the discussion had got away from him, and now he was trying to think more than a sentence ahead. "Well, Mrs. Robbins, your husband's job. Oh, my."

"I'd like to earn a living instead of being handed charity."

"Your independence does you credit. I admire your courage, but courage and recklessness often look a lot alike. When you say you want your husband's job, are you sure you know what you're asking for?"

In the corner next to the window there was an American flag on a wooden staff with a gilded eagle carved on top. When Mr. Johnson spoke of independence, I started concentrating on that eagle, because I was afraid that if I kept looking at him, his doubts would cause me to lose my nerve.

"Yes, Mr. Johnson, I know exactly what I am asking. I've been thinking on this ever since I started trying to figure out how to go on without Albert. I've been praying about it too."

He had formed all his ideas on women from the well-to-do ladies like his wife. She was kindness itself, but I couldn't imagine her working either. I'll bet Mr. Johnson wished he had gone home for lunch so that someone else would have had to deal with this. With me. I said "praying about it" on purpose, to suggest that any objection from him would be arguing with God.

He stopped tapping the pencil. "Well, ma'am, I don't hold with women working, especially not if they have young children, but times are hard, and I can see that you don't have many other choices. If you're bound and determined to work, maybe we can find something more suitable for you to do."

That made me wary. I couldn't bring myself to smile, but with downcast eyes I did manage to murmur a thank you—no point in being rude to anybody who meant well, even if you took offense at what he said. All the same, if he said he would get me hired to clean the courthouse, I intended to head for the door. That flash of spirit didn't last more than a few seconds, though. I let go of that prideful resolution as soon as I remembered Eddie and Georgie needing town schooling, and shoes, and food on the table. Since I had to be the breadwinner now, if Vernon Johnson offered me honest work, even as a cleaner or a washerwoman, I would have to swallow my pride and take it. If it came to that, I would accept whatever job I was given, but not before I had done all I could to be allowed to serve out Albert's term. The sheriff's job would pay better than anything the commissioners would consider women's work.

"I have given this a lot of thought, Mr. Johnson. I could do my husband's job."

I'm sure that all the commissioner saw was a pale, quiet little woman hunched in the chair in front of his desk. He couldn't believe that I would be equal to the task of dealing with lawbreakers. I could tell he was trying—and failing—to picture me as a peace officer, but I didn't think I'd have to get in any fistfights or anything worse than a shouting match. I didn't suppose I'd ever be able to do that, but chances were I wouldn't have to. For one thing, most of the men around here would die of shame if they were to try to fistfight with a woman. And Albert once said that if you could scare people just by looking mean it would save you a lot of time and trouble in dealing with them.

Mr. Johnson gave me a half-hearted smile, but it was plain that he was humoring me rather than agreeing with me. "It's brave of you to be willing to try it, Mrs. Robbins, but perhaps you feel you have no choice. After all, desperate times call for desperate measures. It's a tough job, even for a man. Do you really think you could go out and arrest people? A little lady like you? Be honest now."

"I know how to shoot."

"Oh dear. Do you?"

"I'm tolerably good at it, too, if that matters. Better than your Mr. Snyder, I'll wager."

The thought of that other candidate, the one that nobody wanted, brought him up short.

"You think that you could deal with a violent and dangerous job?"

I sneaked another look at the gilded eagle for reassurance. "I'm willing to try, sir. Maybe I couldn't have dealt with John Dillinger or

Pretty Boy Floyd, but the kind of lawbreakers we have around here? I could handle them. If you think it would ever come to that."

"You ought to assume that it may. And if you went up against some desperate men—say, bootleggers—who fought back, there wouldn't be anything you could do about it. We'd be afraid you'd get hurt—or worse. Remember what happened to poor Sheriff Tyler? Why, you'd be risking your life. Think of your sons, ma'am. They have already lost one parent. Are you willing to risk making orphans of those poor boys? Shouldn't you think of them?"

Shouldn't you stay home with the children? I knew I'd hear that sooner or later. "I am thinking of them, sir. Their schooling in town is important. Albert would have wanted them to stay and get a good education. And as for the job of sheriff being dangerous? I suppose it is, but just lately I learned a hard lesson. Life is dangerous, no matter what you do. My husband took sick and died within a week. It wouldn't have mattered if he'd been a sheriff or a preacher or a railroad bum. He still would have died."

"All the more reason for you not to take any chances with your life then, Mrs. Robbins. You don't want your sons to be orphans."

"I don't want them to starve, either, and that's more likely to happen if I don't do something. Look, sir, the sheriff's department has two full-time deputies on each shift, most of them big as bears and twice as mean."

That wasn't strictly true. Falcon Wallace had the height and bulk that people expected of a peace officer, and the air of calm authority needed to reassure ordinary citizens in times of trouble. Albert always sent Falcon out to look for lost children or break up a fight between man and wife. He was a strapping, towheaded farm boy, as loyal as a hound to his boss, according to Albert. He wondered if Falcon obeyed orders without question because doing so kept him from having to think too much. He said he had finished the eighth grade in a one-room schoolhouse and then lit out for "the big city" (by which he meant this jerkwater town of five hundred souls, which was all of seven miles from his family's farm). Falcon Wallace was indeed tall and he had the farm boy's well-honed muscles, but, like a big shaggy dog, he had a gentle nature—peaceable because a big dog didn't feel the need to prove himself the way the little ones did. When he wasn't arresting people he seemed to be a kind man. I knew a little about Roy Phillips, but Albert never said much about the other two. That was all right. I was betting that Vernon Johnson didn't know much about them either.

I did know all of them well enough to speak to, anyhow. One or the other of the day shift deputies was around nearly every time I stopped by the office to talk to Albert. Roy Phillips was the short, bandy-legged fellow, with hair like black seaweed. He didn't look fearsome, but Albert said he was about the best shot anywhere around and that he never fell for a sob story from anybody. Albert had called Roy Phillips "the smart one." If a report had to be written up by the arresting officers, Roy took care of it. When they weren't busy in the office Roy would have his nose stuck in a Zane Grey dime novel. He went through two a week. He told Albert he'd rather have books than cigarettes. Of course, it didn't take much to be the smart one in a little county sheriff's department. At best, Roy had gone to high school a year or two longer than the other deputies and reading had educated him even more, whereas Albert had stayed on to get his diploma, even though his father had insisted that he do his share of the farm work. On top of all his other duties, I doubted if Roy Phillips could have handled the book work and the ciphering a sheriff was expected to do. I even had to help Albert with it now and again.

Falcon Wallace was the deputy Albert hired when he replaced Sheriff Tyler, and he was happy to have found him, because every law enforcement department needed somebody like Falcon. And, if they were lucky, at least one employee as *unlike* Falcon as possible. Tyree Madden was his opposite number. If a suspect tried to resist arrest,

Tyree brought him down. He broke up fights, herded drunks into jail cells, and took an ax to the whisky stills they found in the woods. But Albert preferred that the other deputies raid the stills instead of Tyree, because he suspected Tyree of keeping some of the confiscated moonshine instead of pouring it out on the ground.

"I am acquainted with the other officers, ma'am."

I hadn't seen as much of the other two deputies as I had of Falcon Wallace and Roy Phillips. Usually when I stopped by the office and Tyree Madden was on duty, he'd get up and walk out without a word, leaving me to pass the time with Albert and whoever else was on duty. He didn't strike me as shy, though—I knew what shyness looked like, and Tyree Madden wasn't it. He was just indifferent to other people's society and even more so to their feelings. Albert said it might be because he didn't have to be polite to people in his job, but I thought that might be the very reason that some people became lawmen in the first place.

It was fine with me for Tyree Madden to avoid me. I didn't try very hard to have a conversation with him. He was always cold and silent—Albert said he'd never seen the man smile, except when other people were crying. A time or two I had seen his pale shadow of a wife bringing his lunch in a paper sack when he had gone off without it. He never thanked her. She cringed like a whipped hound, which I took as a sign that Deputy Madden behaved at home just the way he did on duty. He was usually paired to work on either shift with Galen Aldridge, who really was as burly as a bear cub, and about as fearless as one to boot, but since he was about seven inches short of six feet, maybe his short temper was a form of self-defense. He looked like the sort of fellow who had been bullied by his schoolmates, and Albert and I wondered if he sought out a job that gave him a gun on account of that. I hoped he'd never be called on to arrest one of his old tormentors.

Until recently there had been a jailer, too. Forrest Burdette, who had once been a deputy, before he got too old and unsteady to do the job. He was still spry and alert enough for light work indoors, but he looked like an old turtle with that beaked nose on his leathery face, and his skinny neck poking out of the gaping collar of his uniform. Nobody wanted to fire him, though, on account of his many years of service, so he was kept on by the department to guard the prisoners and to take them their meals—which usually meant tending to a couple of drunks, a job no more taxing than minding a flock of chickens. If they thought they had somebody more dangerous in the cell, the deputies would put him in irons when they brought him in. Nobody had wanted poor old Mr. Burdette to get beaten to death trying to deliver a bowl of pinto beans to a prisoner.

Finally, though, age and infirmity forced Mr. Burdette to quit on his own, so now there were just the four deputies to share the duties of jailer among themselves. Falcon Wallace was probably best at it. The prisoners never gave him much trouble, perhaps because most of them had known him, or someone like him, all their lives. He did his best to be kind, but mostly because he smiled most of the time. I learned that the usual run of prisoners—young men who got locked up for drinking and fighting—were often first-timers. When they sobered up in a jail cell they were confused and afraid. One of them even tried to hang himself with his belt, but Falcon saw him in time and went for help. What the remorseful drunks needed was a friendly face, not an angry and scornful lawman who would make them feel even worse.

Big as bears and twice as mean. That was stretching the truth to the breaking point. Still, two of them were rather big and one of the others was mean, so what I said was mostly true, and I hoped it would convince the commissioners to appoint me sheriff. Whatever it took. If that didn't work, I would have to make them feel sorry for me, but that was a last resort.

"About these sheriff's deputies, Mr. Johnson. I believe you said you're acquainted with all of them?"

"I am, yes, but what about it?" Vernon Johnson's pause before he answered made me sure that he had taken no particular notice of the deputies, but that he was too proud to admit how little he knew. It didn't matter, though. There were four of them, so even if they had been Barbary apes their very existence helped my argument.

I smiled, feeling on safe ground for the first time since I entered the office. "Those deputies are the answer, sir. I'm saying that it is on account of them that I can do the sheriff's job. The way I figure it, those deputies can take care of the warrant serving and the arresting—anything that involves dealing with the people arrested. According to my late husband, they generally do that anyhow. But that still leaves a lot of supervisor's work for the sheriff to do. Paperwork mostly. Drawing up schedules, dealing with money matters, and talking to ordinary folks who have problems."

He smiled in spite of himself. "Old ladies with lost dogs."

"I saw how it worked when Albert was sheriff. Sometimes of a night he'd tell me what went on at work that day, and I'd help him with the paperwork, so I know."

"And you are proficient in reading and writing, Mrs. Robbins?"

"I'm no professor, but I like to read. And I'll wager I am better at both reading and arithmetic than any of those deputies. Albert even said I was better than him, and he would know. We went to the same school and I made better grades than him."

He smiled, and I could tell he didn't doubt my word, because it wasn't saying much to claim you could read and write better than any of them. "Well, this isn't the Wild West, of course. Our sheriffs aren't like the ones in the cowboy movies."

I smiled, remembering Albert telling the boys exactly that.

"And I suppose that in the past we have had sheriffs who behaved like the railroad foreman: overseeing the heavy work, but not doing it personally."

"Yes sir. It's a shame Mr. Tyler wasn't one of those." He had been getting up in age himself by the time Albert signed on as deputy. Maybe if he had stayed in the office doing the paperwork, he could have lived another ten years and died in his bed instead of getting shot and bleeding to death out in the woods.

"Yes, I take your point, but nevertheless you are female, little lady. What if one of those deputies wants the job? Your late husband did."

"These deputies don't." I blushed to sound so brash before this man who could decide my future, even though I doubted that he'd care much one way or the other.

"They're experienced peace officers. What makes you think they don't want it?"

"I asked them." I had asked Falcon and Roy anyhow. Tyree wasn't any more partial to talking to bureaucrats than he was to talking to felons, women, or anybody else. "None of them wants to be sheriff. They're the ones who believe in cowboy movies. I reckon that's why they wanted the job. They don't like the idea of sitting at a desk, writing out reports. They'd rather be working outside. Anyway, I think they actually enjoy the danger."

The commissioner steepled his fingers and looked down at his desk, apparently deep in thought. When he looked at me again, his expression was stern. "That's as may be, Mrs. Robbins. I don't doubt your word. But it seems to me the real question is whether a bunch of strapping young men will consent to taking orders from a woman. Why they might just quit in disgust, and then where would we be? The county would have no lawmen at all."

I decided there was no use arguing that point. Either it was true or it wasn't. Neither of us could say for certain. "Ask them yourself, Mr. Johnson. Ask them yourself."

chapter ten

Roy Phillips's answer surprised his fellow deputies almost as much as it had the chairman of the board of commissioners. "A lady sheriff, huh?" He shrugged. "Well, a boss is a boss, I reckon. Especially seeing how it's the sheriff's widow."

Falcon nodded. The three of them were alone in the little station, Falcon and Roy Phillips working the day shift, as they mostly had been since Albert Robbins died, and Galen Aldridge passing the time because he had woken up early after pulling the night shift, and there wasn't much else to do that day. The cold rain coming down in steady sheets made all of them reluctant to do anything that required leaving the office, unless they received an urgent call for help, so they sat near the telephone, hoping that nobody would be out in the bad weather needing their assistance. It wasn't the sort of day you'd choose to rob a bank or go looking for trouble.

"The sheriff's widow. Yep, that certainly does make a difference. I'll tell you what I told that Mr. Johnson when he stopped me on the street. I says to him, *"Since you asked me about giving the Widow Robbins her husband's old job, I think it makes sense."*

Roy was cleaning his pistol, more out of boredom than because it needed cleaning. He was short and bandy-legged, with the sharp brown eyes of a weasel, and a blank expression that made it hard to know what he was thinking, except that you were sure that he was thinking, about a mile a minute. When he wasn't reading dime novels, he passed the time in pistol cleaning. Short and almost comical looking—like that Buster Keaton, people said—but they seldom mistook him for stupid. Aldridge was almost as quiet as Madden; neither of them ever said enough to give anybody much evidence from which to form an opinion about his intelligence.

Aldridge nodded. "Yeah, that's what we thought, Tyree and me. We talked it over one night when business was slow. Giving the job to the sheriff's missus does make a certain amount of sense." He took a sip of bitter coffee. "Maybe a woman sheriff could improve on the coffee-making."

They all laughed at that, but nobody thought it was a bad idea.

Falcon pointed his pencil at Roy. "Now that's a point in her favor, isn't it, boys? I'm not saying that she'd be the ideal person for the job, of course—" On a blank notepad Falcon was doodling outlines of trees with thick trunks and rounded blobs for foliage, but despite this show of unconcern, he had been listening carefully.

"No, the little lady's sure as hell not the perfect candidate for sheriff, and in the ordinary way, I'd be trying to elbow both of you aside to get the job, because I *am* the perfect candidate." Roy's tight smile did not mean that he was joking.

Galen laughed. "That's mighty brave of you, Roy, to consider taking the job, seeing that the past two sheriffs died in office."

"Well, I figure that reduces the odds of it happening to the next one. Anyhow, if danger concerned me, I wouldn't be a deputy, would I? Mind you, if I wanted to work in an office all the time, I'd be a bookkeeper, but I'll pass on the job for one reason: I can't see that Mrs. Robbins has got any other way to feed her children. Has she?"

"None that we know of," said Falcon. "I talked to Eddie, and he didn't seem to know what they were going to do next, but he did say that his mother wasn't too keen on going back where they came from."

"No, I didn't think she had anywhere to turn. So, qualified or not, she could use the money more than we could."

"Speak for yourselves, boys." Galen yawned and reached for his coffee mug. "It's not like any of us is rich, you know. Not on our salaries. More money always comes in handy. I know you two don't have any kids to support . . ."

Roy snickered. "None that we know of, anyway."

"But I do. Me and Willadene have two growing boys, and a little girl just learning to walk. Feeding that crew ain't cheap. Willadene plants a garden and keeps chickens and between that and my paycheck, we can just about get by."

"Makes me want to swear off having a family, ever." Falcon shuddered. "All those people depending on me. Imagine having to think how something would affect your family every time you were fixing to do something."

"Well, the sheriff's widow also has two boys to feed, and you've still got money coming in these days, Galen, but she doesn't." Roy never agreed with Galen if he could help it. "I figure she deserves some help in taking care of them, and I can't see any other way for her to get it. As far as I'm concerned she is welcome to the job."

This unexpected generosity made Falcon wonder if he had misjudged his fellow deputy. Roy had a cantankerous pride, and very little use for the weak or the shiftless. He wasn't big on conversation, but the other deputies knew they could trust him when they ran into trouble on the job, and really that was all that mattered.

"She needs the money, right enough, and like you I don't begrudge it to her, but . . ." Falcon scribbled another bushy tree on the notepad, and under it he sketched a tombstone. "Still, it wouldn't do for her to go getting shot, neither. Then where would poor Eddie and Georgie be? Clapped into an orphanage, like as not."

Galen shrugged. "Oh, there's bound to be a relative somewhere who would take them in. They might not like to do it, but most people do end up doing their duty in the end, like it or not. But the bread of charity can be bitter, no question about it."

"Like I told you before, that county commissioner, Mr. Johnson, asked me what I thought about it, and I said I'd let him know after I talked it over with you fellas. Galen, maybe you could tell Tyree how we feel about it when he turns up for duty tonight."

Falcon drew a curved line representing a hill behind the lolly-pop-looking trees. At the top of the hill he drew a smaller tree with stick branches and only a few short slanted lines for leaves. "If it's all right with you two, I'd like one of us to tell the commissioner we all support the idea. He needs to know pretty soon. Those sons of poor Sheriff Robbins are fine boys. Let's do what we can for them. Maybe Eddie can still come and do odd jobs around here. I reckon I could use the help mopping out the cells."

"Well, better him than me." Galen hated doing chores. "Do you boys think it was Commissioner Johnson who thought up the idea of appointing the Widow Robbins to serve out her husband's term?"

"He says not, Galen. According to him, Miz Robbins asked for the job herself, and he wanted to sound us out about how we felt. I think he was still mulling over what he thought of the idea himself. Considerate of him to ask us about it before he made up his mind, though."

Galen grunted. "Careful, more like. The commissioner is afraid that all of us might dig our heels in over the prospect of working for a woman, especially if one of us wanted to be appointed instead. Then we'd walk off the job. And, what with the sheriff dead and all, if we did quit, the county would be in a bind until they could find some more men willing to sign on."

"Right," said Roy. "No telling what kind of lawlessness would start happening here if there was nobody wearing a badge and ready to put a stop to it. That commissioner asked my opinion because he's testing the waters, to find out if we would be willing to work for her or not."

"But is it up to him? What about the rest of the board?" said Falcon.

"From what Sheriff Robbins said, I think Mr. Johnson usually gets his way."

"But you wouldn't mind a lady boss, Roy? How about you, Galen?"

"Not if it was little Miz Robbins," said Roy. "I don't have nothin' against her."

They both looked at Galen, who stared at the ceiling awhile before he said, "I'll go along with you. Can't afford to quit anyhow, on account of my wife and kids. Now, mind you, I wouldn't want to work for some bossy old heifer who would try to throw her weight around to let everybody know she was in charge. If Mrs. Robbins was like that then I would walk off the job, paycheck be damned. But I don't see the sheriff's widow behaving like that, a quiet little lady like her."

"Amen to that," said Roy. "I took that into account when I said it was all right by me. I expect we'll get a lot of say in how things are run. Anyhow, it's one thing to have a boss foisted off on you, and quite another to have a say in who gets appointed."

"Okay," said Galen. "Fair enough. I reckon the rest of us can stick it if you can, Roy—considering the circumstances."

"I can. I'm glad to hear you're both in favor of it."

Galen laughed. "Being a deputy is one job that never changes much, no matter who the boss is. Anyhow, what other job is any of us gonna get in times like these? I reckon we'd have to work for a blind mule if they happened to appoint one."

"And knowing the commissioners, they might," said Roy.

Falcon put down the notepad. "Okay, then, we're all in favor of the commissioner's proposal; all of us for the same reason: because the sheriff's widow and sons need the money." He hesitated. "But one thing to keep in mind: those boys need their mother to stay alive, too. She's all they've got. There ought to be some way we can work it so that she gets the sheriff's salary, while we manage to keep her out of harm's way. I don't think anybody expects her to go out and arrest people."

"The paperwork, Falc. That's safe as houses. She can do it without leaving the office." Roy set his reassembled pistol on the desk. "Well, I reckon everybody has already thought of setting her to write up the reports and such, else the commissioner wouldn't be thinking of letting her have the job."

"Same here," said Galen. "The money would be nice, but as far as I'm concerned, she's welcome to be sheriff, on account of the paperwork, which is one part of a sheriff's job that I never wanted. All that writing is women's work anyhow, if you ask me."

Falcon wondered if Galen was even educated enough to do the paperwork. You never saw him reading anything, not even a dime novel or a newspaper. Oh, he could sound out arrest warrants, and scrawl his name wherever he needed to, but composing lengthy, accurately spelled reports was in all likelihood beyond his ability. If that were the case, it might have a lot to do with his not wanting to attempt the recordkeeping, but Falcon saw no reason to embarrass him by bringing it up.

"It suits me," said Roy, who had been doing the paperwork for the past couple of weeks. "I can do it all right—have been doing it, on top of my other duties—but clerking is not the job I signed on for. You didn't see Wyatt Earp doing paperwork. It's having to report to the county bosses that would sour me on higher office."

"I wouldn't want to sit here pushing a pencil, either," said Falcon. "I just hope she wouldn't think we were giving her the job as charity. I doubt she'd take it then."

"I'll bet she would," said Roy. "I'll bet she'd take it no matter what. Like as not, she's the one who came up with the idea in the first place."

Falcon was still stewing about the possibility that the sheriff's widow would refuse their help. "You know, letting Miz Robbins take the job wouldn't be charity, really. We need to make sure she knows that. We ought to tell her that we need her help to run the office. She needs to know that she'd be earning her pay and doing all of us a favor, because it would save us a world of bother if we let her handle the desk work so that we could get on with the real job."

Galen scowled. "That would be fine, provided that's all she did. You don't think she'd actually *want* to go out arresting people, do you?"

"With a pistol on her hip? A little lady like her? I can't imagine she would. I think she's only trying to find a way to feed her children, and she wouldn't want to take any chance of leaving them orphans," said Falcon.

Roy nodded. "As a rule, women tend to be more cautious than men. Anyway, I don't think she'd be obnoxious about being the one in charge around here. Not from what I've seen of her. She's bound to realize we know a lot more than she does."

"That's what I thought," said Falcon. "So we're all agreed then? Roy, you can go ahead and tell the commissioner that we say it's okay for him to give the job to the sheriff's widow."

"What about Tyree?" asked Galen. "Doesn't he get a say?"

"Well, if he's against it, it'll still be three against one, so I don't reckon it matters. One thing, though . . ."

"What's that, Roy?"

"Have we made sure the sheriff's office is," he hesitated, considering his words, ". . . clean?"

"I'll take care of it," said Falcon. But, what with one thing and another, he didn't get around to it, and finally it slipped his mind altogether.

My swearing-in ceremony was nothing like the formal event Albert's had been. Punch and cookies did not follow, either. Everyone would probably have expected me to bake them myself. The commissioners had not even suggested having a reception, and as a recently widowed woman in mourning, I suppose I would not have accepted the offer had it been made. I officially became the new sheriff in a hasty, private event in an office in the courthouse with only a few people present.

The decision to appoint me came quicker than I had expected. Late one afternoon Vernon Johnson had stopped by the house to tell me he had met with the men of the sheriff's department, and none of them had objected to my appointment. I was glad of that. Once all the deputies had agreed to work for a lady sheriff, the commissioners had held a private meeting that very night. According to Mr. Johnson, there was only a brief objection from two of the oldest and most hidebound members of the board, but the majority agreed to allow me to serve out the remainder of my late husband's term as sheriff.

When he brought me the news, Vernon Johnson told me that the swearing-in—lasting all of five minutes—would take place in the courthouse the next afternoon. "We'll put a little notice in the newspaper announcing your appointment. We might even send word to the *Knoxville Journal.* They might want to talk to you, too. After all, a lady sheriff is news. Do you have a picture we could send in with the notice?"

"No, sir. And I surely would not want the newspapers to run one."

"As you wish." As he was leaving, he stopped at the front door and smiled. "Since you were dead set on his, I'm glad we were able to do it for you, and all of us wish you well. But don't you go doing anything rash, Mrs. Robbins. We don't want you trying to be a hero. We won't pay you enough for that."

He meant for me to smile back, so I did, and I promised to be careful. Being appointed so quickly pleased me, not only because it meant money coming in again, but also because it seemed the surest way to get on with my life. It suited me just fine to begin the job at once with as little fanfare as possible. I didn't need any distractions.

The day after the commissioners made the appointment official, I got to the sheriff's office an hour early. Before I went to work, though, my day began as it always had: getting out of bed well before sunup, making a fire in the woodstove, and starting breakfast. The only difference now was that instead of sending Albert off to work, I would go myself. Just past daybreak I woke the boys and took them a bowl of clean water to wash with. Then I packed lunches—one egg sandwich for myself and one for Eddie—in brown paper sacks saved from the grocery store. That task was much the same, only now I would be eating the sheriff's lunch instead of just packing it. I looked forward to the time when lunch-packing became just another part of the morning routine instead of a source of bitter memories.

Later, after I had made sure that both the boys were fed and checked to see that Eddie was properly dressed for school, we all left the house together. First we walked Georgie, still clutching his battered red fire truck, to Annie Slocombe's house. She would give him lunch and look after him until Eddie came home. She couldn't get any kind of job because she had three children of her own and that restless, unreliable husband, who, when he was docile and sober, almost counted as a fourth child himself. At least he hadn't laid a hand on her recently. Things at the Slocombe place had been quiet since our last encounter. I decided it would be a good thing to remind him that I would be looking in on them every day—and that I still had a gun.

Annie had agreed to look after another young'un for two dollars a week, which was all I could afford to pay out of the sheriff's salary of one hundred dollars a month. Once they let me know that I could have the job, I sat down and worked out a budget in one of Eddie's exercise books from school: food, rent, light bill, clothes for the boys, odds and ends. There wouldn't be much left over, and no reserve for emergencies, but I knew we would get by. We had managed on that amount of money when the salary was Albert's, and now the family had one person less to support with it.

The first thing I had thought when I came in the door of the station was, *I wonder who does the cleaning around here.* Typical woman's reaction, Albert would have said. I doubt if he would have even noticed. Whoever the cleaner was, he wasn't doing a very good job. The floors still had traces of spring mud here and there, as if somebody with a mop had given the room a lick and a promise and called it quits. If they thought that, being a woman, I was going to do the housework around here, they all had another think coming. Cleaning a room was one thing I could claim to be an expert on, and I intended to supervise the next pass one of them made with a broom or a mop and bucket. But I wouldn't be doing the cleaning myself.

After I'd spent a few minutes looking around, I went to Albert's old office. It looked just as it had on the times I'd dropped by to see him, but now it felt empty. Since I thought I knew the deputies' schedules, I had planned to get there ahead of them and spend some time alone in Albert's office, in case my emotions got away from me. I wondered how long it would take me to think of it as *my* office. I thought I might need just a little time at first—half an hour at most—to put aside the memory of this office as a place belonging to my husband. It wouldn't do for the deputies to catch me crying, but my guess had been right: nobody was here yet. I meant to be done with my grieving by the time they came in.

For the time being, I decided to think of the room as "the sheriff's office," not Albert's and not mine—just a working space for a county official.

I glanced through the filing cabinets, and riffled through the pile of papers on the desk. In a tin ashtray beside the desk blotter I found a key ring holding a dozen keys, none of them labeled. Later, when I found out what opened what, I would put a little tag on each one so I wouldn't have to fumble through the whole set whenever I wanted to open something.

Finally I sat down in the swivel chair, trying to convince myself that I had really been appointed sheriff. But being given the title and having the authority are two different things. If I wanted to earn the respect of the deputies, I had to work in this office with no maudlin grief to hamper the work. Now that I had talked the commissioners into giving me the job, I meant to do it well and to make it clear to everybody that I neither needed nor wanted charity or pity. I was also going to take care not to ask for any more help from the deputies than I had to. That was another reason to come in early: to make sure I could find my way around the station and the jail without relying too much on them.

There wasn't anything fancy about the sheriff's private office. The wooden desk and swivel chair were ordinary pieces of furniture that could be found anywhere from a doctor's office to a pastor's study. I would have had to stand up to reach more than halfway across the desk, though, and if my arms had been a few inches longer, I could have touched the walls on either side of it.

The room was a small square windowless box. (I could hear him saying it: *"A sheriff doesn't want a prisoner's angry relatives shooting at him through a window. If I want a view, Ellie, I'll just look at the calendar."*) Sure enough, the wall calendar in the office offered prettier scenery than you'd get looking out a window at the row of old buildings that lined Main Street. A smiling blond girl in a fringed turquoise cowgirl outfit—complete with boots and hat—held the reins of a palomino in a field bordered by woods, and in the background were gray snow-capped mountains. Not our mountains. In east Tennessee the mountains are rounded instead of sharp, and mostly covered with hardwood trees. The bare peak on the calendar looked like the kind you see in westerns, jagged and treeless. I thought the scene might be in Wyoming or Montana—not that I'd ever been west of Knoxville myself. A line on the calendar above the year said that it was a gift of Saunders Feed & Seed, which is here in town, so I guess they didn't take the picture themselves.

The deputies had not quite disposed of all traces of Albert, and it had not occurred to me to go to the office and collect them. I suppose I would have remembered to do it eventually, after I had finished all the more necessary tasks that come with a death in the family. I had not considered that, when I took over his office, I would be haunted by small reminders of him, some of which could not be filed away. There were only a few personal items in the office. A chunk of quartz he had used as a paperweight, a framed photo of George and Eddie, dressed in their Sunday best, sitting on a log behind our house—the same log I'd used for target practice. Beside it, full of pencils, was the brown glazed Blue Ridge coffee mug from the Erwin pottery that the boys had given him for Christmas. I had supplied the quarter for the purchase, but they picked out the mug. Sooner or later it would be just another mug to me, I supposed, but I couldn't bear to touch it now. There was also a thick white china coffee mug, and I decided to use that one. It was the sort of mug that diners served coffee in; maybe that's where he got it.

The wide oak desk occupied most of the room. When I looked at the stack of papers still on it, I caught my breath at the sight of Albert's spiky handwriting, scribbled in the margins of the topmost report. Tucked in a corner of the desk blotter was a photograph I hadn't noticed before: a snapshot of our family, posing in front of a stand of laurels—Albert, all smiles, standing with his hand on Eddie's shoulder, and me holding baby George in a fleecy white blanket. Albert's dad had taken that photo a couple of years ago at a family picnic. I wish somebody had taken one of us with him, because he died a little while after that outing. I looked at that picture for a good while before I put it at the back of the top drawer. No distractions; no looking back. But the framed snapshot of Eddie and George could stay.

I spent most of that first hour sifting through the papers on the desk, reading a few of them, trying to decide what I ought to work on first. I had no idea which things were important, which ones had to be done sooner than the others, or even who to send them to when I did finish them. I was tempted to ask one of the deputies—probably Roy Phillips, "the smart one"—for advice. Would he take my asking him for help as a sign of weakness—or worse, an invitation to take charge? Albert had only been in charge for a short time. How did he learn the ropes of being in charge and maintain his authority over men who used to be his coworkers, while he was getting the hang of it? I wished I had thought to ask him. I suspected, though, that a man's asking for help was a different matter from a woman doing the same.

The cells were empty right now, so no one else would be around until eight o'clock. I knew that whenever we had prisoners one of the deputies on day watch acted as jailer, and a prisoner in the jail meant that he had to come in earlier to bring the inmates breakfast, such as it was. In the ordinary way of things, no one watched the prisoners overnight. I guess if we had some modern-day Jesse James in custody, someone would have to stay.

When I asked about that, Roy Phillips told me that when somebody locked up a prisoner, they took away their belt and shoelaces, but, since the department budget didn't stretch to round-the-clock guards, all we could do was hope the prisoners wouldn't find a way to get into mischief during the night. Since our typical inmates generally ran to drunks and petty thieves, most of them repeat offenders, they were unlikely to be ashamed enough to kill themselves over an infraction that would cost them, at most, a couple of weeks in jail.

But what did a deputy do when there weren't calls to answer or prisoners to tend to? Surely, as tight as the budget was, the department couldn't pay him to sit around doing nothing. When the answer occurred to me, I smiled: *the cleaning.*

According to the schedule book on the sheriff's desk, the day shift would be Falcon and Roy, as it usually was, and they would arrive after they'd had their own breakfast—Falcon at the boarding house and Roy at the local diner. At about the same time, the night shift deputies, Tyree and Galen, would stop by the office to report on the evening's events and sign out. One of them should have been here now in case the phone rang, but I suspected the night deputies might have joined Roy at the diner, and that they'd all come in together. I had arrived well before they would. All of this information about departmental routines I had heard from Albert. It was lucky I had listened.

Falcon Wallace was the first to arrive. He looked startled to see me there, but after a moment he recovered his composure and said good morning, trying to act as if a lady sheriff was the most natural thing in the world.

I supposed that we should have begun with some small talk about the weather and such, but I was too preoccupied with everything else, and I couldn't think of any. I could have thanked him for his kindness to Eddie and George after Albert died, but I didn't want to talk about Albert unless I had to.

"I didn't expect you to be here so early, ma'am," he said. "I have been meaning to tidy up the sheriff's office for you, but what with one thing and another, I didn't get around to it."

"Don't worry about it. I'll see to it myself. I probably should have come and taken away his belongings earlier, but, like you said, what with one thing and another . . ."

"Well, I wish you would let me . . ."

"I hope we have more important things to concern us. But speaking of cleaning, do you all take it in turns to mop the floors and so on?"

Falcon hesitated. "Well, we do our best."

"Maybe we should spread the chores around. I'll draw up a list of who should do what each week." I smiled, because women have to smile when they're being firm. "Just because you have a woman sheriff doesn't mean you also got a cleaning lady. I might pitch in, same as the rest of you, but no more than that."

Falcon nodded uneasily and glanced at the telephone. "Has anybody called yet?"

"No. It hasn't rung since I got here. I guess nothing's going on."

"Well, Galen says something is always going on. It's just a matter of whether or not they've been caught. This is about the time we hear from people whose property was stolen or damaged in the night. They get up first thing in the morning and discover that the cow is gone, or their mailbox has been smashed, and then they want us to drop everything and go over there to set it to rights."

"And do you?"

"More often than not. It's not as if we have any more pressing demands on our time. Neither Dillinger nor the Barrow Gang ever got this far east that I know of."

"Well, they're dead anyhow, so unless somebody around here goes into the outlaw business, I guess we can go on worrying about cows and mailboxes."

"Suits me. Nobody's going to shoot one of us over a cow."

"It's a little after eight. What happens now?"

"Generally, when Roy comes in, I'll go out on patrol, and he'll stick around in case there's an emergency." He caught his breath. "I mean, if that's all right with you. You're the sheriff. That is if you want to bother with all this stuff. If you don't, then we can just carry on like we have been. We're doing our jobs the way your husband wanted it done, you know. Roy says routine doesn't change much, no matter who the sheriff is."

"I expect it's all right then, but let's see how it goes, Falcon." There was no point in making a decision until I had enough experience to know if there was any way that would work better than what they had always done.

"Will do, ma'am. Anything I can do to help you get started . . . well, anything any of us can do, really . . ."

He had that sorrowful look that people get when they are pitying someone, but I wanted none of it. "You mustn't feel sorry for me. Not for a minute. I may be here on sufferance, and I may need a little help at first, but I don't take charity. I intend to prove myself and do this job as well as I'm able."

"Yes, ma'am. Understood."

I smiled. "No need to go calling me *ma'am*, Falcon. *Sheriff* will do, or—" I almost told him to call me *Ellendor*, but then I realized that allowing people to call me by my first name would not help anybody to see me as the person in charge. Next thing you know they'd have me mopping the floors every morning. "Or you can say Mrs. Robbins, I suppose."

He nodded. "I'll try to remember, ma'am—*sheriff*, I aimed to say . . . Are you finding everything all right so far?"

"I'm taking it as it goes, and I may ask for explanations every now and again—not too much, just a nudge in the right direction. I'd like for somebody to tell me what needs to be done until I learn more about what to do. You could let me know if there's something that ought to be attended to. I'd appreciate that."

He brightened. "Well, that's good. Any of us would be happy to help any way we can. The laws about prisoners and arrests and all are written down in a manual, but routine is mostly common sense. One thing is the schedules. We set them up for a week at a time. Usually, I'm on with Roy, and Galen works with Tyree. We're on day shift, Roy and I, but one week a month one or both of us swaps with the others for night duty."

"Just to keep from getting stale?"

Falcon smiled. "Well, that's what the sheriff always said. Mr. Tyler, I mean. He was the one who started the switching around, and Sheriff Robbins just kept on with it. Roy says it's to make sure none of us is letting anybody get away with anything on our shift. You know, like not stopping a moonshiner who's heading off to Knoxville to deliver his product, or looking the other way when a whore—" He stopped, and his expression said he had remembered that he was talking to a lady.

I pretended not to notice. "Don't worry about what you have to say to me concerning department business, Deputy. I know we're not dealing with angels, and I'm better off knowing the facts."

"Well, anyhow, the old sheriff figured that swapping shifts means that we'd get caught if we tried to let anything slide on a regular basis."

"I see that."

"Not that we're doing anything we shouldn't, though."

"No, I would hope not."

Ever since I knew I'd gotten the appointment I wondered how I ought to dress to carry out my duties as sheriff. Albert had not worn a uniform, but ever since he got elected he was careful to dress in a formal way so that people would know he was somebody in charge. He usually wore his church clothes—a starched white shirt and his dark suit. He had wanted a black Stetson hat—they weren't just for wearing in cowboy movies; we had even seen railroad executives wearing them, and Albert thought it made a man look like someone who was not to be trifled with. I had thought about using some of the housekeeping money to buy him one for his birthday, but that never came around, so to the end of his life he wore his brown fedora. After he died I put the hat away in the wardrobe. At the time I told myself I was doing it in case Eddie should ever want it, but I think I really kept it because I could not bear to get rid of his things so soon. It had not yet been long enough to let go.

Some women these days wore trousers, if the ladies' magazines were to be believed, but in rural Tennessee it would have caused comment if I had done it. After all, nobody expected me to go chasing bandits or breaking up stills. I didn't need any special clothes to sit at a desk and write all day, and new clothes cost money, which was the most important point of all. On that first day I wore my light-blue dress, the one I most often wore to church, but I tacked on a white lace collar instead of the dime store pearls Albert had given me one Christmas, and I left off the little squashed hat with a few inches of net veil. All I owned were high heels and old house slippers, and neither seemed exactly right to wear on the job. I would have to think some more about footwear, but that day I wore the black high heels, because, being short, I decided that a few extra inches would add to my authority.

"Well, Deputy, if there's anything you think I ought to be doing . . ." But before I could finish that thought, the telephone box on the wall began to ring.

Falcon nodded toward it. "You could start by answering that. Or I will if you'd rather."

"No. Time I got to work."

I put the receiver to my ear and stood on tiptoe to say "Sheriff's office" into the mouthpiece. "This *is* the sheriff speaking . . . Yes, ma'am, I truly am. Are you needing any help from us today?"

From then on, my side of the conversation mainly consisted of a series of yeses, followed by an occasional *when* and *where*. The woman talked a mile a minute, and I didn't have much choice but to listen without interrupting. I caught myself nodding a few times out of habit as if the caller could see me. I didn't promise anything, though. When the caller finally got around to saying what the problem was, I told her not to worry and said someone would look into it.

When I hung up, Falcon was looking at me expectantly. "Trouble?"

"The lady on the phone seemed to think so. She said her name was Crabtree, I believe. From what I could tell, she sounded elderly. She was calling from the community store out in Bitter Creek where she lives."

Falcon smiled. "Oh, we know her of old, ma'am—*sheriff*, I mean. That must have been Robert Crabtree's widow. She lives over on Bitter Creek, like she told you, by herself on their old farm that's mostly hillsides and apple trees. That house has seen better days—well, so has she."

"By herself? Doesn't this Mrs. Crabtree have family?"

"There are a couple of grown sons, but they're out and gone to the car factories up north. The poor old lady gets nervous every so often, and we have to go out there and assure her that the burglar was only a shutter banging in the wind, or whatever ordinary thing has set her off at the time. We're polite to her, though. The old sheriff was very particular about that. He said she pays taxes, same as everybody else, so he reckoned she was entitled to turn to us when something frightened her. She seems to think me and Roy are a cross between handymen and destroying angels."

I smiled at the thought of Roy Phillips in long white robes and eagle's wings. "I wish you were. I'll bet she could use some of both. I know I could."

"Well, we do our best. What did she want this time?"

"She said a thief broke into her chicken coop and stole two laying hens. What should I have said?"

Falcon grinned. "Well, Sheriff, I reckon I would have told her that we don't arrest foxes, but I'll drive out there and soothe her ruffled feathers."

I made it through the first day.

chapter eleven

My first month as acting sheriff was as hard on the deputies as it was on me. I was still learning my way around, and the deputies were trying to get accustomed to working for a woman. We all spent the first couple of weeks walking on eggshells—me, trying to be in charge without being seen as the wicked stepmother, and them trying to accept my authority without feeling like overgrown schoolboys.

After a while, though, we got used to each other, settled into a routine, and got on with our jobs. I got more confident about doing the paperwork; all those times I'd helped Albert paid off. I had even begun to figure out when to give orders and when to rely on the deputies' judgment. Maybe that was easier on account of me being a woman. A male sheriff might have felt honor-bound to lock horns with the deputies to prove he outranked them, but I didn't care about that. I just wanted us to work together well enough to do a good job.

The sheriff's private office had ceased to conjure up painful memories every time I set foot in it. Working there day after day must have laid Albert's ghost to rest for me; by the second week I had got so used to being there that I began to treat the office as my own. I took in a mason jar for garden flowers and set it on one side of my desk next to the framed picture of Eddie and George. In the top drawer I put a comb and a powder compact. Albert's old shaving mirror hung beside the calendar now. I had no hopes of ever looking more than tolerable, but at least I intended to make the effort to keep my face from looking haggard and to make sure that my hair didn't look like a rat's nest.

In those first weeks, as I got better acquainted with each of the deputies, I learned perhaps the most useful thing of all: who was good at what. If we needed an armed and dangerous lawbreaker arrested, Tyree was the man to send, but he was no good at reassuring nervous old ladies or delivering bad news to the next of kin. Falcon Wallace was the best one at dealing with lost children or animal problems, like cows getting through the fencing and blocking the road; we always had a lot of those. Maybe farmers couldn't afford to buy new fencing nowadays. I'd send Galen Aldridge to handle drunks and fighting—which was often the same thing, and Roy Phillips could deal with businessmen and the more complex financial or technical matters. Not that we had much of that, either because it wasn't happening here or because the men behind it were too slippery to get caught. Roy was best at figuring out clues, too, in case the culprit wasn't an obvious choice, and he would help me with the reports if there was too much for one person to do and time was short. I couldn't always send out the one I wanted to, of course, because sometimes the deputies working the shift were not the ones I would have chosen to tackle the problem, and then we had to make do with whoever was available and hope for the best.

It was all working well enough; at least I never heard anybody making any complaints. I even made the coffee every now and again, once I was certain that all of us knew who was in charge. Maybe it was easier because I felt older than all of them, but even the married ones with families of their own seemed like big kids a lot of the time.

Either becoming a widow had made me older than my years, or else women grow up and most men never quite do. Falcon Wallace was the only one who was much younger in years than me, but the others seemed younger, too, so it was easy to be in charge of them—sometimes it felt just like looking after Eddie and George. If I sounded calm and firm and sure of myself, they listened.

I was lucky for those first few weeks: we didn't have to contend with anything more serious than a few fistfights and a couple of fourteen-year-old ne'er-do-wells stealing some farmer's plow mules to play cowboy with. There were times when I thought a vinegary spinster schoolmarm could have done the job better than all of us.

One morning just after I arrived at the office a call came in from an excited woman wanting to know if Falcon could come over and help her with a problem.

"He has the day off," I told her. "I'll come myself. Give me the details." Actually, I was expecting him to walk in any minute, but, as good a fellow as Falcon seemed to be, I was a little uncomfortable with the idea of citizens asking for a particular officer when they had a problem, so I thought I'd better go and see what was going on.

"We got a call just now, and I'm going to take care of it myself," I told Falcon when he came in five minutes later. "They asked for you."

He didn't look fazed by this information, which I took to be a good sign. He just smiled and said, "If you're sure you want to bother, I'll just drink my coffee and answer the phone then. Send word if you need help. Where are you headed?"

"To the diner."

His face changed then, maybe just a flicker of something, but it was gone so fast that I couldn't tell what it meant. I didn't ask him, though. I just nodded and closed the door behind me. But I filed that look away in my mind for future study.

The town's only diner is an old metal-sided railroad car, painted silver and edged with boxwood shrubs around it to hide where the wheels had been. A strip of neon around the top surrounded its name: City Diner. Since this little burg had never been a city, and I doubted it ever would be, either the owners were optimistic or else they got the sign cheap from somewhere else, same as they had the building itself. It was parked on a corner lot within sight of the hotel, just down the street from the train depot, and it stayed in business by keeping late hours and catering to people passing through, waiting here between trains and such.

I had only been in there once. When Albert and I first came to town looking for a place to live we had a bite of lunch there, because we knew he was going to be working for the railroad, and it tickled him to take me to eat in a real railroad car. I never went back, though. Housewives with two little boys don't have the time or the money to eat away from home. I knew they were open early and late, though, to accommodate the train schedule, so maybe the deputies stopped in for coffee and pie in the evening or a hot breakfast before the day shift every now and then.

I never thought about the diner much, because we didn't get any nuisance calls from there. They didn't serve liquor or allow gambling or billiards in the place. It was just an ordinary little eatery with a long counter with a row of stools like mushrooms along its side, and half a dozen booths set next to the front plate-glass windows. Its gravel parking lot, fringed by trees, would hold about ten cars, but it seldom did these days.

When I got there the place didn't look crowded. I wondered what kind of problem they could be having at the diner so early on a sunny spring morning. Surely it was too early for drunks or hoboes. Travelers didn't usually cause trouble unless alcohol was involved. I hoped their problem wasn't serious because I had forgotten to take a weapon. I wondered if a man would have forgotten. Probably not, but women are more inclined to try talking before they go to brandishing weapons anyhow. I hesitated for a moment on the steps, and then I went in, trying to look more confident than I felt.

A couple of men in overalls were sitting at the counter, hunched over pancakes, either railroad shop workers or farmers on an early errand to town. In the booth nearest the door a man in a black business suit had a Knoxville newspaper propped up in front of a plate of congealing scrambled eggs.

A motherly-looking waitress in a faded green uniform was wiping down the counter near the cash register. She had put on a mechanical smile when she heard the door open, but it faded when she saw that it was only me and not one of her regular tippers. I wasn't in uniform, but after a moment she must have realized who I was, because she nodded toward a booth in the back corner and then went back to mopping down the counter.

Two people were sitting in that back booth, and one of them was crying.

I headed back there, thinking as I did that the only two women in the diner—the waitress and I—were the only people working. The skinny boy with his back to the wall, dabbing his face with a paper napkin between sobs, looked about twelve, but not much taller or heavier than my Eddie. To someone not used to being around young'uns, he could have passed for much younger, but I could tell. He had feathery dark hair that could have used a trimming, and an old work shirt that looked like a hand-me-down. The scowling, heavyset man sitting in the booth across from him was wearing a dingy white apron over a tee shirt—he must be the cook here, I thought, but it didn't look like there was any connection between the two of them, because the cook wasn't making any effort to console the boy. He just sat there glaring at him. When the boy tried to take a fresh paper napkin out of the dispenser, the cook slapped his hand away, saying, "Those things cost money," which only made the boy's tears flow that much harder. He wasn't making any noise, though;

just sitting there with his fists clenched, shaking silently, while tears streamed down his face.

It was all very matter-of-fact and quiet. Neither of them had a weapon and there didn't seem to be anything threatening going on, aside from the unauthorized appropriation of paper napkins.

I slid into the booth beside the tearful boy. "Is there a problem here, gentlemen?"

The cook glared at me. "I don't know that it's any of your business, lady."

"I believe it is, sir," I said, trying not to laugh in his face. "I'm by way of being the sheriff around here, and somebody sent for me. So you need to tell me right now what's going on."

After the cook got used to the idea of a peace officer being female, he brightened up considerably, and I suspected that he had been threatening the young fellow with some sort of legal action. "You're the sheriff? Good deal. Just who we needed to see. Did you bring your handcuffs?"

"Tell me what's going on, and we'll go from there."

"All right, *Officer.* I'm Ike Bonham. I own this place. This morning I caught this here crybaby punk stealing out of the garbage cans out back. It's been going on for the better part of a week. At first, when I saw the trash had been disturbed, I thought it was a raccoon, or maybe even a bear, but when I came in this morning I opened the back kitchen window on purpose to keep an eye on the garbage cans, and a little while ago I caught this kid back there trying to help himself."

I nodded and held up a finger to signal the cook to stop talking. "Thank you, sir. I believe I am clear now on your side of the situation. And what about you, young man? Let's start with your name."

The boy wiped his eyes with another paper napkin. "Davis Howell, ma'am. Are you gonna put me in jail?"

"I'm not done listening yet, Davis Howell. What's your side of the story?"

"It ain't stealing, is it? When people throw things away, then them things don't belong to them anymore, do they? So how can anybody *steal* 'em?"

The cook slapped the table with the flat of his hand. "The trash cans still belong to me, by God, and you broke into them! Breaking and entering. That's illegal, for starters. And then there's trespassing. And vagrancy. The kid doesn't have a cent on him. Isn't that a crime around here?"

When I took a closer look at the young thief, I could tell that a bright red lump on his left cheek was going to turn into a bruise in an hour or two. I touched the boy's arm, and he flinched and tried to draw away. "That mark on your face, did he do that?"

Davis Howell touched his cheek and winced. "Yeah. He smacked me when he pulled me away from the garbage can. I reckon there'll be one on my arm, too, where he grabbed me and shook me. He punched me in the stomach, too, when I tried to run away."

I considered it. "Seems to me, gentlemen, if you want to get the law involved in your little set-to, the way this officer sees it, your offenses are about even. You charge this boy with vandalism of property or some such crime, and he can turn around and get us to arrest you for assault and battery." I had done some reading up on Tennessee law on nights when I couldn't sleep, but what I was spouting right then was just plain old common sense. Most of the time when two men are fighting, the rights of the matter are pretty evenly divided between the two sides. You'd be surprised how few really innocent people a lawman ever sees, excepting victims of burglary or theft, I suppose.

"You mean you'd arrest me for protecting my own property? Me?" The cook was flabbergasted.

"I still want to hear the rest of what the boy has to say, sir." I tapped Davis Howell's arm again. "Go ahead. Don't mind him. If he tries to hit you while I'm here, I'm taking him straight to jail. You tell me what's going on."

He shook his head. "I took food, like he said. Put me in jail. You all feed prisoners, don't you?"

That set me back for a minute. It isn't often that we get people volunteering to be locked up. "You're hungry then?"

He shrugged. "I don't mind so much about that. But if I went to jail could I take somebody along with me?"

The cook made an unpleasant noise that was probably a laugh. "They're not running a hotel over there. Nor a soup kitchen."

I ignored him and kept watching the boy's tear-streaked face. "Well, I'm not saying that you could do it, mind, but if I put you in jail, who would you want to bring along?"

He hesitated, wondering if he was about to land himself in more trouble. "My little sister. She ain't but three."

"A jail is no place for a little girl. I have a son about that age, and I won't even let him come down to visit me there. Where are your parents?"

"My mama died last winter. Pneumonia. So then it was just Daddy and Grace and me. We was all right at first, because I had helped Mama around the house enough to know about cooking and keeping things clean. But then about two months ago, Daddy got to drinking real bad and staying gone all the time. About ten days ago he just took off and never did come back. We ain't seen him since. We used up all the food in the house, but when it ran out I had to get something to feed Grace."

"What about your neighbors? Could you get some help from them?"

"We don't live in town. We live out the road a ways going up the mountain, but we allus kept to ourselves. Anyhow, I was a-skeered of anybody finding out we was on our own. We don't have any kinfolk to take us in, and I don't want us going to no orphanage. Grace might get adopted—she's a pretty little thing—but they'd never take me in the bargain, and then we'd be separated forevermore."

He had worked it all out carefully, and I couldn't argue with the logic of any of it, except for his alternate plan, which was stealing food from garbage cans and trying to get by on his own.

"What about school, Davis?"

He shrugged. "I never went all that much, even before Mama passed. I don't reckon they ever missed me. If I coulda left Grace on her own all day, I wouldn't have gone to school, I'da got me a job."

"Hey, sugar. What's goin' on?"

I glanced up. A plump blond woman in a tight uniform was standing in the aisle a few feet away from the booth, but the expression on the cook's face made it plain that she wasn't talking to me. He peered at her over his shoulder, and his scowl deepened. "Kinda late, aren't you, Shel?"

"Yeah, well, I gotta get some rest sometime, sugar. Had to do my hair. It's not like we're busy . . ."

"You'd better not be cattin' around, Shel."

"At this hour of the morning?" Her eyes widened, and she pushed a strand of stringy hair out of her eyes. "And me a married lady."

"Some excuse for a wife you are," he muttered. "Worse at that than you are at being a waitress. Cattin' around with half the county. I don't know what I was thinking, divorcing Cora for the likes of you. I should have listened to your ex-husband."

"Which one?" She was still looking around, and the conversation sounded so pat that it must have been one the two of them had often, because nothing in her face or voice indicated that she was anything but bored, that is, until she recognized me.

I recognized her too. Her cheeks and her lipstick were redder than when I had seen her last, and now there wasn't a drizzle to make her bleached blond hair frizz up, or a cloth coat to smooth her shape, but I knew where I had seen her last: in the mist on that grassy hillside after Albert's funeral.

Her smile wavered for a moment, but then she gave me a cheerful nod. "Well, hello there, Missus Sheriff. Haven't seen you around here as I recall. What's going on here? Anything to worry about?"

Before I could answer her, her irate husband slapped his hand down on the table again. "Well, Sheriff? I haven't got all day. Are you going to arrest this little punk or not?"

I stood up to go. "I'm taking him with me anyhow. Come on, Davis Howell. We'll get you sorted out somewhere else."

The waitress seemed to lose interest in all of us then. She pouted for a moment, as if waiting to see if anybody else was going to speak up, and then with a shrug, she turned and walked behind the counter and through a swinging door that led to the kitchen.

I took Davis Howell by the elbow and walked him to the door of the diner. "Come on, let's see if we can find an alternative to robbing trash bins. You can't take care of a little child all by yourself."

"I wasn't expecting that man—the cook—to be out there at the trash bins. I was hoping it would be her again."

"Which *her*?"

"Shelley. The blonde you was just talkin' to. She was out back there the other morning with some man, and she gimme a hunk of bread and cheese to clear out and not say nothing about it. I was hoping she'd give me some chores to do so's I could earn some money."

"You're too young to be having to worry about that. Come on."

"Are you taking me to jail?"

"I would if we had the makings of a decent meal there, but since we don't I'm going to turn you over to the minister of my church. He's bound to know somebody in the congregation who can look after you and your sister, maybe even give you a home." If that failed, the government people would come and put them in an orphanage, but I thought they'd be better off staying around here.

When I got back to the office Falcon was still at the desk. "Everything go all right at the diner, ma'am? Ike must have been on the warpath again, but I figured he wouldn't hit you. He's not above hitting women, but not *you*."

"Hitting women?"

He nodded. "Every so often Ike and that wife of his go for each other's throats, and then Mildred—the other waitress—calls us to come over and break it up. Who got the worst of it this time?"

"He caught a kid pilfering the trash bins. That's why he called. But he and his wife had words while I was there. Looks like they deserve each other."

"Glad to hear he wasn't walloping her. That Shelley is a handful. 'Course he should have known that when he married her, because fooling around with him broke up her marriage in the first place, but, believe it or not, he is crazed with jealousy."

"Maybe that's why."

"I guess. He says he'll cut her throat if he catches her with another man, which I don't understand, because he must have known what she was like. If he wanted a good woman he should have married one. At least he hasn't caught her—yet. I just hope he doesn't kill her. Then we'd have to arrest him, and I'd sure miss the diner."

⟷

If there was a murder case that everybody was talking about that spring, it was the one that was about to end in execution in New Jersey. It had been four years since the Lindbergh baby had been kidnapped and found buried in a shallow grave not far from his parents' mansion. It had taken the investigators more than two years to find the kidnapper. Then came the trial, which was a three-ring circus of reporters and newsreel photographers covering every minute of the proceedings, because everybody in the world seemed to want to know all the details about the famous aviator's family tragedy. Finally, though, Bruno Hauptmann had been convicted of the baby's murder and sentenced to death. He went to the electric chair in early April, and some people claimed he was innocent, but, after all, somebody had to pay for that poor child's death, so nobody objected to the execution too much that I ever heard. Anyhow, that's what people were talking about that spring.

All of us talked about the Lindbergh case every now and then, when the paper reported something more important than what the condemned man had for breakfast, but Roy Phillips was the only one of us who really got interested in the story. It wasn't the ghoulish details or the question of Bruno Hauptmann's guilt that mattered to him—it was the technology involved in the execution.

"An electric chair." He set the newspaper down next to his coffee mug. "Don't that beat all? I sure would like to see that thing in action, boys."

Tyree glanced at the newspaper's drawing of the chair and shrugged. "Killing a man with electricity. I wonder if it hurts."

Roy grinned. "Not for long."

"Well, you'd have to sit there and wait while they strapped you in and fiddled with the controls, wouldn't you? I reckon all told a rope is quicker."

"Depends on if the executioner knows what he's doing. They say that if the hangman puts the knot in the wrong place when he slips the noose around the prisoner's neck, it can take a good quarter of an hour for the man to die. Strangulation. Twisting in the wind. Mighty slow. And not many hangmen *would* know what they were doing, would they? Most lawmen don't hang more than one or two prisoners in their whole career. The electric chair wouldn't be so difficult to—" he grinned, "to get the hang of."

Tyree was never in favor of changing things that weren't broke. "Yeah, but I've heard that the first jolt of electricity doesn't always kill the condemned man either. That could take awhile too. Stop. Listen for the heartbeat. Start over."

"Seems cleaner, though," said Roy. "More modern, I guess. Just a bunch of white-coated technicians in a little room with a switch on the wall—that's how I picture it, anyhow. I wonder why we don't use an electric chair in Tennessee?"

"Maybe they don't think we have electricity down here."

"Electrocution would be easier, though, don't you reckon? Just flip a switch instead of having to build a platform and fit up a trapdoor, and put the rope around the poor fellow's neck? And then there's all the calculations to contend with."

"What calculations?" I think they'd forgotten I was there, because they both looked startled when I chimed in, but I thought I'd better ask, because anything within law enforcement was my business nowadays.

Roy glanced over at me and reddened a bit, looking like he wished he hadn't brought it all up, but before he could change the subject I asked him again, and after he hemmed and hawed he finally said, "Oh, the calculations . . . Well, Sheriff Tyler always said there was a formula you had to follow before you strung somebody up."

"Did he ever have to hang a prisoner?"

"If he did, it was before my time. Maybe a long time back when he was a deputy. I don't know. But he knew right much about it, seems like. Maybe he heard people talking about it."

"What did he say about calculations, Roy?"

"According to him, it had to do with ratios. He said you had to match the weight of the condemned man to the length of the rope, because if you got the ratio wrong—well, never you mind. It's not something you'll ever have to worry about. But from what I've heard, an electric chair would be easier on everybody involved."

"It's not up to us, though, is it? The state legislature gets to decide that."

Roy nodded. "They'd probably be more interested in costs than in making things easy on anybody."

"Just throwing a switch," said Tyree. "Can't get much easier than that for the executioner. I don't see any point in making it easy on the prisoner, though. That fellow they had on death row in New Jersey killed a helpless little baby. I reckon I'd turn on the juice on him myself and not lose a minute's sleep over it."

I thought about it. Maybe I had never seen an execution, but I had watched Albert die, and that was bad enough. I couldn't imagine having been the cause of it. "I don't think it would be easy to kill a man no matter how you went about it."

Tyree may have known what was in my mind. "Well, Sheriff, you'd just have to bear in mind that anybody an executioner is called on to—well, I won't say *kill*, because a legal execution isn't murder. It's not personal. Anyhow, the murderer has it coming. The way I see it, nothing you could do to the condemned man is a patch on what he put his victim through when he committed his crime."

"And at least he knows it's coming," said Roy. "Your convicted killer has got months to say his good-byes to his family, wrap up his earthly business, and make his peace with God, if he's a mind to. The victims had none of that, did they? There they were, looking forward to many more years of living, same as anybody, and then, out of the blue, the poor unsuspecting souls are put down like so many stockyard calves, with no choice in the matter, no time to settle anything, and no lawyers to try to get them a second chance. I'd feel sorry for the victims if I were you."

I reckon most lawmen feel that way. They wouldn't be lawmen if they didn't. I could see the sense of it, too. Maybe Albert hadn't had a chance to say good-bye when he was dying, stricken with pneumonia like he was, but at least I had most of a week to come to terms with his passing. It would have been a deal worse if I had just opened the door one day to find a stranger on the doorstep telling me my husband was gone. But still . . .

"I don't say that a convicted killer doesn't have it coming, Roy. I'm just saying that I'd find it hard to be the one to make it happen. I know the law wouldn't count it as murder. It's called protecting society when a peace officer does it on the orders of the court, and I agree with that. Even the church sanctions punishing the guilty. But—I don't know. I guess I'd wonder if taking that life was any of my business. Judging somebody, I mean. Without knowing all the facts."

"What if you *did* know all the facts?"

"Well, if I thought that I could stop them from hurting other people, then maybe I could. If I knew the facts for myself."

"But you don't have to know! That's why the state's executioner *can* do it, ma'am." Roy would worry a subject worse than a dog with a bone. "Because he's just carrying out orders from the decisions made by somebody else. The way I see it, if you were to go trying to decide for yourself who deserves it and who doesn't, why, vengeance would be likely to creep into the mixture. And then justice is bound to get tainted. I wouldn't want to have any say-so at all in the matter of who gets executed. No choice, no blame."

Tyree nodded. "That's right. If we wanted to take responsibility for the law's decisions, we'd have the judge's job—or yours."

They both laughed then, and we talked of other things while we finished our coffee. It was just an idle conversation to pass the time, that's all. Shooting the breeze about a case in New Jersey that had nothing at all to do with us.

Except, as it turns out, it did.

The commissioners generally left us alone, too, at first, for which I was uncommonly grateful. I guess they were waiting to see if I could handle the job or not, or whether the deputies could manage to work for a woman. When neither of those things proved to be a problem, they still held off, giving me time to decide whether or not I wanted to quit on account of having young children to raise. But if anything, I was growing more sure of myself as acting sheriff, better at making decisions and faster with the assignments and the paperwork. I got accustomed to talking to strangers and making them believe that they could trust us to take care of their troubles. In fact, as the days passed I was beginning to think that the job wouldn't give me much trouble at all.

If only Lonnie Varden hadn't killed his wife.

THE KILLING

She wasn't looking at him, or even at the uneven path beneath her feet. He had warned her once to watch where she was going, but she was too busy looking at the trees, her new camera dangling from a strap on her wrist.

"Look at that redbud over there under the poplars. With the sun hitting it, it looks like stained glass. The trees are mostly bare, but the forest is aflame. See the new leaves? The ones that are the shade of yellow green that only lasts a week or so."

"Yes. You said that last year, too, Ceil."

"But don't you think it's glorious here in the spring? I've lived here all my life, but every April the beauty of it still takes me unawares."

"I guess I stopped noticing."

"But you're an artist! You should notice it more than anybody."

"Used to be." He had worked at the sawmill for more than a year, and the feeling of being connected to some universal ideal of art was long gone. The only painting he was expected to do anymore was to hand-letter the signs for the office and the prices on cards for each lot of lumber. He had wanted to settle down with Celia, but when they did marry, life changed for both of them more than either had quite expected. By the time he had finished painting the mural of the frontier fort on the post office wall they had settled into being a couple, recognized as such by the community. By then, avoiding marriage—

even if he had wanted to—would have been like swimming upstream against a strong current. Celia Pasten was intelligent and easy to talk to, and she thought he was a wonderful artist—all qualities that had been lacking in the girls he had previously known. With her he was no longer lonely, and that counted most.

At their wedding reception in the church hall, when one of the Greers went through the receiving line, she leaned in close and whispered in the bride's ear, "You see, Celia? Dropping that old knife at the Dumb Supper didn't do you a bit of harm. Here you are, married after all!"

With a frozen smile, Celia went on shaking hands, but she remembered very little of the reception after that. She would tell her new husband about that silly courting tradition. Someday.

Remembering the Dumb Supper made her wonder if her new husband really had been a gift from fate, conjured up by the ancient ritual. He wasn't very tall, but he was as handsome as she could have wished for. He wasn't rich or trained for a grand profession, like medicine or law, but he was an artist, which was more than a profession, really. To her that meant he had been touched with some sort of divine gift for creation; the less she understood his vocation, the more she was in awe of it. Aside from that, her new husband seemed gentle and serious, and perhaps most wonderful of all, Celia thought he looked rather like a prince out of a fairy tale. Because she had never thought of herself as anything but timid and plain, Lonnie's air of quiet confidence and his calmness around people seemed as great an accomplishment—and as difficult—as wing walking or sword swallowing: fascinating to watch, but not something you'd ever attempt yourself.

She had known she would have to resign from teaching when she married, but she hadn't quite realized how much her job defined who she was. Before she became a bride she had been the community's schoolmarm, respected for her knowledge and her independence, as exalted and different from the other women as a pagan priestess, but now she had surrendered all that to become just another wife, no better than the women who had not gone to college, perhaps even outranked by them, because they had children and she did not. It chafed a bit to be dependent on someone else, no matter how beloved, when you had been accustomed to earning your own money and spending it as you pleased, without having to take anyone else's preferences into account.

For his part, marriage meant settling down. People thought that artists could draw anywhere, anytime, and maybe some of them could, but for him the unfettered, itinerant life of a freelance painter had turned out to be the part of the vocation he had valued most. When he lost that, the desire to create art seemed to go with it. He didn't miss it at first. He was happy with Celia, and he would not say that he regretted choosing a life with her over the one he had before, but sometimes he wished he didn't see his future as a straight line leading directly through the decades to the grave—no turns, no shadows, no surprises, except, perhaps, unpleasant ones. Maybe that was why he had done what he had—just to put a curve in that monotonous straight line.

And now he couldn't think of anything else. There must be some way to tell her, but he had been unable to find one. The burden of all this worry had driven all thoughts of nature and beauty out of his mind.

"Spring doesn't inspire you?"

He shrugged. "Not particularly. Anyhow, it doesn't last long."

"No. Two weeks at most, but I wish I could make it last forever."

He looked down at the little Brownie camera his wife was holding. "Well, I guess that's what cameras are for. So you'll remember. But a blurry little snapshot in black-and-white? I don't think that's gonna do it, honey."

"Well, the pictures won't mean anything to anybody else, but at least they will help me remember how it was until next year. I wish you'd draw a picture of spring for me." She pushed a bare branch out of her way, and stepped off the path, aiming the camera at the pink-flowered tree lit by a shaft of sunlight. She took a few more steps, peered through the viewfinder, went closer and backed away again, turning the camera this way and that. After a few more tries, she looked back at him, frowning. "I don't know. Maybe you're right. Without color, it might just look like ordinary leaves. I'm trying to think in black and white."

"Just think of the movies." The woods looked mostly black-and-white to him, anyway: dark tree trunks and barren limbs, brown underbrush still locked in winter, and above it all a clabbered sky the color of milk. You could make them interesting in a painting, but not in a snapshot taken with a cheap camera.

They had a quick lunch after church, and then she suggested a Sunday afternoon stroll through the woods and up the ridge. He went along, because it wasn't worth saying he wanted to stay home and having a discussion about it, since it didn't matter where he was, really. He knew he would barely notice the signs of spring, scarcely hear her voice, trapped as he was inside a fog of his own thoughts. Like clouds, it moved away sometimes, especially when something else distracted him, but it always came back. He couldn't talk about that, though. Better to walk along in the April sunshine, see her joy in the coming of spring, and try to feel a little of it himself. He just hoped he would remember to answer when she spoke to him.

The little box camera had been his gift to her at Christmas, but the winter had been harsh, giving her little chance to use it. The lens needed so much light that it was best to take the photographs outdoors, but there weren't many pictures worth taking in freezing, wet weather, even if you were willing to brave the elements, which Celia wasn't. She put him in mind of a cat—staying inside when it was cold, and always looking for the warmest place to sit. Now, though, she was venturing out on this damp, cool day, because she was so anxious to try out the camera. He was surprised by how much she liked it. She had always seemed most pleased by gifts of jewelry or perfume. Once, early on, he had given her a mechanical carpet sweeper for her birthday, thinking it much more effective than a straw broom, but she'd cried when she saw it. Sometime after that, he worked out why: she never thought she was pretty, no matter what he said to the contrary, and any present that did not honor her femininity diminished her even more.

He thought Celia's problem was a lack of confidence. Someone else he knew had a cheap prettiness concocted with hair bleach and dime store lipstick and rouge, and the blowsy plumpness that made her look like a slattern no matter what she wore, but that one never doubted her attractiveness, either from vanity or from the certainty that free and casual offers of sex was all the beauty that most men required. That woman and Jonella were as different as chalk and cheese, and he had taken too long to realize that they were much the same after all.

Maybe he should have bought his wife a string of glass pearls or a flower brooch, but somehow it would have felt like lying. Instead, after several birthdays and Christmases of costume jewelry and drugstore perfume, he had risked buying her the camera, hoping that she would use it to focus on something besides herself. Much to his relief, it seemed to have worked. She was delighted. Having never had sisters or any serious girlfriends before her, he never knew what to do or say when a woman cried. The sight of her tears was so unsettling that he would do almost anything to avoid causing it—or at least to keep her from finding out that he had given her cause to weep. He trudged after her through the wet woods, scarcely noticing the faint signs of spring.

The trees were still mostly bare and the ground was muddy from the March rains, but nevertheless this windy, sunny afternoon made a welcome change from the bleak chill of the weeks preceding it. It was good to get outside again. They had been married nearly three years, long enough for this walk in the woods to be a picture-taking expedition and not a romantic outing. It wasn't that they didn't care for each other, he told himself, just that eventually the newness of anything wears off, and you settle into a familiar routine without thinking much about it anymore. Their silences were companionable, a sign that they were comfortable together. Mostly they suited each other very well. He had just lately come to realize that, and to wish he had known it sooner.

The day had been sunny when they set out from home, but the wind had blown clouds across the valley and shrouded the ridge they were climbing toward, dimming her hope of seeing a vista of spring. She didn't complain, though, or suggest turning back. After a long winter cooped up indoors, it was good to be out. Besides, the weather was changing so quickly that it was hard to tell how the ridge would look when they finally reached it.

Now the sun was playing hide-and-seek, changing the light so much from one minute to the next that taking photographs in the forest would produce uncertain results. The camera was a cheap one, all he could afford, and, because it was intended to be used for family snapshots, its lens could not be adjusted to accommodate changing conditions. She had been pleased by it, though, and that was all that mattered. He hoped the quality of the pictures would not change that.

She was still giving the redbud tree an appraising stare. There were only eight pictures on a roll of film, and what with the cost of developing, she wouldn't want to waste any. After a moment she shrugged and turned away without taking the picture. "You're right, Lon. The flowers are beautiful, but in black and white that tree won't look any different from the ordinary green ones." The clouds shifted, and the ray of sunlight no longer illuminated the tree. "Maybe you ought to try to draw it instead of me trying to photograph it."

"Take your picture and we'll see. I can use your snapshot as a model and do the colors from memory."

She smiled happily at this compromise and went back to looking for ways to make the tree worth photographing. She tried kneeling down to see if an upward angle made a better shot, but after a long look through the viewfinder, she stood up again. "I don't know. Maybe the sun will come back. I guess I could take just one picture to see how it comes out."

"But by the time you get the pictures back from the drugstore, the redbud will have stopped blooming."

"Yes, but then I'd know for next year." She looked back at the tree. "It might look pretty against the bare branches of the tall trees. I wonder why they call it a redbud when its flowers are bright pink."

He shrugged. "It has other names. My granddaddy used to call them spicewood trees, because people used the green twigs from them to season venison."

"Really? What did that taste like?"

He shook his head. "I don't really remember. I never ate venison without it. Anyhow, it's been awhile since I had any. There aren't so many deer about these days."

"I guess people are shooting a lot of them, and making them scarce. It stands to reason: not many can afford to buy beef these days. We're lucky you still have a job."

He looked away. "Let's try to find a redbud out in the sunshine. If you want to take any pictures of them, you'd better do it now."

"I know. The weather this time of year can't be trusted, can it? This may be the last fine day for weeks. I just wish their flowering season lasted longer. Ten days from now that redbud's color will be gone, and then it will be just like every other tree in the woods."

He sighed. "I reckon people are like that, too."

But she wasn't listening. "There's another redbud with the sun shining on it over there. I hope I can get the picture before the clouds block the light again." She fumbled with the camera and looked up frowning. "It looks so plain over there all by itself. Lonnie, why don't you go over and stand next to it? I know you'll look good even when there's no color in the photograph."

He winced, but he was careful to keep his face a blank. He remembered when being told that he looked good made his blood race, but now all he felt was shame. "Me? I don't know about that."

"Oh, go on over there. It won't take a minute. We can put the picture in the family album. There aren't many pictures of either of us, and someday we may have a family who'll want to know what we looked like when we were young."

Dutifully he waded through the knee-high brambles, and positioned himself stiffly beside the redbud tree. Before she clicked the shutter, she waited until he had put his hand on a redbud branch and summoned a plaster smile. She took the photo and lowered the camera. "Here come the clouds again. But maybe I should take another one anyway. Maybe if you turned sideways . . ."

"There might not be enough light here to make a clear picture when it's cloudy, Celia. Maybe a newspaperman could get a good photo, because they have fancy flash attachments on their cameras. But regular people have to settle for whatever light there is. Let's keep going."

She leaned in close to him and began to hum a tune. The words of the old hymn sprang to his mind: *"Lord, they tell me of an unclouded day,"* and he laughed, hugging her playfully. Celia had a quick, dry wit that still surprised him sometimes. She had never been beautiful, and she wasn't even slender anymore, but she could always make him laugh, even now, when his troubles were on the verge of overwhelming him.

For another quarter of an hour they walked along the path

through the woods, but it was still too early in the spring for there to be many pleasing scenes to photograph. Just a few trees with tiny green leaves scattered among more redbuds. Finally, even Celia had to admit that if you'd seen one, you'd seen 'em all.

She leaned against a still bare poplar, sighing with impatience. "Well, you were right, Lonnie. It's probably too early to get any decent pictures, but I still have five shots on this roll before I can take it to town to get developed. The first one is Helen Watkins and the new baby at church. She's so anxious to see it that I don't have the heart to wait."

"If you're in that much of a hurry, you could just point the camera at anything, just to use up the film."

"We can't afford to waste money like that, Lon. Anyhow, I still have the second roll you bought me to go with the camera. I could use it, too, if we find some good views. I know you think I'm silly for being so particular with a little camera that I've barely learned how to use, but taking pictures is a little like being artist, isn't it?"

"I guess."

"I want to get an idea of what it feels like—of what you see when you look at the world. I want to understand. Besides, I can't draw; my quilting is pitiful; and I can't play the piano, so maybe *this* was meant to be my gift. Not just a Christmas gift from you—and the best one I ever got—but the gift of showing me a way to be creative. I'd like to be able to make something beautiful, the way you can. I mean to try to do it well. Can we go a little bit farther?"

"As far as you like, Celia."

"We could still go up to the ridge."

He offered no suggestions of other scenes to photograph. They walked for a while in silence, separated on the path by a few yards, but neither of them seemed aware of it: Celia because she was trying to see the woods as a camera would, and Lonnie because he was tangled in his own imaginings.

She frowned at a mud puddle blocking the path. "I'll be cleaning shoes all evening, but it's worth it to spend a day outdoors, isn't it? The winter seemed to last forever. Spring is like being born again."

They picked their way single file through the mud and underbrush, closer together now because they were walking more slowly, but still not saying much beyond occasional offhand remarks about the scenery or the shifting clouds. Sprigs of briar were sticking to the back of Celia's coat, and there were twigs in her dark hair. A few feet beyond the path he saw a small patch of purple flowers beside a fallen log, but he didn't call her attention to it. The flowers were too small to show up well in a colorless photo. Three paces later he had forgotten them.

She looked back at him and smiled. "We haven't really spent a day just by ourselves in ages, have we? I was sick for that couple of weeks in February, and you've been working so long at the sawmill these days, it's bedtime before we've even finished supper. As many extra hours as you've been working lately, I would think they'd pay you more."

"Well, they haven't."

"Maybe you ought to talk to the foreman about it. You're a good worker; I know you are."

He scowled. "I'm not going to ask them for more money. There's plenty of men out there without any job at all, and I'm sure the mill could replace me in a flash, if I was to be troublesome."

"Well, don't snap at me about it. We'll be all right on what you earn. There's just the two of us, and we still have canned vegetables from last summer yet to eat. I just wish you had more time for yourself. You haven't done any painting in ages."

Nothing that she had seen. He had drawn one portrait and given it away, working on it in the evenings when she thought he was still at the sawmill. He regretted it now.

After another quarter mile of tramping through woods Celia

stopped and turned to him, her face alight. "I know the perfect place. What about The Hawk's Wing? It's just a ways farther up the ridge, and you can see for miles from up there."

"Yes. You can. We'll go if you want to. I don't mind."

She nodded. "There will be more light there. The valley and the dark mountains will stand out against the cloudy sky, even in black and white, don't you think?"

"I guess. I could make it look that way in a painting. I don't know that much about taking pictures. It's not all that far, though, if you want to try it out." It might rain, of course, but there was no point in saying that.

She walked faster now, so intent on reaching the rock ledge that she barely glanced at the redbuds or the bare black trees that stood along the path like dancers frozen in place. He ambled along just behind her, staring at the familiar tendrils of brown hair spilling over the collar of her cloth coat. The wind had picked up, and he wondered if it would rain before they could start back, but he said nothing because she wanted to finish the film before they started back.

The woods ended at a clearing that ran along the edge of the ridge, and beyond it was sky. It was only when you walked closer to the edge that you could see the steep slope and the fields fringed with trees on the floor of the valley half a mile below. The pattern of fields and woods ended perhaps ten miles away, where a line of mountains on the horizon walled off the valley from the one beyond it.

The Hawk's Wing was a local landmark, popular on the postcards sold in roadside diners and at the souvenir shops that sold gimcrack crafts: beaded headbands with dyed chicken feathers and toy tomahawks, supposedly made by Cherokee artisans. A massive outcropping of granite, flat and smooth, The Hawk's Wing thrust out from the side of the mountain like the prow of a ship, extending fifty feet out over the valley, and suspended half a mile above the valley floor. You could see it from miles away, and sometimes its shadow created a patch of shade covering the land beneath it. The rock was mentioned in the writings of the region's earliest settlers, and crudely drawn on the oldest maps, a testimony to its long-standing stability. It had jutted out from the ridgeline for centuries; the proof of that could be found in the pen-and-ink sketches set down in the travel journals of eighteenth-century explorers. The Cherokees had a tale about a giant bird of prey that snatched a warrior from the mountain, and when the warrior prayed to the eternal mother Selu for help, the goddess turned the bird to stone, allowing the warrior to escape. Tradition had it that the promontory was the wing of the giant hawk, and that the rest of its body lay trapped inside the mountain. Pioneer legends claimed that Daniel Boone himself had ventured out on The Hawk's Wing to look at the landscape so that he could plot his way farther west.

Lonnie wondered why no one had suggested that scene for the mural in the post office.

The ancient rock was nearly thirty feet wide, large enough to allow half a dozen people to walk out on it in order to see, and in this century to photograph, a panoramic view of the landscape—provided that they were not too afraid of heights to do so. One look downward at the sheer drop from the front and sides of The Hawk's Wing had sent many a timid sightseer creeping on all fours back to the safety of the ridge. The braver tourists, who were usually foolhardy young men, liked to sit on the very tip of the rock with their legs dangling over the edge so that their friends could photograph them against the backdrop of the magnificent mountain vista, or just to frighten their sweethearts with their bravado. The stunt was usually good for a few hugs and kisses when they walked back to the ridge.

In the summer, when travelers from the coastal region took to the hills for the cool mountain air, the rock was generally swarming with sightseers, while more waited on the ridge for their own turn to venture out over the valley. Now, though, in the damp chill of early spring, the place was deserted. For the moment the clouds had broken, and the landscape was bathed in sunshine. Its rays created bands of light and shadow on the distant mountains, giving them the appearance of a tapestry woven with different-colored threads.

Lonnie wished he had thought to propose to Celia on the ledge of The Hawk's Wing, knowing that it would have been a beautiful spot to seal their romance, but he had not seen it then, and, besides, there hadn't been time for long hikes because he was still working on the post office mural. In the end, he simply asked her over dinner in a booth at the diner. The irony of that gave him chest pains, and he put that vision out of his thoughts.

Celia stopped at the edge of the trees and surveyed the scene. "Lonnie, it's beautiful! Look—the fields in the valley are that brief yellow green of early spring. A week from now it'll be gone. I can't capture it on film, though. I wish I could."

He was silent for a few moments studying the scene. "No, the fields will just look like a washed-out gray, but look how the light makes patterns in the clouds and on the mountains over yonder. They're mostly brown and gray, because the trees on the slopes are still bare, but it seems to me that they would make a fine picture on account of the different shades of dark and light. Try to capture the contrast with the clouds."

She looked back at him, surprised that he had finally offered an opinion. She smiled and patted his arm, and he kept very still, resisting the urge to turn away. Then she turned back to face the end of the rock and lifted the camera, aiming it first at the fields below, then at the wall of mountains, and finally up at the clouds. "You're right, Lonnie. When I look through the viewfinder, I think I can imagine how it would look in black and white. The distant mountains should still be clear and striking, even without any color."

He shrugged. "Well, you have a better chance here than you did with the redbud."

"I can use up the rest of the roll taking pictures from here, and maybe some of the second roll, too. I hope one of the shots will be good enough for us to get an enlargement made so that we can frame it. Wouldn't that be wonderful? Like my first work of art. We could hang it in the living room."

He nodded toward the rock. "So you're going farther out there to take your pictures?"

She hesitated for a moment. "Well, I was. It would be easier to take pictures of the mountains from out there."

"I guess it would if you're not scared."

"I'm not worried about the height. If the rock was icy or the wind was blowing, I might not chance it, but there doesn't seem to be much wind right now. Don't you think it would be all right?"

He closed his eyes for a moment. "I'll go out there with you."

"You will? Oh, thank you, Lonnie. I want so much to do this."

"I know. Go on, then. Walk in the middle until you're sure about the wind. Mind the wet spots, too. They aren't frozen, but they might be slippery all the same. Don't worry, though. I'll be right behind you."

She gave him a quick, grateful smile, and then she squared her shoulders and stepped out onto the rock, dangling the camera from one hand, and angling her arms away from her sides for balance. She walked slowly at first, looking down at the rock, and pausing between each step in order to avoid the puddles in the shallow depressions on the surface of the rock. A puff of wind ruffled her hair and made her shiver at first, but it was no more than a gentle breeze, incapable of disturbing anything heavier than the dry oak leaves scattered across the rock. He stayed where he was, looking down at the scrubland below, nearest the slope.

After half a dozen steps, Celia relaxed and lifted up the camera in both hands again. She called back to Lonnie. "It's not too bad out here. A little windy, I guess, but not enough to be scary. And the sun is warm. I'm going a little farther out. Are you coming?"

He stood there for a moment, staring out at the fields and forests beyond, and then at Celia's back, hunched a little as she bent over the camera. He could call out to her, tell her to come back to the ridge. There was a fallen log there at the edge of the woods. He could sit her down there, and say—what? He had never tried to work out what to say to her—not on the walk that afternoon, and not in the past few days when he knew that somehow it would have to be dealt with. Each time he tried to come to grips with it his mind shied away from the subject.

Then she called to him again and the moment passed.

He started forward, stumbling on a tangle of dried vines spilling into the path. "Coming? Oh yes."

chapter twelve

He might have got away with pushing her off The Hawk's Wing and claiming that she fell accidentally, but it was his misfortune that a courting couple from the local college had decided to brave the chill and go hiking that afternoon. They had just reached the edge of the woods on the summit of the ridge when out on the rock they saw a young woman in a brown coat, holding a camera up to her face. She was standing close to the tip of Hawk's Wing, turning this way and that, apparently trying to choose the best scene for a photograph. Behind her, a few feet away, stood a sturdy, dark-haired man with his back to the ridge. He was looking in the woman's direction, first shaking his head and then clenching and unclenching his fists, but making no sound. Before the couple could get any closer, the man took a step forward with his arms straight out. He grabbed the woman, lifting her up by the back of her coat, and flung her over the side of the rock. As she fell, he took a step back and turned away, as if he did not want to see what was happening, but the pair on the ridge kept watching, though perhaps they wished they hadn't.

As the woman fell forward, she let go of the camera just as her companion pitched her over the edge of the rock and into thin air. The watchers said she didn't make a sound when she fell, but for an instant they saw her hand reaching up as if she was trying to catch hold of the tip of the rock. She had fallen too far forward to grab it, though, and a moment later she was gone.

The couple heard no scream, and no noise when she hit the ground—the valley floor was too far below for any sound to reach them—but they heard it in their heads. It was the college boy's sweetheart who started to scream, and that's when the man on the rock looked up and finally saw them standing there. For a moment they froze, afraid he would either take a run at them or hurl himself over the edge, too, but whatever spurt of fear or rage had possessed him a minute before was gone now, and he sank down in the middle of the rock, covered his face, and wept.

First the young man persuaded the girl to stop screeching, knowing that her screams would only make matters worse. When her sobbing subsided, he let go of her hand and crept as close to The Hawk's Wing as he dared. When the boy was a dozen feet from the rock, he called out to the weeping man. As calmly as he could he offered to help, as if they were unaware of what had just happened. The man gave no sign that he heard.

He sat still, his body shaking with sobs, but the wary student ventured no closer to him than the edge of the ridge where the outcropping of rock began. He hesitated to get too close to a man they had just seen kill someone, and he knew it was no use going out there to look down to see what had happened to the woman. Nothing and nobody could have survived that fall, and he didn't want to see what was left of her, not even from a vantage point hundreds of yards above.

The student kept talking to the man, trying to sound unconcerned and sympathetic, not because he felt calm, but because he decided that there was no use in speaking any other way. Presently the man's cries subsided, and he began to stare off at the far mountains as if he couldn't hear anything at all. The student kept talking in quiet, reassuring tones to him anyway, while he tried to work out what he would do if the man rushed at him or made a lunge for the edge of the rock.

Just as the sun was beginning to set behind the far wall of mountains, the student managed to coax the man back onto the ridge. The couple could see that he had no weapon, but even so they stepped back toward the trees as he stumbled toward them like a sleepwalker. The man was staring past them, as if barely aware that they were there at all. Once he was safely back on the solid ground of the ridge, they herded him along the path, one on either side of him, talking soothingly about the weather and the fact that it was getting dark. They suggested getting hot coffee and finding a warm place to sit down. The pair hurried him along as quickly as they dared for a few hundred yards, until they were well away from the ridge and into the woods farther down the mountain, where the trail wound down into a dense forest of poplar and oak.

There, the college boy sat down beside the man on a fallen log next to the path and waited for him to catch his breath. A few feet away the girl leaned against a tree, wondering if she ought to take the chance to run. The man had stopped crying by then, but he had not spoken a single word to them. He made no excuses or protestations of innocence, and he hadn't made any threatening moves toward them either. But there was no getting away from what they had seen. As a precaution, the college boy fumbled in the pocket of his leather jacket until he pushed open the blade of his pocket knife and grasped the hilt of it. Since the dazed man had no weapon and barely seemed to know they were there he felt safe enough to tell his girl to leave them and head down the mountain for help. When she opened her mouth to protest, he gave her a look, and she stepped away from the tree and stumbled off down the trail alone.

Now there was nothing to be done but to watch the sky grow darker and pass the time with the dazed man until help arrived.

The student waited for a bit in silence, thinking that surely the man would start talking soon. It was only human nature to want to explain yourself, especially if your actions put you in a bad light. He ought to have some justification for what he did. But the silence stretched on until the boy found it unbearable. He kept thinking about the woman being pitched over the edge of the rock. He couldn't bring it up, though. No telling what would happen if he did.

After giving the matter considerable thought, the boy decided that he would keep talking to the distraught stranger (he was careful not even to think the word *murderer*, because that ominous word would hinder his resolve to stay calm), whether he got any response from the fellow or not. He told himself that regardless of what he and his sweetheart had witnessed out on the rock, they really didn't know the facts behind the situation, and in any case, even spouting nonsense was better than waiting in this strained silence. In a friendly, casual tone, he started to talk, not to anyone in particular, it seemed, just thinking out loud really. He didn't sound concerned about what had just happened; he was just prattling about inconsequential things. He talked about the movie that was playing last week, and the subject of the term paper he was writing for American history. He went on to grouse about the cafeteria food at the college and to speculate about baseball season. He started to talk about his sweetheart, but after a sentence or two he stopped. The subject of girlfriends might bring forth unhappy memories for his listener. He hadn't even asked the man's name, nor given his own.

By the time half an hour had passed, the student had run out of personal observations and current events to comment on—one-way conversations didn't take up as much time as he'd hoped. Now he was telling his silent companion the story of "The Brave Little Tailor," a folk tale he had been assigned to translate for French class. *"Sept d'un coup,"* he said, miming the swatting of imaginary flies. "That means seven with one blow." *Swatting flies* . . . When he realized the ominous implications of the tale, he hastened to add, "Of course, it was only houseflies. People saw the phrase carved on his belt, you see, and they thought the tailor was a giant-killer, but he was just swatting flies, that's all." He fingered the handle of the knife hidden in his jacket pocket, but the man maintained the dazed silence he had kept since he came down off The Hawk's Wing. The college boy didn't know if the man was listening or not, but at least he was keeping still, sitting on the log and staring at the ground. Occasionally he shivered. There was no wind, but since sunset the air had grown colder.

After nearly an hour a flash of light on the woodland trail caught his attention: bobbing lantern lights were advancing steadily toward them, and a minute later the reinforcements, a stout, red-faced farmer and his hired man, emerged from the trees, advancing cautiously. When they got close enough, the boy stopped telling the story. He stood up, nodding for his girl to go back down the trail again by herself—just in case there was trouble. They would meet up later on level ground at the bottom of the mountain.

As the farmer and his hired man approached the log, the student noticed the younger fellow was angling his body in order to conceal the length of rope behind his back. Satisfied that they were prepared to handle the situation, the student nodded to them and then took no more notice of them. He continued to tell the story of the brave little tailor, focusing his attention on the dazed man until the others were close enough to act. Only when they grabbed him did the student slide out of their way to watch from a safe distance while they trussed up the prisoner and hauled him to his feet.

"I told my wife to call the law," the farmer announced. "Told her to have them meet us down the mountain, at the trailhead. The two of us can handle this fellow now, sonny, if you want to go off home. He'll not get away." But the student stayed, determined to see it through. To leave now would be like walking out of a horror movie before the ending resolved the danger: he would always wonder how it ended.

He followed a few paces behind the two men as they half led and half pushed the prisoner along the path. By the time they reached the field at the base of the mountain a sheriff's car was waiting.

A few hours later the searchers found the woman's body by lantern light. She had landed on her back, between a boulder and a laurel thicket, and her eyes were closed. The ones who found her hoped this meant she had passed out before she hit the ground, that she hadn't seen it coming and died in terror. Mercifully, the darkness concealed most of the damage to the body, but they could see the blood clotted around her nose and mouth.

The incident at Hawk's Wing took place on a Sunday evening, when I was home with Eddie and George, but as soon as Tyree Madden brought in the prisoner and settled him in a cell, he sent Galen Aldridge to fetch me. Nobody really expected me to do anything, I suppose, but sensational murder wasn't something that happened very often in a little mountain county, and people would expect the sheriff to be on hand to mark the occasion.

"I don't know how long you'll need to be there," said Galen, hat in hand on my doorstep. "But I thought we could drop your boys off with Willadene on the way over. I know she'll be glad to give them supper."

"They've eaten already. Hours ago."

He smiled. "I never saw a young'un yet that couldn't eat two dinners. I'll bet they have room for pie, anyhow. After that, Willadene can put them to bed with our boys until we're done at the office. Or—late as it is—maybe we ought to leave them there for the rest of the night, and we can take Eddie on to school in the morning. Willadene can watch young George."

I nodded. Galen seemed to have thought of everything. "All right, then, Sheriff, let's round 'em up and go."

The county had its share of killings, same as everywhere else, but mostly they were fights that got out of hand, or domestic troubles, or a falling-out among lawbreakers about dividing the spoils, or splitting the profits, or a simple distrust of the principle of honor among thieves. This was different. A violent murder at a local landmark, witnessed by two horrified young people, generated more notoriety than a sheriff was likely to see in an entire term in office.

The wet streets shone in the car's headlights. The rain that had been threatening all day had finally arrived. As we headed for the station, Galen told me as much of the story as he knew—that the fellow's name was Lonnie Varden, and what had happened in general, based on the hasty account he'd been given by Tyree who had brought in the prisoner. The search-party members who stopped in later added their accounts of recovering the body. Tyree had sent the courting couple back to the college, after making sure he knew where to find them the next day.

When they had reached the office, Tyree put the prisoner in a cell, sent the searchers to deliver the victim's body to the county hospital, and ordered Galen to fetch me, even though it was quite late by then. He knew that between the town gossips and the radio station everybody around here would know most of the story by tomorrow afternoon, but of course, as sheriff, I needed to know ahead of everybody else. The prisoner wasn't Tyree's responsibility; he was mine.

"We just thought you ought to be there, seeing as how you're the sheriff and all."

"Of course I should."

"And it ought to be safe."

"What do you mean, safe? The prisoner is locked in a cell, isn't he?"

"Well, it wasn't so much him that we were worried about," said

Galen, carefully keeping his eyes on the road. "It's the possibility of a lynch mob."

"A lynch mob?"

He glanced at my stricken expression and went back to watching the road. "Oh, we're pretty sure there won't be one. After all, it's just a man and wife killing, from what I hear, but you never know. Depends on who the wife's family is. Sometimes the grieving relatives get likkered up when they hear the news, and anything could happen then."

"The relatives? You think they might storm the jail to get at him?"

Galen sighed. "Well, I don't. That kind of thing usually happens when some stranger has raped a local girl, which hasn't happened for as long as I can remember, either. But we didn't think you'd want to take any chances."

"You mean lock the door and pass out the rifles?"

He smiled. "Cowboy movies don't have a lot to do with real life, do they? I expect, though, that just having all of us here in the office would be enough of a deterrent to any crew of drunks. Of course, unlocking the gun cabinet wouldn't hurt."

Unless the mob was to get inside, I thought. But the idea of a gang of local folks trying to break in and lynch a prisoner seemed more farfetched to me than any movie. Especially if the killer wasn't a stranger preying on an innocent girl, which apparently he wasn't. "But this murder—why did the man do it, Galen?"

He just shrugged. "I asked Tyree that myself. People always want to know why, don't they? But sometimes even the killer himself doesn't know why."

"Somebody must have asked him about it, though."

"Asked, but not answered. Tyree said the man hadn't responded to any questions at all. Tyree said he reckoned that what he did was cheaper than a divorce."

I didn't say anything. By now I had come to understand that peace officers often made grim jokes about the tragedies they had to deal with—like whistling in the dark, I guess.

When we got to the office, Falcon and Roy were also there. Tyree must have sent someone to fetch them, too. They were sitting around the reception desk, with mugs of coffee in front of them, watching the front door and talking quietly among themselves. When Galen and I came in, they all stood up, which wasn't something they did for me as a rule, but I suppose the seriousness of the occasion seemed to call for it.

Tyree nodded toward the door that led to the cells. "Prisoner's in there."

I hesitated, because I wasn't sure whether I ought to sit down and get a briefing from Tyree as the arresting officer, or interview the prisoner for myself. A stranger and a killer—we didn't often have either one to contend with. "Should I go to talk to him now?"

"I wouldn't bother. When I brought him in an hour ago, the fellow was crying so hard I reckon even your boy Eddie could have arrested him singlehanded. He couldn't have fought a June bug by then. Then ten minutes after we clapped him in the cell, he was sound asleep. Guess throwing his wife over that cliff took everything he had."

The Hawk's Wing wasn't anywhere near the settlement where Albert and I grew up, but like everybody else in these parts, we had gone out there every now and again, usually for a summer picnic or a church outing. You could see all creation from the rock, but it wasn't hard to imagine what would happen to somebody who fell off it. I wondered if the man's poor wife had any idea what was happening, or if her last conscious thought had been *Why?* I shuddered.

Tyree caught my expression. "That's right. Threw her off The Hawk's Wing. And the dern fool did it in front of a couple of witnesses."

"Well, I expect that will save the prosecutor some time at trial." It shocked me, but I couldn't let on. "Too bad *you* weren't out there on the rock with the fellow instead of the wife."

Falcon laughed. "That would have been a different story, all right. I don't think anybody could throw Tyree here off a cliff with a pitchfork."

Roy took a swallow of coffee. "The killer wouldn't have tried to attack Tyree, though, you know. I've noticed that the kind of man who beats up on women or children doesn't usually have too much sand when it comes to taking on grown men. Bullies are cowards."

"And he didn't ever say why he did it? Did it look like they were fighting out there on the rock?"

"Witnesses said not. You can talk to them in the morning too. A college boy and his girlfriend were the ones who saw it happen. Spoiled their walk in the woods, that's for sure. But they did just fine. The boy stayed with the killer while his girl went to get help."

"So the college fellow spent time with the prisoner? Did he have any idea why he did it?" I wasn't really asking those questions as part of my job. I just wanted to know, same as every old gossip in town would come morning. Maybe it was because until a few weeks back I had been a wife, and whenever there was violence between a married couple, women couldn't help but have a *there but for the grace of God* feeling.

"The killer hasn't said anything to anybody. Period." Tyree smirked. "I expect it was the woman's fault, though—bound to be. She wasn't pretty, by the way—I saw the body before they took it away to the morgue, and her face was blood-streaked, but not much damaged, but, I mean, even before she hit the ground she wasn't pretty."

"That might have been reason enough," said Galen, but he laughed as if he wanted us to think he was kidding.

Falcon considered it. "The guy married her, though, so he must have thought she looked all right at one time—unless he married her for some particular reason, like maybe her daddy had money or there was a baby on the way."

Tyree shrugged. "Maybe she was unfaithful, or ill-tempered, or a sluttish housekeeper—one way or another, you have to figure she must have had it coming."

Galen nodded. "Stands to reason. You don't just pitch a woman off a cliff unless she was asking for it, one way or another."

I didn't rise to the bait there, but I was tempted to say that if the woman had killed her husband, instead of the other way around, the men in the community would have found a way to blame her just the same. At that point I don't remember having an opinion at all about the whys of the incident. It's amazing how many things are none of your business when you get right down to it. Most people don't feel that way, though, more's the pity, especially when it comes to big news in a sleepy little town. Pretty soon everybody I met on the street would be asking me for all the gory details about the killing, and the whys and wherefores besides. If they didn't get any answers, they'd invent them.

"I'll go back there and see the prisoner first thing in the morning," I told the deputies, stifling a yawn. "Maybe I can get him to talk."

Galen shook his head. "You can try, Sheriff, but he doesn't seem real partial to women."

He was making another joke, but I didn't laugh.

It was nearly dawn by the time I got home, but I wrapped myself in our old bear-claw quilt and slept on the sofa, because I was too tired to lie awake thinking up ways to interrogate the suspect. I wasn't even sure it was my job to question the man. We had eyewitnesses, so it hardly mattered why he did it. That was a problem for the court to hash out. But I wanted to talk to him, and I had the right to do so, so I would. I was thankful that the Aldridges had kept Eddie and George for the night, because it gave me an extra hour of sleep.

I didn't know what to expect at the office, having a bona fide murderer locked up in the jail, and on the way to work I wondered what sort of folks I would have to deal with—newspaper reporters, bossy defense lawyers, anguished relatives, or worried county commissioners. None of them were on hand when I arrived, though. Tyree, looking rumpled and cross, was just getting off work when I came in.

"It's been quiet since you left, Sheriff," he said between yawns. "Roy stayed over, because we figured we ought to have somebody watching the prisoner, in case somebody tried to break him out of jail, or if he finally realized the seriousness of what he'd done and tried to do away with himself in his cell. I thought a woman-killer might take the coward's way out. Not that a suicide wouldn't have saved the state a lot of time and effort, but it would have looked like he outsmarted us if he died on our watch."

"I guess it would. Is the prisoner awake yet?"

"I doubt it. I came back last night and drank coffee with Roy for an hour in case the killer tried to give us any trouble, but he never even woke up. This morning Roy told me that he went back there to check on the prisoner a time or two during the night, but every time he looked, the fellow was sprawled out on his cot, dead to the world. Best thing for everybody, I reckon. I'd hate to be him when he wakes up, though, and remembers where he is and why."

I looked back at the closed door, bolted now as an extra precaution. "He slept? After what he'd done? How could he sleep?"

Tyree yawned again and scratched his head. "Well, I'm not sure I can make sense of it for you, but it happens a lot with prisoners. You'd be surprised. A fellow spends weeks stewing over something he's mad about, and then when he finally lashes out against whatever was deviling him he gets more relaxed than a baby bottle-fed on bourbon. It's over then, and the pressure is finally off for him, I guess."

Maybe the pressure was off then, but I thought that was the place where conscience ought to come in. Apparently it hadn't. "Well, it's morning now, and this is a jail, not a resort hotel, so go wake him up and tell him I'll be back there to question him."

"By yourself, ma'am?"

"Yes, by myself. The cell door is locked, isn't it? And you can hear me if I yell. Now roust him out."

At a little crossroads east of Elizabethton, there's a gas station that keeps a full-grown black bear in a cage of iron bars. That old bear must weight two, three hundred pounds, but people buy candy bars and bottles of soda pop and hand them to him inside the bars, and he gulps them right down and smacks his lips, just as if he were an old man instead of a beast. Now if that bear was to get out of the cage, I reckon he could tear those gas station cowboys limb from limb, but he's been in that cage as long as I can remember, and all he wants these days is his afternoon treats. Things in cages aren't as fearsome as they are in the wild. So was I afraid to face this man who had pitched his wife off a mountaintop? Not particularly, I decided. Right now he was a caged bear, and anyhow, he wasn't the first murderer I'd ever been acquainted with. He'd be the first one I ever saw in jail, I guess, but when Albert and I were growing up in the settlement, there was a farmer who had got into a feud with his neighbor over a calf that had been killed by the other one's dog. The cussing gave way to shouting, and the shouting gave way to shooting, and in a trice the other fellow was as dead as his slaughtered calf. All the relatives were mad about it, of course, but the farmer never did go to jail for the murder. He claimed the shooting was self-defense and since nobody could prove otherwise, they didn't even arrest him. The folks at church were leery of him ever after, though. When he was a youngblood and a drinker, the farmer had been known for having a fearsome temper, and some people said that getting away with murder might teach him a lesson he hadn't needed to learn. But although the settlement waited a long time to see if he'd strike again, that turned out to be the end of it. The farmer went right on about his business as if nothing had ever happened, and now, years later, there's hardly a one of us who hadn't shaken his hand or passed the time of day with him at the store, same as if he was just anybody. He didn't ever seem sorry about what had happened, but he treated everybody else just fine, so by and by people came to forget that he had ever done murder at all.

I guess it's not always like a dog killing chickens. Maybe some people just get caught up in a bad situation . . . maybe it wasn't even their fault.

But that cell door was going to stay locked all the same.

Instead of heading home, Tyree insisted on staying an extra half hour and walking me as far as the locked door that led to the cells. He unbolted it and stepped back, sitting down behind the extra desk beside the door. He swiveled the chair toward the door. "I'll be out here cleaning my weapon, then. If I hear anything going on in there, I'll be inside in two seconds."

I smiled. "With a disassembled gun, Tyree?"

"I'll clean a rifle then." Even the gentlest teasing rankled Tyree, especially when it came from women.

"All right, Tyree, but I'll be fine." I tried to smile, knowing he meant well. His overprotective attitude might be a sign of things to come, though. When the commissioners appointed me sheriff, they hadn't bargained on this either.

chapter thirteen

The jail corridor wasn't more than forty feet long, which didn't give me much time to think about how I expected the prisoner to be, or what I was going to say to him. It didn't matter, though. I wasn't there to interrogate him, but just to see him for myself, since he was housed in my jail. Just before I went in, it crossed my mind to ask Tyree for a weapon to take with me, but I decided that a gun would be more dangerous than helpful. If I was unarmed, the prisoner could not reach through the bars and take a pistol away from me. I would stay past arm's length from the bars and take things as they came.

The reek of ammonia and washing powder in the corridor almost masked the stale odors of urine and sweat, but there wasn't a lot we could do about that, since the only toilet in the cell was a bucket in the corner that was emptied once a day. Although I didn't go back to the cells any oftener than I had to, the sour smell didn't disturb me after the first shock to my senses. It had knocked me back at first, but when I realized that the smell reminded me of Georgie's diaper pail from a year or so ago, I didn't mind it so much anymore. It might be a different story in here, though, come summertime.

No sound was coming from that one occupied cell, but I stopped a few feet away and watched. The prisoner wasn't sleeping. He was sitting hunched over on the end of his bunk, staring down at the floor. If he had heard me come in he gave no sign. I stood there for a bit, watching him out of curiosity.

I didn't know him, had never laid eyes on him before as best I could remember. Galen had already checked the records in the file cabinets, but he hadn't been arrested before—at least not in this county. He was a short and wiry fellow—the men from around here generally are. His hair was straight and dark—not Indian black, but the walnut brown that is also common around here. I'd have bet that when I could see his face, his eyes would turn out to be blue. He kept staring at the floor—not weeping, or praying, or doing anything that gave me indication of his state of mind. How are you expected to act after you've killed somebody and gotten caught? How do you feel? Sorry you did it, or just sorry you didn't get away with it? I didn't know what to say to a jailed murderer. I was too busy telling myself not to be afraid.

"Do you need anything?" As soon as I said it, I thought, *Now there's a typical woman's question.* Acting as if he was a houseguest, and I was ready to bring him a bar of soap and some fresh towels.

The prisoner turned to look at me then, and I could see that he was somewhere around thirty, but because of what he'd been through he looked older: ashen-faced and haggard, with dark circles under his eyes. Though he had slept last night, it hadn't done him much good. I thought back to the days after Albert died when I must have looked like that. It struck me as odd, though, that the prisoner would seem so distraught over his loss when he had been the cause of his wife's death. If I could have saved Albert, I would have; surely I was more entitled to mourn than someone who had not just lost his mate, but killed her. Or maybe he looked haggard from grieving over himself, knowing that his life was over as surely as hers was.

He looked at his scratched and grubby hands. "I'd like to wash up, if that's allowed."

I nodded. "I'll see that you get a pan of warm water, and some soap and towels. I'm the county sheriff." I thought I'd better make that clear, in case he mistook me for a housekeeper. I reckon to most people I looked more like one of them than I did a sheriff. "Name's Robbins."

That news seemed to take his mind off his troubles. "A woman sheriff?" He peered at me through the bars as if I were an apparition. "Never thought I'd see the day. And in these mountains too. Who did you run against? A billy goat? No, wait, I remember. You're the last sheriff's widow, aren't you?"

"Appointed to finish his term. But, be that as it may, I am the one in charge here."

He rubbed his eyes, seeming to be searching his memory. "Appointed. That's right. I heard about that. Nothing against you, ma'am, I'm sure you're doing a fine job. It's just that in the general way the men around here don't seem too partial to putting a woman in charge of anything."

At least they don't usually kill them, I was thinking. But there wasn't any point in baiting the prisoner. "And you are Lonnie Varden, according to the arrest warrant."

That reminded him of his situation, and he stopped looking at me and went back to staring at the floor. "The *late* Lonnie Varden, maybe. I don't reckon I'll be anybody for much longer."

I didn't know what to say to that. Was he trying to tell me he was planning to kill himself in the jail cell? I glanced down at his feet. Muddy boots. No shoelaces. I ought to have a word with the deputies, just in case. I thought about asking a minister to step in and have a word with him, because counseling murderers was something I had no idea how to do and didn't have much taste for anyhow. A wife-killer. How was I supposed to react to that? I couldn't very well tell a killer that what he did would be forgiven—at least not in this world—and I couldn't assure him that everything was going to be all right, because he and I both knew that it wouldn't be. There are people who get away with murder sometimes, but mostly they are either rich or well-connected, or else they have the good sense to kill somebody that nobody much minded about, like a horse thief caught in the act.

"You asked me before if I needed anything."

"Yes. You asked if you could wash up. I'll arrange it directly."

"I guess a bottle of whisky is out of the question. Or a steak. But how about some paper and pencils or colored chalk?" He must have seen my surprise, because he hastened to add, "I'm by way of being an artist."

"Paper and drawing pens? I don't know if that's allowed." I didn't know what was allowed. Most of our prisoners didn't stay long enough to want anything, other than a few hot meals. Once in a while someone would want a pencil and paper to write a letter, or a magazine to help pass the time, but little else.

"Would that worry you?" He smiled. "In case I was to draw a door over there in the wall, open it up, and escape through it? I'm an artist, but I'm not that good."

I smiled to be polite, but I didn't approve of a killer making jokes in a jail cell. I knew that his lightness didn't necessarily mean he was heartless, though—not if he was from around here, and I thought from his way of talking that he was. Among mountain folk, if you got your foot shot off and people asked you how you were, you were supposed to say something like, *"It only hurts when I laugh."* I thought that was likely to be the prisoner's code of conduct: never show your pain, no matter what. Maybe that was because you didn't want people pitying you on top of everything else, or maybe it was supposed to prove how tough you were. Sometimes I think that men came up with codes of bravery because they didn't have childbirth to provide them with the opportunity to suffer pain and risk their lives.

After considering his request for art supplies, I offered him an alternative. "I could get you a book."

"Instead of paints and canvas, you mean?" He shook his head. "I doubt if I could keep my mind on the story. But drawing makes me concentrate. Maybe if I could draw, I might manage to forget—"

"So you're a real artist?" I wanted to keep him talking about things that wouldn't upset him. "Are you from around here?"

"Used to be." He shrugged. "Am I from here? Same mountains, anyhow. I've lived here a couple of years, though. I don't make my living being an artist anymore—mainly because you can't make a living as an artist these days—not that it was ever easy, even at the best of times. I expect you have seen a sample of my work, though."

I shook my head. "Couldn't have. There aren't any museums around here."

"You won't find my work in any museums. My painting is over in the post office. The mural of the pioneer fort on the wall above the post office boxes. It was the first one I did when the government sent me to this area to paint scenery in public buildings. Well, one of the last ones, too, because that's when I met Celia and decided to settle down. Can't support a wife and family on what an artist makes. I couldn't, anyhow."

"You have children?"

"No. But back when we got married, we thought we would—same as everybody, I guess. But no babies had come yet. If I had known different in the beginning, I guess I could have kept trying to be a painter. We could have gotten by for sure if the state would let lady schoolteachers keep working after they got married. When I first met her, Celia was making ninety dollars a month. Then we got married, and it was all on me. So I got a real job working at the sawmill. Instead of having a gallery full of paintings, I have a wall in a backwoods post office."

"I've seen it many a time," I said. "It's a good picture. Folks can tell right off what it's supposed to be, and you drew it just the way I always thought it would look. I think I mighta had an ancestor in that fort; at least I told my boys that, and they like going to see it." I wanted to ask him how somebody could paint such a beautiful scene and yet treat another human being so cruelly, but I guess it only takes a minute to do something evil that you can't take back, and, fair or not, that one action can cancel out all the years of your life you spent doing good. If that was what happened to him, I could feel sorry for him, but I didn't know anything about why he had killed that woman, and even if I had known, forgiveness was no part of my job.

"My youngest boy always wants to go with me to the post office so he can look at the Tennessee cowboys, as he calls them. Georgie's a great one for westerns."

He looked pleased at that. "I'm happy he likes it, and glad you think the mural is good. Being from around here you'd be more likely to know if I got the details right. My—my wife helped me figure out how the fort ought to look." His voice shook a little when he said that, and I knew that for a few minutes he had forgotten she was dead. I tried to think of something else to say on another topic, but it probably didn't matter: sooner or later whatever we talked about would lead his train of thought back to the killing.

"Celia. My wife," he spoke very softly now, staring at the floor. "She liked it too. When we were courting she helped with the planning of it, so I put her in it as a way of thanking her. One of the pioneer women down by the river has her face. The one in the brown dress."

"I remember." I did recall the figure in the brown dress, but not what her face looked like. Next time I went to the post office I would look again. Had she been pretty? Did it matter whether she had been or not?

"I guess you could say that painting of the fort is my legacy. I don't reckon I'll ever paint any more murals now."

I couldn't think of anything to say, because I was pretty sure he was right about that, so I said, "I just came to look in on you, now that you're awake. I wanted to see how you're faring. They tell me that last night you said you didn't need a doctor."

"A doctor?" He shrugged, rubbing a scabbed-over scratch on the side of his face. "I walked into some briars on the way down the mountain. It was near dark by then. Felt like a horsewhip at the time, but I reckon I'm all right now." He looked around him at the tiny cell. "Considering."

The meal tray, on the floor beside the cell door, held an untouched metal bowl of watery oatmeal and a tin cup of cold black coffee.

"You weren't hungry?"

He managed a wry smile. "It wasn't too hard to resist this morning's offerings."

A few more hours in captivity would make him less finicky about what he ate. Or maybe he just didn't want to admit that what he had done had taken away his appetite. Anyhow, he had other things on his mind—or he ought to have had. I wanted to ask him why he did it, but nobody around here asks prying questions if they can help it. It's not fitten. We keep ourselves to ourselves. Whys aren't any of my business. Such questions are for courts and judges. It did seem odd, though, to have a soft-spoken, cultured painter locked up for murder. I thought artists were peaceable sorts. Now a likkered-up logger or a young lout with a temper and a mean streak—that wouldn't have surprised me, but a mild-mannered artist is not what small towns usually get in the way of killers.

"Have you got you a lawyer yet?"

The question didn't seem to interest him. "A lawyer? Don't know any. Don't trust any either. Besides, I doubt they accept payment in the form of a painting—unless one of 'em is mighty fond of his dog."

"You're charged with murder. You have to have a lawyer, like it or not. Maybe your family can contact somebody for you. Do they know you're here? Do we need to get word to anybody?"

"I left my family a long time ago. I don't want to see anybody. Not anywhere, but especially not here."

"If you have people, they're bound to find out, so you might as well get word to them. Even if you parted with them on bad terms, like as not, they'll come through for you now. Families mostly do. I hope they can help you, because the sooner you get a lawyer the better off you will be, it seems to me."

"I'll think on it."

"Do that. It's not my place to give you legal advice, but common sense ought to tell you it won't do you any good just to sit here and do nothing."

He stifled a yawn. "I'm tired. I just want to sleep. When I sleep, all this goes away. The nightmare is being awake."

Sleeping wouldn't solve anything, but I knew how tempting it was, because I remembered those days after I lost Albert, when sleep was the only refuge there was from sorrow and pain. After a few weeks it got better, but I wasn't sure it ever would for this prisoner, because his grief was tempered with guilt. "If you'd like a preacher to stop in and see you later today, I think we could arrange that."

"No, thanks. I don't know what I'd say to a man of God."

"I suppose he could help you to pray."

"Don't you think I'm past praying for, ma'am?"

"They say nobody is. You might try praying for somebody besides yourself, though."

"A preacher would want an explanation, and I don't want to talk about it. I already admitted to doing it. That should be enough."

"I doubt the Lord is very happy about what you did, of course, but maybe you had your reasons. If so, He must already know what they were."

I thought the prisoner was about to say something else then, but the door at the end of the corridor opened and Tyree hollered out, "Telephone for you, Sheriff!"

I didn't believe that for a minute—Tyree was just worried that I'd get my throat cut if I lingered too long with a dangerous prisoner—but I turned to go, anyway. I had about run out of things to say to a murderer, except for the one question that would be on the tip of everybody's tongue, which was the very one he didn't want to answer: *Why did you do it?*

"Who's on the phone?" Tyree and Falcon were still in the office when I came back from the cells: Tyree drinking coffee and Falcon paging through the sports page of the Johnson City paper.

"Oh, the phone call?" Tyree had the grace to blush. "It turned out to be a wrong number. Sorry to disturb you. Did you get on all right back there?"

"He's not violent. I'd say he might be a danger to himself, and we should keep a close watch on him for that, but the rest of us are safe enough. Has anybody asked to see him?"

They both shook their heads.

"Any family? A lawyer?"

"Not that we know of," said Falcon.

"I'm headed off home now, but if his in-laws stop by, I don't reckon you ought to let them in." Tyree said this straight-faced, but I recognized it as the first of many jokes that would be made at the expense of the wife-killer.

I ignored him. "Shouldn't we find out more about who this fellow is?"

"We don't have to, Sheriff. All we have to do is keep him locked up here and make sure nobody breaks him out or lynches him. All the rest of it—*if* he did it, *why* he did it—that's for the lawyers."

Falcon shook his head. "No, Tyree, the sheriff is right. We need to know more about the prisoner: who his friends are, where he worked, and how well liked he is. Because who knows how long we're going to have to hold him in here. Those things will tell us if we need to worry about a lynch mob coming to get him or a bunch of his pals from work trying to slip him a knife or storming the jail to get him out. We have to know who we're dealing with."

I was pleased to see Falcon come up with such logical thinking. Maybe he'd make sheriff himself one day. "Why don't you go and see what you can find out about him then? I think it's better for us to know. He told me he works at the sawmill. Start there."

Falcon came back in time to eat his lunch—an orange and a can of beans from McInturf's Store—at the reception desk. "Did you know that fellow's an artist?" he asked me, between spoonfuls of beans.

"He told me that. He's the one who did that mural in the post office. But he doesn't make his living at it anymore. I guess the hard times are what made him go to work at the sawmill."

Falcon grinned. "Well, he don't work there anymore. The owner of the mill told me they fired him last week."

"What for?"

"If you wasn't the sheriff, I don't believe I'd tell you, Miz Robbins, but, seeing as how you are—" Then he stopped and looked up at the ceiling, trying to work out some delicate way of explaining it to me.

I sighed. "So he wasn't let go for stealing or for general incompetence?"

"No. Well . . . that's a matter of opinion. I reckon the girl's father—he's the foreman there—might call it that. Seems the young lady always took her daddy's lunch to him, and she got in the way of talking to some of the men who were taking their lunch breaks as well."

"How old is this girl?"

"Oh, seventeen or so. Old enough to know better. Maybe she thought she'd catch a husband by making eyes at the sawmill workers. Well, she did, but, unfortunately, the one she caught was somebody else's husband. Anyhow, last week the foreman caught her and our Mr. Varden back there on some burlap sacks in the equipment shed—"

"Making hay?" I said, before he could phrase it in a cruder way.

"Making trouble, that's for sure. The foreman went in to get a screwdriver and caught them in the act. He fired the loverboy before he could even get his pants up. I suppose they didn't think they'd get caught."

"Or maybe one of them was hoping they would." Women need a lot less protecting from the unpleasantness of life than men seemed to think. "I wonder what he told his wife about getting fired?"

"I don't think he told her anything. Maybe he killed her because he wanted to go off with his girlfriend."

"Why couldn't they just run away together? I don't think he had much to lose from a divorce. They didn't have much money or land or anything."

Falcon shook his head. "Beats me, ma'am. I reckon you'll have to ask him."

People around here assuming that woman's death was her own fault didn't mean they were going to let her killer get away with it, though; not when there were two horrified witnesses who were able to describe exactly what they saw: no quarrel, no blows exchanged, no provocation that anyone could see—just a plain little woman holding a camera, her back turned to the man behind her, suddenly thrown from a mountain outcrop and smashed to pieces on the boulders below. The law wouldn't let an act like that go unpunished, even if people had wanted it to, and, because this was a God-fearing place, mostly they didn't. At least, despite Galen's warning, we never heard any talk about people wanting to lynch the killer. That was something to be thankful for, not on his account, but because if a mob stormed the jail, some of the deputies were likely to get hurt trying to protect the worthless wife-killer. The speculation went on for a few more days, but Lonnie Varden never said a word about what happened—not to the officers of the sheriff's department, not to his court-appointed lawyer, not even to Rev. McKee, who came to the jail to pray for him, more out of Christian charity than sympathy.

The incident had been a nine days' wonder when it happened, even attracting newspaper reporters from as far away as Nashville.

A few weeks later everybody here more or less forgot about him, because shortly after the arrest, whoever makes such decisions arranged for the case to be tried in Knoxville, and they took him to the jail there to await trial. I wondered why he ended up in Knoxville. I suppose either they thought he wouldn't get a fair trial in a town where a lot of people knew him, or else they thought a murder case was so serious that they wanted it tried by a more experienced prosecutor than the one we had. I asked Roy, but he didn't know either. "I figure our job is to catch lawbreakers. What happens to them after that is somebody else's problem."

I was too busy doing my job and taking care of my sons to give much thought to the trial of a stranger happening a hundred miles away. It didn't seem worth wondering about. It wasn't as if there was any doubt about whether or not he did it, after all.

LONNIE VARDEN

"The way I figure it," Lonnie Varden told his cellmate, "if I could just bust outta here, I'd have two choices: I could either jump a freight train down at the rail yard, ride it until I can catch another one heading west, and another one after that, until I got all the way to south Texas and then I could jump the border, where the law couldn't get me . . ."

"Or?" The grizzled old man with the pock-marked face didn't care, really. Every inmate whiled away some of the time dreaming up escape fantasies, and men on trial for their lives dreamed even longer and harder.

This little chicken hawk of a fellow—the old man judged him to be on one side or the other of thirty—was a stranger. He was just somebody who had happened to be put in the same cell with him, waiting for trial. Now, it turned out he was the talkative kind, nervous to be trapped in jail with a dangerous felon, and hoping he could muster enough charm to keep himself from getting murdered in the night. The sort of fellow who would end up telling you secrets his mama don't even know, if you are a stranger, because strangers were the only ones safe to confide in.

He said again, "Or—what?"

The chicken hawk still didn't answer. He sat on his bunk, staring out the cell door, perhaps regretting that he had blurted out that admission. Maybe he wasn't as cocky as he pretended to be. Something was chasing him, anyhow. His nails were bitten down to the quick, which told the old man that this kid had two things that he didn't: more trouble than he was accustomed to and good teeth.

The old man thought of the boxcars, where he often sat among the crates on the straw floor, swaying with every lurch of the train, and watching brown-stubbled fields flicker past. Above the clatter of the train, the tramps would talk in fits and starts. Here there was only the noise made by the men in other cells, sometimes howls or sobbing, because the state didn't seem to differentiate between madmen and felons.

At least this young man kept talking calmly, and, even if he had preferred otherwise, the older one didn't have much choice but to listen. Well, that was all right. Listening to a talker was as good a way as any to pass the time. Food or smokes would have been better, of course, but just now those things were past praying for. Sometimes when he'd been out on the rails he might get a windfall—a crate of canned goods in an unguarded boxcar or a moonlight raid on somebody's orchard or garden. If he ever got hungry enough, he could make a few dimes chopping wood, or burning trash, or digging out some flower beds—whatever the housewife had wanted done. Here he was as helpless as a penned-up hog. All he could do was wait for whatever his captors chose to dole out, and he didn't even have the choice in the company he kept.

In the long silence, swallowed by all the noise from outside, the old tramp had nearly managed to drop off to sleep again, but then his young cellmate stirred, apparently remembering he wasn't alone. He looked over at the old man with a faraway smile. "You're a traveler, aren't you? Riding the rails, I mean."

"When I can. It's a life."

"Funny, I used to hop trains as a kid. Never thought I'd still be wishing I could do it when I grew up."

The old man shrugged. "That right?" His garrulous companion of twenty-four hours' acquaintance had been hauled into the cell the day before, feet shackled together and wearing handcuffs attached to chains around his waist. The manacles were gone now, and the young man seemed to be neither insane nor violent, which made his cellmate wonder what all the fuss had been about. There had been no point in asking the guards who'd brought him in. Guards made a point of ignoring anything a prisoner said. From the sound of him, though, the young man himself would be telling him all about it, sooner or later.

Off and on since the kid's arrival they had made unintrusive small talk, but they hadn't yet bothered with names. The old man liked it that way. Part of the lure of the open road was the chance to be nobody for as long as you wanted. You could invent a new past every day for all anyone cared, and best of all, you could run away from the real one.

The nameless chicken hawk didn't want to know his life story, which was just as well, but after the initial alarm at being locked up wore off, he became bored in the bare cell. When he found out his companion was a railroad bum, he passed the time by asking the sort of questions a new traveler generally wants to know: how to survive while riding the rails—where to get clean water, how to avoid the railroad guards, and how to keep well if you have just a few clothes in bad weather. (*"You don't."*) The old man humored him, knowing that his answers to these questions were fuel for the escape fantasy the chicken hawk would have started constructing in his head.

Before long the chicken hawk seemed to think that their chance meeting made them friends, and the old man did not disabuse him of this belief. What would be the point?

He sized up the new prisoner. He was a polite, clean-cut fellow, and, despite the superficial friendliness, he was worried about something—why else would a good-looking fellow be in jail in the first place?—but the way he covered his troubles with a ready smile and a flow of amiable chatter would fool most people. Out in the world that might have been worth something. If they had met on the rails, and the chicken hawk had been determined to tag along, he would have found a way to turn that charm to their advantage. On the road, you learned to use whatever comes to hand.

Too bad they were locked away instead of free to roam the countryside. The chicken hawk's baby-faced innocence would have been useful in getting them handouts from motherly housewives. Like as not, the ladies would have been so taken with that tight little body and chiseled face that they'd miss the coldness in his companion's eyes. The old man had taken the newcomer's measure right off, from force of habit, because sizing up people was life and death to a hungry traveler. He had been traveling for so long that he had nearly forgotten what came before it; if he hadn't been good at reading strangers he'd have been dead long ago.

The young man smiled, but he was staring off into space again. "Yessiree bob. I sure wish I could be riding the rails like you did, like I used to pretend I was doing when I was a kid. You ever do that, mister? Hop trains as a kid?"

"Never did."

"Well, I guess you had to live out in the country, near the railroad tracks, to do it. And, Lord knows, there wasn't much else to do where I grew up, except hunting and farm chores. Maybe town boys play sandlot baseball, but we chased trains. We called it playing Pony Express. Ever heard of it?"

"Can't say that I have." The chicken hawk was angling for information with that mention of town boys and baseball, but the old man did not take the bait. Best to keep him talking about himself; it was too soon yet to get the truth out of him, but sooner or later those idle reminiscences were bound to end up in revelations.

"Well, a bunch of us pals would ride our bikes to the railroad tracks . . ."

"Oh, you had bikes?" Something in the old man's voice said that he hadn't had a childhood, much less a bicycle, but the chicken hawk was too wrapped up in memories to notice.

"Some of the fellas did. If their daddies could afford to buy them one. I built mine out of scrap parts. Garden hose for tires. It didn't look like much, but I could keep up with the rest of them."

"Pony Express on bikes, you said . . ." The old man shook his head. "*Pony Express.* Y'all delivered the mail then, did you?"

"Naw. We just called it that 'cause we rode hard, same as those Wild West riders once did. We got all that from the dime novels about cowboys and outlaws. When we played Pony Express, we'd ride our bikes through the woods to a steep hill next to the tracks, waiting for a train headed up that long grade. Going slow, you see."

The old man nodded, imagining a ribbon of trees unwinding outside. It was hard to tell if he was listening or not, but the young man was oblivious, caught up in his tale and smiling as he remembered it. He had forgotten where he was—and why.

"Mind you, it had to be a freight train—well, that's about all we ever saw out our way, anyhow. Hopper wagons full of coal, flat wagons, and finally that long chain of boxcars—that's what we were waiting for. We'd let the locomotive and the coal cars pass, and we'd try to spot the freight brakeman so we could stay out of his way. Then we'd scratch off on our bikes, trying to keep level with one of the boxcars. We'd be pedaling hard, and reaching for that outside ladder."

The old man nodded, picturing the metal ladder on the side of the boxcar.

"The trick was to grab on to it, kick your bike away from the train, and ride along a half mile or so, hanging on to the ladder. Then you had to jump down before the train picked up speed again."

The old man considered it. "Sounds dangerous. You lose many bikes? Or many chums for that matter?"

"The danger was what made it fun. You don't believe in death anyhow when you're that age."

"Falling under a train would convince you quick enough."

The chicken hawk grinned. "A time or two somebody's bike would fall the wrong way and get smashed to pieces by the boxcar wheels—it never happened to mine, though. Worst I ever got was a twisted ankle jumping down on a hard place and landing wrong. Looking back, I reckon it would have been easy to lose the grip on the ladder and fall under the train, but none of us ever did."

The old man snorted, unimpressed. "God protects drunks and fools."

"I reckon He does. Sometimes. Most of us quit chasing freight trains about the time we turned fourteen."

"Better things to do then?"

"Different things, anyhow. Work or school. Chasing girls instead of trains."

"Well, that's safer."

The chicken hawk gave him a look. "Don't you believe it." He yawned and stretched. "Yeah, I never thought I'd be wishing I could catch a boxcar again. Just goes to show, don't it? Fifteen years pass, and here I am—lower than a bum."

Bum. The old man narrowed his eyes. Now he was paying attention. *Traveler . . . wayfarer . . . vagabond.* Even when he hadn't eaten for a day or two, asking for a handout at some citizen's back door, the old man was particular about what people called him, and it stung him that he had never heard any citizen refer to him by any word as polite as any of those perfectly respectable words for a wanderer.

When the lady of the house, holding a cold potato or a hunk of cornbread, invariably asked, *"How long have you been a hobo?,"* he would smile to soften his answer so that he'd get his handout, but even at the risk of having the door slammed in his face, he always said: *"Not a hobo, dear lady. Hoboes travel from job to job, working whenever they can get work, which I confess I do not. To the hobo, travel is merely a means to an end. But I am not a bum, either. Now, you see, your bum, he doesn't ride the rails at all. He stays put in one place, but he doesn't work. Just bone lazy, I suppose. No, madam, properly speaking, the correct name for my species is tramp. I work when I plain flat have to, but I am traveling all the time. To us tramps, the journey is the end, not the means."*

If the lady hadn't slammed the door in his face by then, next she would ask him how he came to be down-and-out, and then he would have to size her up quick to figure out which yarn would be likeliest to land him a plate of choicer leftovers. The one where the wicked banker cheated him out of his inheritance usually went down well. Most everybody these days hated bankers.

This cold-eyed young buck currently horning in on his boxcar fantasy wouldn't have thought up any good yarns yet. He had been demoted from citizen to felon quite recently, if the old man was any judge. He was too clean and too jaunty to have been in the system for any length of time. Less than a week, most likely. *Mark-of-Cain* guilty or just naughty and unlucky? Too soon to tell; maybe the chicken hawk didn't even know yet himself. His way of talking said he was a little short on education and probably not too far from home, because he sounded like the folks from these parts. That, too, might have been handy for getting some local lady of the house to part with a slab of pie, as long as the chicken hawk wasn't afflicted with that stiff-necked mountain pride that made the hill folk think themselves above taking charity, no matter how hungry they were. No hillbilly would last long on the road if he tried to hang on to his pride. Begging or stealing. Take your pick. If they had been in a boxcar instead of a jail cell he would have given the chicken hawk some pointers in panhandling before the next stop. It would have been a shame to waste those clean-cut looks of his.

He wondered what the chicken hawk's story was, but he didn't much care. On the outside he would have wanted a cut of whatever the chicken hawk could charm out of the pantries of sentimental small-town matrons. In here, though, since neither of them had a scrap of food or a single fag to smoke, he figured he'd lean back on his bunk and keep listening to the flow of talk. It kept his mind off his empty stomach. Maybe even put him back to sleep, if he was lucky.

"What's your name, son?" he asked when the silence had stretched on for a few more minutes. He judged that their acquaintance had lasted long enough for trivial confidences. Maybe he'd learn enough to verify that hunch he had about the newcomer.

The cool stare the chicken hawk gave him instead of an answer told the old man what he already suspected: this fellow was in here for something so serious that he didn't want anybody knowing who he was. Too late now, of course, but maybe there had been a reward out for him—not that he would have bothered trying to collect it. Even attempting to do the town cops a favor could land you in trouble; best to steer clear of them altogether. When the silence had stretched out for too long, he added, "I ain't the law, son. I'm just your cellmate, trying to be civilized. Getting acquainted. You can call me Ulysses."

The fellow shrugged. "After the general?"

So that name made the chicken hawk think of the Union general rather than the wanderer in Greek mythology. That squared with what he figured about the fellow's education—or lack of it. "Okay." He couldn't be bothered to teach a cellmate any lessons in world literature. He wasn't all that bored. "Now how about yourself?"

"Name's Lonnie Var—" He stopped before he said it and grinned. "Just make it Lonnie."

"Look around you, son. You're not running from something. You're already penned up, and if I don't know your name, I'll be just about the only person in these parts that doesn't."

"Varden then. Lonnie Varden."

"Okay. And you're in a world of trouble, aren't you?"

"I didn't say so."

"I don't hear you denying it."

Lonnie Varden sighed. "Well, these days who isn't in trouble from something? Between the bank foreclosers, the revenuers, and the tax collectors, I reckon the likes of Dillinger and Pretty Boy Floyd got nothing on the rest of us when it comes to trying not to get caught for one thing or another. But there's nothing I'd like more than a chance to go home. Well—nothing except not being locked up. I reckon I want my freedom more than I want to go home."

Ulysses smiled. "Most people in here feel the same. Only most of them don't have homes to go back to anymore. Now a good while back, I believe you said you had two choices, and it doesn't sound like going back home is one of them. What do you reckon your other choice is?"

"Well, like I said, my first choice is to ride some old freight train, and the next one, and the one after that, all the way to south Texas, and then stroll across the border into Me-hee-co." He shrugged. "Either that, or else I got to learn how to talk to cops and judges without sounding stiff-necked and unrepentant." He sighed. "Hellfire, General Ulysses, no matter how sorry I really am, acting *stiff-necked and unrepentant* just comes naturally to people from my neck of the woods, but that attitude won't win me any favors with the potentates of this world, will it?"

"Sure won't." That observation was certainly true; a man in charge usually set store by servility, which meant that unless you ate crow, you weren't likely to get anything else. Still, since life usually came up snake eyes, he'd bet that in the end Lonnie Varden would not be able to do either of those things. If he managed to escape he'd get caught and jailed again, and if he tried to talk his way out of trouble, he'd look weak as well as guilty. The old man didn't point that out, though. People seldom thank you for telling them the truth.

"Well, son, there is a precedent for the freight train option, anyhow, considering who your ancestors were."

He stiffened, trying to work out the insult, but pretty sure that had been one. "How the devil would you know—"

"I don't know your pedigree, son. I was speaking of your mountain people in general." If he talked about history, his cellmate might let down his guard about personal matters. "The way I heard it, after the War Between the States, your mountain ancestors—*that is, the ancestor of everybody in these parts*—were about evenly divided between one army and the other, which made for a lot of bitterness both during and after the fighting."

"We have long memories."

"You didn't have any big battles up in these mountains, did you? Not like Gettysburg."

"Not that I ever heard of, no."

"I thought not. Elsewhere the war meant anonymous armies shooting at one another, but who'd want to stage a big battle in these mountains?"

"Yeah, but there was still a war."

"Indeed there was."

"We don't talk much about that war."

"I don't doubt it. Do you know why? Because around here the war was personal. When the enemy is your neighbors or your cousins, you know exactly who has burned down your house or stolen your cows."

"They mostly got away with it, too. All the surrendering in the world can't erase the bitterness of that. I can't say I blame folks for feeling like that."

"That was the general consensus, I believe. It didn't make it any easier to keep living around here, though. Appomattox didn't settle any personal scores. Many a man tried to escape the bitter aftermath by taking off for foreign parts, someplace where nobody knew them, and where kinship ties were not iron shackles."

Varden shook his head. "*Kinship . . . Iron shackles . . .* You sure do talk like a teacher, mister."

Ulysses smiled. "Or someone with too much schooling, perhaps. Sometimes for me another life seeps into this one."

"What are you doing locked up in here?"

"I was attempting to redistribute the wealth on a small farm not far from here, and in my attempt to evade the farmer who interrupted me in his barn, I pushed him aside as I ran, and he injured himself—not my intention, just an unfortunate mishap."

"What happened to him?"

"He fell backward onto his pitchfork. I didn't do it, but the authorities have seen fit to blame me anyway."

The young man whistled and shook his head. "That sounds bad. I'll bet you wish you had stayed in your former life, whatever it was."

"You're hunting another life, too, aren't you? Seventy years later, you are trying to get away from it all, just like those men who slipped away after the war. People used to say *'Gone to Texas,'* whether they had or not. It just meant starting a new life without having to die."

"That would suit me just fine."

"I suppose they all felt like that, but I wonder how many of them managed to achieve it. A fellow might just possibly get down out of the mountains, change his name, go someplace else, and hope that trouble wouldn't follow him. But that would be unlikely."

"Why? What's wrong with it?"

"Well, what if the fugitive had no money, damn little education, and no particular skills that would serve him anywhere else?"

Lonnie Varden shrugged. "Then I reckon you're right. Going away would be mighty hard, but for me the other alternative—explaining yourself to your so-called betters, and sounding humble and sorry—now that would be flat-out impossible."

"Why? It's just words. Words don't cost you anything."

"Well, it would stick in my craw to say it because I don't believe the bosses in this world are any better than me. I did what I did, all right, but it was just two weaknesses coming together and making a tragedy. I didn't mean for any of it to happen. It's not that I'd be lying if I said I was sorry, General, but I'd have trouble begging for mercy and showing how much I regret what I did. Other fellas who felt like I do—maybe they could bare their feelings in front of a bunch of holier-than thou authorities, but I couldn't."

"Maybe you'd better start practicing then, because your attitude in court could mean the difference between getting out someday or not."

"Getting out?" Varden's laugh ended in a sob. "I killed my wife. I murdered her without provocation in front of two witnesses, and I never even bothered to deny it. It doesn't matter what I say in court. I'm a dead man."

Probably true, but it wouldn't do to agree with the fellow. Living with a distraught cellmate was harder time than anybody deserved. The old tramp shrugged. "Maybe you could tell the court she had it coming."

"Tell lies about my Celia and sully her name?" The prisoner shook his head. "I've already killed her once, General."

chapter fourteen

Bruno Hauptmann had kept his appointment with the electric chair in New Jersey on April 3, and, along with the rest of the country, we had promptly forgotten all about him. A few months after that I came into the office a little later than usual. late. The yellow daylilies in the yard were blooming and we had stopped to pick some that morning. Eddie took some to school for his teacher, with the lilies' stems wrapped in wet newspaper, and I brought a few to work for my desk.

Roy said good morning when I came in, taking no more notice of the flowers than I'd expected him to. He wasn't much for small talk either. He held up an open envelope from the stack of morning mail. "Got a letter here that says they're sending Lonnie Varden back to us by the end of the week."

I just nodded and began putting some water in the Mason jar I used for a vase. "Guess the trial is over then."

"If you ask me, they should have called us instead of writing a letter. We're lucky that we got word before the newspaper reporters showed up."

I took the office scissors out of the drawer and started to cut the stems of the lilies so they'd be short enough to fit in the jar without making it topple over. "About Lonnie Varden?" I was barely listening to him, because I had just noticed a little black spider crawling along one of the lily stems, and it was taking all my concentration to keep from screaming. I was the sheriff, though, and I was at work, so it wouldn't do for me to start squealing like a day-old shoat at the sight of a tiny bug. I held my breath, pinched it between my fingers, and flicked it into the wastebasket. Roy was still talking.

"Why would reporters show up here if the trial's over? Everybody knew he was guilty before he even went to court."

"That's right."

"Well, I expect that saved the prosecutor some time at trial. I suppose they wrote it up in the Knoxville paper, but I never saw it, did you?"

"No. Knew he did it. Knew the court would find him guilty. Everything else they wrote would just be . . ." He tapped my flower. "Gilding the lily."

I smiled. "I should have kept up, since he's from this county." I should have, but the past few months had left me feeling like a bed sheet in a windstorm. Between cooking and washing and taking care of my sons, and doing my job, so that nobody could say I was taking charity, I barely had a thought to spare for cases we had already disposed of. *Sufficient unto the day is the evil thereof.* "But you said they're sending him back here?"

Roy tapped the letter. "So they say. He's been in Knoxville for trial, but I reckon they're done with him now."

"Why isn't he going to the penitentiary then?" I should have had a mug of coffee before we started talking. I was barely listening to what Roy was saying, just making the right noises whenever he paused, because I was concentrating too much on my flower arranging and not enough on the realities of state law.

Roy stiffened and made a kind of noise, so I looked up at him to see what was wrong. He blinked uncertainly. "Well, he's not going to the penitentiary because they found him guilty, ma'am. Of first degree murder."

"Well, of course they did. They had everything but a movie of him doing it. What of it?" There was one lily that wasn't quite straight in the arrangement: its stem was too long, I decided, and I turned my attention back to that.

Roy watched me fiddle with the flower for a few moments before he said, "Well, you see, a first degree murder conviction means they intend to hang him."

I looked up then, holding the scissors in one hand and the last lily in the other. "But you said he's coming back . . . They're going to hang him? *Here?*"

Roy reddened and looked down at the letter, and I could tell that he bitterly regretted having started the conversation in the first place, but it couldn't be helped. I'd have to know sooner rather than later, and it was his duty to tell me. "Well . . . I figured—*I hoped*—you already knew. I guess somebody will be along to talk to you about it. I'm sure they will."

"About the hanging? Does the state handle it or what?"

Roy sighed. "No. We do. Well, I guess you could say that we represent the state, but what I mean is that executions are the responsibility of the county in which the offense occurred. So the local sheriff's department carries out the sentence. That is, you do. State law says the hanging is performed by the sheriff of the county in which the offense was committed."

"So I have to decide which one of you performs the execution . . . maybe Tyree?"

"I don't think you can. Not unless they approve a special exemption." Roy kept looking past me at the door, as if he were hoping that somebody would arrive and save him from this conversation. He groped for words to soften the blow. "And they might grant an exemption, of course. They might. All things considered."

"You mean because the sheriff is female?"

"Well, yes. It's a special circumstance. Nobody would argue with that. But if for some reason they don't grant an exception . . . the fact is that you would have to perform the hanging. Yourself. Personally."

"Me? But doesn't it take strength?" I must have had a dozen other objections, but that was the first one that came out.

"To unbolt a trapdoor? Not much. They'll start building the scaffold in a couple of days. Well, somebody will. We may have to get the plans from somewhere and hire local carpenters. Lord knows they could use the work. It will have a trapdoor, so they'll have to work out how to manage that. If that thing got stuck during the execution we'd all look like fools. Anyhow, when the gallows platform gets assembled, you can go and have a look at it, see how it works."

I tried to picture myself practicing to perform an execution, but the idea made me shiver. Then I remembered something else. "The hanging is supposed to be public, isn't it?" Roy had said we'd all look like fools. That's what he meant: besides a whole crowd of ghouls to watch the grisly spectacle, there'd also be radio and newspaper reporters there to witness the execution on behalf of their audience who couldn't attend in person. It wasn't that any of them cared about seeing justice done for that poor dead woman. Everybody just wanted a chance to see a free spectacle they could brag about in later years. Watching a man die—how many chances did an ordinary person have to do that? Some people liked to watch animals being torn to pieces—coon hunts, cockfights—and for people like that this hanging might provide the same sort of grim thrill, only more intense. I wondered if there was any way to deprive them of their blood feast and to spare myself the ordeal of having to perform the act in public. "So the hanging will be done outdoors somewhere, and anybody that wants to can come and watch?"

"Apparently so. State law says it has to be public." He blushed a little.

"There'll be fools wanting to bring their kids to see a hanging. There'll be drunks making a party of it. Can't we stop that?"

"Not as far as I can tell, but I could check. We have a book on the state's law-enforcement regulations in the top file drawer, and I read up on executions awhile back. Didn't see any point in bringing it up until now, though. I was hoping you already knew."

"No. I didn't know. Nobody bothered to tell me. When is it supposed to happen?"

He held up the letter. "According to this, there has to be time to build the scaffold and make the arrangements for an attending physician, figure out who will claim the body, all that. The letter covers a lot of the details. The execution date is in three weeks, it says. They'll be sending him back here by the end of this week, though. He'll stay here in jail until the hanging. But we have a couple of weeks to get ready."

"What do you mean, 'get ready'?"

"Well, I told you. Getting the scaffold built is the main thing. We ought to see if we can find somebody who has officiated at an execution before, because there may be things we wouldn't think of on our own, like stretching the rope. We ought to study up on the procedure as much as we can."

I nodded. "I suppose we will need a preacher in case the condemned man wants one. I hope he does. I'd like him to be at peace with the Lord before he dies."

"I'd be more at ease knowing we had a doctor there. We will have one, of course, because there has to be a doctor on hand to pronounce the prisoner officially dead, but I hope he can see his way clear to giving the poor devil a sedative before we take him to the gallows. Not on his account, mind you. I don't care if the prisoner suffers or not, after what he did. I just don't want him to go to his death fighting and screaming and making things worse for you than they already will be."

I wondered what I would do in his place. Could I go to my certain death calmly and with dignity, the way people did in storybooks? I suspected that if I did, it would only be in order not to give the spectators the satisfaction of seeing my terror and grief. Death ought to be a private thing, and if it isn't, at least you ought to try to keep your feelings about it to yourself. I think I'd mind the staring strangers worse than I would the rope. "Maybe you ought to make a list, Roy. The main thing, though, is building the gallows. There isn't one around somewhere already, is there?"

"No. Seems wasteful, doesn't it, to keep rebuilding the same structure instead of just building a sturdy one and keeping it maintained? You'd think there'd be a permanent one in every county, but there aren't too awful many hangings, so they just put one up when they need it and tear it down afterward. I guess that's one benefit of this execution—the local carpenters could do with the work."

"I wonder how long it takes to build a gallows?"

"I don't suppose you're the right person to speak to, really." The plain young woman twisted her hands in her lap, shredding a paper handkerchief and looking anywhere but at me. She had on a straw hat, a purple-flowered church dress, and thick cotton stockings, which was probably her going-to-town outfit. It was clear that she was embarrassed about having come—probably never been in a sheriff's department before in her whole blameless life, and I was sure she wouldn't be here now if there hadn't been a woman in charge. I wondered what she wanted.

When I arrived that morning a few minutes before eight I had found her pacing back and forth on the office porch with an expression of such distress that I nearly grinned, picturing her trying to confess to blowing up the *Lusitania*. I couldn't imagine her mixed up in anything more serious than killing a neighbor's chicken by mistake.

But I didn't ask her any questions to begin with. Instead, I ushered her in and offered to make her coffee while she made up her mind to tell me what was troubling her.

"I'm afraid I don't drink coffee, ma'am," she said. "I don't suppose you have any tea?"

I shook my head. "Nobody here drinks it. Do you mind if I make some coffee for myself?"

"Please do." She pulled up a chair next to the reception desk, took off her hat, and settled herself while she waited for me to fix the coffee. She studied the yellowing wanted posters on the board beside the desk until I sat down, ready to listen.

"I heard tell the county had a woman sheriff now," she said, peering at me curiously.

"That's so, ma'am. My husband died and I took his place. Is there something we can help you with?"

She sighed and pulled another paper handkerchief out of her pocketbook. She didn't blow her nose with it, though. She just started picking it to pieces while she talked, staring at it instead of at me. "It's about this execution that's going to take place. I just felt like I had to tell somebody. My sister calls it a jest of fate, and I know what she means, but I'm not sure I can bring myself to believe it. Do you believe in fate?"

"I guess I believe that when things happen to people, most times they bring it on themselves. Maybe you'd better tell me what you're getting at. And you might start by telling me your name."

She blushed. "I'm Eunice Greer. I've come about that man who flung his wife off The Hawk's Wing. Honestly, I think my sister is gloating because Celia broke the rules and didn't deserve a husband, but she got one anyway. We are the only spinsters left, my sister and I, but I think it's quite tragic that Celia died because of a silly old game, and people ought to know about it. In case that makes a difference, you know."

She wasn't making any sense. I suppose she was so nervous that she'd been working out her story in her head, and by the time she got to tell it to me she was already in the middle of it, so she just kept on going. I tried again. "Are you saying that your sister thinks the hanging is a game?"

"No, no. Not the hanging. That's a tragedy. Even she admits that. It's what may have caused it that is such a terrible thing. Ever since he killed her, I've worried about whether or not I ought to say anything. I expect most people will think my story is pure foolishness, but I hoped that you'd understand—being a woman and all—because women know there isn't always a straight line between one thing that happens and the next."

I wished there was more of a straight line in her explanation, because I still wasn't following it. "Go on."

"Besides, you're from a community up the mountain yourself, aren't you? I'd heard that."

"That's so. Before we moved to town, my home was a little settlement up the mountain. I was born and raised there. But just what is it you hoped I'd understand?"

She sighed. "Well, it's about Lonnie Varden, that prisoner you're fixing to execute."

"Lonnie Varden? What about him?"

"His wife, Celia, grew up in our settlement. We'd known her all our lives."

"Did you come to visit Mr. Varden? He's not here yet, you know. I expect a couple of marshals will be bringing him in toward the end of the week. Is he also a friend of yours?"

"Oh no. I barely know him by sight, and I don't think it would do either of us any good if I were to visit him. He didn't grow up anywhere around here, as far as I know, and Celia married him just a few years ago."

"But if you don't know him . . . Do you know anything about the state of their marriage?" I knew that such a question had no bearing on my duty as a peace officer, and maybe I had no business asking it, but when a man murders his wife it's only natural for outsiders to wonder what problems there had been between them. *Why* is a woman's question, I guess, but we always want to know.

She shook her head. "I never really spent any time with the two of them together. All I know is that the marriage was cursed before it ever happened, and that's why he killed her. My sister says it was fate."

I wanted to ask her more about that, but the conversation felt too much like gossiping for me to let her keep going without first setting her straight about legal procedure, as best I understood it myself. "Well, Miss Greer, I'm sure that your story is very interesting, and I suppose the prosecuting attorney might have been able to use information about the victim's past—or, more likely, the defense would have, but here in the sheriff's department the details about the crime are none of our business anymore. After the arrest the courts decide what to do with him. We just carry out their instructions. The hanging is in a couple of weeks. I'm sure you're anxious to see the killer punished for what he did to your friend."

"But that's just it. I'm not sure that Lonnie Varden should even *be* punished. I mean I know he killed her and all, but we think he was fated to do it."

I'll bet the defense would have thought this story was a Christmas present, except that Eunice Greer would have been the world's worst witness, and her tale of fate might have proved so fanciful that they'd have been laughed out of court.

A minute or two later she finally worked her way around to the beginning of the tale. "Back when we were young girls in the settlement, we had a Dumb Supper. You know about them, I suppose?"

"Yes. Never went to one, but I know the custom. You cook a meal for your future husband, and if you do the ritual right, he's supposed to show up, either in person or in spirit."

"Well, we had one for a lark nine years ago, and Celia broke the rules. She told me about it a year later—how she had dropped a place knife when she was setting the table, and when she went to put it back, she turned and faced the table."

"Facing the table is forbidden, isn't it?"

"Yes. It ruins everything. She should have stopped right then and told the rest of us, but she didn't. Why, it's a mercy the misfortune didn't taint the other girls as well. Of course, we don't know what's to come, do we? It makes me glad I never tried to wed."

"Celia Varden dropped a knife playing at a Dumb Supper years ago, and you think that's why she was killed?"

She nodded. "We do. As soon as Celia was killed, I told my sister what had happened at the Dumb Supper, and she wrote to the others to let them know. She says Celia got what she deserved for being deceitful and trying to cheat fate out of a husband, and that she got what was coming to her for that deceit. I don't know. Maybe my sister is just bitter about staying a spinster, no matter what she says to the contrary. But it's Celia's poor husband who concerns me. I'm sure she didn't tell him anything about the Dumb Supper when she married him. So now she's gone and gotten both of them killed."

It should have been funny except that the story was going to end with a hanging. I thought Eunice Greer was talking pure foolishness, but I could see that she was sincere in what she was saying. There's people from all over who believe things even sillier than that, but it wouldn't be right to mock them for it. Finally I said, "We're not given to know if fate makes people do things or not, so in this world we have to hold people responsible for what they do, no matter why they did it."

She blushed. "Well, being a woman I thought you'd understand, anyhow. I'm sorry for him, but I don't know what I can do about it. Maybe he couldn't help it."

"Maybe there's a reason why anybody in the world does anything, but we usually don't know what those reasons are. I think we have to judge people by their actions, because they have a choice. At some point, curse or no curse, a person has to decide to do what he does. If there's more to it than that, then his lawyer ought to bring it up in court and let the jury decide if it matters."

"It's too late to talk to him, though, isn't it?"

"The trial is over now, yes."

"But the trial was miles away, and I couldn't possibly have got there. The lawyer was a man, though, and I doubt if he would have listened to a word I said. It's only when I got to thinking about them hanging him and knowing it was going to happen here that I felt I had to come and tell somebody."

I thought about it. "Would it be all right with you if I told your story to Mr. Varden when he gets back? Maybe it would give him some peace to think the crime wasn't altogether his fault."

Eunice Greer looked relieved. She stuffed the remains of the paper handkerchief back in her purse and stood up to go. "Thank you, Sheriff. Yes. I suppose I can't hope for any more than that. You tell him that. And tell him that we will be praying for him. All of us from the Dumb Supper. We'll be praying for his soul."

In these mountains there is a kind of cricket called a cicada that hardly crosses your mind most of the time, but every seventeen years an enormous brood of them hatches out of the ground and takes flight. Then it is like living through one of the ten plagues of Egypt around here. The last time it happened was four years ago, after we had moved to town. The newly awakened cicadas swarm like black smoke, covering everything, and blundering into anyone who is working outside in a field near trees or bushes, so that it's a misery to venture out until they finish their natural cycle and go to ground again.

The newspapermen made me think of them.

A few days after it was announced that wife-killer Lonnie Varden would be publicly executed by a sheriff who happened to be female, a great swarm of journalists seemed to rise right up out of the ground and descend on this little town just like the plague of cicadas. They tied up the telephone at the office until we began to be afraid that some caller with a genuine emergency would be unable to get through. Finally Roy started taking names and threatening to arrest any reporter who called more than three times. Then they took to dropping by the office and trying to waylay us on our way in and out the door. They offered the deputies everything from a cup of coffee to a five-dollar bill for a five-minute interview with the prisoner. We told them all to get lost, but we might as well have been swatting at cicadas.

I ate lunch in the office every day, so generally the only time I had to worry about them was going to work and leaving at the end of the day, but it didn't take them long to figure that out, and at five o'clock one afternoon I opened the door and an explosion of flashbulbs sent me stumbling back into the office with blue dots blinding me for the better part of a minute. Even with the door shut behind me I could hear them yelling my name—my *first* name, mind you, as if these total strangers were my old-time buddies—and bawling out questions, some of which struck me as so peculiar that I wondered if they had taken leave of their senses.

"*What are you going to wear to the hanging, Ellie?*" "*What's your favorite color, Ellie?*" "*Are you going to kiss him good-bye before you string him up?*"

I stumbled to a chair next to the reception desk. "I don't know what to do! We can't run them out of town, can we?"

Falcon shook his head. "As far as I can tell, being annoying isn't illegal. Besides, a lot of folks in town think these fellows are a godsend. They've filled up the depot hotel, and on account of them, all the local eateries have been doing a landslide business all week."

"Wait until they read the stories those reporters churn out. I'll bet they could go over those articles with a divining rod and not find a scrap of truth about this town or anybody those newspapermen talked to."

"They're making a lot more work for us, I'll give you that," said Falcon. "They are almost as hard to keep out as ants, and they don't take no for an answer."

"We ought to try to say as little as possible to them. Seems like no matter what we say they'll twist it around to whatever they want. The more we can steer clear of them, the better."

Easier said than done.

I was walking home that afternoon a little before six, thinking about home, as I always did. Most days, as soon as I got away from the office and got to the wooded path along the creek that led to the house, I went from thinking like a law officer to being an ordinary woman again, with a house to run and children to look after. I was thinking about fixing beans and cornbread and sliced tomatoes for supper—wondering if we had enough tomatoes in the garden and whether the milk would last us through breakfast if I used some of it in the cornbread—when someone fell in step beside me. I hadn't noticed anyone around, but suddenly there he was: a stocky man wearing a shiny brown suit, a necktie, and a battered fedora that had seen better days. The town banker, the railroad directors, and the undertaker dress that way on workdays, but somehow I knew this fellow was not any of them, because when they did dress up, their clothes were not as shabby as this fellow's.

"Good evening, madam. You'd be the sheriff, wouldn't you?"

There's no law against talking to an elected official on public land, and even if there had been, I had been raised to be civil to everybody in the world, as long as they didn't give me a reason to behave otherwise.

"That's right, sir. I'm off duty now, though. Just heading off home." I quickened my step a little, but he took it in stride, even managing to dodge the mud puddle in the path.

"I reckon you got more of a job than you bargained for when they appointed you sheriff, madam."

"The hanging, you mean? I'll manage. It's my job to do it—but not to talk about it."

"I see that you have divined that I am a journalist, Sheriff. You know, there are people all across the country who are interested in your story. How you feel about doing a man's job. How you take care of your family while trying to do your work. You'd make quite a story. And as pretty as you are, you'd make the cover of *Life* magazine, if you'd give us some time to make a proper feature story of it. Let a photographer do a series of pictures of you at work and at home, say."

"Not interested."

He paused for a moment, sizing me up probably. "My editor has authorized me to pay you a tidy sum for exclusive rights to your story, madam. Surely, a newly widowed lady such as yourself could find a use for some ready money."

I kept walking just as fast as ever, wishing I wasn't tempted by his offer. It would feel like selling my soul to the devil, but I had two boys to feed and clothe, and no idea what the future would hold once I finished my late husband's term in office. A bankable sum of money would be an answer to prayer, really. And where was the harm in it? No one said it was against the rules. Finally I turned to look at the man in the shiny brown suit, half expecting him to have sprouted horns and a cloven hoof, but he looked just the same: weary and a little out of breath, but quite alert to my every expression.

"Give me your business card and tell me where you're staying. I'll have to think about it."

"Got another sack here," said Roy, slinging a canvas bag on top of the reception desk. He mopped his brow with a dingy cotton handkerchief. "Good thing you don't pick up the mail yourself, Sheriff. When the postmaster handed this load over to me just now he looked like he wanted to spit in your eye."

"Did you sort out the ones for me?"

He grinned and pulled a handful of envelopes out of his hip pocket. "Those in the sack are *all* for you. This here's the department's share. I'll look through them and leave that batch to you." He ambled back to his desk, still laughing.

I loosened the cord on the mailbag and pulled out the first dozen letters. Some of them had been sent to THE COUNTY SHERIFF, with only the name of the town and the state written beneath it, but the postal officials had no trouble figuring out who the letters were for. There had been a couple hundred just like them beginning a few days after Lonnie Varden arrived. Practice makes perfect.

The ones addressed to MISS ELLENDOR ROBBINS (spelled forty different ways) were usually marriage proposals. The rest didn't want to rescue me from widowhood; they just wanted to save me from the unwomanly task of executing a prisoner. I suppose they meant well, but it was hard to see how, for example, a professor from Bloomington, Indiana, or a plumber from Harrisburg, Pennsylvania, could think they were more qualified, much less legally authorized, to execute a convicted felon for a state they didn't even live in.

I tore one open. I don't know why. We had been getting piles of letters for more than a week, and they all said pretty much the same thing.

Dear Madam,

I read of your present troubles in the newspaper, and I was shocked and saddened to learn that a poor widow woman with no experience in law enforcement was expected to dispatch a dangerous killer in a public execution. If anything could make this prospect more terrible, it is the knowledge that you are also the mother of two young children whose images of their gentle mother must surely be tainted by this deed. My horror at imagining this appalling scene leads me to offer my humble services so as to spare you from this fate. Thus, madam, although I live several hundred miles from your little mountain county, you may consider me at your disposal . . .

The ones from the doctors and professors mostly sounded like that. The ordinary farmers and mill hands and such usually said something like:

Dear Lady Sheriff

I heard about yore having to hang a man in public. It is a turrible thing, and I would gladly do it for you . . .

None of them asked for any money to take my place at the execution. That surprised me. People these days were looking for a way to make money out of anything, because nobody seemed to have any, but these self-appointed knights appeared to be set on rescuing a fair lady, with no other catch to the offer. When the first couple of letters came in I thought about answering them because my upbringing had given me strict rules about thanking people for offers of help, whether you had wanted that help or not, but before I could work out a civil answer, the trickle of letters became a stream and then a flood, so I gave up the idea of responding at all. If I had tried to answer—or even read—all the correspondence addressed to the office or to me personally, there wouldn't have been time for anything else.

I did wonder, though, how Eddie would take the news, and I knew he would hear it at school if I didn't tell him first, so one night after Georgie had fallen asleep I sat Eddie down in the kitchen with a glass of milk and tried to explain.

"I guess you heard about that man who threw his wife off The Hawk's Wing last spring?"

"Some of the fellers at school talked about it. They were talking about hiking up there to see where it happened." Just as I reached for the dishcloth he wiped the milk from his lips with the back of his hand. "Could I go along with them?"

"No. If you didn't get nightmares, you'd go telling Georgie, and he would." I'd had nightmares myself a time or two thinking about it.

"Why did the man do that?"

"He hasn't said. And he doesn't have to."

"Bobby Hardesty said he reckoned the man's wife had another sweetheart."

"That's nobody's business, Eddie. Least of all the pupils of the fifth grade. And you can tell them I said so."

He hung his head. "Yes, ma'am."

I knew he wouldn't tell them, though. I may have been the county sheriff, but to Eddie I was just his mother, and he wouldn't want to deliver any scoldings from me to his friends. A sheriff for a daddy is one thing; a mama who's a sheriff is something else again. It didn't matter to me, though. I didn't want to be important—just independent.

"It doesn't matter why that man killed his wife, Eddie, and it doesn't matter what she did or didn't do, because nobody has a right to take another person's life. The fact is he did it. People saw him do it, and they gave him a trial downstate, and the jury found him guilty. After listening to the witnesses, the jury decided it wasn't an accident, and he wasn't crazy at the time, so they sentenced him to death. Do you understand?"

Eddie stifled a yawn. "Uh-huh. Can I have that last biscuit from supper?"

"No. You can have it with breakfast." I tried again. "The state believes it has a right to execute that man for being a murderer. Do you know why?"

He shrugged. "Stop him from doing it again?"

"That's right. And we hope that it would make other people think twice about killing anybody, too."

"Can people go and watch the hanging?"

"Yes. The courts think that seeing such a terrible thing will convince people not to risk such a fate for themselves, and so the execution is done in public."

"Here in town?"

"Yes. You know that empty lot over next to the train station? They're building the gallows there."

"Can Georgie and me go and watch?"

"Watch what? The carpenters building the platform?"

"Naw. The hanging. Well, I reckon Georgie is too young for it. It'd give him nightmares for sure, but I wouldn't want to miss it."

"You'd better get used to the idea then, son, because I forbid you to go."

His face crinkled with disappointment. "Awww. Why not? I'm plenty old enough. Anyhow I'll bet Daddy would have let me go."

"He might have tried, but it wouldn't have made any difference. I would not have let you go. Such a thing is not fitten for a child to see." Nor for most adults either, I thought, but there wasn't much I could do about that. Maybe I should have a word with Falcon about making sure none of the town's schoolboys tried to sneak into the crowd. Human nature being what it is, I knew that some parent might be fool enough to bring the child themselves, but we couldn't help that.

chapter fifteen

I had been called on the carpet, not for anything I had done, but for what I would be obliged to do.

When the trial was over, the attorney general's office sent word that Lonnie Varden was being sent back here to the county for execution, and it suddenly dawned on the local commissioners that their newly appointed sheriff, whose job it would be to hang the condemned man, was a woman. The day after we were notified, I was summoned to a meeting in the boardroom at the courthouse. They invited me to sit down, and I did, but I still felt like I was standing. I wore my blue swearing-in dress and my long-brimmed white hat with the black ribbon trim because I knew that this was likely to be an important meeting. I might even have to fight for my job. Even so, I made myself smile at everybody when I went in, and I tried to act calm and unconcerned, but I kept on my white cotton gloves because my hands were sweating.

Vernon Johnson, in a white linen suit and string tie, chaired the meeting. Despite its big windows, which were shut, the upstairs room in the courthouse was hot and stuffy, but even if it hadn't been, Mr. Johnson might have kept mopping his brow with that big silk handkerchief because I think most of the heat he was feeling was coming from the accusing looks of his fellow board members. After all, he was the one who insisted that they appoint me. I bet he was regretting it now, which was a shame, because nobody ought to have to regret doing someone a kindness.

I sat at the head of the scarred oak table facing two rows of stern-looking gentlemen: the railroad executives in dark suits, and a couple of the county's more prosperous farmers wearing their shiny Sunday suit jackets over work clothes and suspenders. One of them had a shaggy brown dog sprawled out next to his chair. Looking at that line of scowls, I started to feel like the condemned prisoner instead of like the sheriff.

Vernon Johnson sighed. "No good deed goes unpunished, I suppose, but heaven knows I meant well. Providing for a widow lady, giving her a paperwork job—and now this."

One of the farmers smiled. "You couldn't be expected to foresee a murder, Mr. Johnson. Nobody blames you. The question now is what's to be done about it."

"We could send him somewhere else, or get somebody to do it as a volunteer. Maybe there are experts in execution procedures."

"I have a suggestion, sirs," I said.

They all turned to look at me with much the same expression they'd have had if the farmer's dog had spoken up.

"I think you ought to let me get on with my job. There haven't been any complaints so far, have there?"

Vernon Johnson sighed. "You have done well, Mrs. Robbins; nobody is saying otherwise, but this business of performing an execution. People are horrified. It's not something we could expect a woman to do, any more than we could ask one to join the army and fight battles."

A few of the other commissioners chuckled politely.

"Do you *want* to hang a man, Mrs. Robbins?"

I waited for a moment, sorting out my words. "I want to do the job I was appointed to. Every job in the world involves things you'd rather not do, doesn't it?" I looked at the craggy old farmer on my left. "I'll bet shoveling cow manure isn't your favorite part of farming, but it's got to be done, doesn't it?"

He smiled and nodded.

"I'm saying that I am willing to do what would be required of any sheriff during a term in office. I'm sorry that an execution has to be part of those duties, but I am satisfied that the prisoner is guilty as charged, and the court has decided what ought to happen to him. Somebody has to carry out their orders, and I am the one sworn to do it. I am willing."

A railroad executive spoke up, addressing the others as if I wasn't there. "But it's a public execution. What if she backs out at the last minute, or makes a hash of it?"

They all looked at me, some looking stern and a couple with pity in their eyes, but nobody looked convinced that I would be able to do it.

I took off my cotton glove and pushed my sleeve up a little. I held my arm out straight so they all could see it. "Do you all see this here scar on my wrist? Let me tell you how I got it." I think Albert fell in love with me partly on account of the fact that I was brave enough to put a red-hot poker over the bite of that mad dog, but I never talk about that time if I can help it, for I nearly drowned in the pain of it. But if I had to show I was brave, I reckon that was the best proof I had. When I finished talking they were staring at that shriveled scar on my wrist, and most of them had gone greenish white.

Before they could recover, Vernon Johnson called for a vote. It wasn't unanimous, but the farmer I spoke to about shoveling manure cast the deciding vote. I would perform the execution, and thereby keep my job.

The clattering went on. I laid down my pen and pushed away the paperwork. I couldn't keep my mind on it. "I wish we could get a radio brought in here," I said to nobody in particular. In the main part of the office Roy was typing up a report, and Falcon had gone out on patrol, but even if anybody had been close enough and paying attention, they wouldn't have heard me. The noise of the hammering outside drowned out everything, and I felt myself beginning to flinch in time with the pounding.

The carpenters hired by the county were building a scaffold.

The hanging was only a week away now, and preparations were well under way. The newspapers were already running stories, and a dozen or so big-city reporters had already arrived in town to cover the event. They passed the time waiting for the hanging by pestering us for interviews, because public executions were becoming increasingly rare. I wouldn't be sorry to see them disappear altogether. We had to keep someone on duty all the time to keep the journalists from trying to get into the jail to interview the prisoner. Some of them offered bribes, too, but fortunately my deputies caught on to the contempt and condescension in the reporters' attitudes toward them, which made them so angry that no amount of money would have tempted them. I had thought long and hard about the offer from the magazine reporter for an exclusive interview with me, but it became easy to refuse the money when I thought of how I'd feel if Falcon or Roy accepted an offer like that. I called the fellow and declined the offer. I suppose he'll write his story anyway, making up quotes and getting someone to take pictures of me when I'm not looking, but at least I'll know I did the right thing as I saw it, and that, I decided, was something I owed Eddie and George more than I owed them new clothes or fancy food.

If the county had given me a say in the decision, the builders would have been constructing the contraption a mile or more outside town instead of practically on our doorstep, but everybody was full of reasons why the vacant lot on the street behind the jail was the ideal place to construct a gallows. Something about the soil and the drainage and the size of the parcel of land being good for limiting crowds. I was wholeheartedly in favor of that last reason, because the fewer spectators we had to contend with, the better. We were likely to have more people attending than the usual hanging because of the novelty of having a woman perform the execution. If in fact I did end up performing the execution. That had not officially been decided yet. Someone in the state government could overrule the county's decision, for all I knew. Still, judging by the phone calls and the letters we were getting, almost every big newspaper east of the Mississippi was planning to send somebody to cover it, and even a couple of radio stations intended to have reporters on hand to broadcast the event. I wondered if their presence would make the ordeal any more terrible than it already would be. I couldn't imagine even sparing them a thought: they would be like flies on a battlefield, annoying but insignificant.

It couldn't have been easy for Lonnie Varden to have to sit there in his cell, listening to that pounding day after day, knowing, as he must have, that the hammers measured out the span of his life same as heartbeats, and that when they stopped, his time would be almost up. Falcon had asked the carpentry foreman when he reckoned on them finishing, and he said they planned to be done by sundown on the day before the execution. The construction boss said they knew they had to allow us enough time to test the mechanism before the ceremony itself.

"The foreman called it a ceremony?" I'd asked Falcon.

"Well, I don't think he likes to say the word execution,*"* said Falcon. *"It casts a pall on his honest carpentry."*

Penned up and listening to his death coming closer by the hour . . . I felt sorry for the prisoner, which wasn't the same thing as believing that he ought to be set free. He hadn't shown his wife an ounce of pity; I was mindful of that. I thought it was all too easy for people to see a sorrowful doomed prisoner and forget all about the poor victim who never had a chance to appeal for mercy. I figured it was our job in law enforcement to remember those who couldn't speak for themselves anymore. But I did think that the forfeit of a man's life was punishment enough. He should not have to listen to the building of the gallows to disturb whatever peace he could find in his last days. I went back to his cell to tell him so.

"I'm gonna go check on the prisoner," I told Roy. I nearly had to shout to make him hear me.

Roy glanced up from his typing and nodded to show he had heard me. "Maybe I ought to check the manual and see if the town has a noise ordinance!" he called back.

Even if they did have a noise ordinance I didn't see what we could do about enforcing it. Roy was joking, though. The din would be worse back in the cell corridor, which was at the back of the building, only a few hundred yards from the construction site.

Roy motioned for me to stop. "Are you sure you want to go back and talk to that fellow?"

"Well, somebody has to look in on him every now and again." I smiled. "He doesn't seem dangerous to me. I know what he did and all, but I think he's safe enough now."

"That wasn't what I was getting at. When I was a kid my daddy let me raise a piglet, the runt of the litter. I had to feed it with a knotted cloth soaked in milk so's it would get enough to eat. When it got bigger, that little shoat followed me around like a puppy dog. Smart too. I was going to teach him to do tricks."

"And?"

"You were raised on a farm. You know, don't you?" I nodded. "I thought you would. Come October, when my piglet got to be a good-sized porker, my daddy rounded it up with the rest of the surplus hogs and killed it for meat to see us through the winter. I flat-out cried for days."

"When we lived on the Robbinses' farm, I never would let Eddie make a pet of something we were planning to kill. Not even a baby chick."

"I'm just afraid that's what you're doing now. Making a pet out of some pitiful creature that you're going to have to kill one of these days. And I remember how much it hurts when it's time to let go."

I shrugged. "Reckon I'm used to letting go by now."

I found Lonnie Varden sitting on his bunk, staring up at the ceiling. A dime novel western lay open facedown on the blanket beside him. When he saw me he tapped the book and sighed. "Just killing time, before it—"

Before it kills me, he almost said. I nodded, glad that he hadn't said it. "I can go if you'd rather read."

"I've quit reading. It doesn't provide any distraction at all. You're supposed to care about whether the cowboy can escape the marauding Indians who are chasing him, but somehow I can't work up any enthusiasm for the fellow's troubles. At least he *has* a chance."

"Yes. I can see how you might think he was better off than you are. Maybe you'd be better off reading something else. Would you like a Bible?"

"I might, sooner or later. But I'm not sure I'd find it very comforting right now either. They're pretty definite about those Ten Commandments, and I think I broke the big one—being a murderer and all." He rubbed his hand over his eyes. "Maybe one or two other important ones, too."

I nodded. "I suppose most people have. I don't have any other reading material to offer you right now, though. I just came to check on you and to apologize for the noise." I had to raise my voice a little to be heard over the clamor.

He shrugged. "I don't suppose you care for it either. Nothing you can do about it, is there?"

"No. They've got to do their jobs, same as the rest of us, and they can't very well see to do it after dark—that wouldn't help anyhow, would it? Then it would just keep you awake all night."

"That wouldn't make the neighbors very happy."

"No. Hammering is not a quiet job, so I guess we'll all have to put up with it as best we can."

"If those are the only choices, then I'd rather have it quiet at night. But it's not much of an improvement. At first, the quiet is a welcome relief, but I don't sleep much, and when it's been dark and silent for a couple of hours, there's nothing I can do but brood about my situation and how it's going to end. I almost miss the hammering then."

"I'm sorry that paperback western didn't take your mind off your troubles. I could get you another one at the drugstore." Or ask somebody for the loan of one. I wondered what Roy read.

He shook his head. "The problem with reading is that whatever's in the book always seems to relate to my situation in real life. Will the hero get the girl? Sure, but so what? In real life, nobody writes *The End* across the sky. There are no happy endings. If it's happy, it isn't the end. So you just keep going until you reach the unhappy ending. And I won't go near a whodunit. Lord, whatever you do, don't bring me one of those. It's hard to read one when you've lived one yourself and to know that instead of being the morally superior detective you're the heartless villain."

I was surprised to hear him say that, because most people have a bucketful of excuses for anything they're ever blamed for. "Do you feel like a heartless villain?"

He didn't look at me, but he thought about the question for a good while. Just as he began to answer there was a break in the construction noise, which was good, because he spoke so softly I could barely hear. "A heartless villain? Maybe I am one, but I don't see myself that way. I feel like I tried to be a good person, but I wasn't always as strong or self-disciplined as I thought I could be. And one day my pride or my weakness got the best of me and took away everything that mattered. Somehow my whole life got balled up into a nightmare that lasted less than a minute out there on that rock. Then it was over, with no going back, and I know that forever after I will be judged by just that one minute and by nothing else I ever did."

"You must have thought a lot about that." His answer had been too pat to have occurred to him right then in reply to my question. I guess sometime or other everybody broods over how they'll be remembered, and knowing exactly when you are going to die must make those thoughts that much more terrible. Maybe I'll be remembered as 'the lady sheriff,' but I'd rather be remembered with respect and love by Eddie and George. That's all that matters, really, and at least, God willing, I'll have time to do more with my life before it's over.

The hammering started up again.

Lonnie Varden put his hands over his ears. "Nobody could read through that din. I wish to God I had something to draw with!"

"So you wouldn't have to think, you mean?"

He shrugged. "It's funny, but drawing *is* thinking, in a way."

I tried to work out what he meant. "You mean you have to analyze what you're drawing so you can figure out how to make things the right shape and make them look like they're supposed to?"

"You do, but that's not what I was thinking about. After you do it often enough, that just comes second nature. What I'm talking about is the fact that sometimes when you start putting things on paper you find out what you really think, even if you hadn't realized it before. You draw a person, just trying to capture the set of the eyes, the angle of the jaw, . . . and when you finally stop and look at what you've put down on paper, you see a faint sneer on the lips, maybe, or a spark of anger in the eyes. Apparently you spotted some emotion while you were drawing that face, but you weren't aware that you knew it."

"Did that always happen when you drew pictures of people?"

"Hardly ever, to tell you the truth. If you know someone well enough to do a portrait of them, usually you know what they're like and what they might be feeling. Most of the time there isn't much emotion at all—except boredom. Posing is generally about as tiresome as watching the paint dry. It happened to me once, though. I drew a woman. I guess she was pretty enough—not like a movie star, not even all that attractive, really, but she had that look, that attitude that said, *'I'm available. Yours for the taking.'* Men mistake that for beauty more often than you'd think. Anyhow, everybody thinks pretty people are also nice, you know. Even artists fall for that. Fairy tales, movies, you name it: we're all trained to believe that beautiful equals good."

"Angels."

"Yeah. Like angels. Just try putting an ugly angel on a stained glass window. Or have the good guy in a western played by some plump ordinary Joe. Anyhow, one time I drew this woman, thinking she was a fairy-tale beauty, and—well, she wasn't."

"Your wife, you mean?"

"No. Somebody else. Somebody I wish had been on that rock instead of my wife." Then he straightened up and shivered a little—a goose walking over your grave, people called that feeling—and I knew he wished he hadn't said any of that. When the moment passed, he turned to look at me, and I could see that he was calm and back in the present. "How 'bout I draw your boys?"

I hadn't expected that. "My boys?"

Lonnie Varden smiled. "I'll bet he didn't tell you. Your son Eddie sneaks back here sometimes when he's supposed to be dumping the mop bucket out back, and we pass the time of day for a couple of minutes. Please don't let on I told you. I didn't mean to get him in trouble."

"I won't." But I did make a mental note to tell the deputies to watch him closer.

"He'll be all right. I wouldn't do anything to scare him. I promise you that. We don't talk about—you know, what's about to happen to me. Nice kid, that boy of yours. Well-spoken. He's got good bone structure too. You ever had his portrait done?"

I shook my head. "Just snapshots with our old box camera, that's all. I don't think even the rich people around here get portraits painted of their children. It wouldn't be easy."

He looked around the bare cell. "I could probably manage to do his portrait for you."

"Oh, I couldn't—"

"I know. You couldn't let your boys come in here and pose for a killer like me."

"Not just that." I was embarrassed that he had guessed my first thought, but there were other reasons as well. "I couldn't allow you to have all that painting paraphernalia in here."

"I don't have any painting paraphernalia anymore. I never went home after it happened, you know, and I heard that Celia's family came down and burned everything that ever belonged to me—clothes, books, painting supplies—even the paintings themselves. It's all gone. So I guess once this hanging is over, I'll disappear from the world altogether."

"The mural in the post office will still be there. They'll probably put pictures of it in magazines, on account of the fact that you did it."

He made a face. "Not the way I wanted to get famous. I wish I could do something more than that."

"You asked me for art supplies before."

"I know, but now that the hammering has started, I thought you might reconsider, just to keep me from going crazy."

I hesitated. "Painting supplies could be dangerous, couldn't they?"

He smiled, bemused at the notion. "Yeah, I reckon I could squeeze the oil paint out of the tube, swallow it, and die of poisoning. Or I might break up a wooden easel and make a sharp lance out of one of its legs."

"I hadn't thought much about it. Sounds like you have, though."

"Just off the top of my head. I was just being silly. But I tell you what: I'm bored out of my skull just staring at these bare walls—and listening to the sounds of the hammering out there. I wish I didn't know what they were building."

"I'm sorry. I can't help that. I told you: none of us much cares for the noise either. We can hardly hear ourselves think."

"At least you don't have to take it personally. For me those hammer blows are like a loud heartbeat. When they stop, I stop."

"I'm sorry. Nobody meant for it to torment you. They just decided to build the scaffold there for practical reasons."

"Tell you what: let's see if we can work out a safe way for me to keep myself from going crazy and for you to get a portrait of your son. My last chance to leave a mark on the world." He saw me hesitate, and his teasing expression gave way to one of regret. "Please, ma'am. I want to be remembered for something besides what I'm dying for."

I was still looking for the snare. My people don't trust strangers at the best of times, and I was afraid that because I was female he'd think I could be easily tricked. "You could turn a paintbrush into a weapon, too, though."

"All right. What about a piece of chalk? Or a stub of charcoal? They're not poison. You know those pills people take for indigestion? Chalk is what they are, more or less."

"Charcoal burns."

"I don't have any matches, though. And I don't see anything in here that I could rub together to make a spark, do you?"

"I guess not. I doubt that would work on bare charcoal anyhow. It sure wouldn't work on coal. But there's not an art supply store within forty miles of here, is there? Where would I get fancy charcoal for making pictures with?"

He laughed. "About fifty yards from here. For free."

"Where?"

"You know that big old willow tree that grows down by the creek? You could break off a limb—about the size of a hammer handle, I guess—and stick the end of that branch into a fire. That'll make the best charcoal there is. Then you sharpen it with a knife so it will have an edge. That's what I'd draw with anyhow. I'll bet you Rembrandt and da Vinci did the same."

"Just ordinary charcoal?"

"*Willow* charcoal. That's what artists draw the shapes with. Underneath all that oil paint, every work of art starts out as smudges of charcoal. It's the bones of the painting."

"But you couldn't have the oil paint or the rest of the materials you'd use."

"I can do you a portrait in charcoal. We'd have to fix it afterward so it wouldn't smear, but it's the best I can offer. Besides, I can't think of any way to do any harm with them, even if I had a mind to, which I don't. Please: fix me a willow branch of charcoal, burn it and sharpen it like I told you, and then get some plain white paper from the butcher shop. If you'll do that, you have my word that I'll do you the finest portrait I can."

"Would you have time to do one?"

"I have nothing but time."

"Well, I can't let Eddie come back and pose for you. It wouldn't be right. And my other boy, Georgie, he's too little to be hanging around a jail, even if his mama works here." That was true enough, but in a corner of my mind I pictured the newspaper headlines if those journalist vultures got hold of the tale: SHERIFF'S SONS POSE FOR CONDEMNED KILLER. No picture was worth that kind of public humiliation.

He thought about it for a moment. "I could work from a snapshot, you know. In fact, it might be easier to do it that way than to try to get two squirming little boys to sit still."

"Have you ever done a picture from a photograph?"

"Sure. A lot of times, when I was painting murals for the government, I had to rely on the illustrations in books, because the real people and buildings I needed to depict were long gone. I'm used to working that way. You can get me a picture of your boys, can't you?"

I couldn't think of anything wrong with that plan. Paper, a burnt stick of charcoal, and a snapshot seemed little enough to ask. I'd be glad of a real portrait of Eddie and George, and I thought it might be a kindness to give the poor man something to do, to take his mind off what was to come. I wouldn't want to be beholden to him, of course, but maybe I could bring him some pie or a candy bar to thank him for his trouble. He wouldn't have any use for money anymore. "I'll think on it," I told him. "But if I can see my way clear to letting you do this, I'd be grateful to have a picture of my sons. You're kind to offer."

He nodded. "It'll be my legacy, I guess. All I want is to be remembered for something besides . . . well, besides what happened up on The Hawk's Wing."

"I wish you'd tell me why you did it. Just so I'd know."

"You wouldn't understand."

"You don't seem like the kind of man who would do such a cruel thing."

He nodded. "I wouldn't have thought so either."

The best picture I had of the boys was the one in the wooden dime store frame on the desk in my office. It was just a family snapshot, but I was partial to it. It was a clear fall day, and the two of them were sitting on the log out behind the house. Eddie was leaning back a little on the log with his arms around Georgie; both of them were dressed in their church clothes and grinning crinkled smiles up at the camera—the kind of smiles people put on when they're having their picture taken so that later you have no idea whether they were happy or not. Albert had taken that picture last fall, and I looked at it for a moment, trying to remember the whole scene: the red and gold oak leaves in the woods behind the log, Albert holding the camera and hollering for the boys to smile, and me standing near the back steps, waving to try to make Georgie look at the camera. But that image in my head was just as much of a picture as the one in the frame. I had taken a picture with my mind's eye, and now it was just as frozen as a snapshot, not a real living memory at all anymore.

I picked up the framed photo, intending to take it back to Lonnie Varden in the cell, when I suddenly found myself looking at it as a law officer instead of as a widowed mother wanting a memento of her children. Both the wooden frame and the thin glass panel could be broken into sharp jagged pieces and used as weapons. I stiffened at the thought. Maybe he hadn't made the suggestion with that idea in mind, but it might very well occur to him sooner or later. Who would want to die at the end of a rope in front of a jeering crowd if there was another way out? Suicide or escape—maybe he wouldn't even care which. But sorry for him or not, I couldn't let it happen under my watch.

Maybe instead of offering to do me a kindness, the prisoner had been trying to trick me into giving him something he could use to cut his own throat, or to hold against the throat of a deputy and force his way out of jail. Lonnie Varden hadn't seemed so treacherous, or I wouldn't have agreed in the first place, but I had to keep telling myself that this wasn't like meeting strangers in church. Almost everybody I met in here would be dangerous in one form or another, and more lives than mine depended on my remembering that. Even the drunks and the petty thieves we usually arrested had tempers or were capable of lashing out in fear. This man hadn't seemed like the sort of monster who could throw an unsuspecting woman off a cliff, either. What did I know about monsters anyway? One time I had heard a preacher say that Satan had been the most beautiful of all God's angels. Or maybe, given the right circumstances, there is a minute in everybody's life when they could be a monster.

I kept thinking it over, because of how bad I wanted a portrait of my sons and knowing this was likely to be the only chance I'd ever have to get one. Lonnie Varden may have been a bad man, but he was a good artist, and it would be a shame to waste that God-given talent while he was still alive to use it. I decided to take the photograph out of the frame and give that to him instead. It was only a piece of coated paper. And the butcher's paper and charcoal were harmless enough, as far as I could tell. I'd tell the deputies to keep a closer eye on him while he worked. He must not be allowed to have cigarettes either. Paper burns.

If the prisoner meant to do me a kindness or to distract himself from what was to come, then I was determined to give him that chance as long as I could do so without endangering anybody. I turned over the frame and pushed the little clasp against the cardboard backing that held it in place. When the cardboard slid away, I picked up the picture of the boys, but as I did so, I found another photo that had been tucked behind it: a studio portrait of a smirking woman with crinkly bleached blond hair and a gherkin nose poking out from between plump rouged cheeks. It was a sepia picture, but the photographer had touched it up by reddening the lips and adding a bright-green tint to the eyes. I had seen movie star pictures tarted up like that, but this was a local job: all the flashy color in the world couldn't make a starlet out of that homely face.

I had never seen that photograph before. But I had seen the face. That piggy-eyed woman was the one who had come up to me at the funeral to tell me how sorry she was about Albert's passing. I had wondered about it at the time. Something about it hadn't seemed right. There were too many other things going on back then for me to dwell on the matter, but I had not quite forgotten it. She hadn't talked as if she was mourning the loss of the sheriff or some friend of the family. She had called my husband "Albert," like whatever connection they had was just between the two of them. She was the waitress at the diner. I wasn't thinking anything in particular when I turned over the photograph, but my hands were shaking.

In a loopy pencil scrawl on the back she had written, *"To my handsome sweetest pal—Ain't we got fun? Shelley."*

I guess that picture frame had been a weapon after all.

chapter sixteen

It's funny how something that has always been true changes everything just because you find out about it. For a long time to come I would be questioning every memory I had, trying to second-guess everything he ever said or did. I had a lot of things to think about that afternoon. I might be mulling over some of them for as long as I lived, and the anger in my gut was a banked fire. Maybe it was a good thing that right then I didn't have much time for thinking. I had all the planning of the execution to focus on, but that was just substituting the state's anger for mine.

I was walking home so wrapped up in my thoughts that I scarcely knew where I was. I stopped beside the creek and stared down into the water, not really seeing it at all, but at some point I remembered Eddie and George, who would be wanting supper, and that reminded me that the decision about the portrait of the boys wasn't something I could postpone for long. Lonnie Varden needed materials to work with.

The butcher paper had been easy enough to acquire. I had slipped out earlier in the afternoon, before the shop closed, bought six yards of it for fifteen cents, and set it on my desk to give to the prisoner when I got his drawing materials. Obtaining the charcoal wouldn't be so easy.

This time of year it stayed light until past eight, so I had taken longer than usual going home from work, because I had to sort out everything in my mind, and I wanted to be done crying before I got home to George and Eddie. I had made it through the entire afternoon at work without shedding a single tear, and as angry as I felt now, any tears I did shed would probably sizzle against my cheeks.

After I found the picture behind the photo of my boys, I searched every inch of that office: desk drawers, folders in the filing cabinet, the pages of the few books on the shelf. My first thought had been to go storming out of the office with the picture of the blond sow and wave it in the face of the nearest deputy. Surely one of them knew something, but of course they'd never admit that to me. I did stay calm enough to realize that confronting them about this would make me look weak and foolish. I don't know what good I thought the knowledge would do me; after all, Albert had been dead for months now, but I just wanted to know how bad it was. Once when I was lifting folders out of the filing cabinet, I caught sight of that scar on my wrist, and I wished there were some way I could cauterize this present wound to keep it from contaminating me, because I knew that what I had just learned about Albert was going to poison my memories of all our years together. I had thought he was the kindest, most honest, most disciplined person I knew, but now I wondered if I had ever known him at all. Maybe all that calm silence that I took for strength was just discontent that he couldn't put into words.

I found what I was looking for, finally, in a blue tobacco tin at the back of the middle drawer of the file cabinet in the sheriff's private office. I set it on the desk and stared at it for a few minutes before I opened it, because I knew that once I found out what was inside, I would lose something I could never get back.

It was a long afternoon. I tried to listen while people complained about drunken delinquents, damaged fences, and noisy neighbors. "We'll do what we can," I kept saying, writing down all the particulars of the complaints, but my thoughts were mostly elsewhere. Suddenly my life seemed to divide into before I found the picture and after, just as before the line had fallen at the point of Albert's death. A bitter thought occurred to me: maybe this new knowing would make me a better sheriff. No longer would I feel inclined to pity people or give them the benefit of the doubt. Never again would I trust anybody.

Heading home that evening, thoughts of Albert kept circling in my mind, but once I reached the place where the path paralleled the creek and remembered what Lonnie Varden had told me about making charcoal, I knew that getting that chore done was the cleanest and calmest notion I'd had all afternoon. I'd be better off finding something to keep myself busy, rather than brooding on the unalterable past. I walked on to the part of the creek where the willows grew, and threaded my way under the low limbs of the largest tree. The limbs themselves were the size of the trunks of other trees—pines and poplars. Balancing myself against the stoutest limb, as near to the water's edge as I dared, I hacked off a sturdy willow branch with Albert's old—with *my*—pocket knife. It wasn't an easy job. By the time I finished it was nearly dusk. I should have gone home and come back with an ax, but there wasn't enough daylight left for that. At last I managed to weaken the branch enough with the knife to break off a foot-long piece.

I carried it home, and while I was fixing supper, I stuck the end of that branch into the fire in the woodstove. When I judged it was burnt enough, I left it sitting in a dry pan on the top of the stove to cool.

That night after I put the boys to bed I stood for a long time looking in the bedroom mirror, thinking again about what I had found that afternoon. What had Albert seen when he looked at me? I saw a pale, plain face, and mouse-brown hair pulled back in a knot at the nape of my neck, which is how married ladies wore their hair up home. Hair curlers and beauty shop permanents were popular here in town, but they were mostly for the wives of the town leaders—and maybe for sluts, I thought, remembering the frizzy-haired blonde painted up like a Kewpie doll. I never did use makeup like the town ladies did, but I was well over thirty now, and maybe I should have. Little girls—look at a four-year-old—have naturally red lips, a pinkish bloom on their cheeks, and a blue haze on their eyelids, but as little girls get older, all that color fades away, or just wears away with life and chores and hardship. I reckon older women paint their faces to try to put back that color that nature gives to little girls, but rouge and lipstick can't give you back what you lost, and it can't stop time. Maybe the pretense was enough, though.

I did wonder what Albert had seen in that waitress. She was younger than me by maybe half a dozen years, but she was a plump, painted, trashy sort of woman who talked too much and knew too little. I wished I could ask him, *Why her?* He set such a store by being a respected civic leader, and by all the trappings of gentility, with his insistence on cloth napkins and serving bowls at every meal. Wouldn't he have been ashamed to go parading around with that uncouth sow on his arm? Wouldn't divorce have made a scandal even here in town? I don't suppose he had intended any of that to happen, though. Albert was a middle-aged man who suddenly thought he had become important, and I reckon it went to his head. He got to thinking he was entitled to anything people offered him for free, be it a slab of pie at the diner or the wet favors of a moon-faced trollop.

I wondered what I would have done about it if he had lived, and for the boys' sake I thought it might be just as well that he hadn't.

I hadn't seen the doctor since the week Albert died, and I didn't need him now on account of anybody being sick, but when I told him why I did need to see him, he came along to the office readily enough. Maybe he wasn't as busy in the summertime, when people stopped coming down with winter ailments. It was high season for farming, though, so maybe the accidents made up the slack. I hated to bother him, but for the kind of advice I needed, there wasn't anybody else around here to ask.

He settled himself in the second chair in my office, and looked me over with a practiced eye. "You look thinner, Mrs. Robbins. Sleeping all right?"

I tried to smile. "I'm not the patient—just the sheriff. So I need to ask you for some advice. You know I have to hang a man next week."

He nodded. "Everybody from here to Timbuktu knows that. It's a barbarous thing, a hanging. We show more mercy toward farm animals when we put them down."

"I don't disagree with you, sir, but it's the state's law, and I am sworn to carry it out. And for that I'd be grateful for some help."

"Well, I don't see how I can be of any help to you. You were speaking of sworn duty just now. When I became a doctor I took an oath, too, and mine begins, *'First do no harm.'*"

"I know. I thought about that, and I figure if you can keep a man from having to endure any unnecessary suffering, that would count as *doing no harm*, wouldn't it?"

He considered it. "I suppose it would. Though I confess I was hoping that all you wanted from me was a bottle of medicine to help you sleep, because I know this execution must be preying on your mind. But what kind of help are you asking for?"

"One of my deputies says there's rules about hanging somebody. I mean, ways to make sure the end comes quick and clean. There may be books about that somewhere, but there aren't any around here. I just thought that since you studied the human body, you might know things that would help me. I've heard terrible stories—about prisoners having their heads come off, or going straight through the trapdoor and touching the ground, so that bystanders have to shovel the ground out from under their feet so they have a few inches of clearance . . ."

"To strangle in." He scowled. "Yes. If anything could make a hanging more barbaric it would be that."

"It's a public execution, too."

He shuddered. "I know. I'll have to be on hand to pronounce the poor devil dead. And since you'll leave him hanging for a quarter of an hour before you cut him down, I hope to God he is."

"There isn't much I can do about that, Doctor, but I want him to die with as much dignity as I can manage. It's like you said: even animals are not treated as cruelly as that. So, as best you can, would you please tell me what I need to know so that I can give that man a merciful exit from this world?"

He was quiet for a minute or two, turning the idea over in his mind. Finally, he reached into his jacket pocket and pulled out a fountain pen. "Give me a piece of paper. I need to show you how to find the carotid artery."

I wasn't glad to see Henry and Elva that evening, but at least they weren't newspaper reporters. I was busy doing the supper dishes when there was a knock at the front door. Before I could call out to warn the boys not to answer it, I heard Georgie shout, "Uncle Henry!" I slapped the dishrag against the side of the dish pan. Too late! I would have to give both boys a talking to as soon as possible, before they turned the parlor into a lounge for newspapermen. The deputies had been telling strangers that I lived on a farm six miles out of town, which deterred most of the reporters, but sooner or later one of them would question some unwary citizen who would tell them where I really lived. Well, at least they hadn't found me yet.

I smoothed down my apron—no point in taking it off just for them—and headed them off in the hall, motioning for them to go into the parlor. Elva sat down on the sofa with Georgie doing his best to crawl into her lap, but Henry went straight to Albert's old Chesterfield chair by the radio and sat down in it as if he owned it. Maybe I wouldn't have let that pass before, but now it didn't seem to matter much. It was just a chair.

I said good evening and sat down at the end of the sofa away from Elva and waited to see what they had come about, because Henry wouldn't make a trip to town just to pay a social call.

Henry looked around, and I wondered if he was looking for signs that I was spending money on new household goods or if he was just checking to see how much I was neglecting my housecleaning chores. Eddie had come in from the bedroom, where he had been reading a Tarzan book, but right away he picked up on the tension in the room, so instead of speaking, he nodded solemnly at his aunt and uncle and slipped down on the floor beside the sofa. Henry nodded back and kept looking around the room. I didn't let on that he annoyed me, though, and I didn't let my nervousness rush me into speech.

After a few more moments of heavy silence, Henry said, "Well, Ellendor, I hear you're still doing the job of county sheriff."

"I'm doing fine, thank you, Henry."

"I expect you're finding it more complicated than you bargained for, though."

"How so?"

Elva looked at me in amazement. "*How so?* Why, the execution, Ellie! People are talking about it day and night. It has even been in the newspaper. Our sister-in-law is actually going to hang some poor man. We hardly know what to say to people."

"Well, you might explain to them that I'm the one doing the hanging, and not the one being hanged." I didn't expect them to be amused by this, and they weren't. I tried again. "Look, I'm doing a good job, as far as I can tell, and I'm taking care of my sons without anybody's help."

Henry leaned forward with that jaw-jutting look of his that meant absolute stubbornness. "That's just it, Ellendor. We have come to offer you some help."

"Really, Henry? What do you propose to do? Carry out the hanging to spare me from having to do it?"

"Me? Why I have to get the Baileys to kill our hogs for us come fall. I am certainly incapable of killing a human being. But, Elva can say what she likes, I'm impressed that you have enough sand to do a man's job and carry through with it even when it turns out to be more than you bargained for. And if anybody dares to complain about it to my face, that's what I'll tell them. No, I'm not offering to do the hanging for you. The help we came to give you is to take George and Eddie back to the farm until all this is over."

We had all forgotten that Eddie was there, sitting quietly on the floor next to the sofa, but when Henry said that, he sprang to his feet, looking from one of us to the other. "No! I don't want to leave town and miss the hanging!"

Henry went on as if he hadn't spoken. "After all, it is summertime. He won't be missing school, and with all the hoopla there is here in town—reporters and whatnot—you might be glad to have one less thing to worry about."

I had been all set to say no to whatever tomfool notion Henry had come to see me about, but as soon as I thought about what he was suggesting, I wondered why I hadn't thought of it myself. I didn't want my children at that execution. I didn't want anybody's children to be there. And the longer Eddie stayed in town, the more likely it was that some enterprising reporter would ferret him out and concoct some kind of fanciful story about the boy whose mama was the hangman. I didn't want him put through that. It occurred to me that a few weeks ago I would have asked myself what Albert would have wanted me to do. In fact, that question would have occurred to me before anything else. But now, I didn't give a fig for Albert's wishes. I did worry, though, that there might be a catch to his brother's new generosity.

"This isn't a trick, is it, Henry?"

"To take the boys away from you for good?" He shook his head. "You've proved that you don't need anybody's help to take care of them, and I reckon Albert wanted them to get town schooling, or he wouldn't have moved here in the first place. Now if they wanted to stay up on the farm with us, that'd be different."

"But we don't," said Eddie.

Neither of them really wanted to go, either, though for different reasons. Georgie was too young to understand about the execution; he just didn't want to leave his mama, but I didn't give either of them any choice in the matter. I packed their clothes and their favorite toys—Georgie's red fire truck, of course—in a flour sack, and gave Eddie fifteen cents pocket money to lessen the disappointment of having to leave. They were better off away from town until all this was over, and, although I would miss them, I wasn't sorry to have one less thing to worry about in a week that already held too much for me to bear.

"Come see us when you can," said Henry, as they headed out the door.

"When it's all over," I said.

The next morning when I got to the office, Galen told me that Lonnie Varden was sleeping, so I decided not to disturb him. Roy or Falcon could give him the paper and charcoal when they delivered the prisoner's breakfast. That morning the execution began to seem more real, because I was summoned to inspect the tangible proof of it.

"Sam Lidaker wants to see you, Sheriff." Falcon Wallace was hovering in the doorway to my little office. The door had been pushed closed, but not shut altogether, and he was probably wondering whether or not he should have knocked.

I wasn't all that busy, though. I was sifting through the pile of letters from this morning's mail, in case there should happen to be some correspondence mixed in there that was actually worth reading. "Who is Sam Lidaker?" I murmured.

"He's the carpenter that the county hired to build the gallows. I think you must have spoken to him when he started on the job."

I remembered now. When we found out that the hanging was going to take place here, I had a whole brood of worries pecking at my heels—jail security for the prisoner, to keep him *in* and a lynch mob *out*; obnoxious city reporters; the execution process itself—and the construction of the scaffold itself seemed to me to be the least of them. Vernon Johnson had given us the name of several local builders and named the sum that we would be authorized to pay for the job of erecting a trapdoor platform scaffold. Roy Phillips contacted the candidates for the job, and of the three carpenters who submitted bids, Sam Lidaker's estimate was the lowest. I had met him for a couple of minutes when he stopped by the office to officially accept the job and sign the contract, but the encounter had been so brief I had nearly forgotten it. After the site had been selected, Mr. Lidaker got on with his noisy assignment and troubled us only with his hammering, not with his presence.

Now he was back, and I wondered why.

A few moments later Falcon ushered him and went back to fielding calls at the reception desk.

"Afternoon, ma'am." Sam Lidaker was a short, bandy-legged fellow with a mop of tight red curls and a pleasant expression that I'd have expected to see on someone who was building kitchen shelves, not a soon-to-be-used scaffold. I wondered if he was planning to attend to admire his handiwork. "I stopped by to tell you that we're purt near finished building your contraption, and I was hoping you had time to go over and take a look at it."

I wasn't anxious to get a close look at the gallows until I had to.

"I'm sure you're doing a fine job, Mr. Lidaker. My duties here are keeping me busy right now."

He nodded. "That's to be expected, but I think you need to take the time to go and look at the structure now, and to make sure you know how it operates. You don't want to wait until five thousand people are standing there watching your every move before you try to make the thing work."

He had a point. Bad enough that I had only been sheriff for a couple of months, and that I'd be doing this execution in front of a gaping mob and a passel of photographers—if I got to the crucial moment and was unable to get the mechanism to work it would be a disaster. Worse, it would mean more suffering for the wretched man appointed to die.

"Will you show me how it works, Mr. Lidaker?"

"That's what I came for, ma'am. After all, if you had difficulty in operating the contraption, it would make me look bad, like I hadn't constructed it right. Come on over there now, and I'll show you how it works."

I saw the sense in what he said, and although the thought of the gallows made me shudder, I knew I ought to see it; at least the walk to the construction site would keep me from having to read any more offers of help from gallant would-be executioners. I was mortally tired of wading through those. I followed Sam Lidaker around the side of the sheriff's office and into the street behind it.

"It wasn't too all-fired difficult," the carpenter was saying. "Except for somebody's tomfool notion to make the thing twenty feet high."

"I think they're expecting a big crowd," I murmured. "They want to make sure that everyone can see the . . . the *proceedings* so that there won't be any pushing and shoving among the spectators. There are likely to be some drunks around, and we don't want to give them any excuse to start a fight. A tall scaffold means that nobody should have to push and shove to get a good view."

"I'm mindful of that, but you need to be all the more careful yourself on account of it. There you'll be on that high platform with a prisoner, who may very well squirm and fight, trying to keep anybody from putting the rope around his neck. In his place, I know *I* would. I worry that if there's a struggle, somebody could get knocked off the platform by accident, and like as not that would kill them just as fast as the rope will kill the prisoner."

I thought about it. "Can you put a wooden railing at waist height around the scaffold?"

"Sure can. Cost you another three dollars, though, for the wood and the labor."

"Do it. Tell them it's on my say-so."

The gallows was constructed of new-milled yellow pine, so recently planed that it glowed in the sunshine, and when I got close to it I detected the sweet smell of pine resin. I wondered if the lumber had come from the sawmill where Lonnie Varden had worked, and if the foreman who fired him had taken a special pleasure in knowing what that wood would be used for. The structure, a high raised platform with steep steps at one side, sat in the red clay of an empty lot, towering above a row of three-room shacks behind it—not a pleasant view for the occupants, but the gallows would be gone a day or two after the hanging, maybe sooner, if the spectators decided to hack it apart for souvenirs. I would be glad when it was over.

"We put in thirteen steps according to custom, ma'am." He took a long look at me, his eyes coming to rest at my hemline. "If you plan to wear a dress and high heels for the occasion, then see that you watch yourself going up and down those steps. It's a long way to fall. I hear tell that the fellow you're a-hanging has already caused one woman to fall to her death. Wouldn't want to see him take out another."

He said this bit of gallows humor so smoothly that I knew it had become his standard jest about the execution. Like as not, the phrase would appear in some newspaper sooner or later.

He touched my elbow and steered me into the space beneath the platform. "What I wanted to show you in particular, though, was the mechanism itself. The trapdoor, that is."

From a distance, the scaffold might have been a porch, and the crosspiece mounted above it could have held a glider or a hammock—or perhaps that was just me trying to see things on a woman's terms, instead of facing the fact that I was looking at a killing device. We were standing directly beneath the platform, under an opening that looked about three feet square.

"The trapdoor," said Mr. Lidaker. "We cut out the square right below the crosspiece of the scaffold. We'll go up there directly and you can see it up close. The gallows is two square-cut posts, nine feet high, with a six-foot crosspiece set between them. In the middle of the crosspiece we cut a deep notch. That's where the rope goes. Are you with me so far?"

I nodded. I could see the crosspiece through the open trapdoor beneath it, but I was trying to look past it at the patch of blue sky beyond.

"Now the whole shebang depends on that trapdoor up there working the way it's supposed to. It has to be strong enough to stand on, and easy to open when the time is right. We put strong steel hinges on one side of the trap, and across from them there's a ratchet attached to a lever—you can see it off to the left—it's that knee-high rod sticking straight up beside the trap."

"I need to make sure I can pull that lever so the trapdoor will open, don't I?"

"That's what we need to know. And if it takes too much strength for you to manage, why then we'll have to consider the alternatives."

I wished he had put hand railings on the steps, but since they were only going to be used once, barring practice drops, it probably wasn't worth the trouble or the expense to alter them. I'd just have to be very careful when I climbed them. The carpenter gestured for me to go up first, "so's if you fall, I can catch you," he explained.

Once at the top, I leaned against one of the support posts for balance and looked out over the rooftops to the sprawl of green mountains beyond. The scenery was better at the Robbins farm, but I had been pent up in town for so long now that the sight of something besides buildings felt like the letting go of a long-held breath.

"Now, ma'am, you need to take care not to step on the trapdoor yourself. It was built to hold twice your weight, at least, but there's no point in taking chances, is there?" He guided me around the upright and put me next to the lever.

I had to stoop just a bit to touch the iron rod. It was warm from the sunshine, and I nearly jerked my hand away as if it were a living thing. "I just pull this?"

Mr. Lidaker raised a forefinger for caution. "All in good time. First you want to make sure that the prisoner's hands are secured behind his back—so's he doesn't try to clutch at the rope, as anybody would. Then someone must tie a rope around his legs below the knees to keep him from kicking out when he drops. The last thing—after he's been offered a chance to say any last words—is that a black hood is placed over the condemned man's head."

I shivered. "Yes. I wouldn't want strangers to see my death throes."

"Well, that's one way of looking at it, but I think it's mostly out of consideration for the crowd. They say the face of a hanged man is a dreadful sight to behold: bulging eyes, tongue stuck out. You wouldn't want folks to have to look on that."

"If they're brazen enough to come to an execution, then I'm not concerned with any unpleasantness they may see, but I'll grant you the hood is a good idea. Where do we get one?"

He shrugged. "I don't reckon there's all that much demand for them. Not much to it. About half a yard of black cotton cloth with eye holes cut in it."

"Thank you. I'll take care of it. But there is one more bit of carpentry that I need you to do, at the county's expense, of course."

"Yes, ma'am?"

"Build a coffin. Just a simple pine box will do."

He nodded. "That's all a man needs."

"It's a bad business, Mrs. Robbins." Rev. McKee shook his head sadly. "I don't say that the poor fellow shouldn't have to answer for his sins, but this business of making his death a public spectacle puts me in mind of the Roman Coliseum."

I nodded. "I can't say I'm in favor of it myself, sir."

I was ticking off things on my chore list to be accomplished before the execution, and when I got to the part about religious services for the prisoner, I decided to ask my own minister to provide them. Lonnie Varden had shown no interest at all in the proceedings, and he probably would have preferred to have no minister at all, but tradition required it.

I found Rev. McKee in an old straw hat and overalls, tending to the tomato plants in the backyard of the parsonage. When I told him my business would not take up much of his time, he went on weeding as we talked, while I settled myself on an upturned wooden bucket and watched. The sun had turned Rev. McKee's bald spot quite pink, and his work clothes were smeared with red clay, but he hadn't let the circumstances impair his dignity.

"I'm sorry that the state requires a public execution, sir, but surely you agree with me that the condemned man is entitled to spiritual counsel?"

"Of course he is. Everyone is. If he repents, his soul can be saved, even though his earthly body is forfeit."

"He hasn't asked for any minister in particular, so I thought seeing as how Albert and I were in your congregation, I'd ask if you'd oblige him."

"It is my Christian duty to minister to anyone in need, Miz Robbins, but I confess that it troubles me that the state's executioner should be a woman."

"I can't help that, sir. I took an oath," and for good measure I added, "before God."

"I suppose you did. And I would say that by and large you have discharged your duties well."

"Thank you."

"That boy you brought to me—Davis Howell—he and his sister are settled with a nice family out on Brummett's Creek. I'm glad you were able to get help for them."

"Anybody would have done the same," I said, hoping that was true. I was glad to know that those children's lives no longer depended on what they could find in trash bins. But carrying out the execution was as much a part of my job as helping those in need, and I was mindful of that.

Rev. McKee spent a couple of minutes picking bugs off the tomato leaves, while he thought things over. Finally he said, "I suppose somebody has to do it. The execution will go forward whether I am there or not."

"That's true, sir. And I know the prisoner will be in good hands with you."

He mopped his brow with a bandana. "I'll do my best." He pulled a big ripe tomato off the nearest plant and passed it to me. "Apprise me of the particulars when you have worked them out."

chapter seventeen

We were now a day and a half away from the execution and already my hands were shaking. I wondered what they would do if I was too sick to go through with it. I sat in my office, trying to figure out how to cope with everything, and flinching every time the phone rang. I reached for the spoon to stir my coffee, and my hand was shaking so much that the spoon clattered to the floor. Seeing that fallen spoon at my feet made me remember Eunice Greer and her peculiar story about the Dumb Supper. I hoped she wasn't around trying to tell it to any of the reporters, but I had promised to pass the story along to Lonnie Varden, and there wasn't much time left to do that.

I went to the cell, hoping to find the prisoner calmer than I was. He wasn't sleeping much these days, but aside from being thinner than before, he seemed to be doing as well as could be expected. He was kneeling on the floor of the cell, hunched over the roll of butcher paper, staring at the images that were beginning to take shape. I couldn't tell much about the picture yet. He had sketched in the shapes of the boys' faces, and the upper part of their bodies, but aside from that only the eyes looked real, but I could tell he hadn't finished with them yet. Eyes must be the hardest thing to get right in a portrait. They're what make a person who they are, I think.

When he saw me, he rocked back on his haunches and held up the stub of charcoal. "It should last me long enough to finish this. The charcoal point keeps getting dull, but I found that by putting it up against the cinderblock wall and spinning it, I can get it shaped into the tapered point I need to make a fine line."

"Well, I'm glad you can get it to work like that, because I couldn't let you have a knife to sharpen it with. I could get you another piece if you need it, though. That willow tree isn't far from my house."

"It looks like this one is going to last—well, I guess it'll last," he laughed a little, trying to sound unconcerned, "longer than I will, I suppose, but this handkerchief I'm using is getting so dirty it's useless. I use it to smudge the lines for lightening and blending effects, so I can't do much without it. I'll need to swap it for a clean one pretty soon. You take this one away and rinse it out, and bring me a fresh one, if you have one about."

"I'll do that." Through the bars he handed me the charcoal-smeared scrap of linen. I was going to stuff it in my pocket, but it was so dirty I just balled it up in my fist for the time being. I could rinse it in the bathroom sink and let it dry on the windowsill. "There's a box of my late husband's handkerchiefs in the top drawer of the desk here."

"You don't mind me using your husband's handkerchiefs?"

I shrugged. "I was thinking about burning them." He looked at me sharply when I said that, but I didn't feel like talking about it. "Anyway, I'll see that you get those clean handkerchiefs. How are you feeling?"

Perhaps it seemed odd to be concerned about how a man was feeling when you were the one who had the job of killing him within a day or so, but, after all, as I had been trying to explain to a raft of people lately, *killing* was the wrong word, because there was no malice at all in it, nothing personal, and his death was not a decision I had made. It was like being a soldier in a war: carrying out orders. There was at least one person in this world who I could have killed with cold delight for my own satisfaction, but that person was not Lonnie Varden. Carrying out his death sentence was simply the most terrible part of a job I had sworn to do to the best of my ability, and I had to do it. But if I could make the man's final days peaceful and free of suffering, I would. There seemed to be no law against doing that.

"How am I feeling, Sheriff?" He was flipping the stub of charcoal idly between his fingers, and I made a mental note to send back a pan of water so that he could clean himself up before suppertime. "I am about two quarts shy of whisky, if you could manage to come up with a jug or two."

"I can't oblige you there, but you are entitled to a last meal, and while I'm here I could take your order for that. Have you given it any thought?"

"Every once in a while it crossed my mind. I doubt I'll be able to eat much of it, knowing what's to come, but I'll bet that's the kind of thing reporters ask people about, isn't it?"

"It might be. I steer clear of them whenever I can."

"I wonder what they'd expect me to ask for as my last supper? Lobster and caviar, to show that I had spent some time as a city slicker, or beans and cornbread, in memory of my *rustic boyhood*?" He said that last part in a mocking tone, and I figured he was repeating the phrase from some newspaper article written about him during the trial.

"I think you ought to please yourself. Like as not, the reporters will just make up whatever they want to write about your last meal, anyway. People tell me they've read outlandish things in the city newspapers that I'm supposed to have said, and those stories were written by reporters I wouldn't know from Adam's off ox."

He smiled. "Good. I'll order what I want, and then you can lie to them about what it was. Tell 'em I had roasted giraffe, truffles, and candied kumquats. What is a kumquat, anyhow?"

"I have no earthly idea, Mr. Varden. I doubt if either one of us will ever find out. But I don't think they sell them around here, so I hope you don't try to order any."

"Well, I haven't reached any decisions yet. I know I have to request something you can get here in town. You won't be sending off to Boston for fresh lobster. 'Course, I'd be happy to wait on that."

"Wouldn't be fresh by the time it got here, anyhow," I said, ignoring his gallows humor about postponing the execution. Was his jauntiness intended to comfort me or himself?

"Yeah. Spoiled lobster would probably kill me faster than the rope would. Wonder if that would be a worse way to go?" He considered it. "Well, never mind. It's not on the bill of fare. How about you, Sheriff? What would you want for your last meal?"

I didn't have to think it over. "Fried chicken. A breast and both drumsticks all to myself. When I was little, my daddy and older brothers got all the best pieces, and then when I got grown, I always gave the breast pieces to my husband and the drumsticks to our sons. Just once in my life I'd like to have the good pieces all to myself, instead of making do with the wings, the neck, and the gizzard."

"Well, I may make do with a hamburger and a milkshake from the diner. Every now and then I get to craving those."

I stiffened when he said *diner*, but I hoped he hadn't noticed. "Well, you give it some more thought, Mr. Varden. What's more important is who you'd like as your minister. I've already requested a pastor to officiate at the execution, but I can change that if you have a preference. Are you a Baptist or a Methodist, or what? Do you belong to a church, and have a pastor who'd come and see you through your last hours?"

He shook his head. "I'm not particular. Repentance is between me and the Lord, not for public consumption. But you have to provide a preacher to solemnize my final moments?"

"It's customary. A doctor to officially pronounce you dead, and a minister to pray for your soul. I asked the minister of my church."

"That'll do. Ordinarily I object to long-winded ministers, but maybe in this case I won't mind so much." He shrugged. "It strikes me as useless, though, for getting me salvation, and of doubtful value as a comfort to my mind, but I'll put up with it. Anything else?"

I decided it was time to deliver Eunice Greer's peculiar message. "I promised somebody I'd tell you something. It may not make a lot of sense, but the lady seemed pretty set on having you told, anyhow. She thinks it may bring you some comfort, I suppose."

He looked wary. "This lady you're talking about—what's her name?"

"Miss Eunice Greer. She was friends with your wife back when they were growing up."

He looked puzzled, but maybe a little relieved too. "I don't believe I know her."

"No. She may have been at your wedding, but she didn't think you'd remember her. She wanted me to tell you about something that happened years ago when your wife was a young girl. She and a group of her friends held a Dumb Supper one night—just for a joke, mostly. Do you know about that old ritual?"

He shrugged. "Heard of it. A bunch of silly girls cook a dinner in an abandoned house and do everything backward, in hopes of finding out who they'll marry one day."

"That's right. It's a game now, but I think that a long time ago it was something more serious."

"So, what happened at this Dumb Supper? I know I wasn't there. Did Celia see somebody other than me?"

"Miss Greer didn't say anything about that. What she was concerned about was that your wife broke the rules of the ritual and didn't tell anybody."

"Broke the rules? What rules?"

"Well, the custom is that you have to do everything backward, as you said, and never face the table while you're setting the places or serving the food. You back up toward the table and keep your hands behind your back."

"That must be awkward, but so what?"

"Apparently, your wife dropped a knife while she was setting the table, and when she went to put it back in place, she accidentally turned around and faced the table. But instead of stopping the ritual, she just played along for the rest of the evening without telling anybody."

"Okay, so? What happened then?"

"Well, apparently nothing. That is, until years later when she got married and—and—"

"And her husband killed her." He sighed and shook his head. "Well, that's a daisy of a story. Do you reckon that jury over in Knoxville would have bought it? *Modern Woman Killed by Ancient Mountain Curse.*"

"No. I don't reckon they would have believed a word of it. I'm not even sure Miss Greer herself believed it was the cause of your wife's death, but she was most particular about you being told. I believe she thought you might find some comfort in knowing that there may have been reasons beyond your control for whatever happened."

"No. I don't believe in such things, and, even if I did, it seems hard lines on poor Celia to blame her for her own murder, though it would be nice to think I had some excuse for what I did, other than lust and fear. But if you see the lady again, tell her I thanked her for her concern."

I nodded. The conversation had set me to thinking about his dead wife and wondering how it all came to pass. Killing her seemed so unnecessary. It wasn't as if he was stuck with her. Divorce isn't the unthinkable act it used to be, and they had no children to suffer the consequences of their separation.

"You could have just left her, you know."

He stiffened when I said that, and I squirmed a little. "I know it's none of my business, but I can't help but wonder. Especially lately. If you wanted to get away from her, you could have walked out, couldn't you?"

"I tried. After I got fired for being caught with Jonella, I thought I might hop a boxcar and get as far away as I could before Celia heard the news from somebody in the community, but I couldn't make up my mind to do it. Then I thought about taking a shotgun out to the shed and doing away with myself, but I pictured her finding my body and a mass of blood, all covered in flies. That wouldn't be easy on her either."

"And killing her was?"

"I didn't know what else to do. I thought that if she found out, it would hurt her more than she could bear, and I wanted to spare her that pain. I guess I figured it was like a mercy killing, like putting a sick dog out of its misery."

"It was a cruel way to die."

"I hope it wasn't. It couldn't have lasted more than a few seconds, and I think she would have blacked out almost at once."

"I don't think that matters. What troubles me is that your wife loved and trusted you, and that in the last moments of her life she knew that you wanted her dead. And maybe worse than that: *she didn't know why.*"

"I don't think I did want her dead, really. It's just that I would have done anything not to have to face her, to see the hurt in her eyes when I told her the truth."

"She might have forgiven you, you know."

He nodded. "I expect she would have. At least, I don't think she would have divorced me. But she trusted me so much. She thought I was brave and honest and honorable. Sometimes I could see myself through her eyes, and I knew that if she ever lost that illusion of me, it would be intolerable for both of us. I needed her to believe in me."

"I thought great artists were supposed to lead irregular lives: drinking and carousing and having mistresses."

"Neither one of us thought that painting a mural in a post office afforded me the right to act like a great artist. I worked in a sawmill, remember?"

"And you got fired from there because some slut tempted you. So why didn't you kill *her*, instead of your poor wife?"

He shook his head impatiently. "Because she didn't matter. Don't you see? She was nothing."

I guess I had to believe him. They say that the Great Plague of London was started by a diseased rat, so maybe things that are of themselves no-account can destroy much more than their own worth. Anyhow, I left it at that.

An hour later when I got time to go back and give the prisoner a clean handkerchief, I found him on the floor of his cell, still working with the burnt stub of willow. I craned my neck trying to see how the drawing was shaping up, but he was shielding part of it with the crook of his elbow. He nodded when he saw me and went on smudging a line he had just drawn. "I'd rather you wait and see it when it's finished. For effect."

"Have you given any thought about where you want to be buried?" We had only just thought of it. Roy said that penitentiaries bury their executed prisoners in unmarked graves somewhere on the grounds of the prison, but we had no place to bury anyone, and I had spent so much time thinking of the execution itself—of getting everything right—that I had no idea what we were supposed to do with the prisoner's remains once it was over.

When I asked him about a final resting place, a look of pain crossed his face. He put down the charcoal and sat back on his haunches. "Burial plans?"

"We need to know what to do after the execution. Have you made any arrangements?"

"I've spent so long now being told what to do that I hardly remember how to make any decisions on my own."

"Will someone claim the body?" I shivered a little to be talking about *the body* to the man whose body it was, but he didn't seem to notice.

He shook his head. "I parted ways with my family a long time ago, and they certainly don't want anything to do with me now. I can't blame them. I can't think of anybody who'd care about me, alive or dead, except—"

"Except your lady friend?"

"No. I never meant anything to her. I was going to say *except Celia*. My wife." He sighed. "I heard that her family took her away to be laid to rest. I don't even know where. They wouldn't let me out for the funeral, of course. I reckon they didn't think I'd care. And if I asked to be buried next to her, they'd laugh, wouldn't they?"

"If I were kin to your wife, I think I'd be wondering what *she* would have wanted."

"I guess there's no way of knowing that, is there? We thought we had years to make decisions about death. Strange, isn't it? Celia is the only one I think about now."

"Not the other one?" I tried not to sneer, I really did, but some of my anger toward Albert bled through.

He was looking at his drawing again. Frowning at the black line of a jaw on the butcher paper, he made another little smudge. "The other one? Well, only if I'm having a nightmare. Look where *she* got me."

I did sneer at that. "Men have been blaming women for their troubles ever since Adam ate the apple. He didn't have to accept the offer, and neither did you."

"Well, never mind about that, Madam Sheriff. Point taken. Blaming somebody else didn't get Adam off the hook in the Garden of Eden, and nothing's going to save me, either. You asked about plans for my burial. There aren't any. I guess none of us ever believes that we're really going to die. Oh, maybe old people do, but when you're still young and strong and pain free, it feels like you can go on forever."

"Well, your forever is hours away, so you need to decide on something."

"I don't guess it matters. I'm best forgotten. Just dig a hole somewhere in the woods and be done with it."

But he was still a human being, and he deserved to be buried like one. "I reckon I owe you something for this portrait you're doing of my boys, and I can only think of one way to pay that debt. I own a burial plot you can use."

He grinned up at me. " 'Cause you don't reckon *you'll* ever need it?"

"Well, I don't need it yet, and when I do I don't intend to be buried next to the man that's already lying there. You're two of a kind, you and him."

Neither of us said anything for a long minute. He kept staring at me, waiting for me to say something else, I guess. Finally he said, "You're talking about your husband? We're two of a kind? When did you find out?"

I took a deep breath. I had brought it up. Might as well answer him. "When I opened the picture frame on his desk to get the photo of the boys for you to use as a drawing model."

He sighed and shook his head. "Well, that's hard lines, you finding out when he's already dead and gone. He never had a chance to explain."

"I'm not interested in any explanations."

"I guess I have no right to tell you I'm sorry, since I'm guilty of the same thing."

"There seems to be a lot of it going around. And yes, he died—only not on account of her." I saw his expression change. "Pneumonia. You knew that's how I got this job."

"But you just found out about . . . You had no idea?"

"What does it matter now? He's gone."

"It matters enough for you to give away your cemetery plot."

"Shouldn't you be thinking about your troubles instead of mine, Mr. Varden?"

"Oh, my troubles will all be over tomorrow, and I'd just as soon not think about the hows and whys of it. If you feel like talking, I got nothing left but time. Not much of it, I guess, but you're welcome to what there is of it."

I hadn't ought to be talking about personal matters with a condemned prisoner, but who else was there? The deputies likely knew what was going on and were covering up. Besides, I'd look weak if I was to try to talk to them about my late husband's transgressions. I didn't have any women friends I'd confide in, either, and I don't know what help the preacher could offer, except maybe to assure me that Albert would have gone to hell for his unrepented sins, which would have been no comfort at all. But this man behind bars would take my secret to the grave, because he would be going there in one more day. I sat down in the hall, at a safe distance from the bars, with my back against the wall opposite the cell. He stayed on the floor and scooted close to the cell door to hear me, because I didn't want to take any chances on anybody eavesdropping.

"I think it was like you said. Not any star-crossed romance. He had taken up with a cheap frizzy-haired blonde who probably offered him a free sample, and he didn't see any reason to turn it down."

He held up a finger, nodding for me to go on. He would still be listening, but he was doing something else as well. He knelt down and tore a palm-sized strip from the end of the butcher paper, just above a practice sketch he had abandoned. He made a few quick, steady strokes on the scrap of paper, looked at it appraisingly for a moment, scribbled more marks, and handed it to me through the bars.

I nearly dropped the paper. In fewer than a dozen strokes, Lonnie Varden had conjured up the smirking face of Shelley Bonham: the small close-set eyes, the puffy cheeks, and the wide, dark lips curled in a sneering smile. I stared at him open-mouthed, and he grinned.

"I'm not a mind reader, Sheriff. But I am used to watching people, and when we were talking about last meals and I mentioned getting a cheeseburger from the diner, you looked like somebody had thrown a bowl of ice water in your face. And, as it happens, I was acquainted with Shelley myself, so it wasn't hard to match your diner reaction to that priceless description you made. What was it? *A cheap frizzy-haired blonde?* That's ol' Shel to the life, all right. The good time that was had by all."

"You—?"

"Oh, not lately. Not since I married Celia. But when I first came to town to paint that mural in the post office, Shelley was the self-appointed welcome committee. I ate a few meals at the diner, and she was on offer as dessert. I forget which husband she was on then. Maybe she did, too."

"Did she . . . charge you . . . ?

He laughed. "For dinner, she did. But for herself? No. With her looks, I doubt she'd get much, and I wasn't looking to pay for it. I was just lonesome. No, Shel's specialty was making a man feel wanted, and then giving him the prize for free. But nobody sticks with her for long—even aside from the fear of getting caught by her legal owner. She's just something to do if you've already seen the movie."

"My husband kept her picture. And notes from her in a blue tobacco tin."

"So? I got a lace bookmark one time as a prize in Sunday school, and I kept that thing in my drawer for a dozen years. Some men like to keep trophies. Proves they won something."

"It's foolish. Look what happened. He died, and I found the evidence."

"I'm sure he's sorry now, Mrs. Robbins. I think you can take my word for that."

"It doesn't matter." I slipped the sketch in the pocket of my dress. "I'll get word to the undertaker about that burial plot. Like I said, I owe you."

"I'll have your boys' portrait finished by morning. I promise you that."

⟜

He would probably be up most of the night finishing the portrait, but maybe it was good that he had something to take his mind off what was to come. I didn't think any of us would sleep much that last night, and, although the execution was set for noon, on account of all the people who would be pouring into town to watch the *festivities*, nobody would go home early.

The prisoner had his last meal about seven o'clock—fried chicken and mashed potatoes with milk gravy. Galen Aldridge's wife is a good cook, so I gave her two dollars to fix the meal for him—more than it cost—and she was happy to do it.

Half an hour later, Galen went back to the cell and fetched the tray. The plate was empty except for a heap of chicken bones. "He sure packed it away, Sheriff." Galen was beaming. "I wonder what that means."

"Well, it means Willadene is a good cook, but you knew that. I don't think it tells us anything about whether he's remorseful or afraid. Maybe he was just hungry."

"If it was me, facing the hereafter with the sin of murder on my soul, I believe I'd be spending my last night in prayer and fasting."

"Maybe it wouldn't do any good. Is he still working on the picture?"

"I'd say so. Doing a good job too. I'd know it was Eddie and George anywhere. I can build you a frame for it, if you want me to."

I felt tears sting my eyes and turned away so he wouldn't see them. "Thank you, Galen. I'd be grateful."

With Eddie and George up on the farm with Henry, there was no need for me to go home at all that night, but a little before nine, after I'd finished talking to the prisoner, I told Galen goodnight and left the office. The town was quieter than I'd dared to hope. Maybe most of the spectators were planning on showing up in the morning. Even the reporters were gone—too late now to file any stories except the big one, and that would have to wait until tomorrow. They were probably congregated in a back room somewhere with a goodly supply of whisky, swapping war stories about their past adventures. We hadn't even had much in the way of petty crime all week, either. When I remarked on this at the office, Falcon said happily, "We've been telling folks that if they do anything to get locked up, they won't be able to watch the execution, so they're all walking chalk this week."

Nobody stopped to pass the time with me as I walked home, although I might have welcomed the intrusion if I'd thought it would take my mind off my troubles for once. The creek was low and running clear again, now that the spring floods were long gone. I stopped for a few minutes to watch the water slide over the rocks in the twilight, and, when I looked over at the willow on the other side of the creek, I wondered if I'd ever be able to see that tree again without thinking of stubs of burnt charcoal and white butcher paper.

I still wasn't used to coming home to a house that was dark and empty, but, except for missing the boys, I didn't really long for companionship, for more reasons than just being tired. There were tomatoes on the drain board that needed to be used up, and a loaf of bread that would get moldy in another couple of days, so I made myself a tomato sandwich and ate it while I skimmed the newspaper I'd brought home from the office.

Afterward I turned on the radio for company and got out my

sewing box. The yard of black cloth I'd bought the day before was sitting on the table next to the leather Chesterfield chair that I was determined to stop thinking of as Albert's.

I'd given a lot of thought to the way the hood should be made. A male hangman might have just cut out a circle of black cloth and tied it under the chin, as Mr. Lidaker had suggested, but I thought that death deserved as much formality as the other rituals of life—say, a wedding—and I decided to make a proper hood, thick enough to hide any fluids that might come forth while he was dying, and secure enough not to come off during the death throes. I sewed two seams in the cloth, shaping the hood like a bag so that it would fit tightly over his head. I even stitched around the circles I'd cut for eyes, to make it look official. It was all part of my resolution to help him die with dignity.

Another thing occurred to me while I was sewing the hood: Lonnie Varden had been wearing regulation prison stripes all the time he had been imprisoned, and with no relatives coming forward to claim him and no possessions left in his old home, he had nothing else to wear. It wouldn't be fitten for him to be executed and then buried in a prison uniform. When he paid for his crime, he deserved to go to the Lord with his God-given dignity. He ought to go to his death in a proper suit of clothes.

Lonnie Varden and Albert were about the same size—two of a kind, again—and I decided that in addition to the hood, I would furnish him the clothes he would die in. Albert had been buried in his good black suit, but the rest of his things were still in the wardrobe in our bedroom, because I hadn't been able to bear to give them away. Now, though, I resolved to see all of them gone before the boys got back from the farm. The church could give the clothes to folks in need of them, but first I would do two things: first, I would get out Albert's second-best trousers, the best white Sunday shirt he had left, and the old navy-blue suit jacket he had worn at our wedding, so that I could take them along to the jail in the morning. Second, I was going to burn all my late husband's underwear in the woodstove so that any taint of *her* would be gone for good.

⟡

The day had come.

I got to the office early on purpose, because I didn't want to have to dodge questions from packs of baying newsmen and fight my way through the crowds. On the door Roy had put up a notice that read, EXECUTION AT NOON, but we expected the spectators to start showing up by nine o'clock, staking out the best places to watch the hanging from. A day or so earlier Tyree said he'd heard that people were renting out spaces at their windows overlooking the gallows. Even the tall sycamore trees by the creek would be occupied. I hoped most of those present would be sober. We had enough to contend with as it was. All four deputies were on duty for the day—the crowd alone would have justified that, but each of them also had a part to play in the ritual of execution. I rapped twice on the front door, and Galen let me in.

"Still quiet out there, Sheriff?"

"So far. How's the prisoner?"

"Calm. I don't think he slept much, but maybe that's good. I wouldn't want to be alert and wide-awake for what he has to face today."

"Has he had his breakfast?"

"I took it back there. He didn't seem interested in eating it, though."

"I'll look in on him later." I hadn't had any appetite for breakfast, either. For what I had to do, I wanted my stomach to be empty so that if my nerves got the best of me, I wouldn't disgrace myself by vomiting in public.

Galen sighed. "It's going to be a long morning."

"Yes." I handed him the paper sack I had brought from home. "I have a change of clothes here for the prisoner so that he won't have to be hanged in his prison uniform. You and Falcon can take it back to him about eleven, when you start getting him ready. One of you stays outside the cell with the shotgun aimed at him, while the other one helps him change. When you're getting him dressed make sure you don't have the manacles and the shackles off him at the same time. First one and then the other."

Galen let the top of the bag fall open until he could see the blue suit jacket resting on top. He recognized it at once. "But that belonged to—"

I nodded. "I won't be wanting it back, Galen. The prisoner will be buried in it. Just see that he gets it on without causing a ruckus. And after he's dressed, one of you needs to stay back there with him at all times just in case."

In my office I had written up a chart listing everyone's duties during the execution, and even the order of the procession. I went over it again and reread the short official speech I was required to make before the hanging began.

A few minutes later Falcon appeared in the doorway, looking smart in a neatly pressed uniform, but he was worried. "Do you think there might be a reprieve, Sheriff? The phone keeps ringing, but it's mostly those damn reporters. I was wondering what would happen if the governor's office tried to call us and couldn't get through?"

"Roy says they won't. There was one appeal, because by law every death sentence has to be appealed, but it was denied. There's no doubt of his guilt."

"I know he doesn't deserve a reprieve, Sheriff, but I feel sorry for him all the same."

"I understand. He seems to be a nice fellow, who did something unforgivable in a panic, and it is about to cost him his life. If it helps you any, Falcon, just remind yourself of Celia Varden falling to her death off The Hawk's Wing. No mercy was shown to her. Anyhow, all you need to worry about is doing what you're told. And remind me to tell Galen that at ten thirty I want him to take the car and drive to Reverend McKee's house. I want him to have an escort here to the jail. He might have a hard time fighting his way through the crowds, and I don't want any delays."

"Yes'm." Falcon looked at me curiously. "Aren't you dreading all this?"

I nodded. "I'll be glad when it's over."

chapter eighteen

The execution was less than an hour away. Falcon found himself thinking about the funeral of the late Sheriff Robbins a few months back. He had been a pallbearer then—for the first time ever—and the calm, but urgent directing of the participants in the ceremony had been similar to this.

Just before eleven o'clock Galen arrived with the minister, and Falcon had gone out to help the two of them push through the crowds blocking the door. Rev. McKee, already sweating and rumpled from his exertions, held his Bible high over his head as they propelled him past a knot of reporters and news photographers, all of whom were trying to get a shot of him as he hurtled along. Finally, they reached the office and slammed the door, shutting out some of the shouting outside.

Ellendor Robbins came out of her office and thanked the preacher for coming. She was calm, but paler than he had seen her since the day of her husband's burial. He thought she had lost some weight in the past few days, too. She was wearing the same brown dress she had worn for her husband's funeral, but now it gaped at the neck and hung loosely over her frame. She was frowning out the window at the milling crowd. "Vultures! You don't think they're fixing to storm the jail, do you?"

Roy laughed. "I reckon that sorry bunch would lynch anybody who tried to *stop* the hanging. They came to see a spectacle, and they won't be done out of it."

Galen nodded. "It's better than the county fair. The people in those little houses between the gallows and the creek have rented out space on their porches. I reckon the sycamore tree limbs were free for the taking, though, for anybody who was spry enough to climb that high up." He hauled himself out of the swivel chair and picked up the paper sack next to the desk. "Eleven o'clock. I'm going to take the prisoner his change of clothes now. Falcon, you come on back and keep me covered. Sheriff's orders."

Rev. McKee started to follow them. "I should go back and see if he wants me to pray with him while there's time."

The sheriff nodded. "*Outside* the cell, though, Reverend, please. Stand next to Deputy Wallace here. And, Galen, you come back when you're done getting him changed, but Falcon needs to stay with the prisoner until we're ready to begin. Understand? I'm taking no chances."

Falcon's eyes widened when she said that, but he picked up the shotgun and led the procession back to the cells. The sheriff turned her attention back to the window. "The doctor's here."

Roy opened the door wide enough to admit him and slammed it shut in the faces of two shouting reporters.

"This whole town has gone mad," muttered the doctor. "I'll bet half of them don't even know what the man is being hanged for."

Roy bolted the door. "Is everybody here now, Sheriff?"

"Yes. Everybody we're letting inside, anyhow. The commissioners, Mr. Lidaker, who built the gallows, and any other dignitaries who plan to attend will be waiting for us outside at the foot of the scaffold. They won't participate in the hanging itself, and they won't go up on the platform. There will be eight of us in the procession. I'll go first. Then Reverend McKee. Then the prisoner, followed by Deputies

Wallace and Madden . . ." She looked around the office. "Where is Tyree?"

Roy coughed nervously. "In the john, Sheriff. He's been in there most of the morning. I think I heard him being sick a time or two."

The doctor stirred. "Should I go and have a look at him?"

"I think he'll be all right, sir, once he finishes getting the liquid courage out of his system." Seeing the sheriff's look of surprise, Roy added, "It beats all, don't it? Tyree is the last one in the world I'd have expected to come down with a case of nerves over this hanging. My money would have been on young Falcon, but there it is."

Ellendor Robbins shook her head. "Maybe Tyree has more imagination than we gave him credit for. I never thought he'd turn a hair at the prospect of an execution. Falcon and Tyree will follow directly behind the prisoner. He'll be manacled, so you'll all need to make sure he gets up the steps without a mishap. Catch him if he starts to fall. And you'd all better keep an eye on Tyree as well."

The doctor frowned. "Am I in this parade of yours?"

"Yes, sir. Just after the first two deputies. You need to be on the platform in case anything goes wrong beforehand. After the trapdoor is released, you'll have several minutes to get down to the area beneath the scaffold so that you can check on the prisoner's vital signs and officially pronounce him dead."

"*Several minutes.*" The doctor spat out the words.

She sighed. "It can't be helped. We're following the law as best we can." She glanced down at her notes. "After the doctor ascends the platform steps, Deputies Phillips and Aldridge will follow, both armed with shotguns. I don't anticipate any trouble from the crowd—expect maybe shoving in hopes of getting a closer look—but we have to be prepared for anything. They will guard the steps while Mr. Wallace and Mr. Madden are preparing the prisoner—adjusting the hood, tying his legs with rope instead of the iron shackles, and so on."

Roy Phillips bit his lip and shuddered a little. "Do you have any idea how long all this is going to take, Sheriff?"

It was the doctor who answered. "Deputy, it will be the longest fifteen minutes of your life."

Galen Aldridge came back from the cell corridor alone, carrying a rolled-up bit of paper. "The prisoner is dressed, Sheriff. That suit fits him pretty well. The preacher decided to stay back there and pray awhile longer, but Mr. Varden doesn't seem overjoyed to have him there. It'll prove a distraction, though. Falcon is standing guard, as ordered." He handed the rolled-up paper to the sheriff. "The prisoner asked if you were coming back there, and I said I thought not, so he asked me to give you this. Said he stayed up most of the night to finish it."

She unfolded the paper, setting an empty coffee mug on the end of it so that it would stay open. Roy took the other end and unfolded it slowly so that the sheriff could see the picture. Lonnie Varden had drawn portraits of the Robbins children, but his work was not an exact copy of the snapshot he had used as a guide. Instead of depicting the two little Robbins boys in their Sunday clothes, seated on a log, he had drawn only the head and bare shoulders of each child, but there were five images in all, both in profile and full face, one of them looking directly out at the observer, with a hint of wings here and there where the shoulders should be. The images were positioned opposite one another, looking off into the distance with gentle, angelic smiles. The likenesses of Eddie and George Robbins were excellent, idealized, but easily recognizable to anyone who knew them. They were the Robbins children as seen through the eyes of a loving mother. The composition of the portrait itself was even more recognizable, though not, perhaps, to the residents of a backwater mountain town. And what did it matter, anyhow? Lonnie Varden, even knowing that this small sketch was his last chance to make art, had copied Sir Joshua Reynolds's *A Cherub Head in Different Views*, familiar to any student of art, even if he had not seen the original, which was in a museum in London.

Ellendor Robbins had not taken her eyes off the drawing. "It's beautiful. A perfect wonder." Gently, she touched one finger to the charcoal-shaded cheek of the younger boy.

Galen nodded. "Like I said, it took him most of the night to finish it. They look like Christmas angels. I wonder what Eddie will think of it? Are you sure you don't want to go back there and see him, Sheriff?"

For a moment she hesitated, glancing back at the door to the cells. "It's best that I don't. I'll thank him when I see him, for he has given me a priceless gift here, but if I tried to see him now I might start to cry and that won't do. I mustn't show weakness."

"Ain't it about time we got this show on the road?" Tyree Madden, red-faced and still far from sober, staggered out of the john, one hand on the holstered pistol at his side.

Galen and Sheriff Robbins exchanged glances. She nodded toward the coffeepot. "Get a cup of coffee down his sorry throat while the rest of us get ready. And see that he washes his face. Then get the rope, go out to the scaffold, and set it in place. Make sure it's well fastened to the crossbeam." She turned to the other deputy. "Roy, please go back there and tell Reverend McKee to finish up with the prisoner. It's time for him to join us out here."

She let the drawing roll up and glanced up at the clock. "It's quarter past eleven. I'll just go and put this in my office and get the hood to cover the prisoner's head. Let's begin in ten minutes. We'll assemble here and have the pastor say a prayer for all of us before we go out."

Tyree put his fist to his mouth to cover a belch. "Are we the Christians or the lions?"

At eleven forty-five the door to the sheriff's office opened partway, and a great roar went up from the onlookers close enough to observe this. Their shouts alerted others that the ceremony was beginning, and the crowd left the main street in front of the office and surged through the grass and gravel alleyways between buildings in order to reach the back lot where the gallows stood. Some of the photographers stayed put beside the steps to the sheriff's office, hoping for one good close-up shot of the condemned man struggling in his shackles, and of the lady sheriff weeping into a lace handkerchief. They were to be disappointed, though: neither the prisoner nor his executioner showed any sign of emotion. They walked slowly, but without hesitation, ignoring the crowd, which parted to let them pass: first the sheriff, shorter than the rest, with her badge pinned neatly to the front of her brown dress. Behind her walked a spare, balding gentleman, obviously a clergyman, because, although he wore no dog collar, he was holding a Bible and murmuring to himself. The prisoner, stumbling a little in his leg irons, stared straight ahead, affecting not to notice the strangers shoving one another in hopes of getting a closer look at him. Their efforts to reach him were thwarted on either side by stone-faced lawmen carrying shotguns. The frowning, fair-haired man in the black suit who trailed them must be the physician, judging by the leather satchel he carried, and behind him two more deputies brought up the rear, preventing the spectators from closing in behind the procession. A three-minute walk, around the side of the building and down the gravel alleyway to the back street, and they had arrived at the foot of the scaffold.

The sheriff stopped for a moment, looking up at the newly built platform, still smelling of pine resin and sawdust. From the cross-beam erected at one end of the flooring hung a thick hemp rope, itself smelling faintly of lard. "You have to grease the rope," one fellow was explaining to his neighbors, "and then tie it to a beam with a weight tied to the end of it, else the bulk of the hanged man will stretch the rope during the execution, perhaps carrying the prisoner all the way to the ground below." Someone else said, "It's a short rope, no danger of it stretching that much." No hope of a quick, clean death by a broken neck either.

Mrs. Robbins took a few steps forward to inspect the bottom of the platform. The supports of the structure were thick and well braced, and the trapdoor was bolted firmly in place. All was in readiness.

From the other side of the dusty lot someone waved to get her attention. She recognized Mr. Lidaker, the carpenter, respectfully attired in his Sunday suit, and she nodded an expressionless greeting. When he was sure she had seen him, he motioned toward the small flatbed truck containing the coffin, hastily constructed from scrap lumber left over from the building of the gallows. The sheriff's expression still did not change, but she nodded again, and then turned to mount the steps—thirteen of them, as required by tradition.

Reverend McKee waited until the sheriff reached the third step before following her on the ascent. His lips were moving, and he stared straight ahead, as if there were no crowd surrounding them. The roaring was so loud now that even if he had shouted his orisons, no one would have heard them.

Lonnie Varden mounted the steps slowly, and when the shouting grew louder, he shuddered a little and glanced about him. He stumbled once as the iron shackles caught on the edge of the step, but the tall young deputy just behind him lifted the chain above the step and watched for the rest of the climb to make sure it did not catch again.

The doctor who followed the first two deputies stopped halfway up the steps to survey the bawling spectators with a look of utter scorn. They paid him no mind, though, and with a sigh of disgust he made his way up to the platform.

The last two lawmen, shotguns in hand, barrels pointed at the ground, went up one after the other, with the last—a scowling banty rooster of a fellow—undertaking to ascend the steps backward so that he could face the crowd, in case someone tried to storm the steps. For a lark a drunken spectator pretended to head for the steps, but the last deputy brought up the barrel of his gun and motioned with it for the man to back off. The joker staggered away, shaking his head at the ferocious response to his jest, and by then the participants were all assembled on the platform, so the crowd quieted down, captivated by the drama before them.

The banty rooster deputy and the heavyset older one stood on either side of the crossbeam, facing in opposite directions, shotguns at the ready. The tall young deputy and the woozy-looking one worked in tandem, removing the manacles and leg irons from the prisoner, and replacing the metal restraints with rope. They tied his legs together (*"So's he doesn't kick once he falls through the trapdoor!"*), and bound his hands behind his back, to prevent him from clawing the rope around his neck. During all these preparations Lonnie Varden stared straight ahead, and the minister leaned in close to him speaking in low, urgent tones. Sheriff Robbins stood by observing the proceedings, glancing down at the papers she held.

When the prisoner was secured and placed squarely on the trapdoor with the noose around his neck, the sheriff walked to the middle of the platform, faced the prisoner, and began to read the official formula required by the state to be delivered before an execution. Her voice was clear and steady, but she spoke softly so that those who were not close to the scaffold had trouble hearing her. The recitation took only a couple of minutes, in any case, and then she approached the prisoner, who was pale but composed. Beads of sweat glistened on his forehead.

"Do you have any last words?" No one beyond the platform could hear her, but that must have been what she said, because the condemned man half turned and surveyed the crowd. He hesitated for a moment, and then a hoarse voice from the back of the onlookers called out, "She fell farther than you will!" A few people clapped and murmured in agreement.

At this display of hostility, Lonnie Varden's face crumpled and he shuddered. Then he murmured something to the sheriff, who was now standing beside him. She replied, and he shook his head.

Why waste a speech on this vicious mob of spectators?

She spoke a few more words and touched his shoulder gently. He nodded.

She handed the legal papers to the blond deputy, who still looked green to the gills. He stuffed them in his pocket, and then she was holding only a black cloth, which turned out to be the hood the condemned man would wear into eternity.

Rev. McKee began to pray louder now, the Lord's Prayer, and some in the crowd joined in.

The lady sheriff slipped the hood over Lonnie Varden's bowed head and drew the ends of the white cord together to close it under his chin. She lifted the noose and tightened the rope until the knot rested tight against the side of his neck.

Any further delay would not be a kindness. She took a few steps back, clear of the trapdoor, until she was standing at the base of the crossbeam, next to the lever that would draw the bolt. A few more breaths, then complete silence, and—before she could touch the lever, the blond, woozy-looking deputy stumbled a little, pushing her aside. Before she could recover her balance, he jerked the lever forward, and the prisoner's body dropped out of sight.

The longest fifteen minutes of your life.

The deputies waited ten minutes before they began to disperse the crowd. The moment the body dropped through the opening the shouting had died in mid-roar. A couple of news photographers lingered to take their last shots of the swaying body, but most of the onlookers had begun to edge away, frightened or sickened by the spectacle of imminent death. Beneath the platform the doctor waited alone, staring at the face of his pocket watch and occasionally glancing at the twitching body at the end of the rope, no more than five feet from the ground.

The deputies cleared a path so that Mr. Lidaker could drive his truck up beside the scaffold, and two of them helped him haul the pine coffin out of the back and set it on the ground nearby, in readiness.

The sheriff shook hands with Mr. Lidaker. "Thank you for all you did, sir. When the coffin is ready, take it to the undertakers. Tell them to bury Mr. Varden on the hillside cemetery, in the plot alongside Albert Robbins."

The carpenter's eyes widened and he started to reply, but the sheriff had walked away to have a word with the doctor. He was still standing near the open trapdoor, watching the body twisting in a shaft of sunlight.

"Four more minutes," he said when he heard the sheriff's approach.

"He's not twitching anymore."

"Do you want to take the chance that he's unconscious and that once you cut him down he'll come to, and you'll have to do it all over again?"

"No."

"Then wait four minutes."

Falcon and Tyree stood together near the steps, keeping people away from the scaffold. Two men had already tried to go up on the platform to steal the rope. The deputies chased them away, because they couldn't be bothered with a minor arrest just then. Tyree had sobered up, but he looked even worse now, bilious and unsteady. "I felt like

I had to do it," he told Falcon. "It just all of a sudden hit me that I couldn't let that little lady be responsible for that man's death. So I just . . . did it. You reckon I ought to tell her I'm sorry?"

Falcon shivered. "I don't know. I wouldn't bring it up unless she does."

"I could tell her I was still feeling wobbly after being sick and that I stumbled and fell into it. She might not believe me, but she could pretend she did."

"I guess she could, Tyree."

"I just couldn't let her do it. It gave me chills to think of it."

"Yeah, I know what you mean about getting the willies. After we tied the prisoner's legs and stepped back, she put that hood over his head, and I looked at him. He was wearing the sheriff's clothes, Tyree! Mr. Robbins, I mean. That was *his* old suit. For a second there, seeing him standing there with his head covered up and wearing that suit, I felt like we were hanging *him*."

"She said she'd be glad when it was over. Do you think she really could have done it?"

Falcon shook his head. "I'm glad I'll never know."

The undertaker's assistant made her say it twice. He leaned against the funeral home's black Ford hearse, staring down at the determined little lady with the badge pinned to her dress. "Yes, ma'am, I remember where we buried your husband. Sure do. Wasn't more'n four, five months ago? Up on the hill near that old weed cedar. There's no tombstone yet, but we have a little metal marker with a card in it, marking the spot."

"That's right."

"And you want the prisoner laid to rest beside him? Beside Albert Robbins? Are you entirely sure, ma'am?"

Ellendor Robbins's expression did not change, but her sigh meant impatience. "Yes. I own the plot. Send the bill for the gravedigging to the county."

"What about a funeral?"

"There won't be one. And don't mark the grave, either. I don't want it to be a sideshow. In fact, dig the grave this afternoon, but don't inter the body until after dark. I don't want any witnesses."

"All right, but ma'am—"

"Now what?"

"The doctor over yonder under the platform is motioning for you to come. I think he's ready to cut the body down."

chapter nineteen

Everything has an ending, and a rope has two.

I had thought about that old saying more than once in the past few weeks, because I had seen more than my share of endings in a few short months, but now I thought that the worst was well and truly over: two men dead, and whether they deserved it or not, I couldn't save either one of them, and I never asked myself if I'd wanted to.

It was almost over, anyhow.

I had already told the deputies not to expect to see me for a couple of days. Tomorrow I would go up the mountain to get my boys from Henry and Elva's farm. Maybe I would even stay for supper and go for a walk in the woods. I had more thinking to do.

I left the sheriff's office a few hours after the hanging, as soon as I thought the day shift deputies could handle things for the rest of the day. The reporters had all checked out of the hotel and were at the depot waiting for the afternoon train, ready to chase some other story into the ground. I went home at four and slept until dark.

An hour later I was at the cemetery, waiting beside the cedar tree, when the black hearse drove up and parked on the gravel road at the bottom of the hill. I watched four men—in work clothes, not funeral attire—get out and haul the pine box up the hill to the newly dug hole next to the grave of Albert Robbins. They looked like shadows in the moonlight, moving soundlessly across the dark grass, swaying a little under the weight of their burden.

Maybe I should have asked Rev. McKee to meet me here, but I hadn't thought of it. I reckoned I could say a prayer myself, though, if I felt like it.

When I stepped forward to meet them, the undertakers' men looked up, startled, and one of them lost his footing, and nearly dropped his end of the coffin.

"It's only me," I said. "I wanted to make sure you had the right place." Of course they did; they had already dug the hole, but I couldn't say why I had really come, because I didn't know myself. I just wanted to see it through, I guess.

They mumbled a greeting and got on with their work. I stood back and watched them lower the box into the ground. One last rope.

They didn't stop to pray or say any words over the grave. Death was all in a day's work to them. After they filled in the hole, they murmured hasty farewells and hurried away. I stood there for a long time, staring down at the freshly turned earth, trying to think of something fitten to say—to either of the two men lying there. But, for different reasons, I couldn't offer forgiveness to either one of them. I had the rest of my life to think of something to say, though. They'd still be there.

I went down the hill, away from the cemetery, and kept walking, but I wasn't going home. Not yet. I followed the creek path back through town, past the office, where all seemed peaceful, past the almost-empty hotel, and across the street to the silver railroad car with the neon sign on top: CITY DINER. I looked through the windows and saw Mildred, the henna-haired waitress, behind the counter. Most of the booths were empty. Now that the excitement was over, people had either gone home to relax or they'd gone elsewhere to look for more excitement. The place had the same drained, empty feeling it had the day after the circus left town.

I crossed the parking lot and went around to the back door of the diner, thinking about Davis Howell rooting through those garbage cans for food. At least now he was safe. As I reached up to tap on the door, the scar on my wrist caught the light from the bare bulb above the stoop. I had lived with that scar for nearly twenty five years, but the mad dog that gave it to me had died before the sun set. Its owner had to put it down, because you have a responsibility to keep the creatures in your care from hurting the community. When they get out of control, you have to stop them.

I tapped on the door and waited.

A moment later a scowling Ike Bonham jerked it open, holding a .32 pistol aimed at my head. I just stared him down, didn't move a muscle. Seconds later, when he recognized me, he grunted and shoved the pistol into the waistband of his pants. "Thought you might be somebody trying to rob us."

Something in the way he said that made me think that wasn't why he'd answered the back door with a loaded gun. He wasn't expecting a robber—or me. I smiled a little.

"Well? What do you want? Nobody here called you."

I stood my ground, despite the mingled stench of whisky and garlic on his breath. "No. I just stopped by to bring something for your wife. That man we hanged today asked me to give this to her. Last request. And I promised him I would. Is she here?" I craned my neck and looked past him into the grease-spattered kitchen. I wondered if the walls were really yellow or just discolored from all the smoke and grease.

"She's in the john." He kept watching me with narrowed eyes, but he made no move to call to her. "What do you mean that killer left her something?"

"It isn't worth anything, but I guess it meant a lot to him."

I reached into my pocket and pulled out the blue tobacco tin and two small pictures: the photo inscribed *Ain't we got fun?* and the little sketch of her that Lonnie Varden had drawn on the scrap of butcher paper in his cell.

"He wanted her to have these to remember him by. You'll see that she gets them, won't you?"

Ike Bonham's hand was shaking when he took the tin, and when he saw the two pictures, his face contorted with rage. He tipped the photo up into the light, and his lips trembled as he read the scrawled message on the back: *Ain't we got fun?*

I waited, but he seemed to have forgotten all about me. Still clutching the tobacco tin and the pictures, he staggered back a step and slammed the door in my face. That was all right. I turned and walked away, headed home.

First thing in the morning I would travel up the mountain to get my boys so that whatever happened in town tomorrow would be none of my business.

It was over now.

acknowledgments

A newly appointed female sheriff is required by law to personally hang a prisoner in a public execution.

How much of this story is true?

Although *Prayers the Devil Answers* was inspired by a true story, it was not intended to be an exact chronicle of the actual events. It is true that in 1936 in Owensboro, Kentucky, a woman sheriff, appointed to serve out the term of her late husband, was obliged to oversee the public execution by hanging of a convicted felon. It was the last public hanging ever carried out in the United States.

Like Ellendor Robbins in the novel, the real widow also had young children to support, and it was for that reason that she accepted the job of sheriff.

The similarities between the stories end there, though. In constructing my novel about this incident, I was primarily interested in the dilemma of a widow with children—a housewife—faced with the prospect of hanging a man before a crowd of thousands of onlookers. I changed the circumstances of the prisoner and the crime, because I wanted to keep the focus on the woman sheriff and her determination to do her duty at all costs in order to honor her oath of office, so that she could keep her job and take care of her children. The grain of truth in this novel is like the grain of sand that forms the heart of a pearl: it so obscured by layers of embellishment that the original germ of inspiration is no longer visible at all.

You always have to do research for a novel, though, even if you are not faithfully chronicling the lives of actual historical figures.

There's very little invention in most works of fiction, but there is some rearranging. The outcropping of rock on the mountaintop, called "the Hawk's Wing" in this novel, is a real place called McAfee's Knob. You will find it on the Appalachian Trail near Roanoke, Virginia.

I'm grateful to Hamblen County, Tennessee Sheriff, Esco Jarnagin for his advice on the operation of a Depression-era Tennessee sheriff's department, and the politics involved for the new sheriff. When I asked him how much he thought a 1930s sheriff would be paid in rural Tennessee, he laughingly answered, "Not enough!"

Award-winning artist Alan Shuptrine of Chattanooga guided me through the steps an artist would take in preparing to paint a mural on the wall of a public building, and he helped me to figure out how the prisoner Lonnie Varden would have gone about drawing a portrait in the confines of his cell. My thanks to him for the wealth of arcane detail about the process, from his explanations about the making of gesso and doing a color wash for the mural, to the burning of a willow branch to produce a stick of charcoal suitable for drawing a portrait. Alan was very patient and thorough in his instructions on how to describe these processes, and I thank him for sharing his expertise with me.

The subject of Lonnie Varden's post office mural, the July 1776 attack on Fort Watauga, was an actual incident in frontier history, and Tennessee's first governor, John Sevier, took part in the battle. Celia's description of those events is correct. You can visit a replica of the fort and see museum exhibits relating to that era at Sycamore Shoals State

Park in Elizabethton, Tennessee. As far as I know, though, no WPA artist ever painted a mural of the scene on the wall of a post office.

I'm grateful to my agent, Irene Goodman, who was captivated by this story and refused to let me *not* write it, and to my editor, Johanna Castillo, of Atria Books for her guidance in bringing the novel to publication. A special thanks to all the kind readers who have expressed great interest in this book and eagerly awaited its arrival.

Sharyn McCrumb
Roanoke County, Virginia, 2015